MARVEL

AVENGERS ASSEMBLE™

LIVING LEGENDS

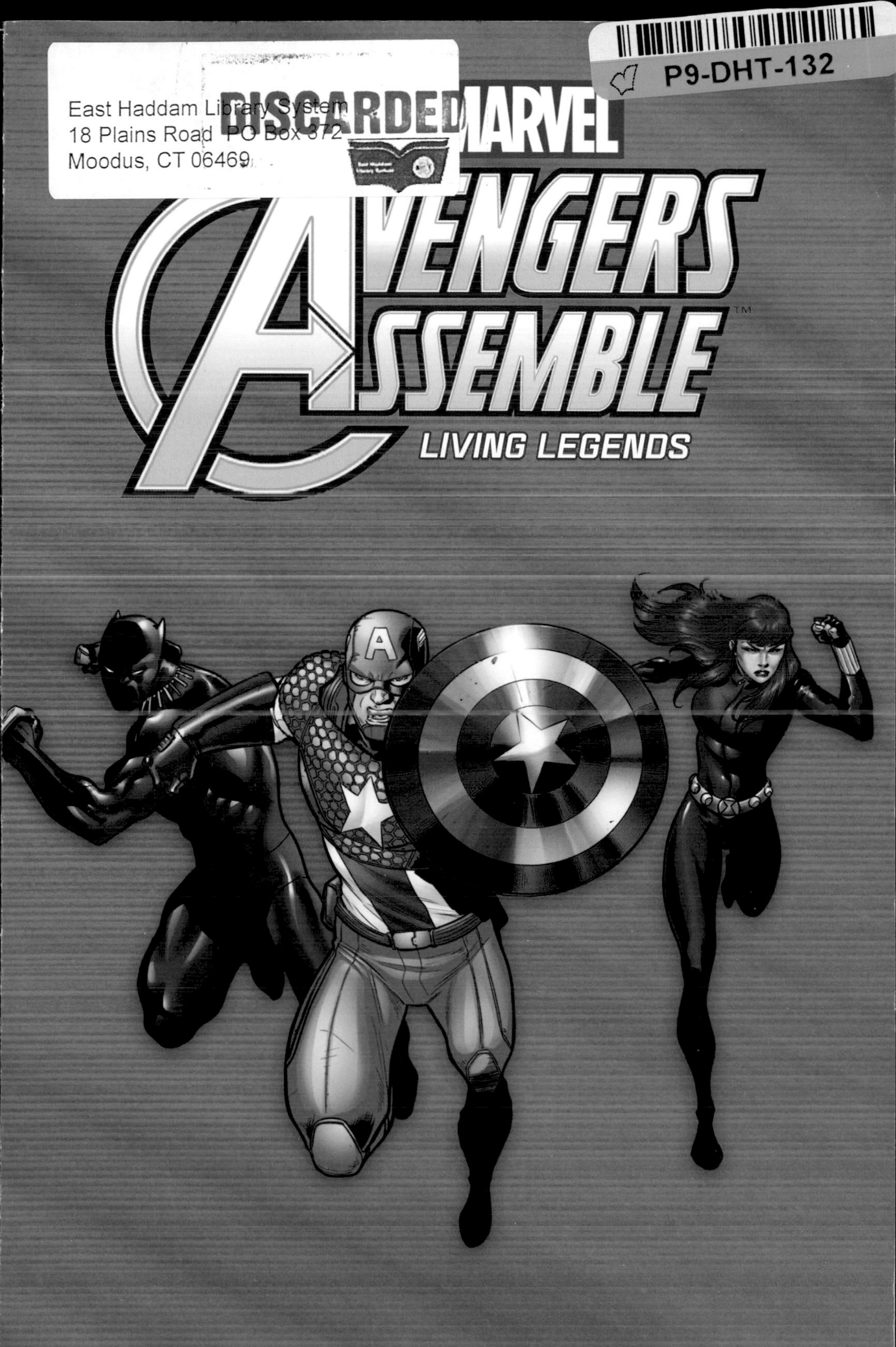

COLLECTION EDITOR: **JENNIFER GRÜNWALD**
ASSISTANT EDITOR: **CAITLIN O'CONNELL**
ASSOCIATE MANAGING EDITOR: **KATERI WOODY**
EDITOR, SPECIAL PROJECTS: **MARK D. BEAZLEY**
VP PRODUCTION & SPECIAL PROJECTS: **JEFF YOUNGQUIST**
SVP PRINT, SALES & MARKETING: **DAVID GABRIEL**
BOOK DESIGNER: **ADAM DEL RE**

EDITOR IN CHIEF: **C.B. CEBULSKI**
CHIEF CREATIVE OFFICER: **JOE QUESADA**
PRESIDENT: **DAN BUCKLEY**
EXECUTIVE PRODUCER: **ALAN FINE**

AVENGERS ASSEMBLE: LIVING LEGENDS. Contains material originally published in magazine form as THOR: WHERE WALK THE FROST GIANTS #1, BLACK PANTHER: THE SOUND AND THE FURY #1, AVENGERS: SHARDS OF INFINITY #1, ANT-MAN AND THE WASP: LIVING LEGENDS #1 and CAPTAIN MARVEL: BRAVER & MIGHTER #1. First printing 2019. ISBN 978-1-302-91638-1. Published by MARVEL WORLDWIDE, INC., a subsidiary of MARVEL ENTERTAINMENT, LLC. OFFICE OF PUBLICATION: 135 West 50th Street, New York, NY 10020. © 2019 MARVEL No similarity between any of the names, characters, persons, and/ or institutions in this magazine with those of any living or dead person or institution is intended, and any such similarity which may exist is purely coincidental. **Printed in Canada.** DAN BUCKLEY, President, Marvel Entertainment; JOHN NEE, Publisher; JOE QUESADA, Chief Creative Officer; TOM BREVOORT, SVP of Publishing; DAVID BOGART, Associate Publisher & SVP of Talent Affairs; DAVID GABRIEL, SVP of Sales & Marketing, Publishing; JEFF YOUNGQUIST, VP of Production & Special Projects; DAN CARR, Executive Director of Publishing Technology; ALEX MORALES, Director of Publishing Operations; DAN EDINGTON, Managing Editor; SUSAN CRESPI, Production Manager; STAN LEE, Chairman Emeritus. For information regarding advertising in Marvel Comics or on Marvel.com, please contact Vit DeBellis, Custom Solutions & Integrated Advertising Manager, at vdebellis@marvel.com. For Marvel subscription inquiries, please call 888-511-5480. **Manufactured between 2/8/2019 and 3/12/2019 by SOLISCO PRINTERS, SCOTT, QC, CANADA.**

10 9 8 7 6 5 4 3 2 1

MARVEL
AVENGERS ASSEMBLE™
LIVING LEGENDS

THOR: WHERE WALK THE FROST GIANTS

Ralph Macchio
WRITER

Todd Nauck
ARTIST

Rachelle Rosenberg
COLOR ARTIST

**Todd Nauck &
Rachelle Rosenberg**
COVER ART

BLACK PANTHER: THE SOUND AND THE FURY

Ralph Macchio
WRITER

Andrea Di Vito
ARTIST

Laura Villari
COLOR ARTIST

**Andrea Di Vito &
Laura Villari**
COVER ART

AVENGERS: SHARDS OF INFINITY

Ralph Macchio
WRITER

Andrea Di Vito
ARTIST

Laura Villari
COLOR ARTIST

**Andrea Di Vito &
Laura Villari**
COVER ART

ANT-MAN AND THE WASP: LIVING LEGENDS

Ralph Macchio
WRITER

Andrea Di Vito
ARTIST

Laura Villari
COLOR ARTIST

Andrea Di Vito & Laura Villari
COVER ART

CAPTAIN MARVEL: BRAVER & MIGHTIER

Jody Houser
WRITER

Simone Buonfantino
ARTIST

Erick Arciniega
COLOR ARTIST

Valerio Schiti & Rachelle Rosenberg
COVER ART

VC's Travis Lanham
LETTERER

Mark Basso
EDITOR

Avengers created by Stan Lee & Jack Kirby

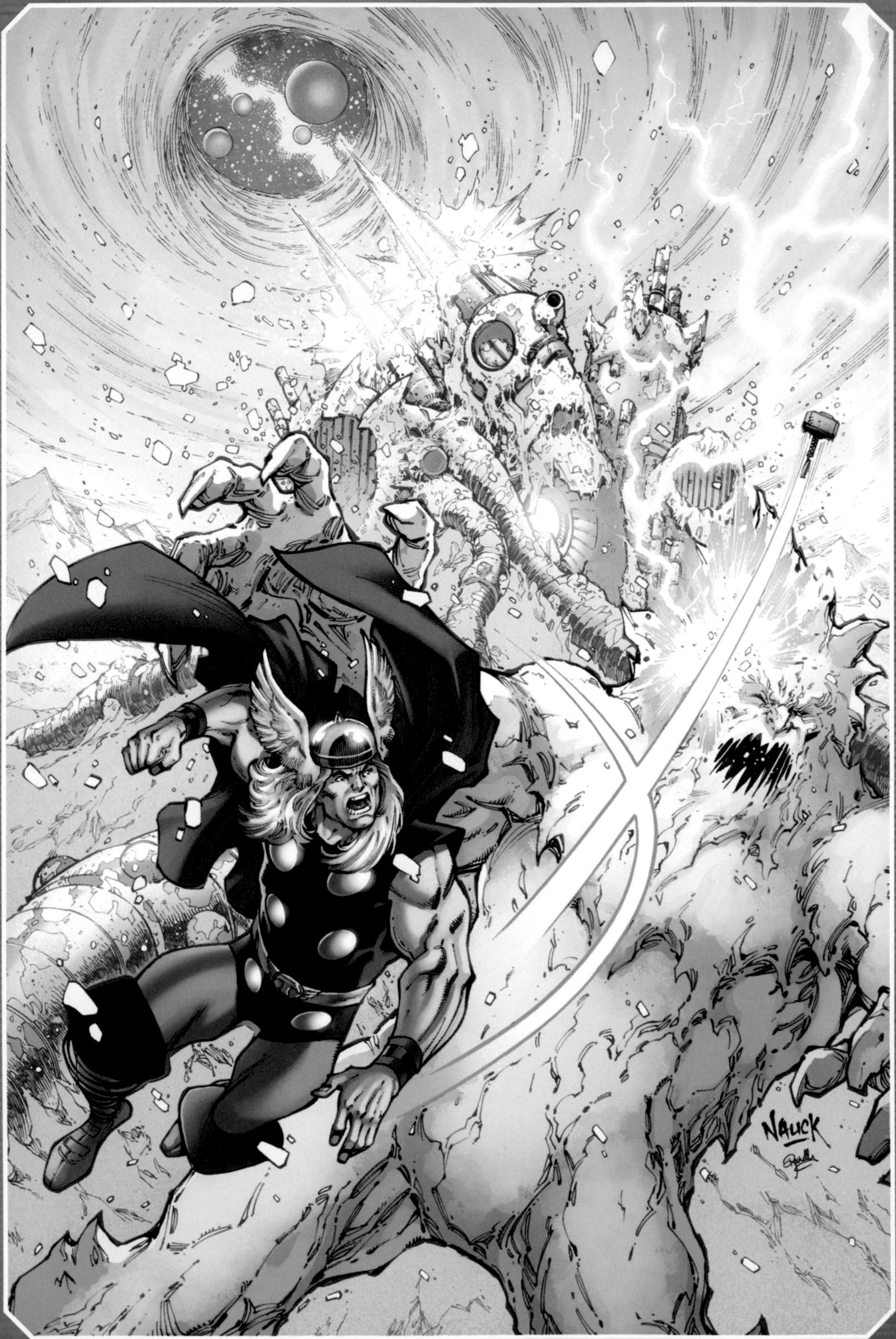
NAUCK

THOR: WHERE WALK THE FROST GIANTS

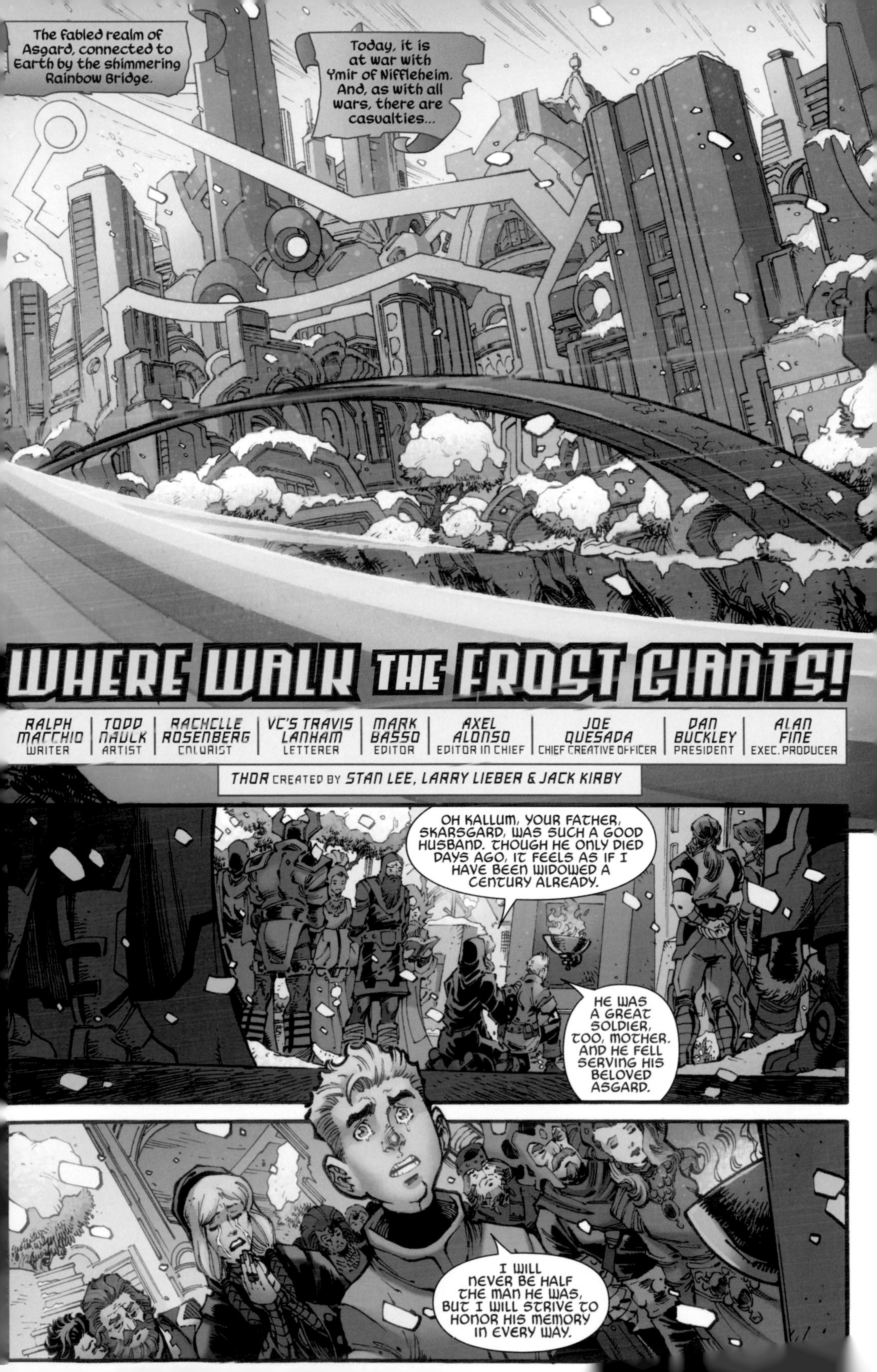
The fabled realm of Asgard, connected to Earth by the shimmering Rainbow Bridge.
Today, it is at war with Ymir of Niffleheim. And, as with all wars, there are casualties...
WHERE WALK THE FROST GIANTS!
RALPH MACCHIO WRITER
TODD NAUCK ARTIST
RACHELLE ROSENBERG COLORIST
VC'S TRAVIS LANHAM LETTERER
MARK BASSO EDITOR
AXEL ALONSO EDITOR IN CHIEF
JOE QUESADA CHIEF CREATIVE OFFICER
DAN BUCKLEY PRESIDENT
ALAN FINE EXEC. PRODUCER
THOR CREATED BY STAN LEE, LARRY LIEBER & JACK KIRBY
OH KALLUM, YOUR FATHER, SKARSGARD, WAS SUCH A GOOD HUSBAND. THOUGH HE ONLY DIED DAYS AGO, IT FEELS AS IF I HAVE BEEN WIDOWED A CENTURY ALREADY.
HE WAS A GREAT SOLDIER, TOO, MOTHER. AND HE FELL SERVING HIS BELOVED ASGARD.
I WILL NEVER BE HALF THE MAN HE WAS, BUT I WILL STRIVE TO HONOR HIS MEMORY IN EVERY WAY.

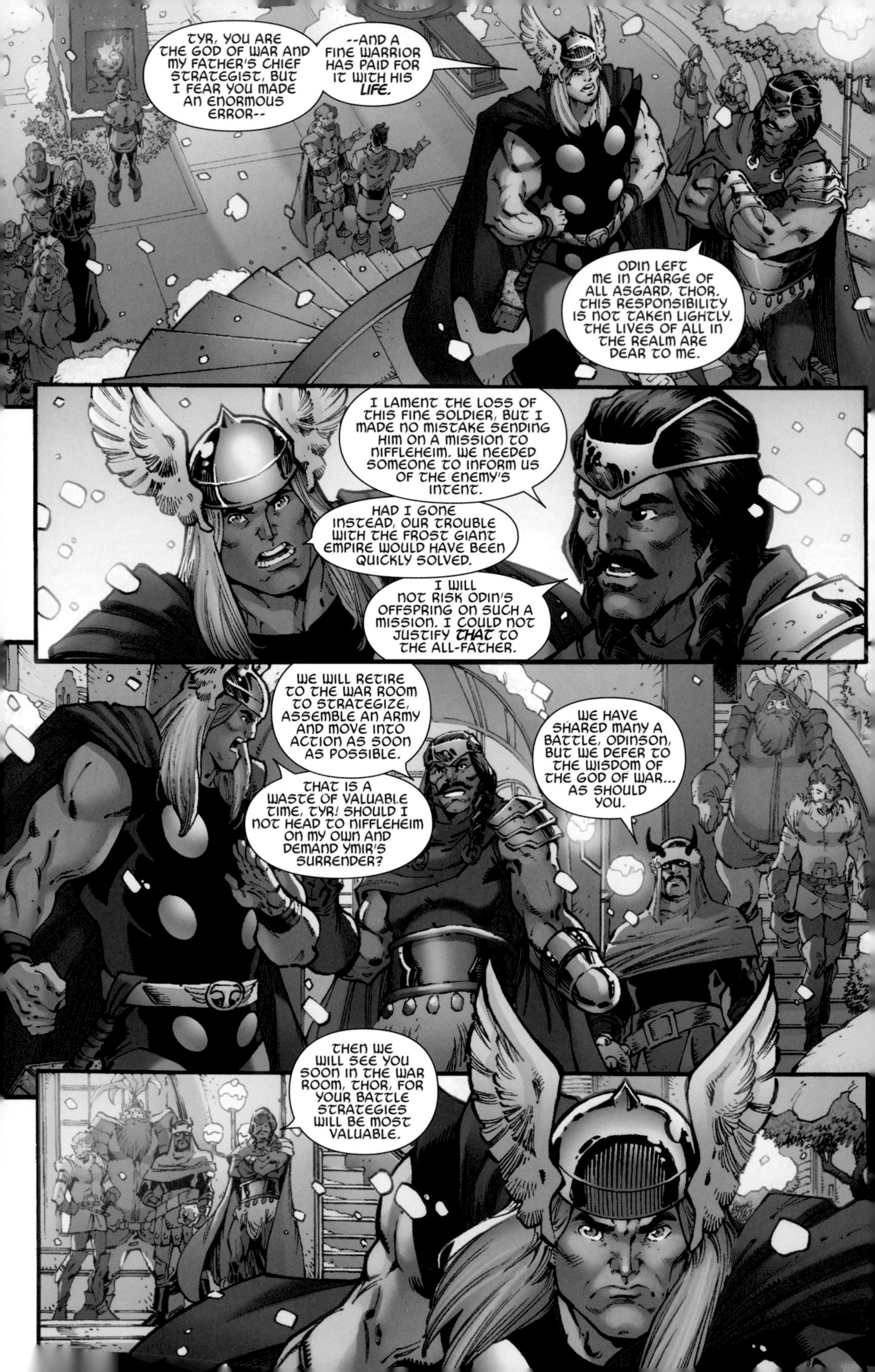
TYR, YOU ARE THE GOD OF WAR AND MY FATHER'S CHIEF STRATEGIST, BUT I FEAR YOU MADE AN ENORMOUS ERROR--
--AND A FINE WARRIOR HAS PAID FOR IT WITH HIS LIFE.
ODIN LEFT ME IN CHARGE OF ALL ASGARD, THOR. THIS RESPONSIBILITY IS NOT TAKEN LIGHTLY. THE LIVES OF ALL IN THE REALM ARE DEAR TO ME.
I LAMENT THE LOSS OF THIS FINE SOLDIER, BUT I MADE NO MISTAKE SENDING HIM ON A MISSION TO NIFFLEHEIM. WE NEEDED SOMEONE TO INFORM US OF THE ENEMY'S INTENT.
HAD I GONE INSTEAD, OUR TROUBLE WITH THE FROST GIANT EMPIRE WOULD HAVE BEEN QUICKLY SOLVED.
I WILL NOT RISK ODIN'S OFFSPRING ON SUCH A MISSION. I COULD NOT JUSTIFY THAT TO THE ALL-FATHER.
WE WILL RETIRE TO THE WAR ROOM TO STRATEGIZE, ASSEMBLE AN ARMY AND MOVE INTO ACTION AS SOON AS POSSIBLE.
THAT IS A WASTE OF VALUABLE TIME, TYR! SHOULD I NOT HEAD TO NIFFLEHEIM ON MY OWN AND DEMAND YMIR'S SURRENDER?
WE HAVE SHARED MANY A BATTLE, ODINSON, BUT WE DEFER TO THE WISDOM OF THE GOD OF WAR... AS SHOULD YOU.
THEN WE WILL SEE YOU SOON IN THE WAR ROOM, THOR, FOR YOUR BATTLE STRATEGIES WILL BE MOST VALUABLE.

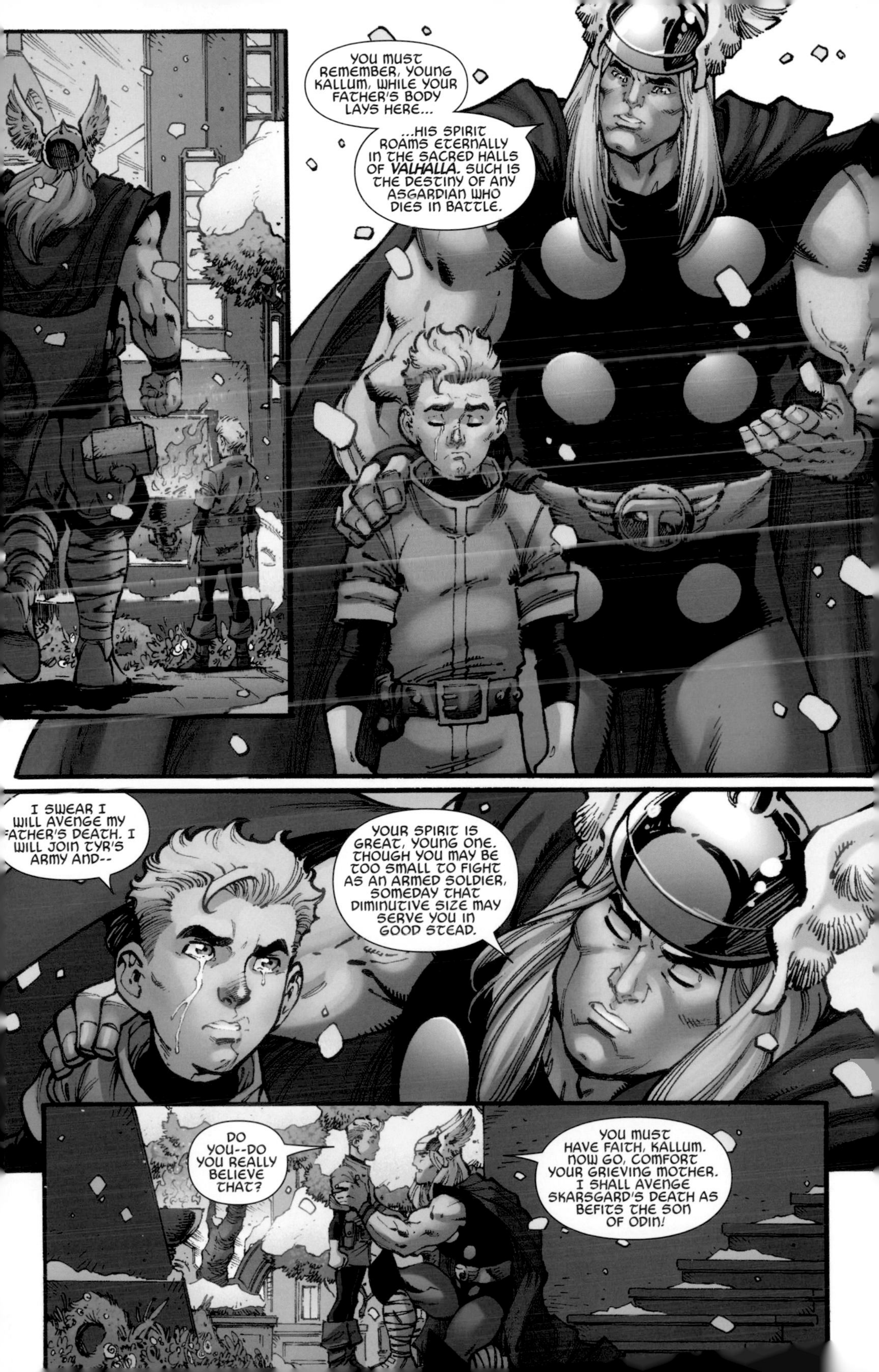
YOU MUST REMEMBER, YOUNG KALLUM, WHILE YOUR FATHER'S BODY LAYS HERE...
...HIS SPIRIT ROAMS ETERNALLY IN THE SACRED HALLS OF VALHALLA. SUCH IS THE DESTINY OF ANY ASGARDIAN WHO DIES IN BATTLE.
I SWEAR I WILL AVENGE MY FATHER'S DEATH. I WILL JOIN TYR'S ARMY AND--
YOUR SPIRIT IS GREAT, YOUNG ONE. THOUGH YOU MAY BE TOO SMALL TO FIGHT AS AN ARMED SOLDIER, SOMEDAY THAT DIMINUTIVE SIZE MAY SERVE YOU IN GOOD STEAD.
DO YOU--DO YOU REALLY BELIEVE THAT?
YOU MUST HAVE FAITH, KALLUM. NOW GO, COMFORT YOUR GRIEVING MOTHER. I SHALL AVENGE SKARSGARD'S DEATH AS BEFITS THE SON OF ODIN!

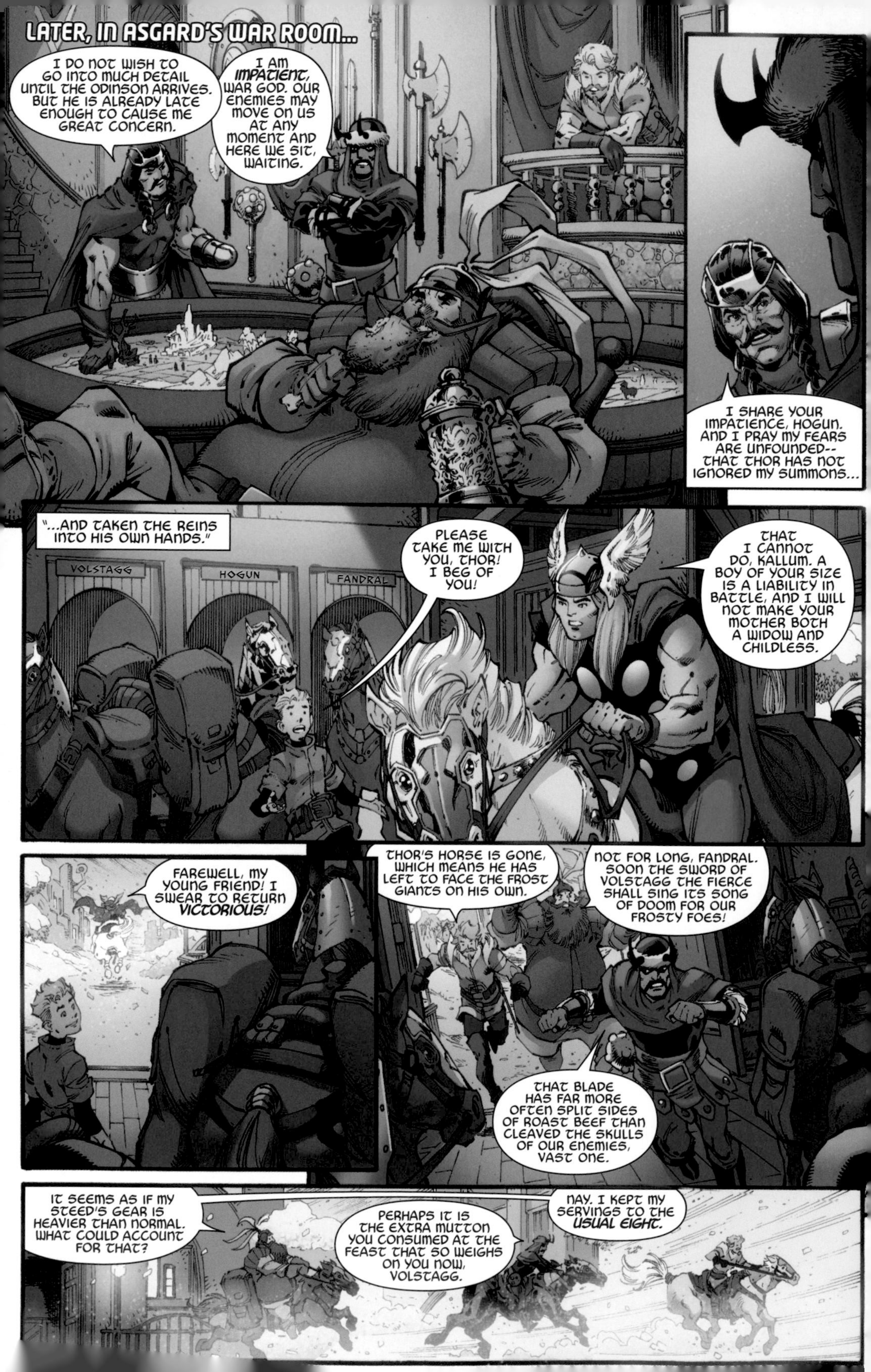
LATER, IN ASGARD'S WAR ROOM...
I DO NOT WISH TO GO INTO MUCH DETAIL UNTIL THE ODINSON ARRIVES. BUT HE IS ALREADY LATE ENOUGH TO CAUSE ME GREAT CONCERN.
I AM *IMPATIENT*, WAR GOD. OUR ENEMIES MAY MOVE ON US AT ANY MOMENT AND HERE WE SIT, WAITING.
I SHARE YOUR IMPATIENCE, HOGUN. AND I PRAY MY FEARS ARE UNFOUNDED-- THAT THOR HAS NOT IGNORED MY SUMMONS...
"...AND TAKEN THE REINS INTO HIS OWN HANDS."
VOLSTAGG
HOGUN
FANDRAL
PLEASE TAKE ME WITH YOU, THOR! I BEG OF YOU!
THAT I CANNOT DO, KALLUM. A BOY OF YOUR SIZE IS A LIABILITY IN BATTLE, AND I WILL NOT MAKE YOUR MOTHER BOTH A WIDOW AND CHILDLESS.
FAREWELL, MY YOUNG FRIEND! I SWEAR TO RETURN ***VICTORIOUS!***
THOR'S HORSE IS GONE, WHICH MEANS HE HAS LEFT TO FACE THE FROST GIANTS ON HIS OWN.
NOT FOR LONG, FANDRAL. SOON THE SWORD OF VOLSTAGG THE FIERCE SHALL SING ITS SONG OF DOOM FOR OUR FROSTY FOES!
THAT BLADE HAS FAR MORE OFTEN SPLIT SIDES OF ROAST BEEF THAN CLEAVED THE SKULLS OF OUR ENEMIES, VAST ONE.
IT SEEMS AS IF MY STEED'S GEAR IS HEAVIER THAN NORMAL. WHAT COULD ACCOUNT FOR THAT?
PERHAPS IT IS THE EXTRA MUTTON YOU CONSUMED AT THE FEAST THAT SO WEIGHS ON YOU NOW, VOLSTAGG.
NAY. I KEPT MY SERVINGS TO THE *USUAL EIGHT.*

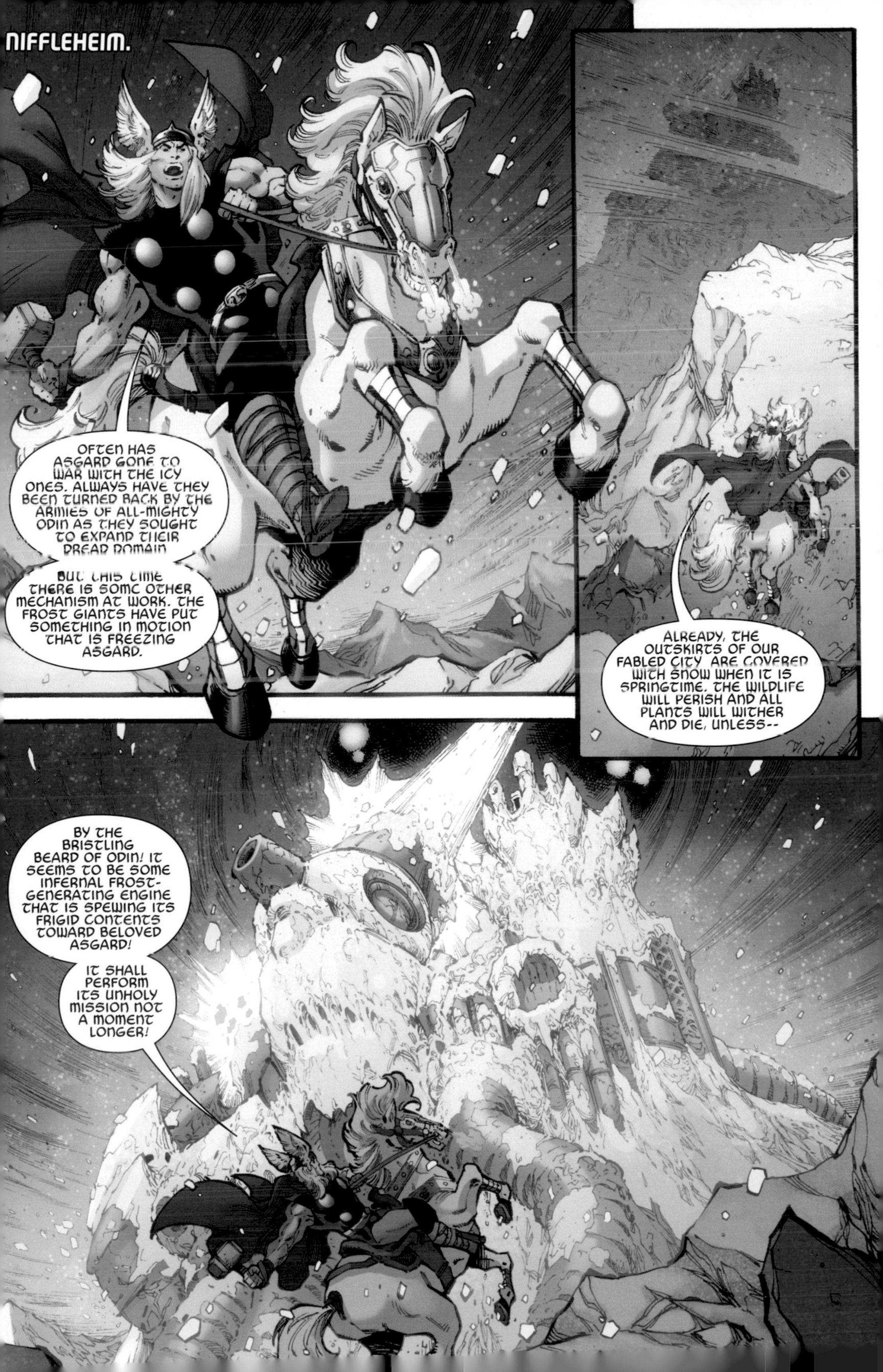
NIFFLEHEIM.
OFTEN HAS ASGARD GONE TO WAR WITH THE ICY ONES. ALWAYS HAVE THEY BEEN TURNED BACK BY THE ARMIES OF ALL-MIGHTY ODIN AS THEY SOUGHT TO EXPAND THEIR DREAD DOMAIN.
BUT THIS TIME THERE IS SOME OTHER MECHANISM AT WORK. THE FROST GIANTS HAVE PUT SOMETHING IN MOTION THAT IS FREEZING ASGARD.
ALREADY, THE OUTSKIRTS OF OUR FABLED CITY ARE COVERED WITH SNOW WHEN IT IS SPRINGTIME. THE WILDLIFE WILL PERISH AND ALL PLANTS WILL WITHER AND DIE, UNLESS--
BY THE BRISTLING BEARD OF ODIN! IT SEEMS TO BE SOME INFERNAL FROST-GENERATING ENGINE THAT IS SPEWING ITS FRIGID CONTENTS TOWARD BELOVED ASGARD!
IT SHALL PERFORM ITS UNHOLY MISSION NOT A MOMENT LONGER!

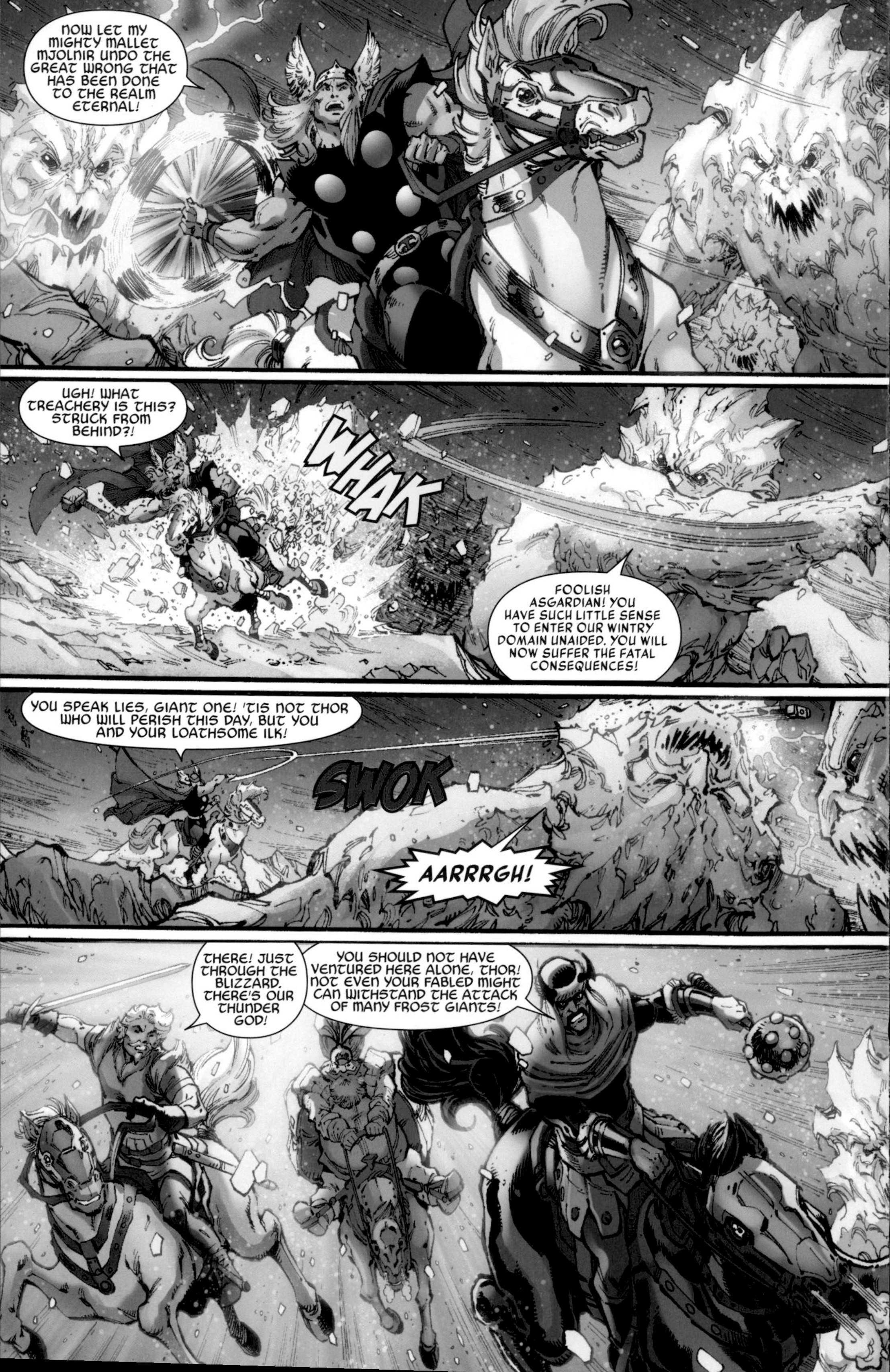
NOW LET MY MIGHTY MALLET MJOLNIR UNDO THE GREAT WRONG THAT HAS BEEN DONE TO THE REALM ETERNAL!
UGH! WHAT TREACHERY IS THIS? STRUCK FROM BEHIND?!
WHAK
FOOLISH ASGARDIAN! YOU HAVE SUCH LITTLE SENSE TO ENTER OUR WINTRY DOMAIN UNAIDED. YOU WILL NOW SUFFER THE FATAL CONSEQUENCES!
YOU SPEAK LIES, GIANT ONE! 'TIS NOT THOR WHO WILL PERISH THIS DAY, BUT YOU AND YOUR LOATHSOME ILK!
SWOK
AARRRGH!
THERE! JUST THROUGH THE BLIZZARD. THERE'S OUR THUNDER GOD!
YOU SHOULD NOT HAVE VENTURED HERE ALONE, THOR! NOT EVEN YOUR FABLED MIGHT CAN WITHSTAND THE ATTACK OF MANY FROST GIANTS!

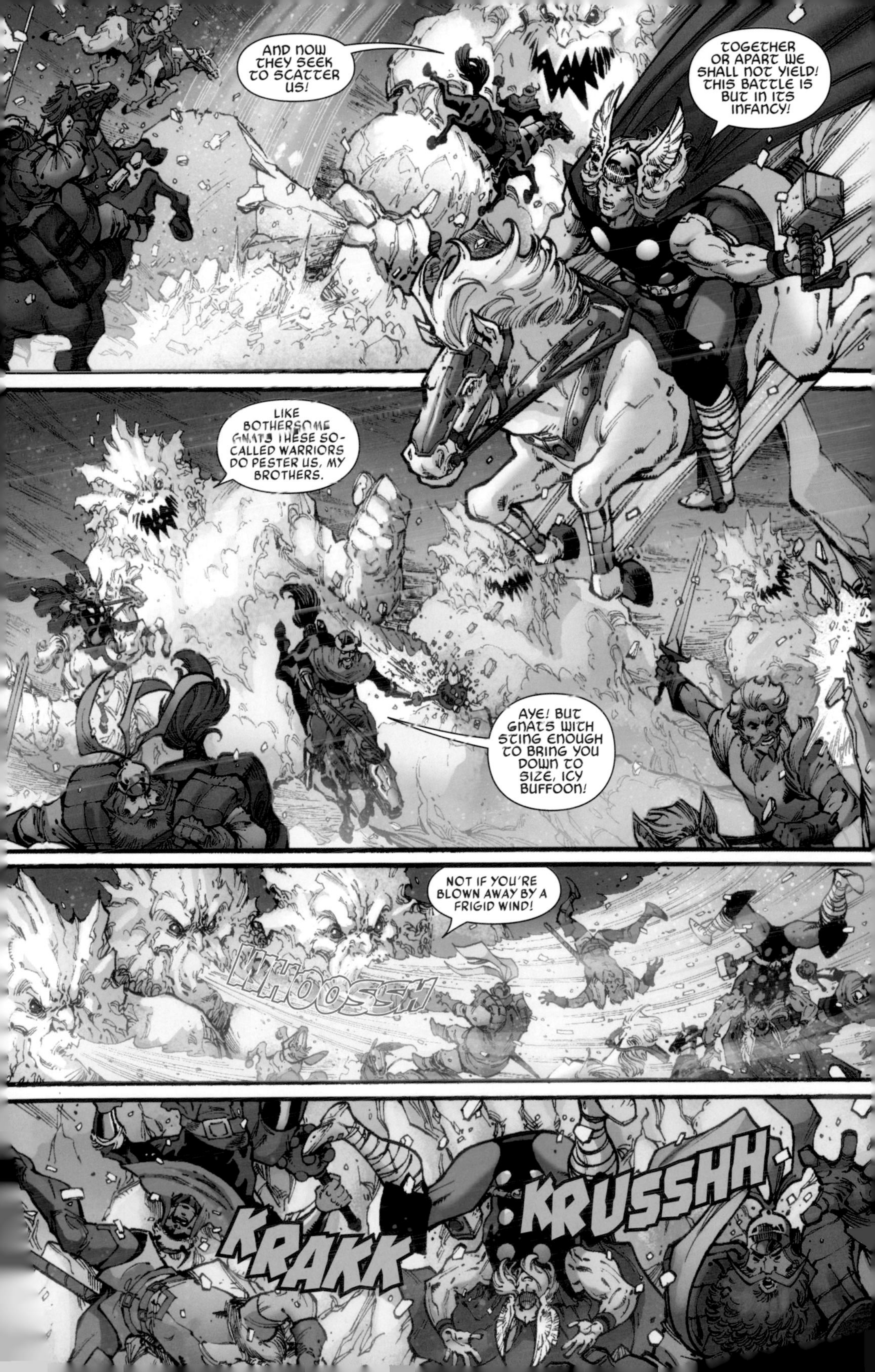
AND NOW THEY SEEK TO SCATTER US!
TOGETHER OR APART WE SHALL NOT YIELD! THIS BATTLE IS BUT IN ITS INFANCY!
LIKE BOTHERSOME GNATS THESE SO-CALLED WARRIORS DO PESTER US, MY BROTHERS.
AYE! BUT GNATS WITH STING ENOUGH TO BRING YOU DOWN TO SIZE, ICY BUFFOON!
NOT IF YOU'RE BLOWN AWAY BY A FRIGID WIND!
WHOOSSH
KRAKK
KRUSSHH

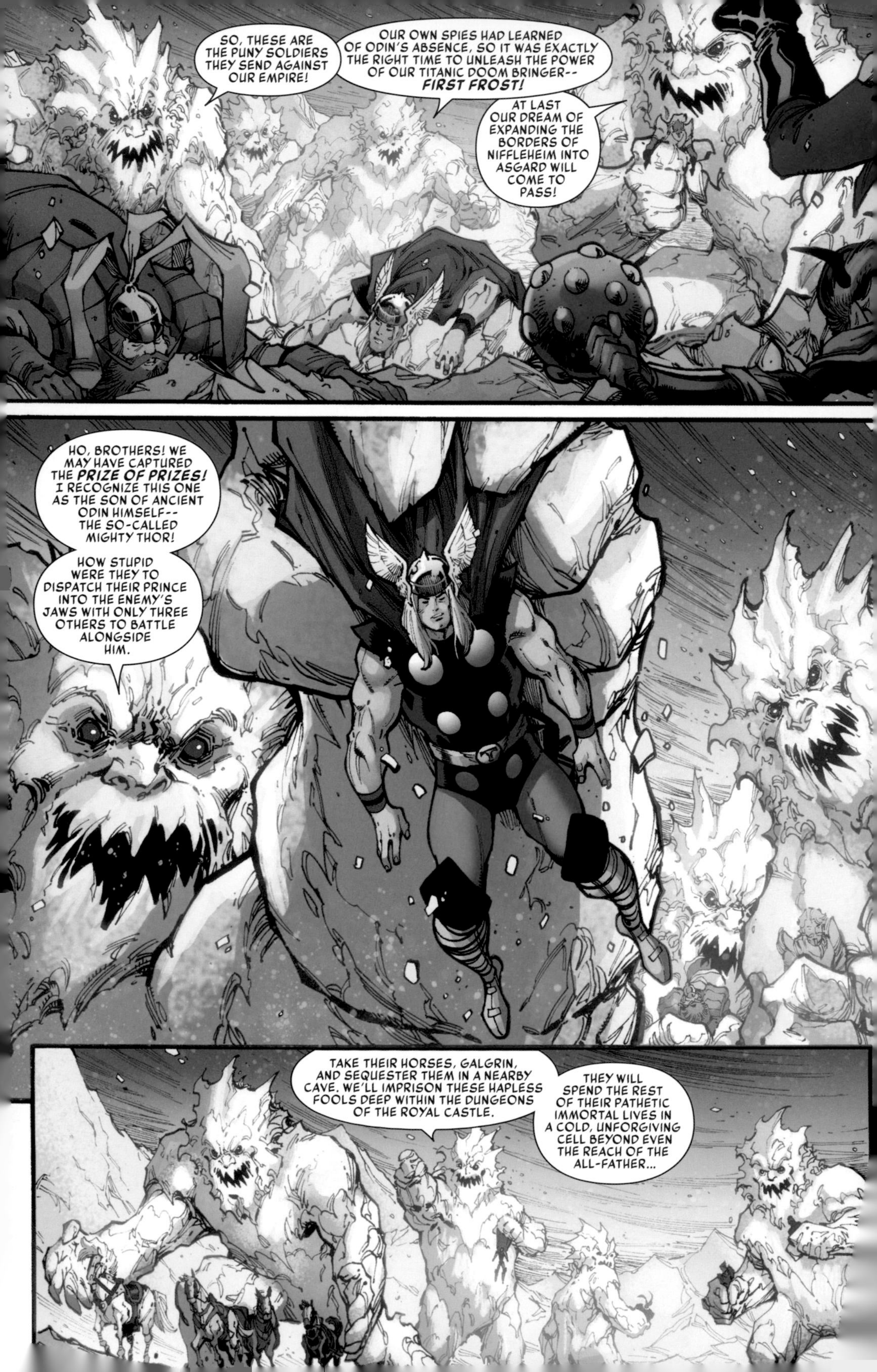
SO, THESE ARE THE PUNY SOLDIERS THEY SEND AGAINST OUR EMPIRE!
OUR OWN SPIES HAD LEARNED OF ODIN'S ABSENCE, SO IT WAS EXACTLY THE RIGHT TIME TO UNLEASH THE POWER OF OUR TITANIC DOOM BRINGER-- FIRST FROST!
AT LAST OUR DREAM OF EXPANDING THE BORDERS OF NIFFLEHEIM INTO ASGARD WILL COME TO PASS!
HO, BROTHERS! WE MAY HAVE CAPTURED THE PRIZE OF PRIZES! I RECOGNIZE THIS ONE AS THE SON OF ANCIENT ODIN HIMSELF-- THE SO-CALLED MIGHTY THOR!
HOW STUPID WERE THEY TO DISPATCH THEIR PRINCE INTO THE ENEMY'S JAWS WITH ONLY THREE OTHERS TO BATTLE ALONGSIDE HIM.
TAKE THEIR HORSES, GALGRIN, AND SEQUESTER THEM IN A NEARBY CAVE. WE'LL IMPRISON THESE HAPLESS FOOLS DEEP WITHIN THE DUNGEONS OF THE ROYAL CASTLE.
THEY WILL SPEND THE REST OF THEIR PATHETIC IMMORTAL LIVES IN A COLD, UNFORGIVING CELL BEYOND EVEN THE REACH OF THE ALL-FATHER...

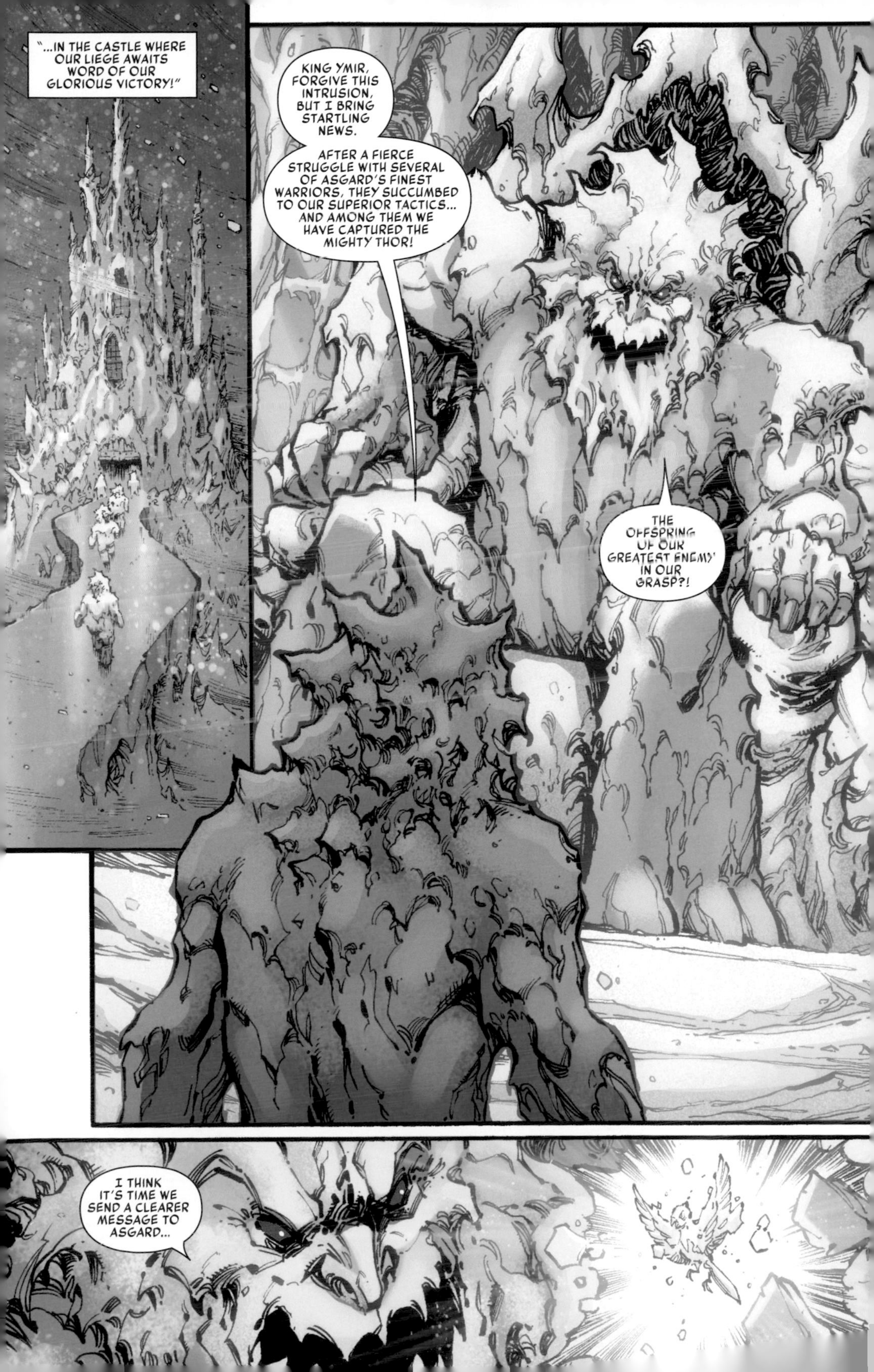
"...IN THE CASTLE WHERE OUR LIEGE AWAITS WORD OF OUR GLORIOUS VICTORY!"
KING YMIR, FORGIVE THIS INTRUSION, BUT I BRING STARTLING NEWS.
AFTER A FIERCE STRUGGLE WITH SEVERAL OF ASGARD'S FINEST WARRIORS, THEY SUCCUMBED TO OUR SUPERIOR TACTICS... AND AMONG THEM WE HAVE CAPTURED THE MIGHTY THOR!
THE OFFSPRING OF OUR GREATEST ENEMY IN OUR GRASP?!
I THINK IT'S TIME WE SEND A CLEARER MESSAGE TO ASGARD...

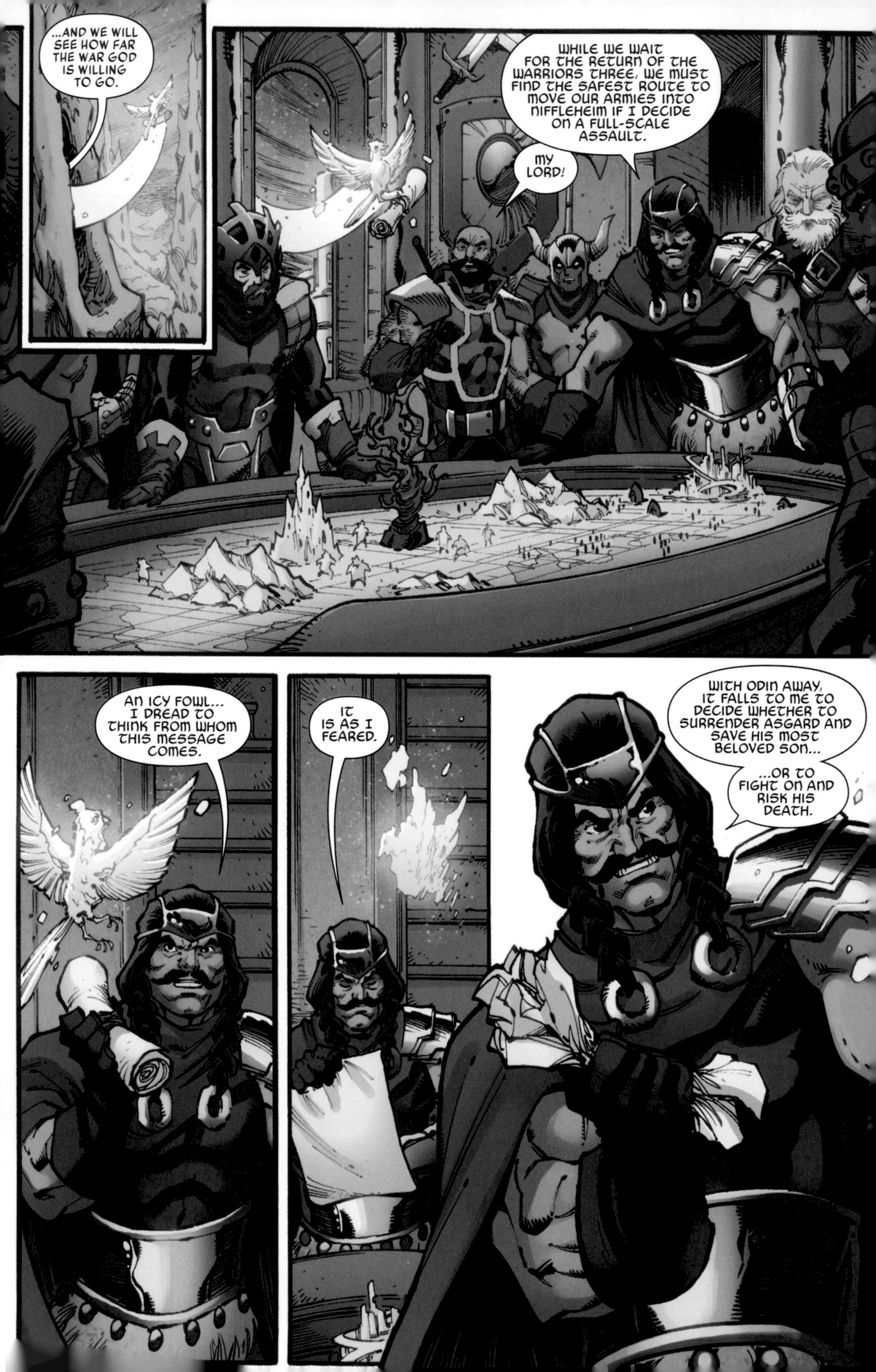
...AND WE WILL SEE HOW FAR THE WAR GOD IS WILLING TO GO.
WHILE WE WAIT FOR THE RETURN OF THE WARRIORS THREE, WE MUST FIND THE SAFEST ROUTE TO MOVE OUR ARMIES INTO NIFFLEHEIM IF I DECIDE ON A FULL-SCALE ASSAULT.
MY LORD!
AN ICY FOWL... I DREAD TO THINK FROM WHOM THIS MESSAGE COMES.
IT IS AS I FEARED.
WITH ODIN AWAY, IT FALLS TO ME TO DECIDE WHETHER TO SURRENDER ASGARD AND SAVE HIS MOST BELOVED SON...
...OR TO FIGHT ON AND RISK HIS DEATH.

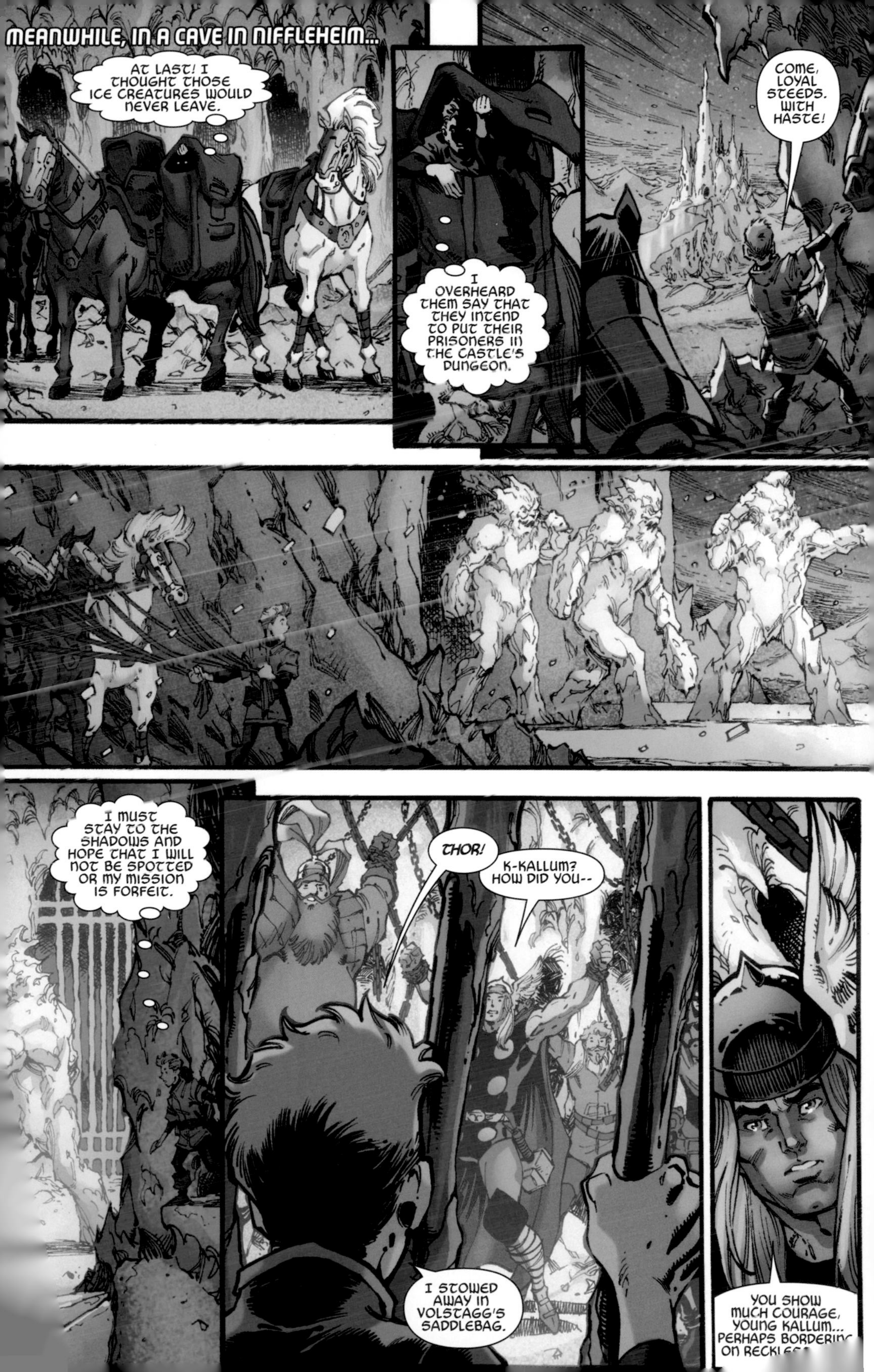
MEANWHILE, IN A CAVE IN NIFFLEHEIM...
AT LAST! I THOUGHT THOSE ICE CREATURES WOULD NEVER LEAVE.
I OVERHEARD THEM SAY THAT THEY INTEND TO PUT THEIR PRISONERS IN THE CASTLE'S DUNGEON.
COME, LOYAL STEEDS. WITH HASTE!
I MUST STAY TO THE SHADOWS AND HOPE THAT I WILL NOT BE SPOTTED OR MY MISSION IS FORFEIT.
THOR!
K-KALLUM? HOW DID YOU--
I STOWED AWAY IN VOLSTAGG'S SADDLEBAG.
YOU SHOW MUCH COURAGE, YOUNG KALLUM... PERHAPS BORDERING

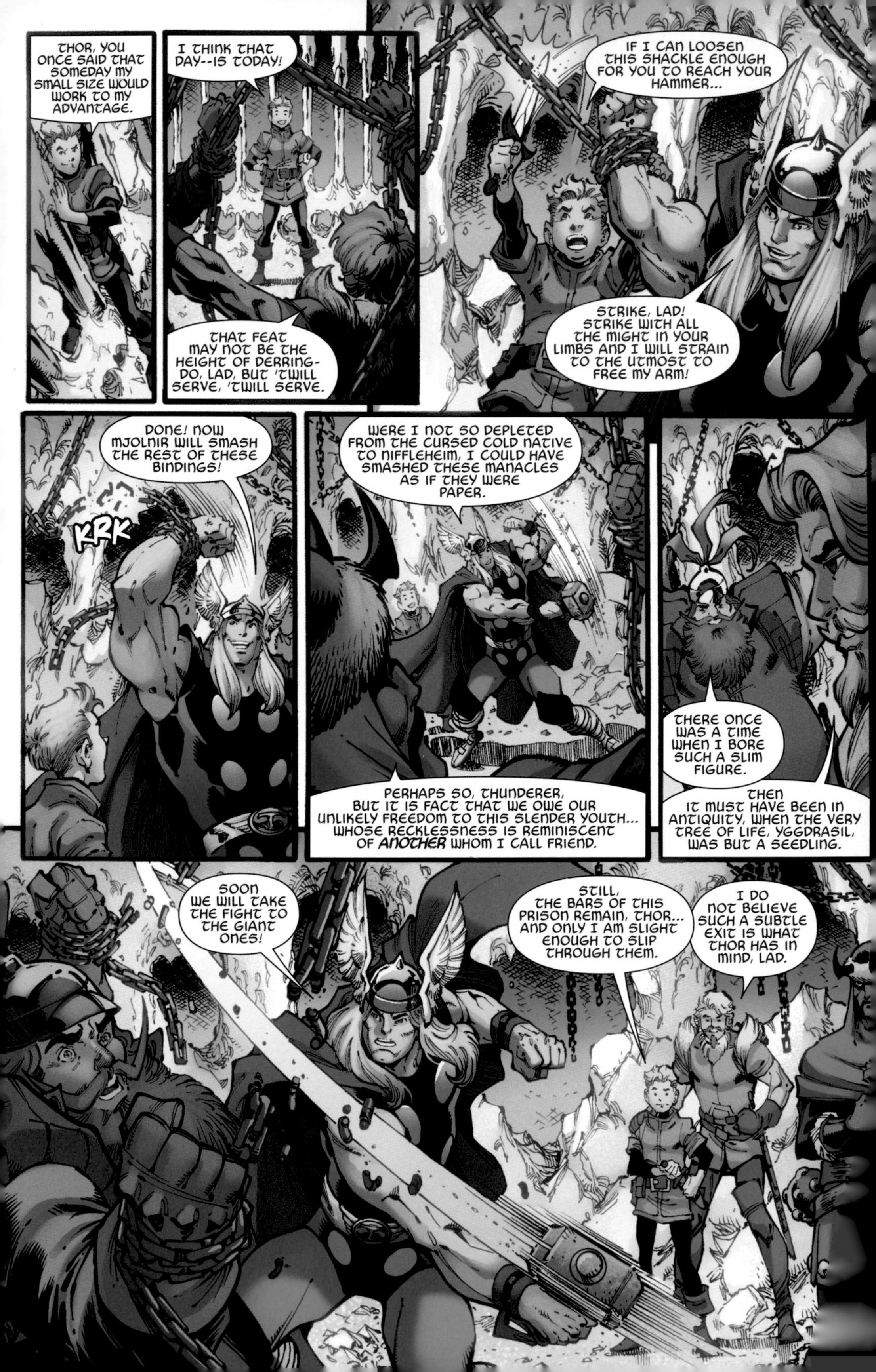
THOR, YOU ONCE SAID THAT SOMEDAY MY SMALL SIZE WOULD WORK TO MY ADVANTAGE.
I THINK THAT DAY--IS TODAY!
THAT FEAT MAY NOT BE THE HEIGHT OF DERRING-DO, LAD, BUT 'TWILL SERVE, 'TWILL SERVE.
IF I CAN LOOSEN THIS SHACKLE ENOUGH FOR YOU TO REACH YOUR HAMMER...
STRIKE, LAD! STRIKE WITH ALL THE MIGHT IN YOUR LIMBS AND I WILL STRAIN TO THE UTMOST TO FREE MY ARM!
DONE! NOW MJOLNIR WILL SMASH THE REST OF THESE BINDINGS!
KRK
WERE I NOT SO DEPLETED FROM THE CURSED COLD NATIVE TO NIFFLEHEIM, I COULD HAVE SMASHED THESE MANACLES AS IF THEY WERE PAPER.
PERHAPS SO, THUNDERER, BUT IT IS FACT THAT WE OWE OUR UNLIKELY FREEDOM TO THIS SLENDER YOUTH... WHOSE RECKLESSNESS IS REMINISCENT OF ANOTHER WHOM I CALL FRIEND.
THERE ONCE WAS A TIME WHEN I BORE SUCH A SLIM FIGURE.
THEN IT MUST HAVE BEEN IN ANTIQUITY, WHEN THE VERY TREE OF LIFE, YGGDRASIL, WAS BUT A SEEDLING.
SOON WE WILL TAKE THE FIGHT TO THE GIANT ONES!
STILL, THE BARS OF THIS PRISON REMAIN, THOR... AND ONLY I AM SLIGHT ENOUGH TO SLIP THROUGH THEM.
I DO NOT BELIEVE SUCH A SUBTLE EXIT IS WHAT THOR HAS IN MIND, LAD.

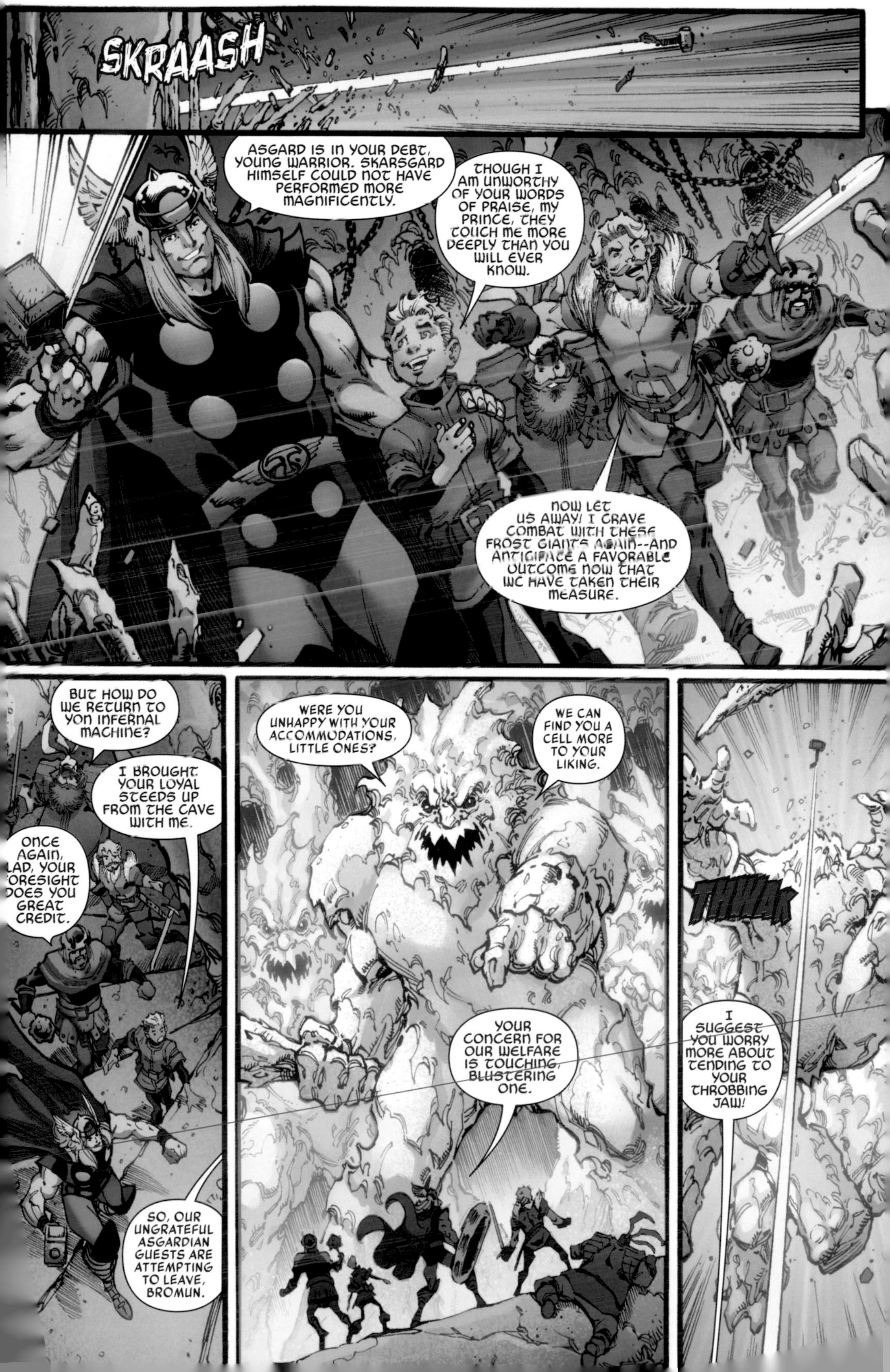
SKRAASH
ASGARD IS IN YOUR DEBT, YOUNG WARRIOR. SKARSGARD HIMSELF COULD NOT HAVE PERFORMED MORE MAGNIFICENTLY.
THOUGH I AM UNWORTHY OF YOUR WORDS OF PRAISE, MY PRINCE, THEY TOUCH ME MORE DEEPLY THAN YOU WILL EVER KNOW.
NOW LET US AWAY! I CRAVE COMBAT WITH THESE FROST GIANTS AGAIN--AND ANTICIPATE A FAVORABLE OUTCOME NOW THAT WE HAVE TAKEN THEIR MEASURE.
BUT HOW DO WE RETURN TO YON INFERNAL MACHINE?
I BROUGHT YOUR LOYAL STEEDS UP FROM THE CAVE WITH ME.
ONCE AGAIN, LAD, YOUR FORESIGHT DOES YOU GREAT CREDIT.
SO, OUR UNGRATEFUL ASGARDIAN GUESTS ARE ATTEMPTING TO LEAVE, BROMUN.
WERE YOU UNHAPPY WITH YOUR ACCOMMODATIONS, LITTLE ONES?
WE CAN FIND YOU A CELL MORE TO YOUR LIKING.
YOUR CONCERN FOR OUR WELFARE IS TOUCHING, BLUSTERING ONE.
THWAK
I SUGGEST YOU WORRY MORE ABOUT TENDING TO YOUR THROBBING JAW!

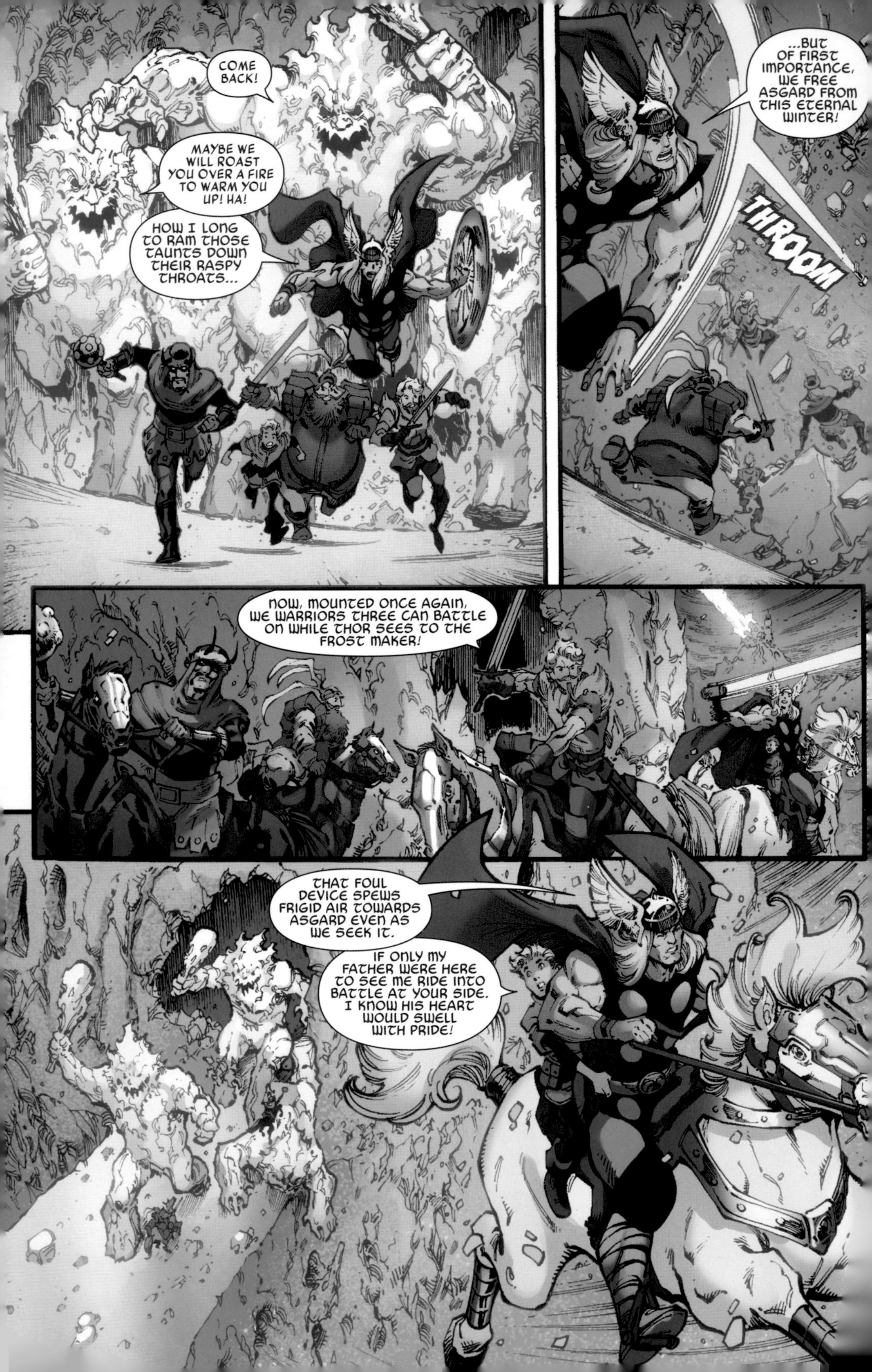
COME BACK!
MAYBE WE WILL ROAST YOU OVER A FIRE TO WARM YOU UP! HA!
HOW I LONG TO RAM THOSE TAUNTS DOWN THEIR RASPY THROATS...
...BUT OF FIRST IMPORTANCE, WE FREE ASGARD FROM THIS ETERNAL WINTER!
THROOM
NOW, MOUNTED ONCE AGAIN, WE WARRIORS THREE CAN BATTLE ON WHILE THOR SEES TO THE FROST MAKER!
THAT FOUL DEVICE SPEWS FRIGID AIR TOWARDS ASGARD EVEN AS WE SEEK IT.
IF ONLY MY FATHER WERE HERE TO SEE ME RIDE INTO BATTLE AT YOUR SIDE. I KNOW HIS HEART WOULD SWELL WITH PRIDE!

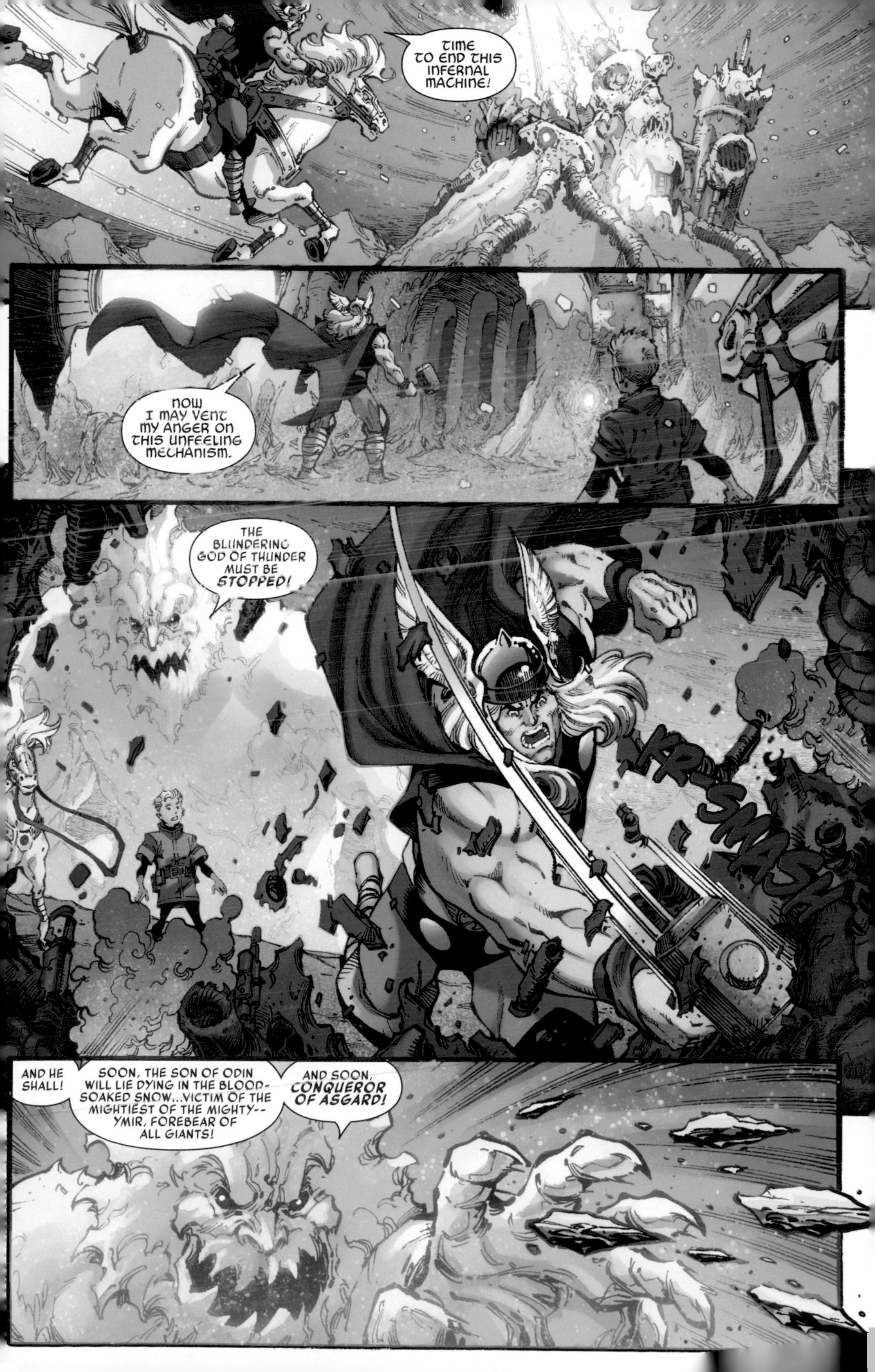
TIME TO END THIS INFERNAL MACHINE!
NOW I MAY VENT MY ANGER ON THIS UNFEELING MECHANISM.
THE BLUNDERING GOD OF THUNDER MUST BE STOPPED!
KR-SMASH
AND HE SHALL!
SOON, THE SON OF ODIN WILL LIE DYING IN THE BLOOD-SOAKED SNOW...VICTIM OF THE MIGHTIEST OF THE MIGHTY--YMIR, FOREBEAR OF ALL GIANTS!
AND SOON, CONQUEROR OF ASGARD!

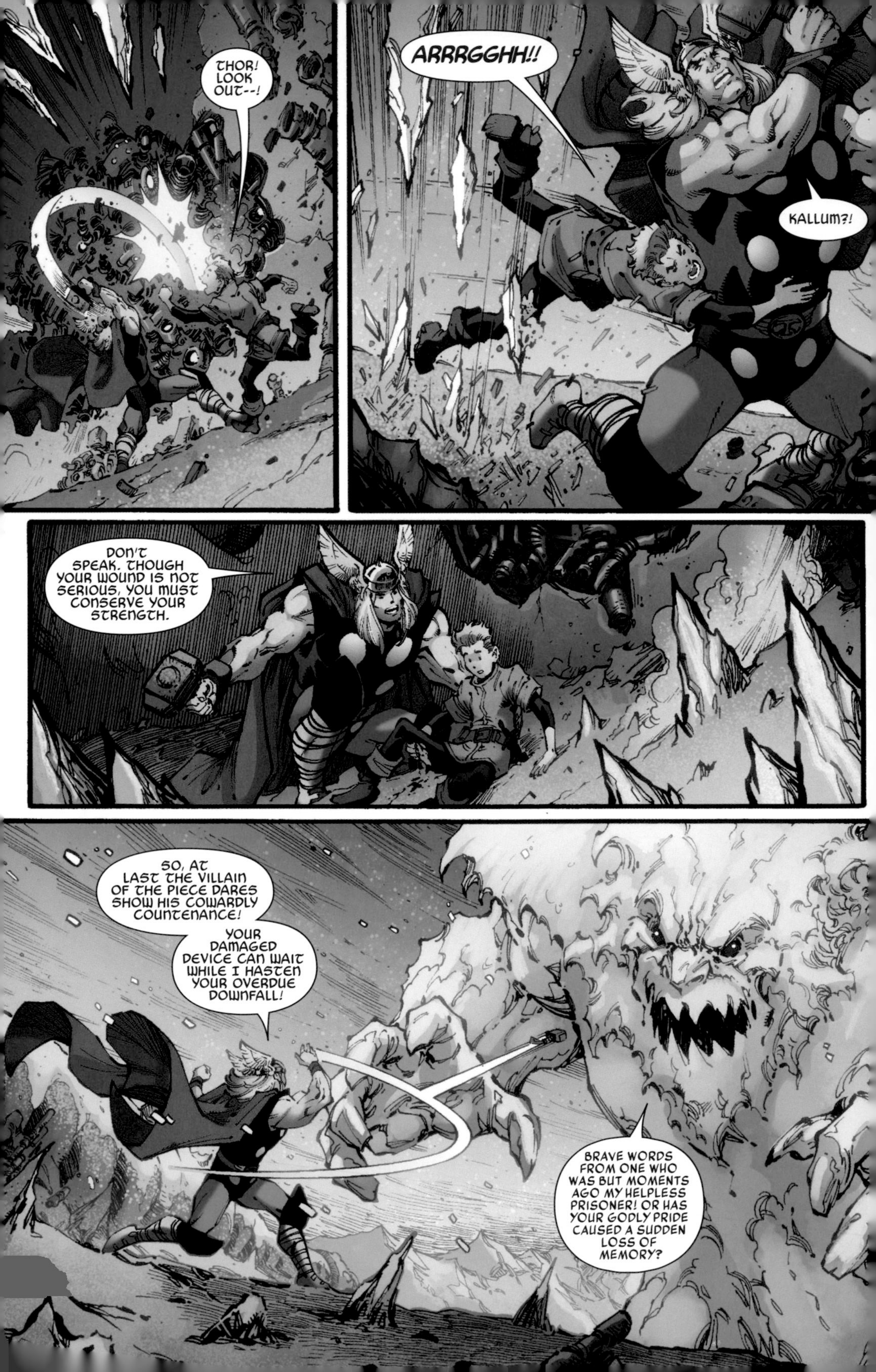
THOR! LOOK OUT--!
ARRRGGHH!!
KALLUM?!
DON'T SPEAK. THOUGH YOUR WOUND IS NOT SERIOUS, YOU MUST CONSERVE YOUR STRENGTH.
SO, AT LAST THE VILLAIN OF THE PIECE DARES SHOW HIS COWARDLY COUNTENANCE!
YOUR DAMAGED DEVICE CAN WAIT WHILE I HASTEN YOUR OVERDUE DOWNFALL!
BRAVE WORDS FROM ONE WHO WAS BUT MOMENTS AGO MY HELPLESS PRISONER! OR HAS YOUR GODLY PRIDE CAUSED A SUDDEN LOSS OF MEMORY?

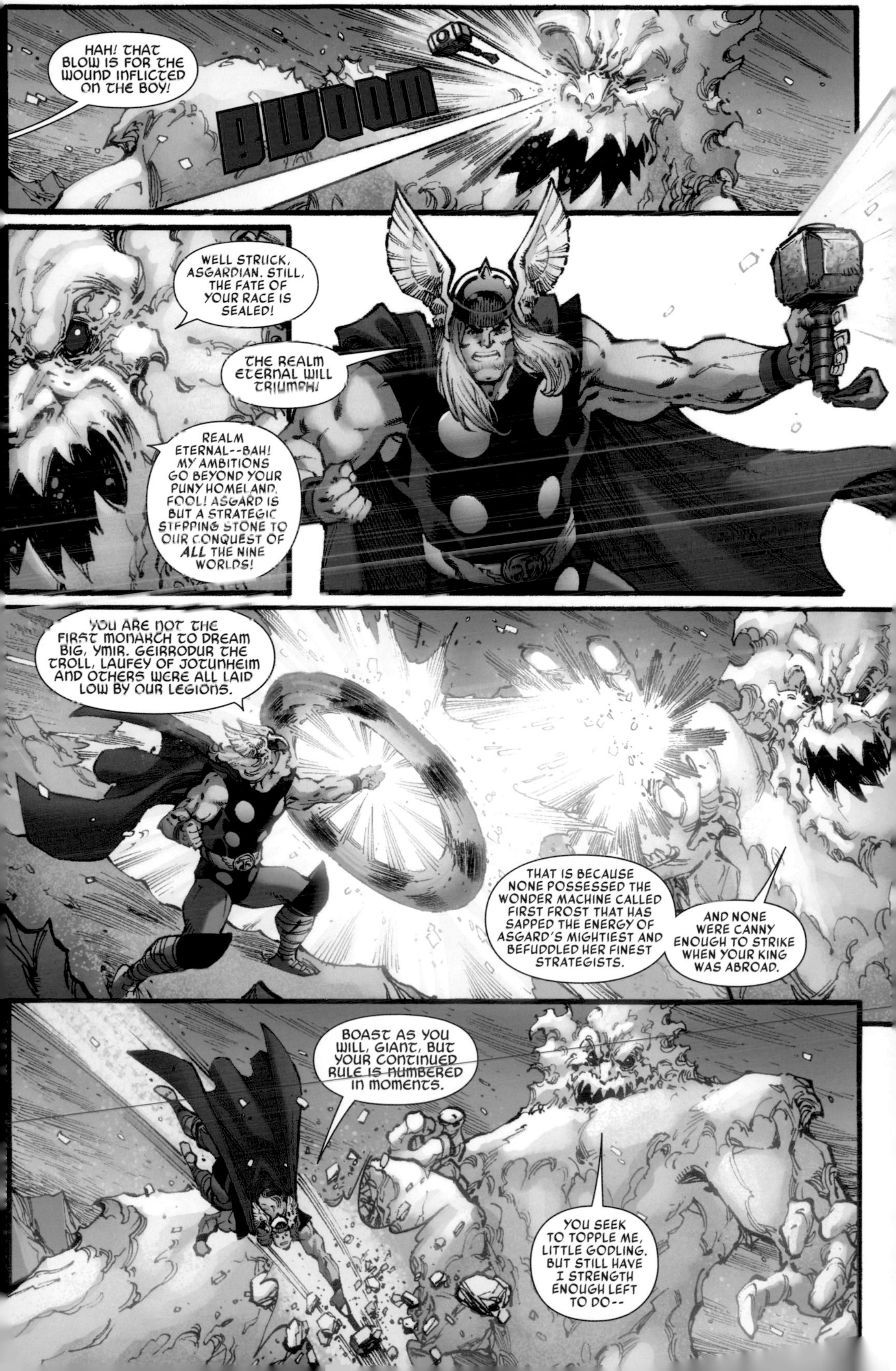
HAH! THAT BLOW IS FOR THE WOUND INFLICTED ON THE BOY!
GWOOM
WELL STRUCK, ASGARDIAN. STILL, THE FATE OF YOUR RACE IS SEALED!
THE REALM ETERNAL WILL TRIUMPH!
REALM ETERNAL--BAH! MY AMBITIONS GO BEYOND YOUR PUNY HOMELAND, FOOL! ASGARD IS BUT A STRATEGIC STEPPING STONE TO OUR CONQUEST OF ALL THE NINE WORLDS!
YOU ARE NOT THE FIRST MONARCH TO DREAM BIG, YMIR. GEIRRODUR THE TROLL, LAUFEY OF JOTUNHEIM AND OTHERS WERE ALL LAID LOW BY OUR LEGIONS.
THAT IS BECAUSE NONE POSSESSED THE WONDER MACHINE CALLED FIRST FROST THAT HAS SAPPED THE ENERGY OF ASGARD'S MIGHTIEST AND BEFUDDLED HER FINEST STRATEGISTS.
AND NONE WERE CANNY ENOUGH TO STRIKE WHEN YOUR KING WAS ABROAD.
BOAST AS YOU WILL, GIANT, BUT YOUR CONTINUED RULE IS NUMBERED IN MOMENTS.
YOU SEEK TO TOPPLE ME, LITTLE GODLING, BUT STILL HAVE I STRENGTH ENOUGH LEFT TO DO--

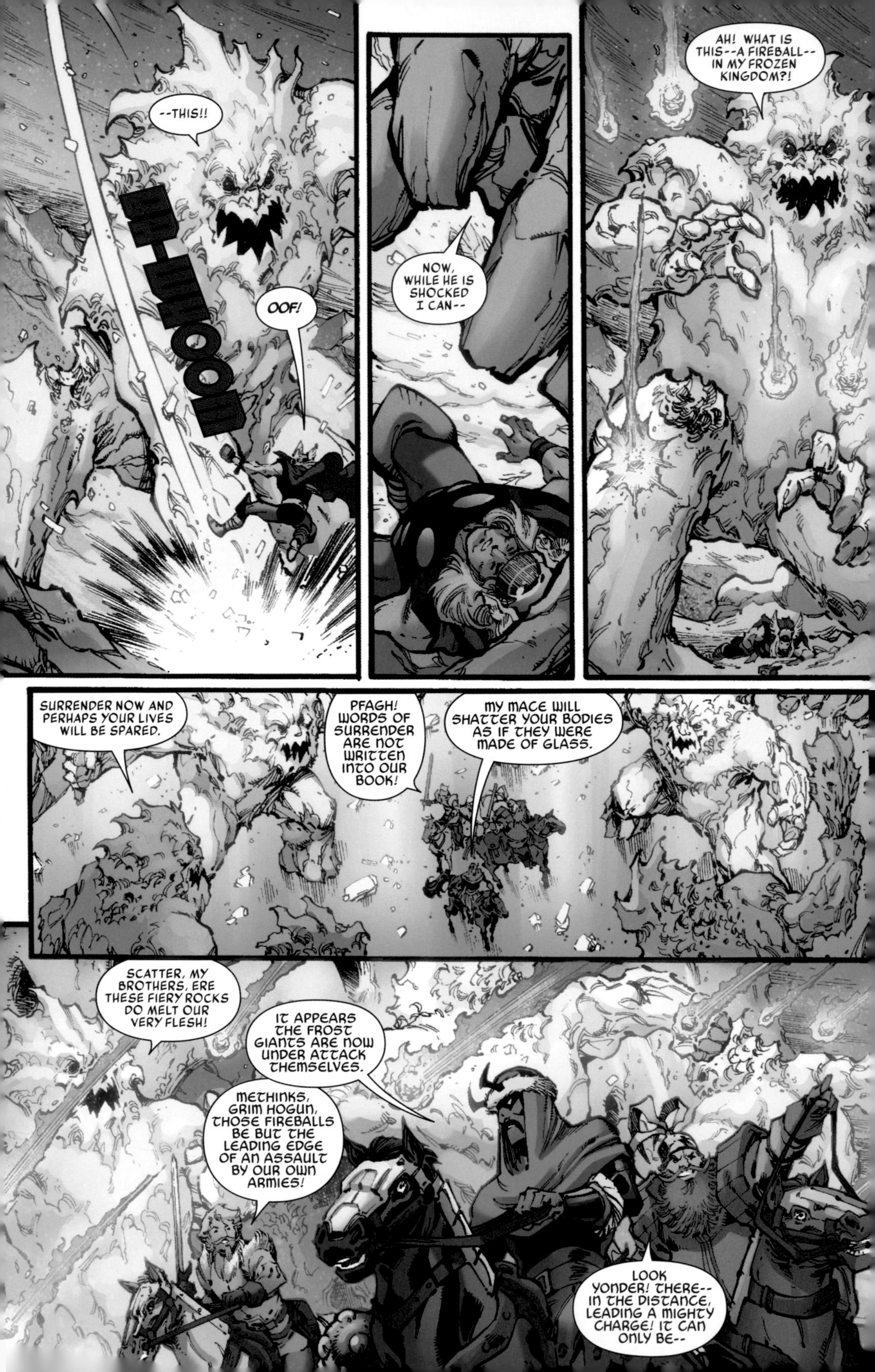
--THIS!!
THWOOM
OOF!
NOW, WHILE HE IS SHOCKED I CAN--
AH! WHAT IS THIS--A FIREBALL--IN MY FROZEN KINGDOM?!
SURRENDER NOW AND PERHAPS YOUR LIVES WILL BE SPARED.
PFAGH! WORDS OF SURRENDER ARE NOT WRITTEN INTO OUR BOOK!
MY MACE WILL SHATTER YOUR BODIES AS IF THEY WERE MADE OF GLASS.
SCATTER, MY BROTHERS, ERE THESE FIERY ROCKS DO MELT OUR VERY FLESH!
IT APPEARS THE FROST GIANTS ARE NOW UNDER ATTACK THEMSELVES.
METHINKS, GRIM HOGUN, THOSE FIREBALLS BE BUT THE LEADING EDGE OF AN ASSAULT BY OUR OWN ARMIES!
LOOK YONDER! THERE--IN THE DISTANCE, LEADING A MIGHTY CHARGE! IT CAN ONLY BE--

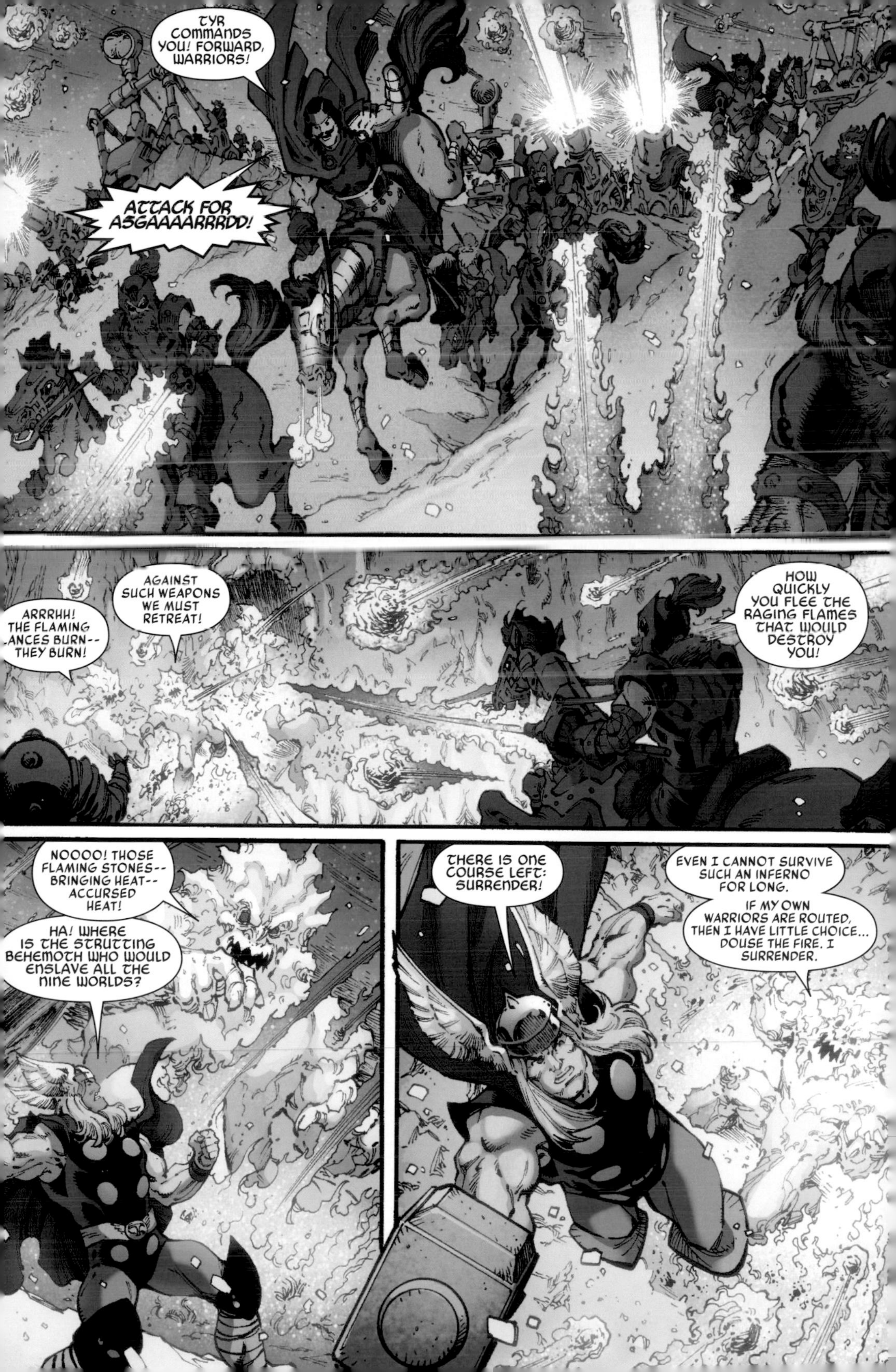
TYR COMMANDS YOU! FORWARD, WARRIORS!
ATTACK FOR ASGAAAARRRDD!
ARRRHH! THE FLAMING LANCES BURN-- THEY BURN!
AGAINST SUCH WEAPONS WE MUST RETREAT!
HOW QUICKLY YOU FLEE THE RAGING FLAMES THAT WOULD DESTROY YOU!
NOOOO! THOSE FLAMING STONES-- BRINGING HEAT-- ACCURSED HEAT!
HA! WHERE IS THE STRUTTING BEHEMOTH WHO WOULD ENSLAVE ALL THE NINE WORLDS?
THERE IS ONE COURSE LEFT: SURRENDER!
EVEN I CANNOT SURVIVE SUCH AN INFERNO FOR LONG.
IF MY OWN WARRIORS ARE ROUTED, THEN I HAVE LITTLE CHOICE... DOUSE THE FIRE. I SURRENDER.

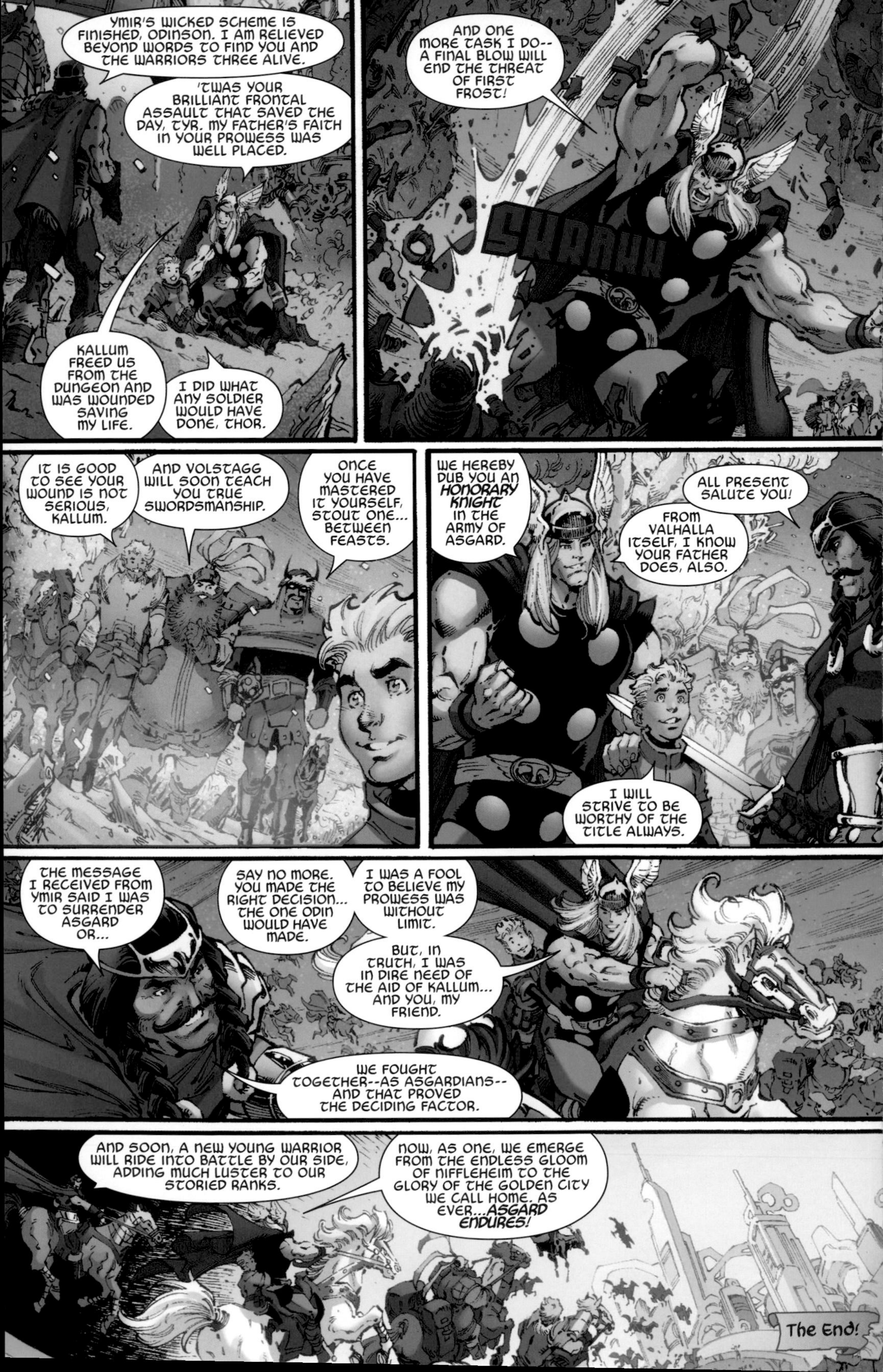
YMIR'S WICKED SCHEME IS FINISHED, ODINSON. I AM RELIEVED BEYOND WORDS TO FIND YOU AND THE WARRIORS THREE ALIVE.
'TWAS YOUR BRILLIANT FRONTAL ASSAULT THAT SAVED THE DAY, TYR. MY FATHER'S FAITH IN YOUR PROWESS WAS WELL PLACED.
KALLUM FREED US FROM THE DUNGEON AND WAS WOUNDED SAVING MY LIFE.
I DID WHAT ANY SOLDIER WOULD HAVE DONE, THOR.
AND ONE MORE TASK I DO-- A FINAL BLOW WILL END THE THREAT OF FIRST FROST!
SKRAKK
IT IS GOOD TO SEE YOUR WOUND IS NOT SERIOUS, KALLUM.
AND VOLSTAGG WILL SOON TEACH YOU TRUE SWORDSMANSHIP.
ONCE YOU HAVE MASTERED IT YOURSELF, STOUT ONE... BETWEEN FEASTS.
WE HEREBY DUB YOU AN HONORARY KNIGHT IN THE ARMY OF ASGARD.
ALL PRESENT SALUTE YOU!
FROM VALHALLA ITSELF, I KNOW YOUR FATHER DOES, ALSO.
I WILL STRIVE TO BE WORTHY OF THE TITLE ALWAYS.
THE MESSAGE I RECEIVED FROM YMIR SAID I WAS TO SURRENDER ASGARD OR...
SAY NO MORE. YOU MADE THE RIGHT DECISION... THE ONE ODIN WOULD HAVE MADE.
I WAS A FOOL TO BELIEVE MY PROWESS WAS WITHOUT LIMIT.
BUT, IN TRUTH, I WAS IN DIRE NEED OF THE AID OF KALLUM... AND YOU, MY FRIEND.
WE FOUGHT TOGETHER--AS ASGARDIANS-- AND THAT PROVED THE DECIDING FACTOR.
AND SOON, A NEW YOUNG WARRIOR WILL RIDE INTO BATTLE BY OUR SIDE, ADDING MUCH LUSTER TO OUR STORIED RANKS.
NOW, AS ONE, WE EMERGE FROM THE ENDLESS GLOOM OF NIFFLEHEIM TO THE GLORY OF THE GOLDEN CITY WE CALL HOME. AS EVER...ASGARD ENDURES!
The End!

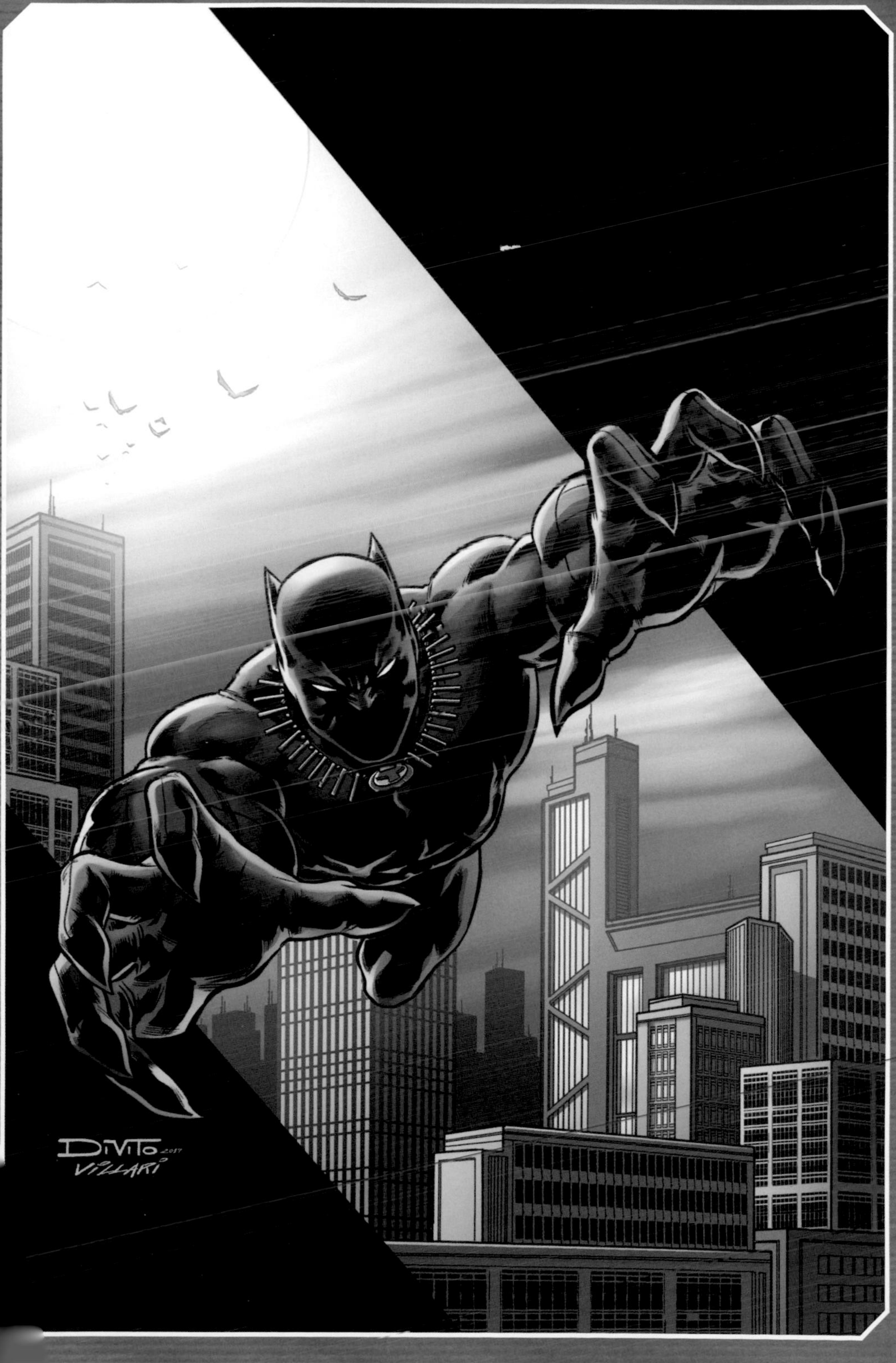
DiVito 2017
Villari

BLACK PANTHER: THE SOUND AND THE FURY

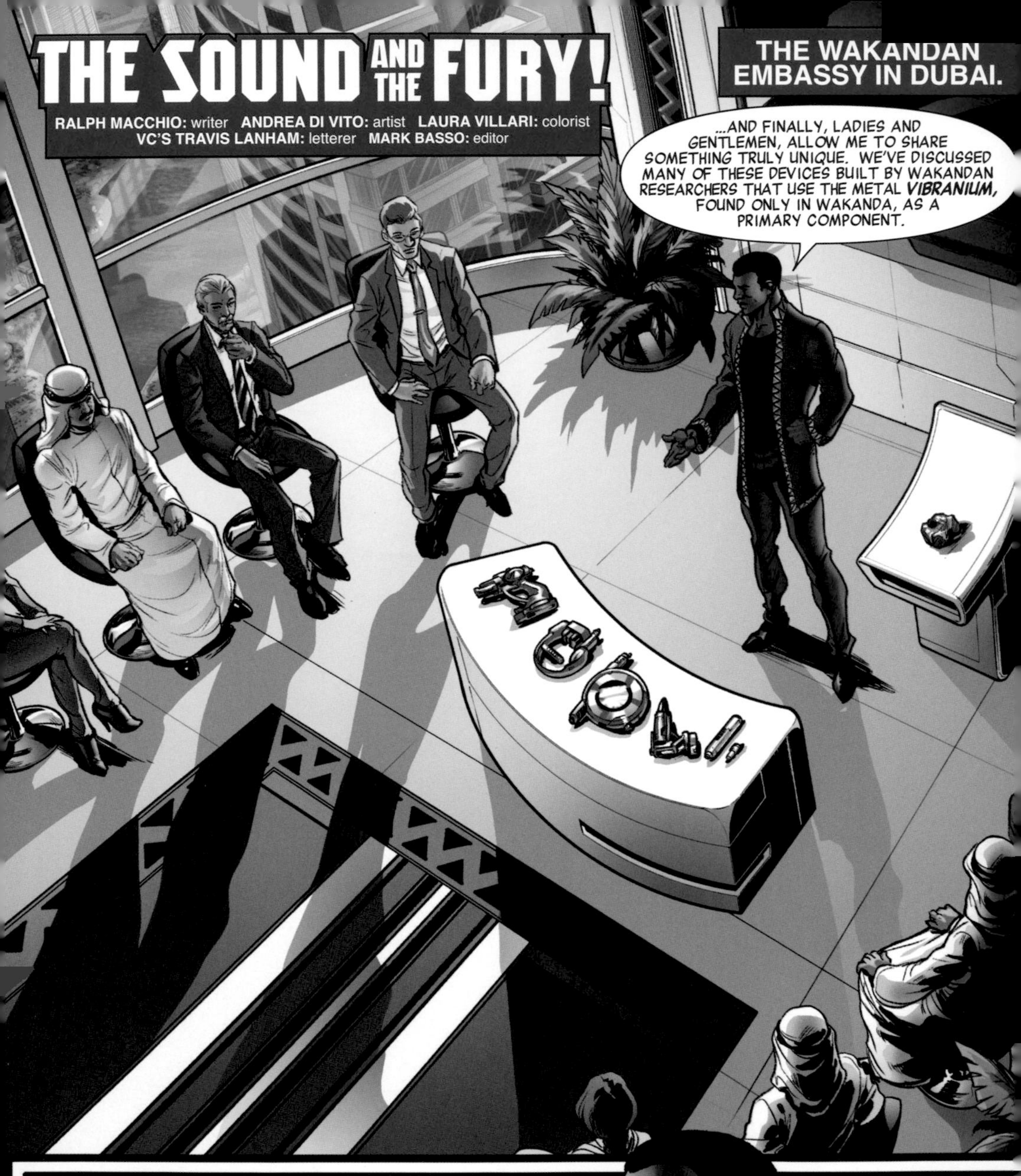
THE SOUND AND THE FURY!
RALPH MACCHIO: writer ANDREA DI VITO: artist LAURA VILLARI: colorist
VC'S TRAVIS LANHAM: letterer MARK BASSO: editor
THE WAKANDAN EMBASSY IN DUBAI.
...AND FINALLY, LADIES AND GENTLEMEN, ALLOW ME TO SHARE SOMETHING TRULY UNIQUE. WE'VE DISCUSSED MANY OF THESE DEVICES BUILT BY WAKANDAN RESEARCHERS THAT USE THE METAL VIBRANIUM, FOUND ONLY IN WAKANDA, AS A PRIMARY COMPONENT.

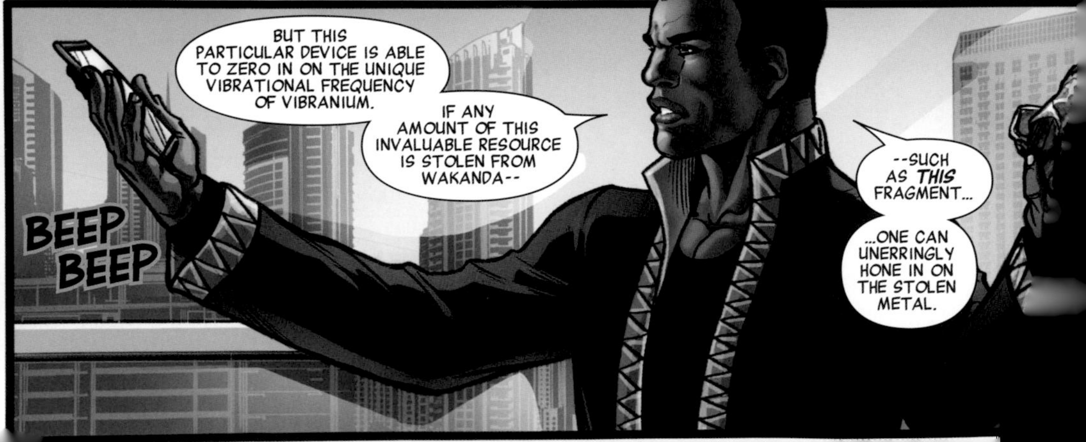
BUT THIS PARTICULAR DEVICE IS ABLE TO ZERO IN ON THE UNIQUE VIBRATIONAL FREQUENCY OF VIBRANIUM.
IF ANY AMOUNT OF THIS INVALUABLE RESOURCE IS STOLEN FROM WAKANDA--
BEEP BEEP
--SUCH AS THIS FRAGMENT...
...ONE CAN UNERRINGLY HONE IN ON THE STOLEN METAL.

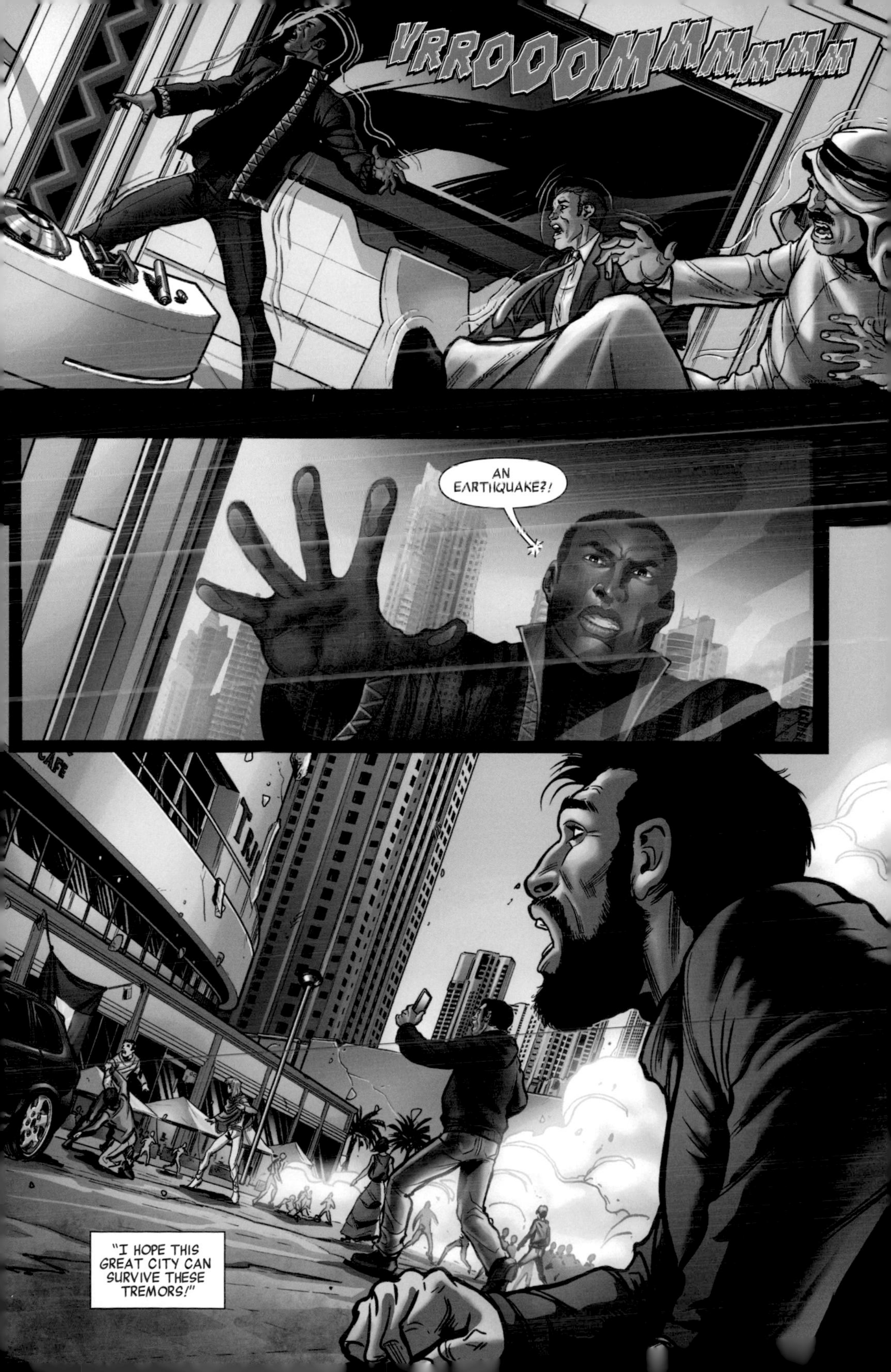
VRROOOMMMMMMM
AN EARTIQUAKE?!
"I HOPE THIS GREAT CITY CAN SURVIVE THESE TREMORS!"

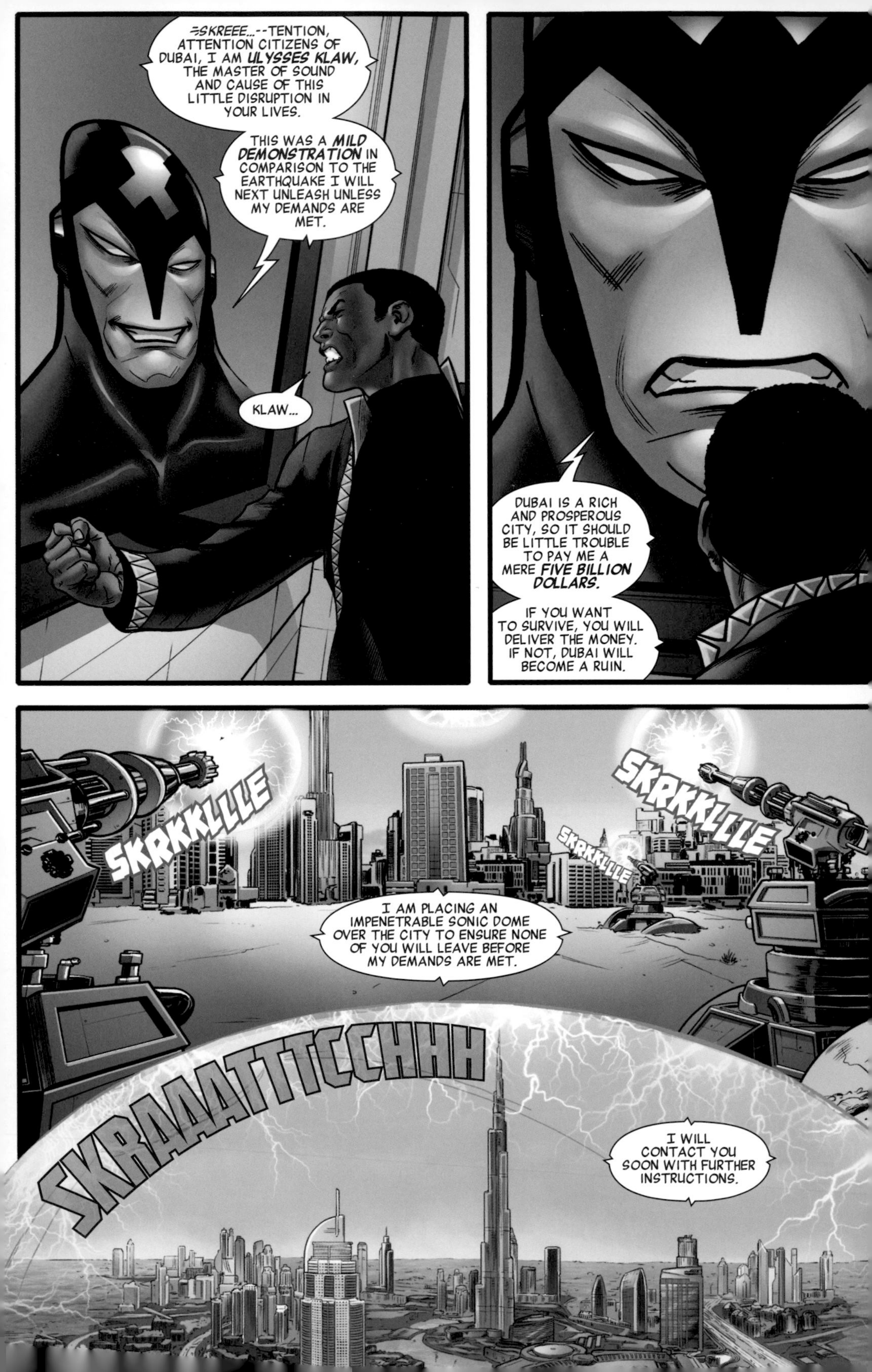

=SKREEE...--TENTION, ATTENTION CITIZENS OF DUBAI, I AM ULYSSES KLAW, THE MASTER OF SOUND AND CAUSE OF THIS LITTLE DISRUPTION IN YOUR LIVES.
THIS WAS A MILD DEMONSTRATION IN COMPARISON TO THE EARTHQUAKE I WILL NEXT UNLEASH UNLESS MY DEMANDS ARE MET.
KLAW...
DUBAI IS A RICH AND PROSPEROUS CITY, SO IT SHOULD BE LITTLE TROUBLE TO PAY ME A MERE FIVE BILLION DOLLARS.
IF YOU WANT TO SURVIVE, YOU WILL DELIVER THE MONEY. IF NOT, DUBAI WILL BECOME A RUIN.
SKRKKLLLE
SKRKKLLLE
SKRKKLLLE
I AM PLACING AN IMPENETRABLE SONIC DOME OVER THE CITY TO ENSURE NONE OF YOU WILL LEAVE BEFORE MY DEMANDS ARE MET.
SKRAAATTTCCHHH
I WILL CONTACT YOU SOON WITH FURTHER INSTRUCTIONS.

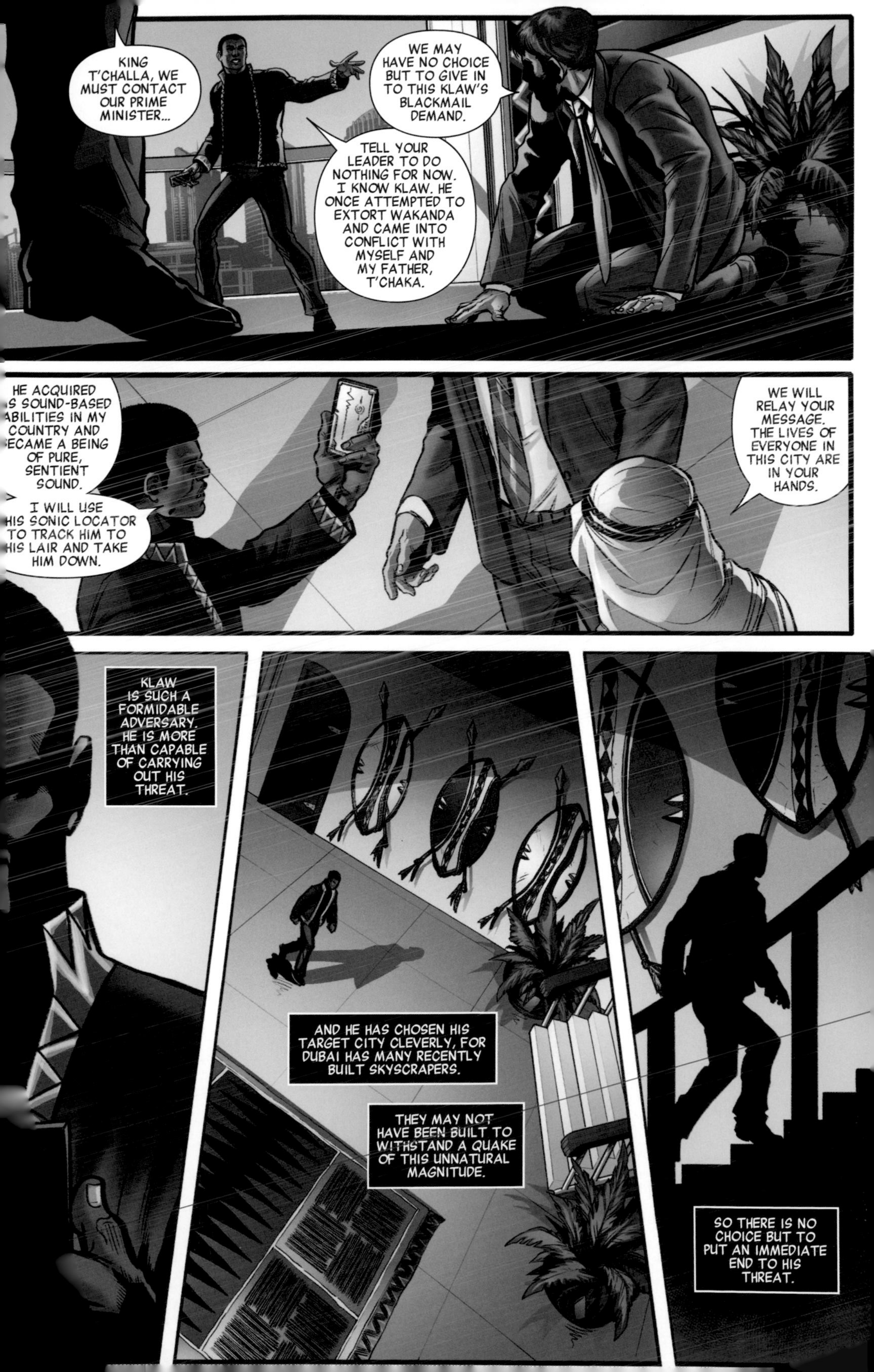

KING T'CHALLA, WE MUST CONTACT OUR PRIME MINISTER...
WE MAY HAVE NO CHOICE BUT TO GIVE IN TO THIS KLAW'S BLACKMAIL DEMAND.
TELL YOUR LEADER TO DO NOTHING FOR NOW. I KNOW KLAW. HE ONCE ATTEMPTED TO EXTORT WAKANDA AND CAME INTO CONFLICT WITH MYSELF AND MY FATHER, T'CHAKA.
HE ACQUIRED S SOUND-BASED ABILITIES IN MY COUNTRY AND ECAME A BEING OF PURE, SENTIENT SOUND.
I WILL USE HIS SONIC LOCATOR TO TRACK HIM TO HIS LAIR AND TAKE HIM DOWN.
WE WILL RELAY YOUR MESSAGE. THE LIVES OF EVERYONE IN THIS CITY ARE IN YOUR HANDS.
KLAW IS SUCH A FORMIDABLE ADVERSARY. HE IS MORE THAN CAPABLE OF CARRYING OUT HIS THREAT.
AND HE HAS CHOSEN HIS TARGET CITY CLEVERLY, FOR DUBAI HAS MANY RECENTLY BUILT SKYSCRAPERS.
THEY MAY NOT HAVE BEEN BUILT TO WITHSTAND A QUAKE OF THIS UNNATURAL MAGNITUDE.
SO THERE IS NO CHOICE BUT TO PUT AN IMMEDIATE END TO HIS THREAT.

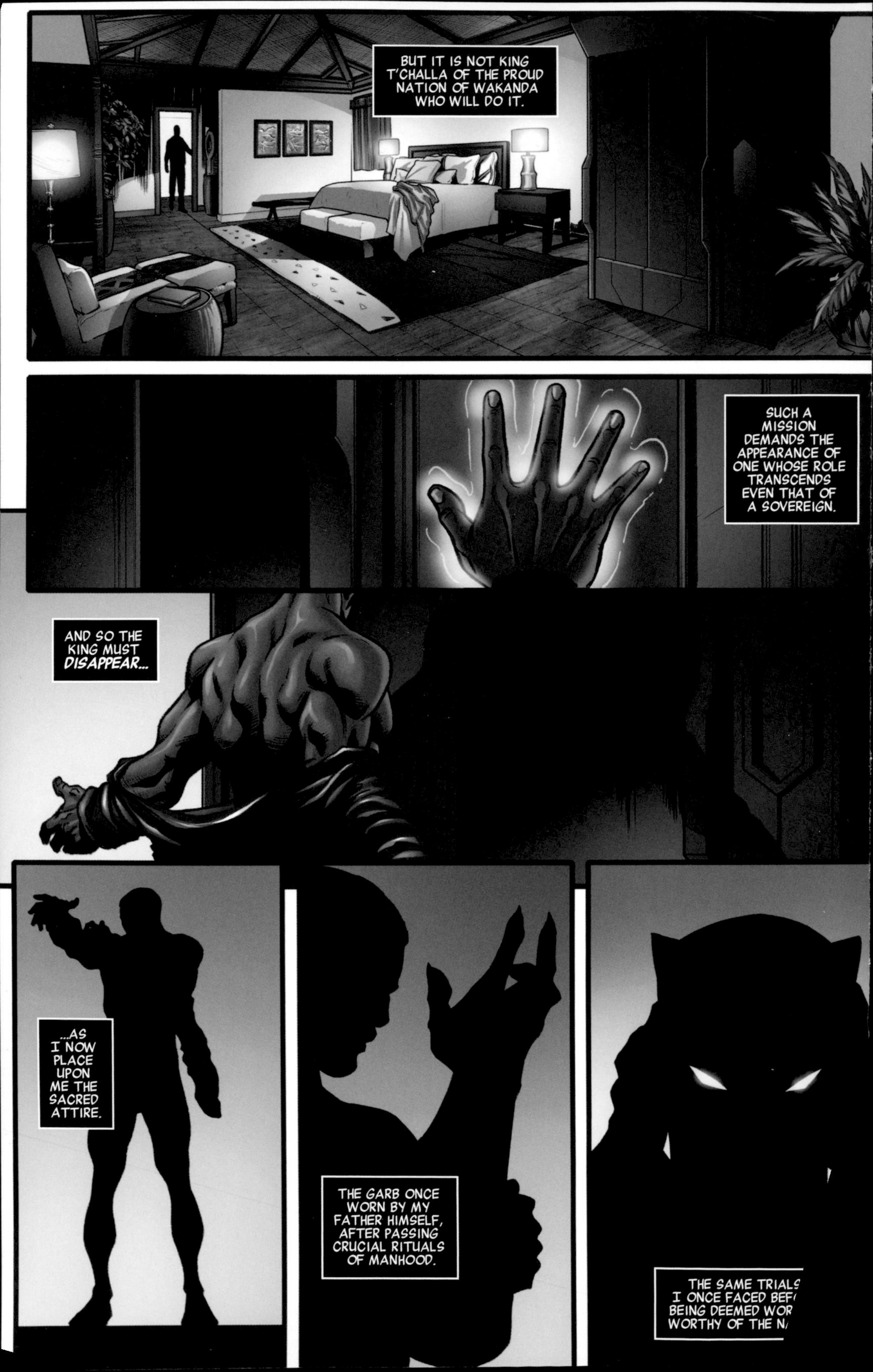
BUT IT IS NOT KING T'CHALLA OF THE PROUD NATION OF WAKANDA WHO WILL DO IT.
SUCH A MISSION DEMANDS THE APPEARANCE OF ONE WHOSE ROLE TRANSCENDS EVEN THAT OF A SOVEREIGN.
AND SO THE KING MUST DISAPPEAR...
...AS I NOW PLACE UPON ME THE SACRED ATTIRE.
THE GARB ONCE WORN BY MY FATHER HIMSELF, AFTER PASSING CRUCIAL RITUALS OF MANHOOD.
THE SAME TRIALS I ONCE FACED BEF BEING DEEMED WOR WORTHY OF THE N

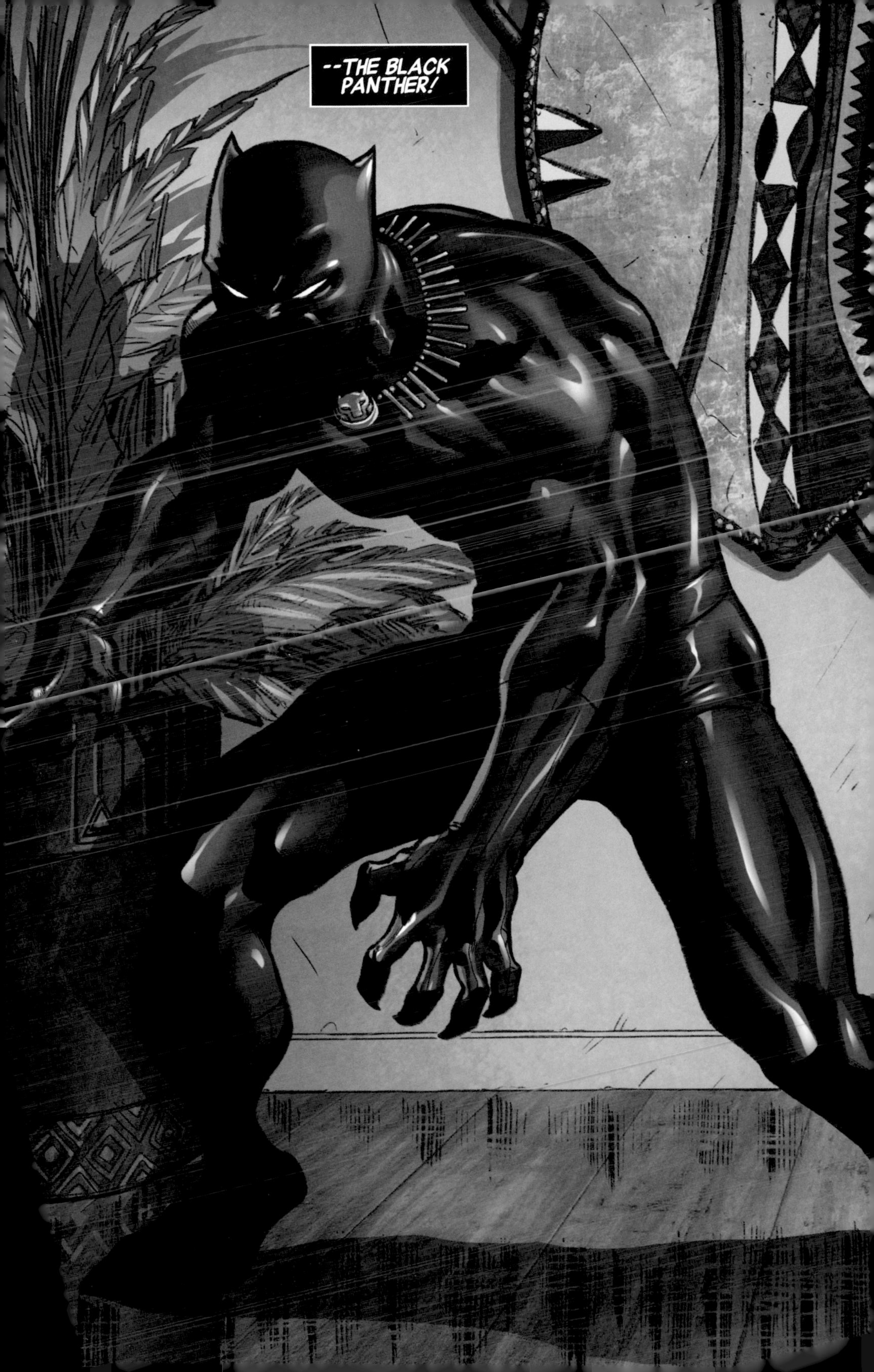
--THE BLACK PANTHER!

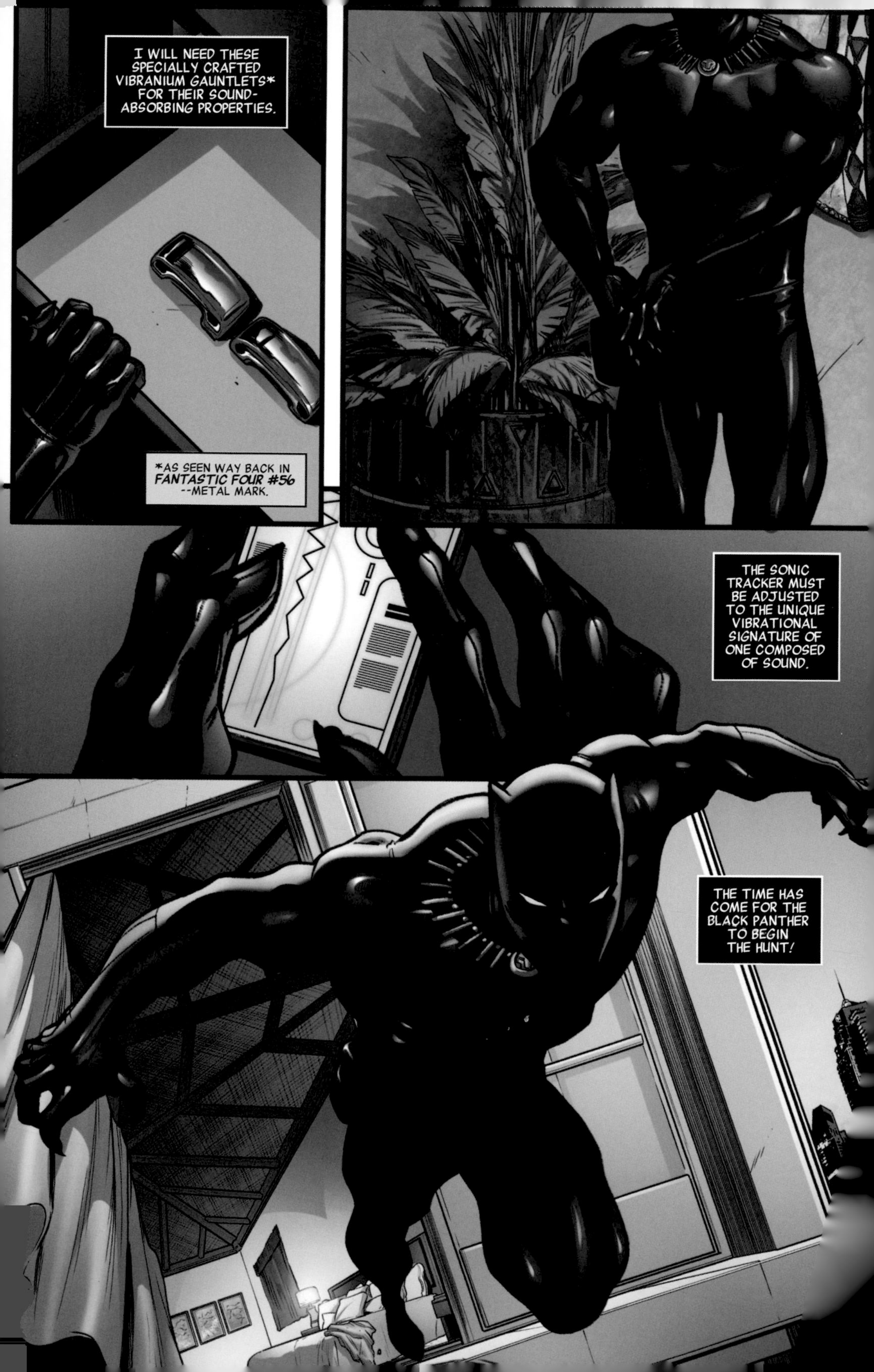
I WILL NEED THESE SPECIALLY CRAFTED VIBRANIUM GAUNTLETS* FOR THEIR SOUND-ABSORBING PROPERTIES.
*AS SEEN WAY BACK IN FANTASTIC FOUR #56 --METAL MARK.
THE SONIC TRACKER MUST BE ADJUSTED TO THE UNIQUE VIBRATIONAL SIGNATURE OF ONE COMPOSED OF SOUND.
THE TIME HAS COME FOR THE BLACK PANTHER TO BEGIN THE HUNT!

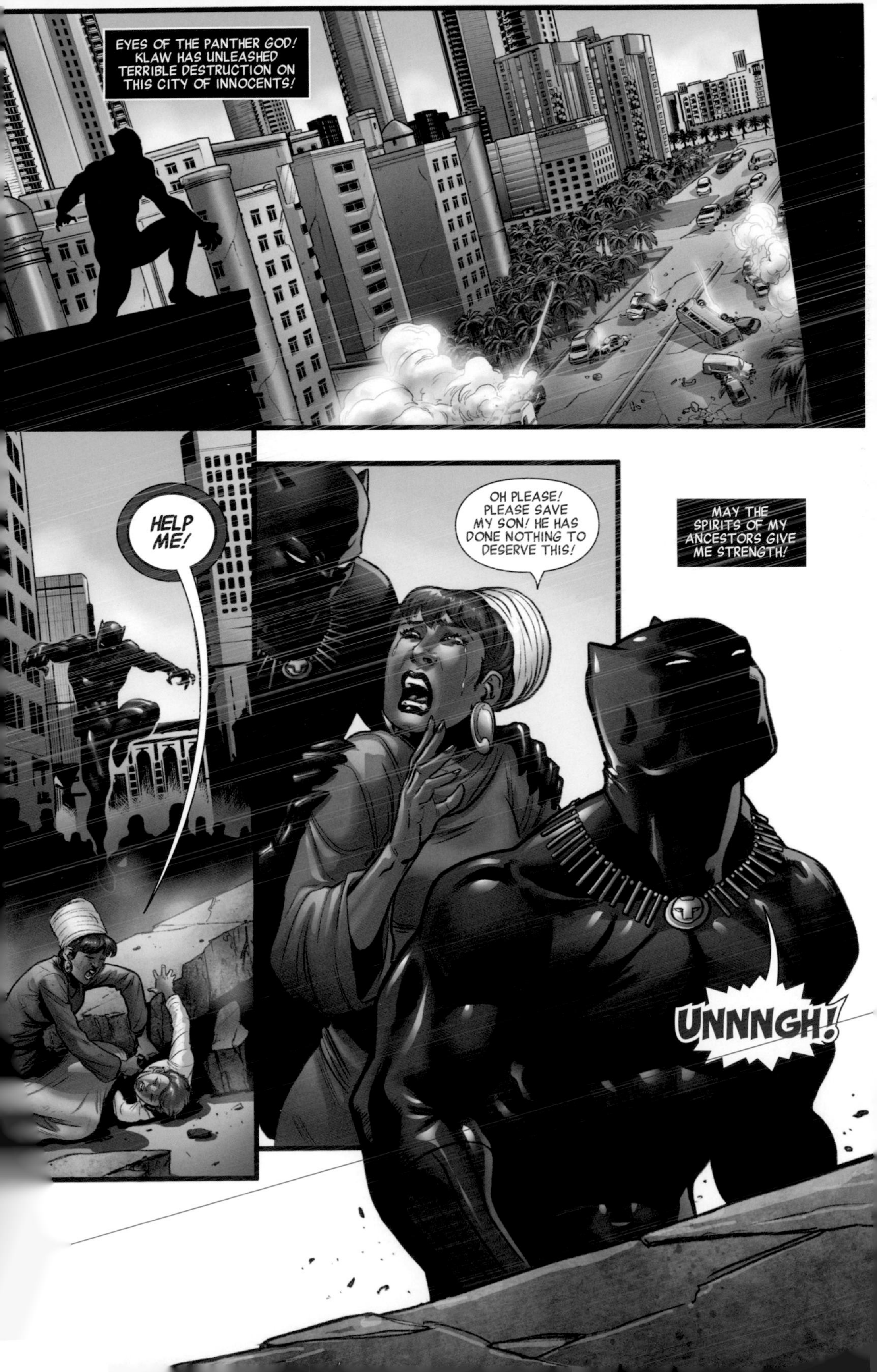
EYES OF THE PANTHER GOD! KLAW HAS UNLEASHED TERRIBLE DESTRUCTION ON THIS CITY OF INNOCENTS!
HELP ME!
OH PLEASE! PLEASE SAVE MY SON! HE HAS DONE NOTHING TO DESERVE THIS!
MAY THE SPIRITS OF MY ANCESTORS GIVE ME STRENGTH!
UNNNGH!

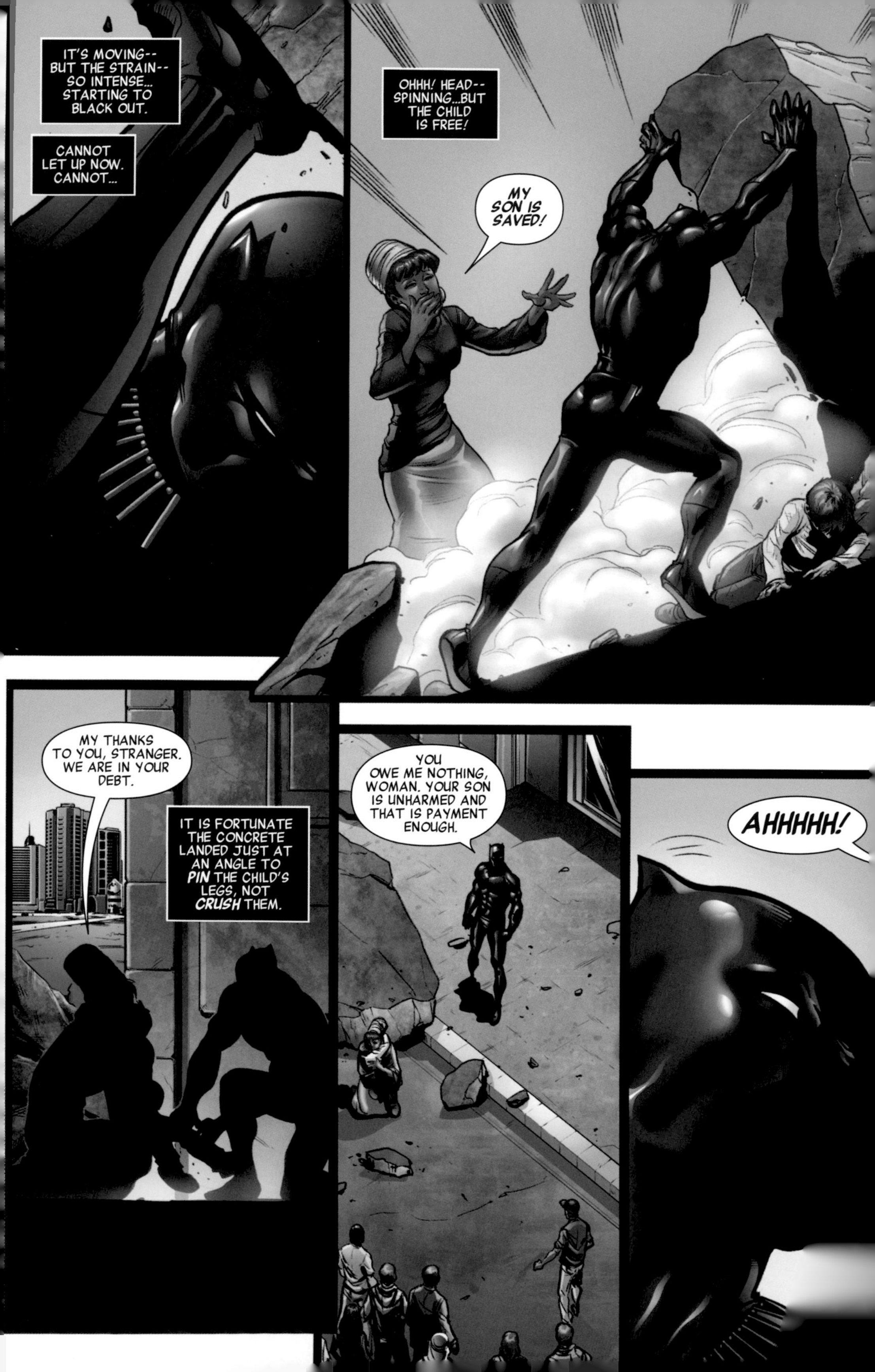
IT'S MOVING-- BUT THE STRAIN-- SO INTENSE... STARTING TO BLACK OUT.
CANNOT LET UP NOW. CANNOT...
OHHH! HEAD-- SPINNING...BUT THE CHILD IS FREE!
MY SON IS SAVED!
MY THANKS TO YOU, STRANGER. WE ARE IN YOUR DEBT.
IT IS FORTUNATE THE CONCRETE LANDED JUST AT AN ANGLE TO PIN THE CHILD'S LEGS, NOT CRUSH THEM.
YOU OWE ME NOTHING, WOMAN. YOUR SON IS UNHARMED AND THAT IS PAYMENT ENOUGH.
AHHHHH!

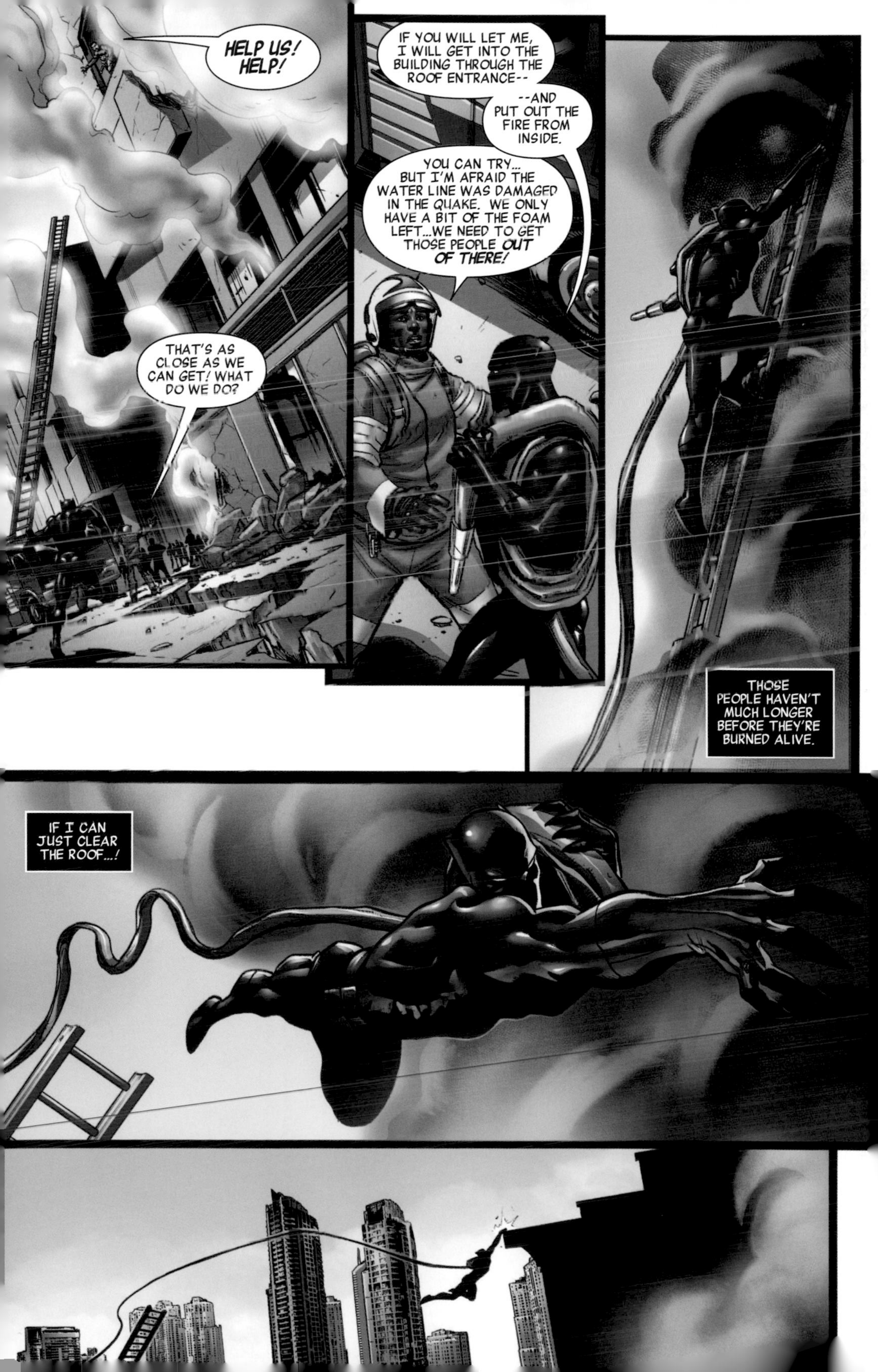
HELP US! HELP!
THAT'S AS CLOSE AS WE CAN GET! WHAT DO WE DO?
IF YOU WILL LET ME, I WILL GET INTO THE BUILDING THROUGH THE ROOF ENTRANCE--
--AND PUT OUT THE FIRE FROM INSIDE.
YOU CAN TRY... BUT I'M AFRAID THE WATER LINE WAS DAMAGED IN THE QUAKE. WE ONLY HAVE A BIT OF THE FOAM LEFT...WE NEED TO GET THOSE PEOPLE OUT OF THERE!
THOSE PEOPLE HAVEN'T MUCH LONGER BEFORE THEY'RE BURNED ALIVE.
IF I CAN JUST CLEAR THE ROOF...!

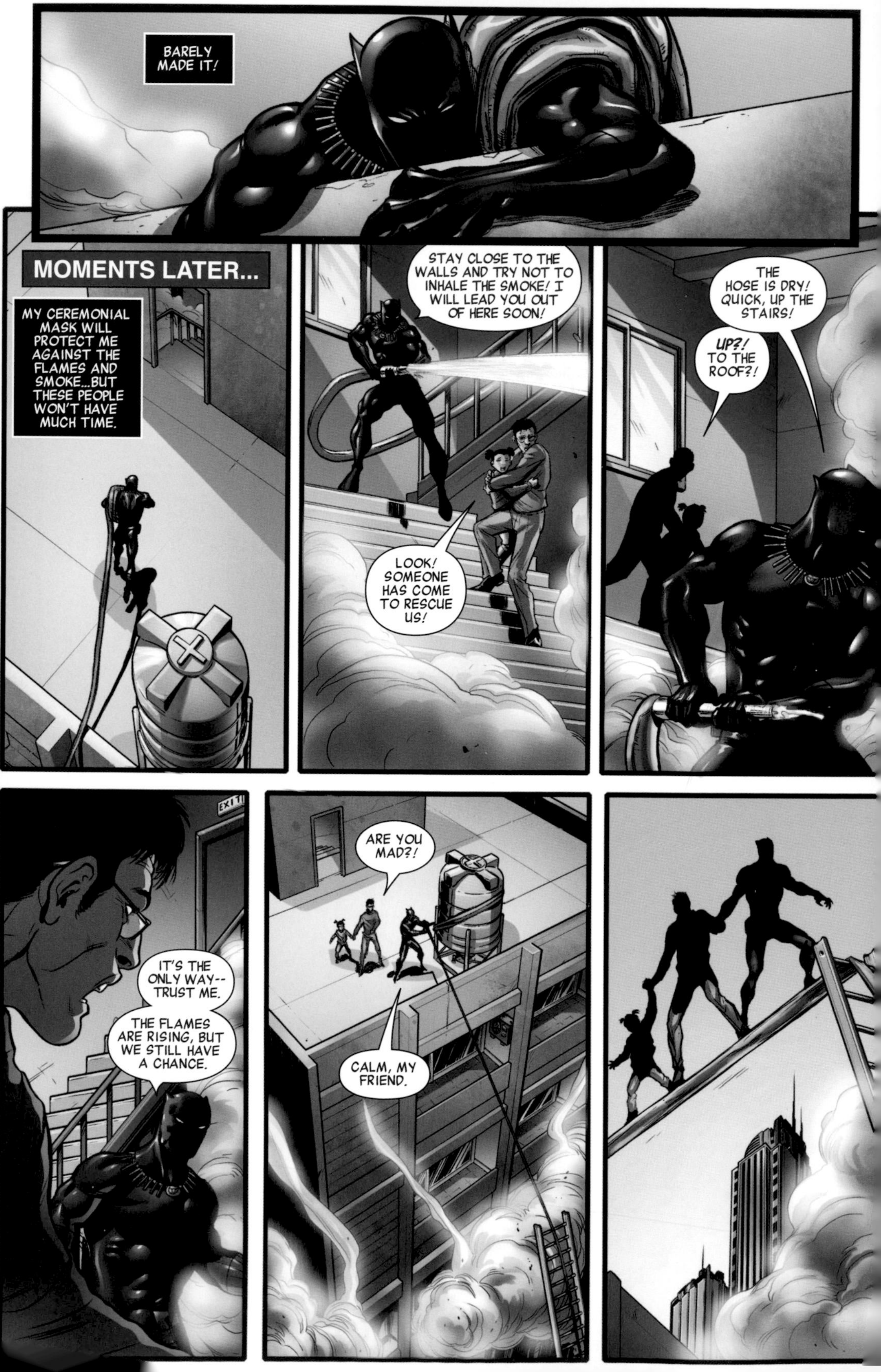

BARELY MADE IT!
MOMENTS LATER...
MY CEREMONIAL MASK WILL PROTECT ME AGAINST THE FLAMES AND SMOKE...BUT THESE PEOPLE WON'T HAVE MUCH TIME.
STAY CLOSE TO THE WALLS AND TRY NOT TO INHALE THE SMOKE! I WILL LEAD YOU OUT OF HERE SOON!
LOOK! SOMEONE HAS COME TO RESCUE US!
THE HOSE IS DRY! QUICK, UP THE STAIRS!
UP?! TO THE ROOF?!
IT'S THE ONLY WAY-- TRUST ME.
THE FLAMES ARE RISING, BUT WE STILL HAVE A CHANCE.
ARE YOU MAD?!
CALM, MY FRIEND.

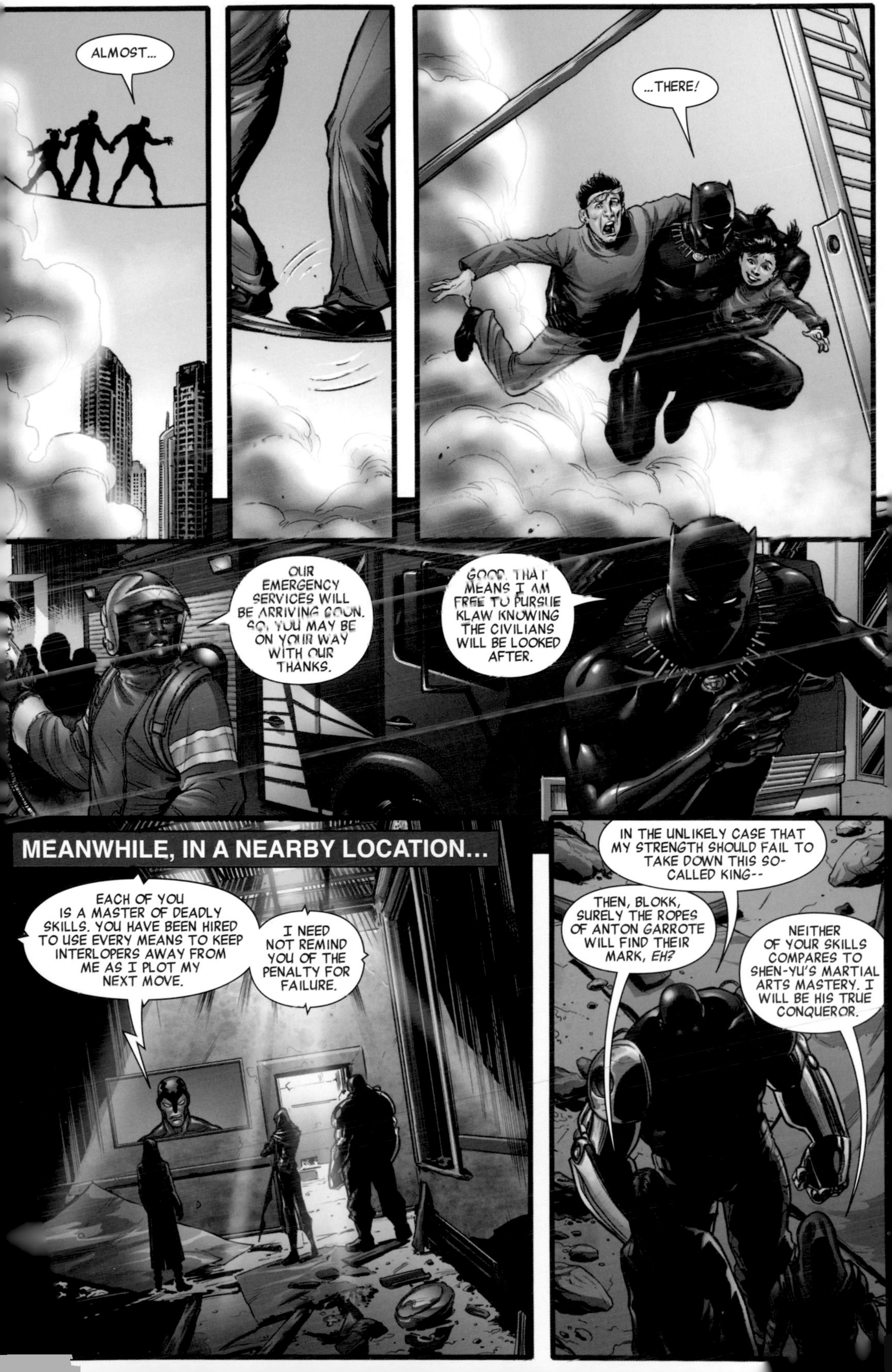

ALMOST...
...THERE!
OUR EMERGENCY SERVICES WILL BE ARRIVING SOON. SO, YOU MAY BE ON YOUR WAY WITH OUR THANKS.
GOOD. THAT MEANS I AM FREE TO PURSUE KLAW KNOWING THE CIVILIANS WILL BE LOOKED AFTER.
MEANWHILE, IN A NEARBY LOCATION...
EACH OF YOU IS A MASTER OF DEADLY SKILLS. YOU HAVE BEEN HIRED TO USE EVERY MEANS TO KEEP INTERLOPERS AWAY FROM ME AS I PLOT MY NEXT MOVE.
I NEED NOT REMIND YOU OF THE PENALTY FOR FAILURE.
IN THE UNLIKELY CASE THAT MY STRENGTH SHOULD FAIL TO TAKE DOWN THIS SO-CALLED KING--
THEN, BLOKK, SURELY THE ROPES OF ANTON GARROTE WILL FIND THEIR MARK, EH?
NEITHER OF YOUR SKILLS COMPARES TO SHEN-YU'S MARTIAL ARTS MASTERY. I WILL BE HIS TRUE CONQUEROR.

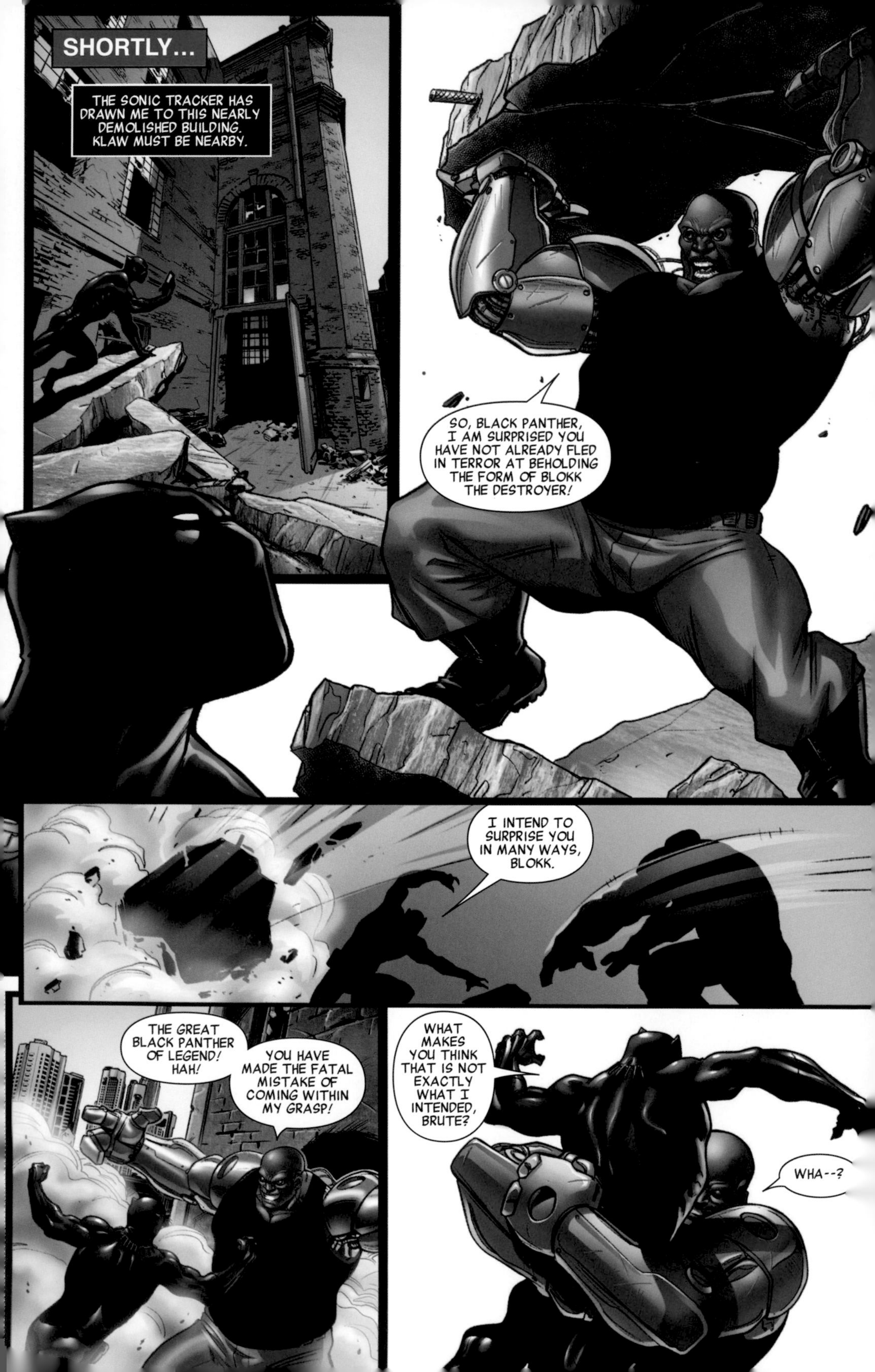
SHORTLY...
THE SONIC TRACKER HAS DRAWN ME TO THIS NEARLY DEMOLISHED BUILDING. KLAW MUST BE NEARBY.
SO, BLACK PANTHER, I AM SURPRISED YOU HAVE NOT ALREADY FLED IN TERROR AT BEHOLDING THE FORM OF BLOKK THE DESTROYER!
I INTEND TO SURPRISE YOU IN MANY WAYS, BLOKK.
THE GREAT BLACK PANTHER OF LEGEND! HAH!
YOU HAVE MADE THE FATAL MISTAKE OF COMING WITHIN MY GRASP!
WHAT MAKES YOU THINK THAT IS NOT EXACTLY WHAT I INTENDED, BRUTE?
WHA--?

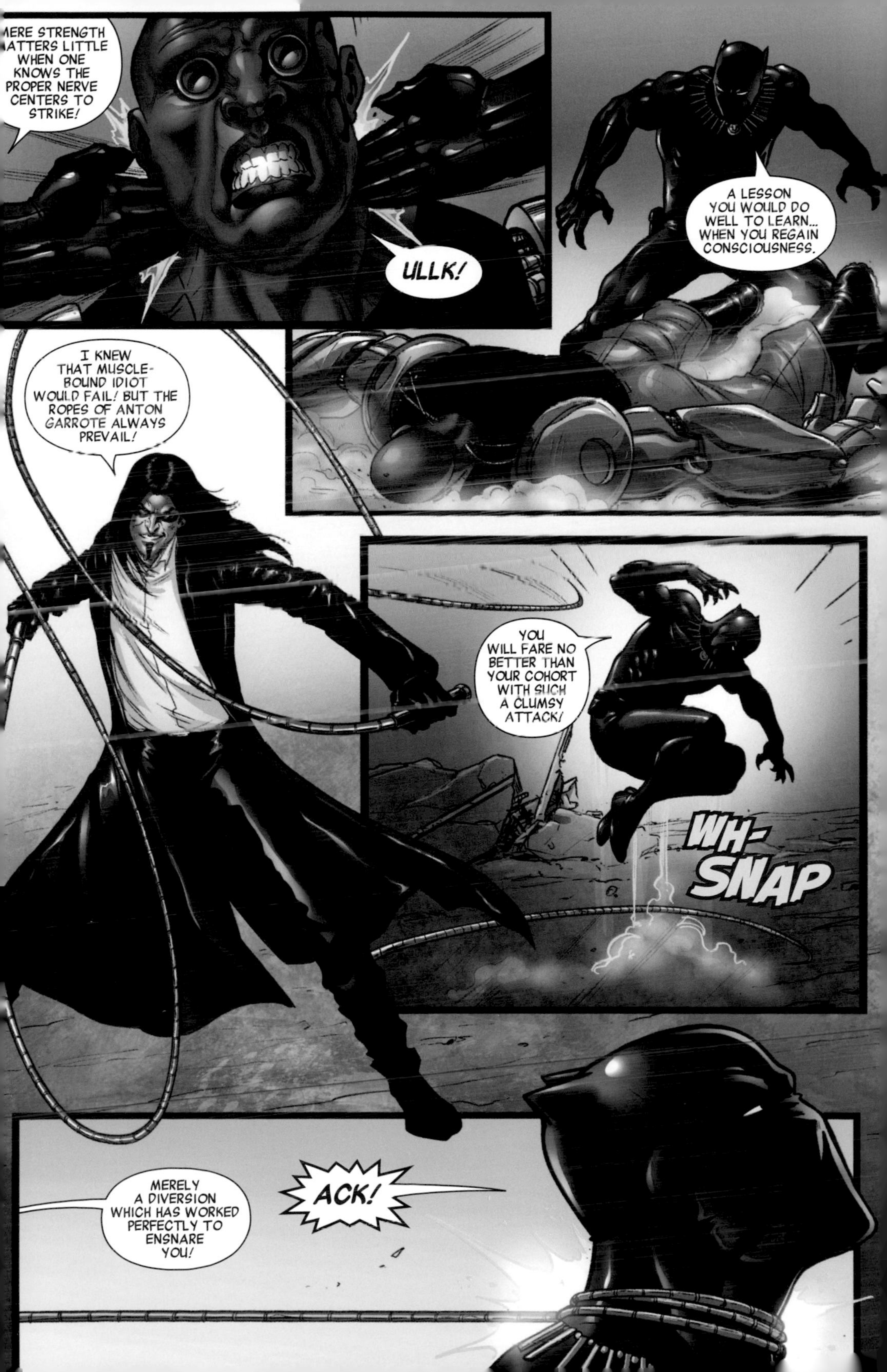
MERE STRENGTH MATTERS LITTLE WHEN ONE KNOWS THE PROPER NERVE CENTERS TO STRIKE!
ULLK!
A LESSON YOU WOULD DO WELL TO LEARN... WHEN YOU REGAIN CONSCIOUSNESS.
I KNEW THAT MUSCLE-BOUND IDIOT WOULD FAIL! BUT THE ROPES OF ANTON GARROTE ALWAYS PREVAIL!
YOU WILL FARE NO BETTER THAN YOUR COHORT WITH SUCH A CLUMSY ATTACK!
WH-SNAP
MERELY A DIVERSION WHICH HAS WORKED PERFECTLY TO ENSNARE YOU!
ACK!

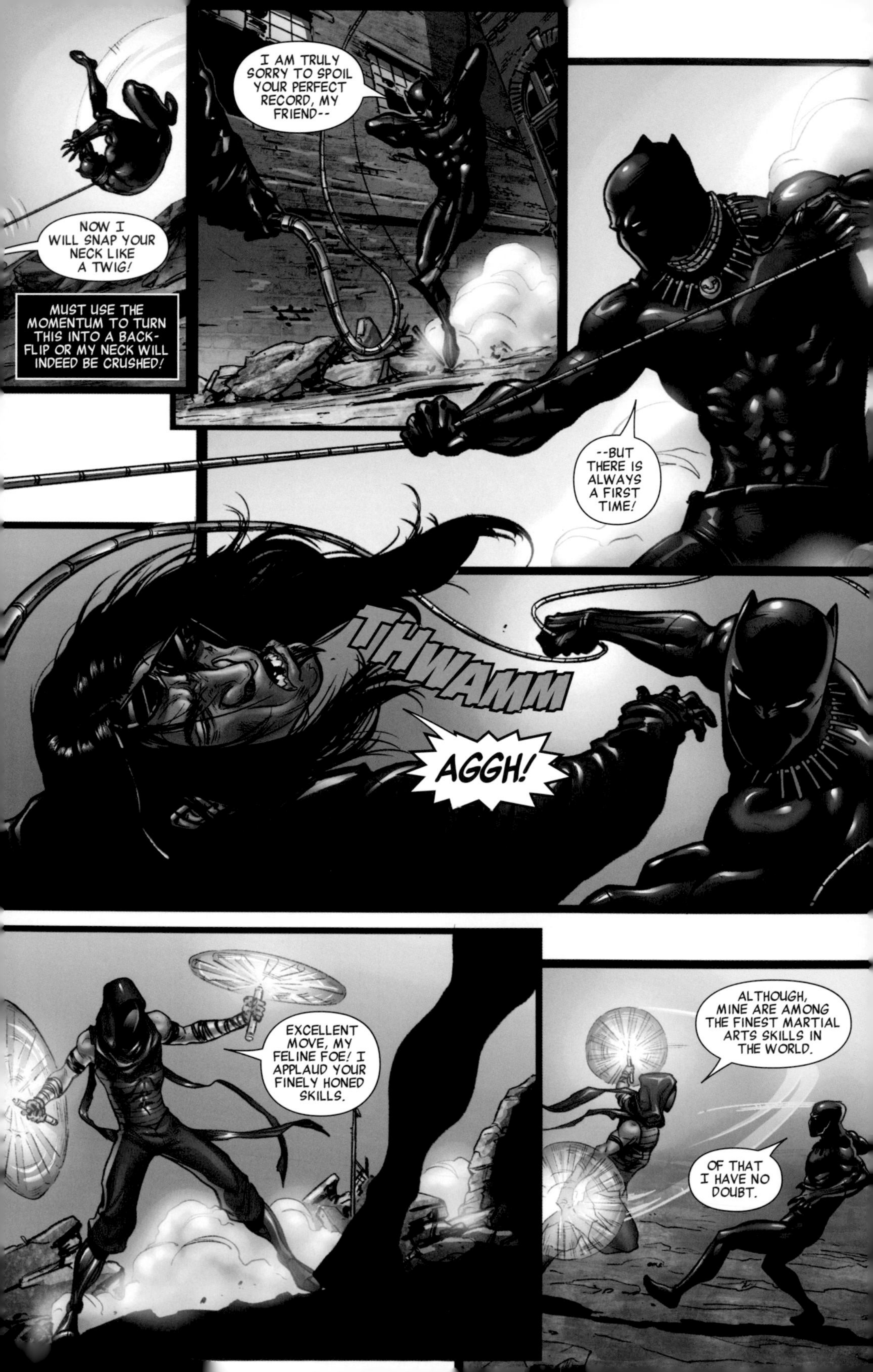
NOW I WILL SNAP YOUR NECK LIKE A TWIG!
MUST USE THE MOMENTUM TO TURN THIS INTO A BACK-FLIP OR MY NECK WILL INDEED BE CRUSHED!
I AM TRULY SORRY TO SPOIL YOUR PERFECT RECORD, MY FRIEND--
--BUT THERE IS ALWAYS A FIRST TIME!
THWAMM
AGGH!
EXCELLENT MOVE, MY FELINE FOE! I APPLAUD YOUR FINELY HONED SKILLS.
ALTHOUGH, MINE ARE AMONG THE FINEST MARTIAL ARTS SKILLS IN THE WORLD.
OF THAT I HAVE NO DOUBT.

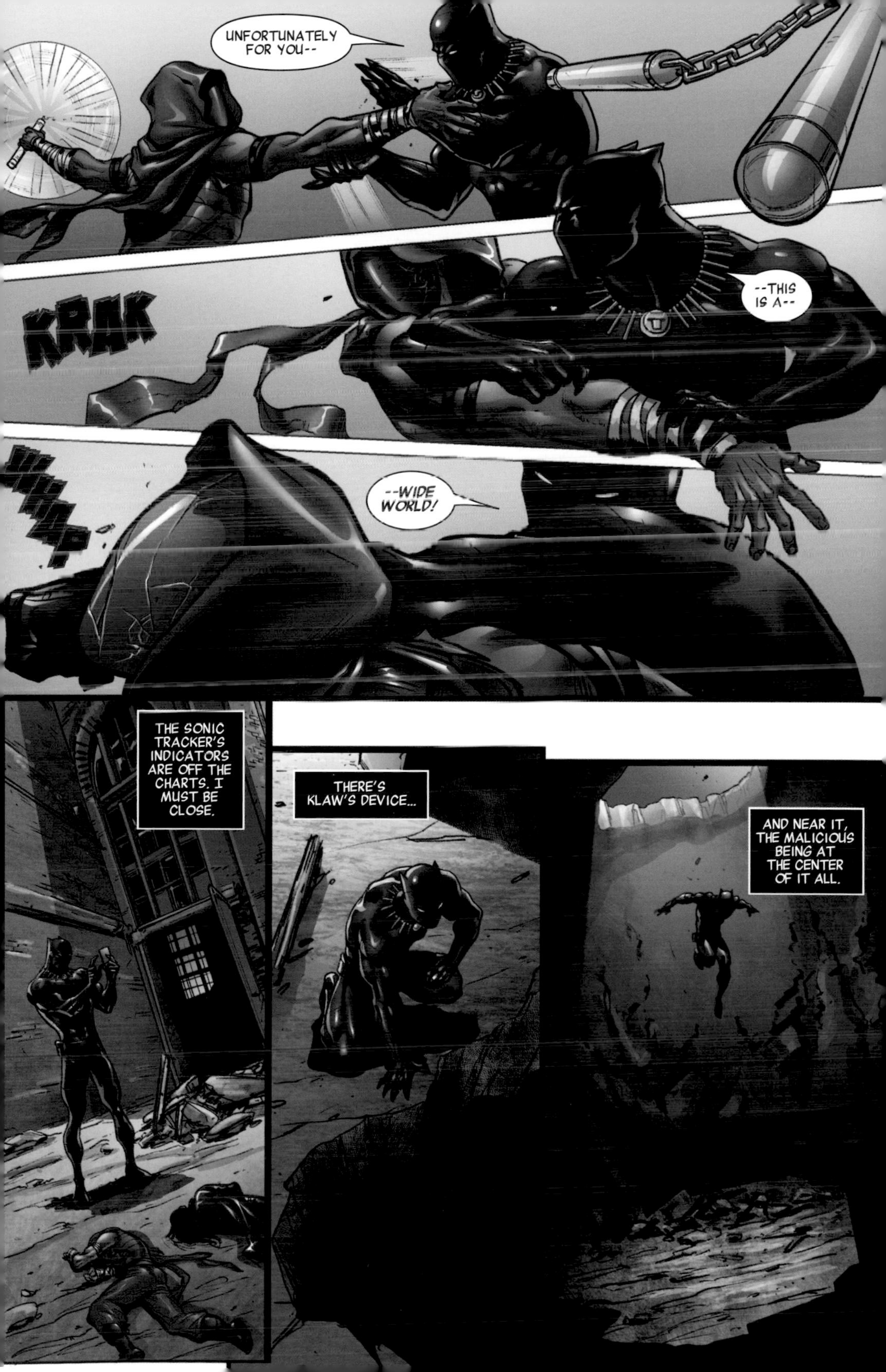
UNFORTUNATELY FOR YOU--
KRAK
--THIS IS A--
WHAP
--WIDE WORLD!
THE SONIC TRACKER'S INDICATORS ARE OFF THE CHARTS. I MUST BE CLOSE.
THERE'S KLAW'S DEVICE...
AND NEAR IT, THE MALICIOUS BEING AT THE CENTER OF IT ALL.

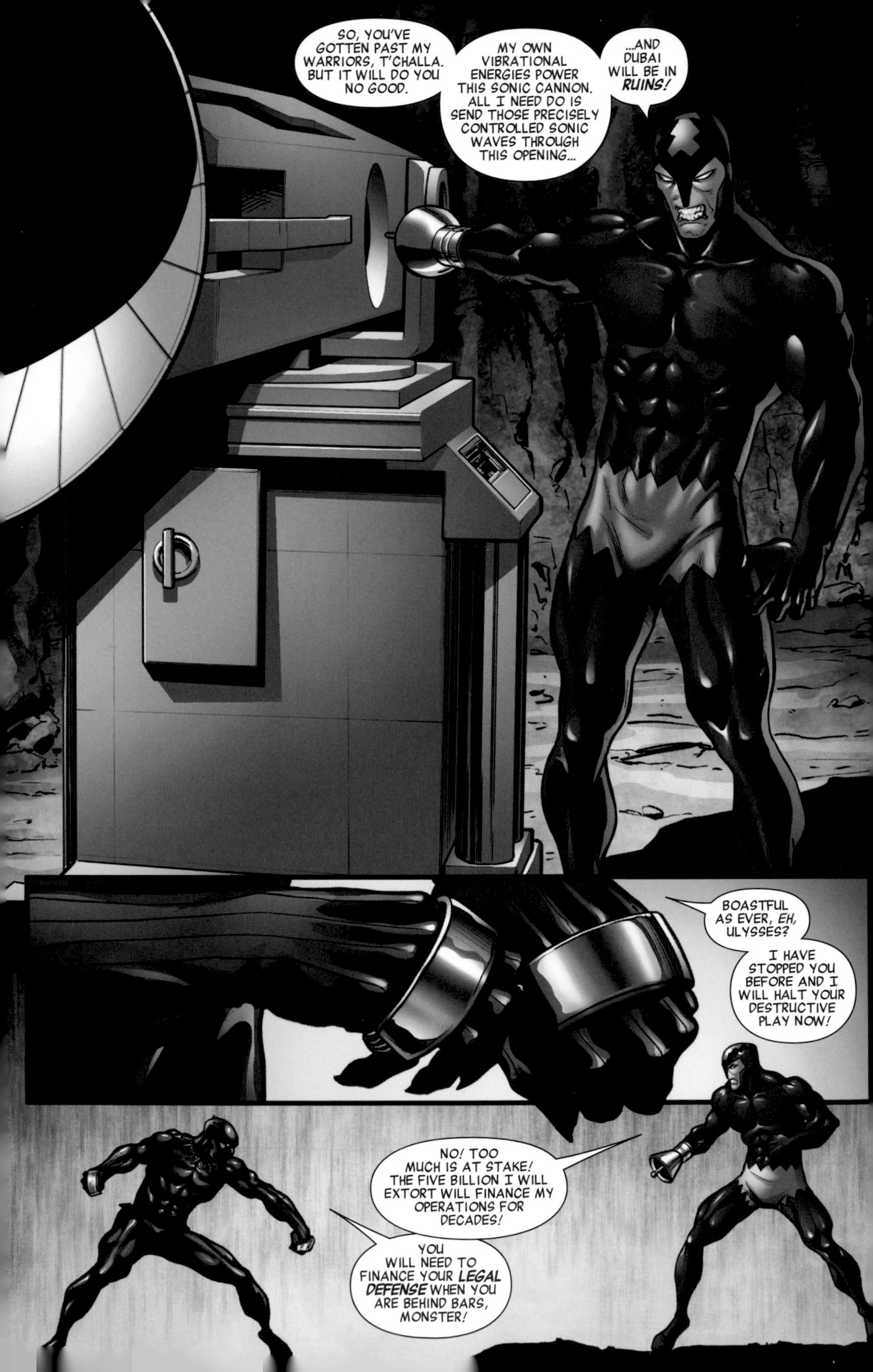
SO, YOU'VE GOTTEN PAST MY WARRIORS, T'CHALLA. BUT IT WILL DO YOU NO GOOD.
MY OWN VIBRATIONAL ENERGIES POWER THIS SONIC CANNON. ALL I NEED DO IS SEND THOSE PRECISELY CONTROLLED SONIC WAVES THROUGH THIS OPENING...
...AND DUBAI WILL BE IN *RUINS!*
BOASTFUL AS EVER, *EH,* ULYSSES?
I HAVE STOPPED YOU BEFORE AND I WILL HALT YOUR DESTRUCTIVE PLAY NOW!
NO! TOO MUCH IS AT STAKE! THE FIVE BILLION I WILL EXTORT WILL FINANCE MY OPERATIONS FOR DECADES!
YOU WILL NEED TO FINANCE YOUR *LEGAL DEFENSE* WHEN YOU ARE BEHIND BARS, MONSTER!

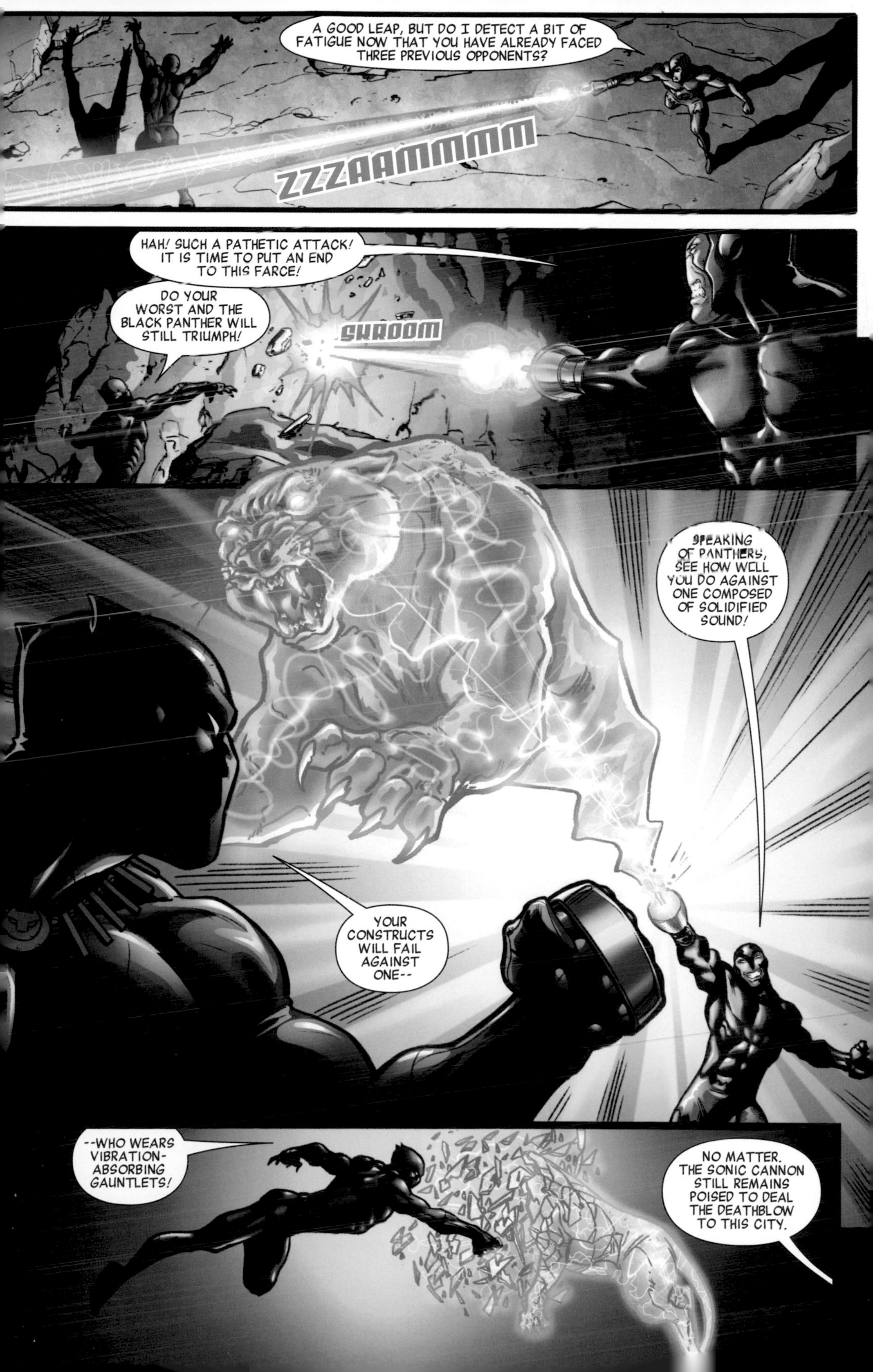
A GOOD LEAP, BUT DO I DETECT A BIT OF FATIGUE NOW THAT YOU HAVE ALREADY FACED THREE PREVIOUS OPPONENTS?
ZZZAAMMMMM
HAH! SUCH A PATHETIC ATTACK! IT IS TIME TO PUT AN END TO THIS FARCE!
DO YOUR WORST AND THE BLACK PANTHER WILL STILL TRIUMPH!
SKROOM
SPEAKING OF PANTHERS, SEE HOW WELL YOU DO AGAINST ONE COMPOSED OF SOLIDIFIED SOUND!
YOUR CONSTRUCTS WILL FAIL AGAINST ONE--
--WHO WEARS VIBRATION-ABSORBING GAUNTLETS!
NO MATTER. THE SONIC CANNON STILL REMAINS POISED TO DEAL THE DEATHBLOW TO THIS CITY.

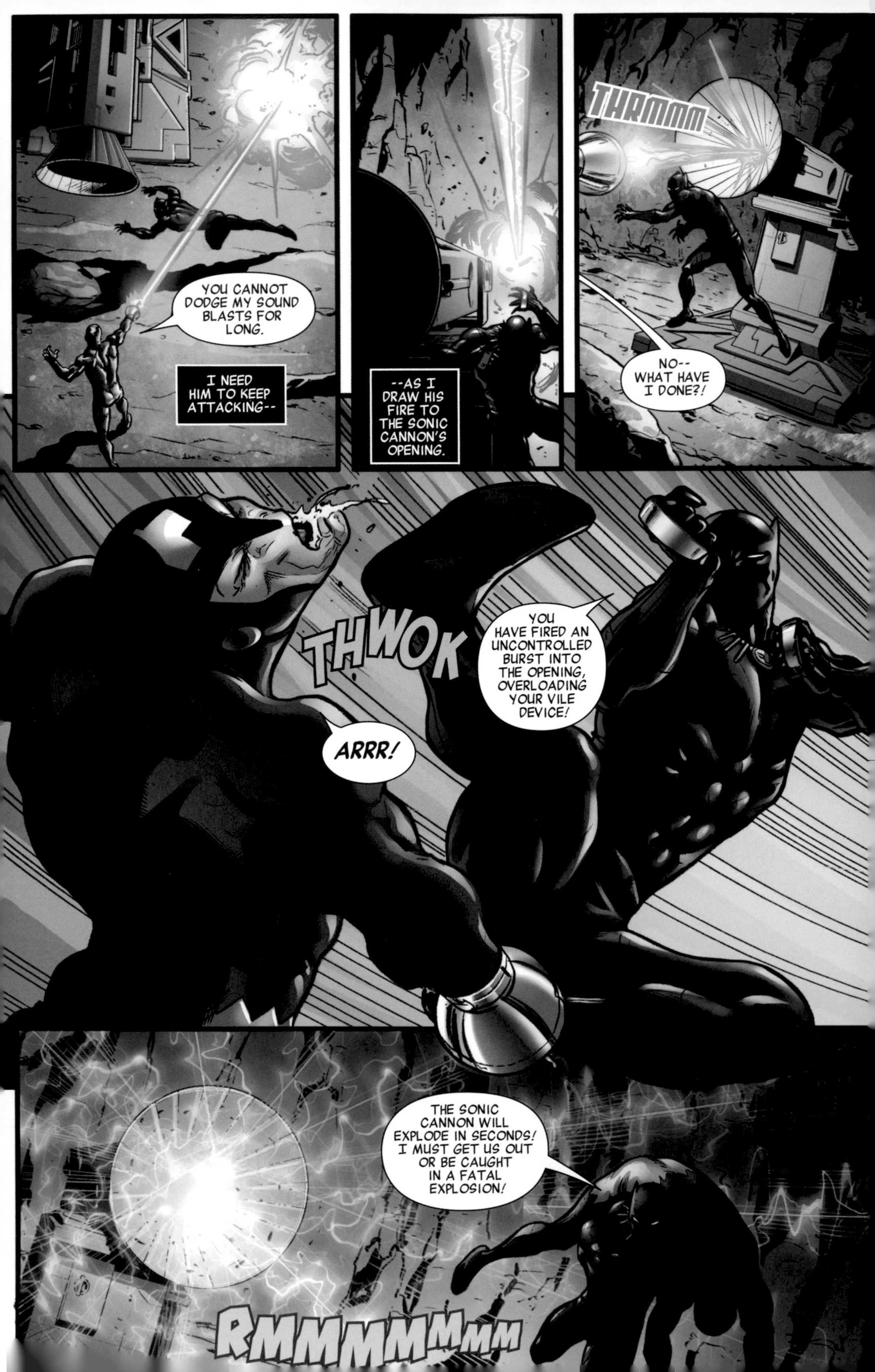
YOU CANNOT DODGE MY SOUND BLASTS FOR LONG.
I NEED HIM TO KEEP ATTACKING--
--AS I DRAW HIS FIRE TO THE SONIC CANNON'S OPENING.
THRMMM
NO-- WHAT HAVE I DONE?!
THWOK
YOU HAVE FIRED AN UNCONTROLLED BURST INTO THE OPENING, OVERLOADING YOUR VILE DEVICE!
ARRR!
THE SONIC CANNON WILL EXPLODE IN SECONDS! I MUST GET US OUT OR BE CAUGHT IN A FATAL EXPLOSION!
RMMMMMMmm

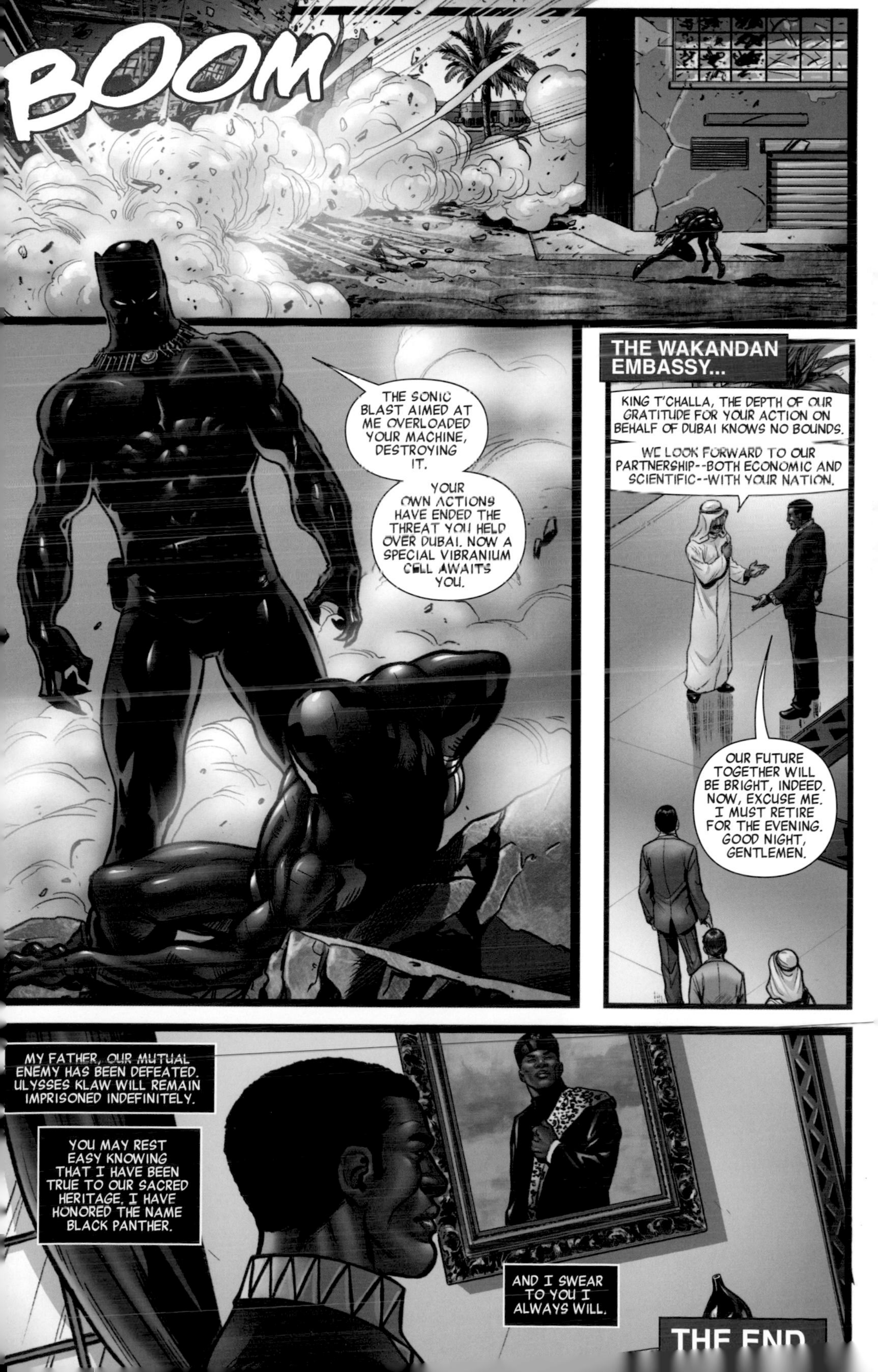
BOOM
THE SONIC BLAST AIMED AT ME OVERLOADED YOUR MACHINE, DESTROYING IT.
YOUR OWN ACTIONS HAVE ENDED THE THREAT YOU HELD OVER DUBAI. NOW A SPECIAL VIBRANIUM CELL AWAITS YOU.
THE WAKANDAN EMBASSY...
KING T'CHALLA, THE DEPTH OF OUR GRATITUDE FOR YOUR ACTION ON BEHALF OF DUBAI KNOWS NO BOUNDS.
WE LOOK FORWARD TO OUR PARTNERSHIP--BOTH ECONOMIC AND SCIENTIFIC--WITH YOUR NATION.
OUR FUTURE TOGETHER WILL BE BRIGHT, INDEED. NOW, EXCUSE ME. I MUST RETIRE FOR THE EVENING. GOOD NIGHT, GENTLEMEN.
MY FATHER, OUR MUTUAL ENEMY HAS BEEN DEFEATED. ULYSSES KLAW WILL REMAIN IMPRISONED INDEFINITELY.
YOU MAY REST EASY KNOWING THAT I HAVE BEEN TRUE TO OUR SACRED HERITAGE. I HAVE HONORED THE NAME BLACK PANTHER.
AND I SWEAR TO YOU I ALWAYS WILL.
THE END

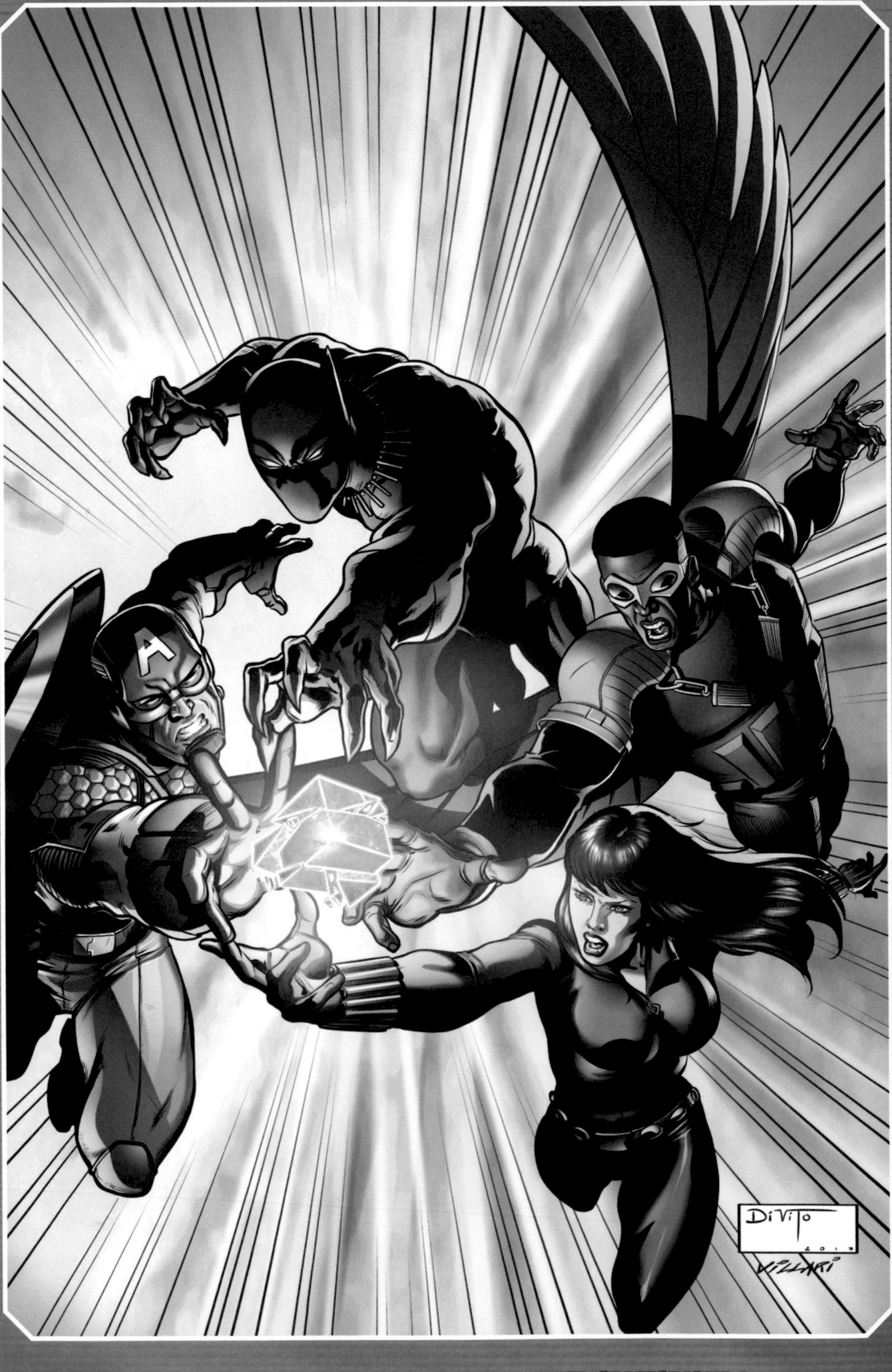
DiVito
Villari

AVENGERS: SHARDS OF INFINITY

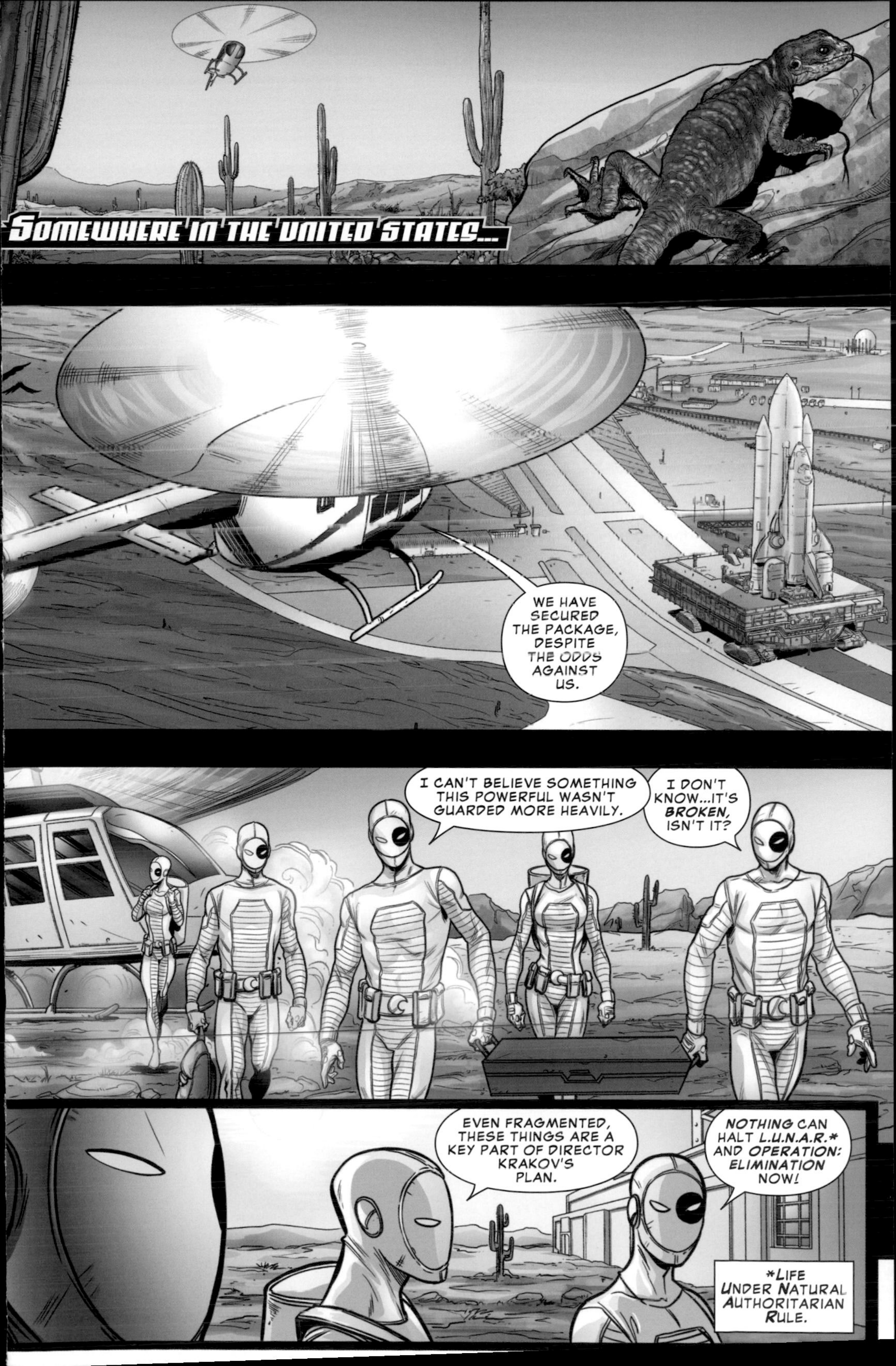
SOMEWHERE IN THE UNITED STATES...
WE HAVE SECURED THE PACKAGE, DESPITE THE ODDS AGAINST US.
I CAN'T BELIEVE SOMETHING THIS POWERFUL WASN'T GUARDED MORE HEAVILY.
I DON'T KNOW...IT'S BROKEN, ISN'T IT?
EVEN FRAGMENTED, THESE THINGS ARE A KEY PART OF DIRECTOR KRAKOV'S PLAN.
NOTHING CAN HALT L.U.N.A.R.* AND OPERATION: ELIMINATION NOW!
*LIFE UNDER NATURAL AUTHORITARIAN RULE.

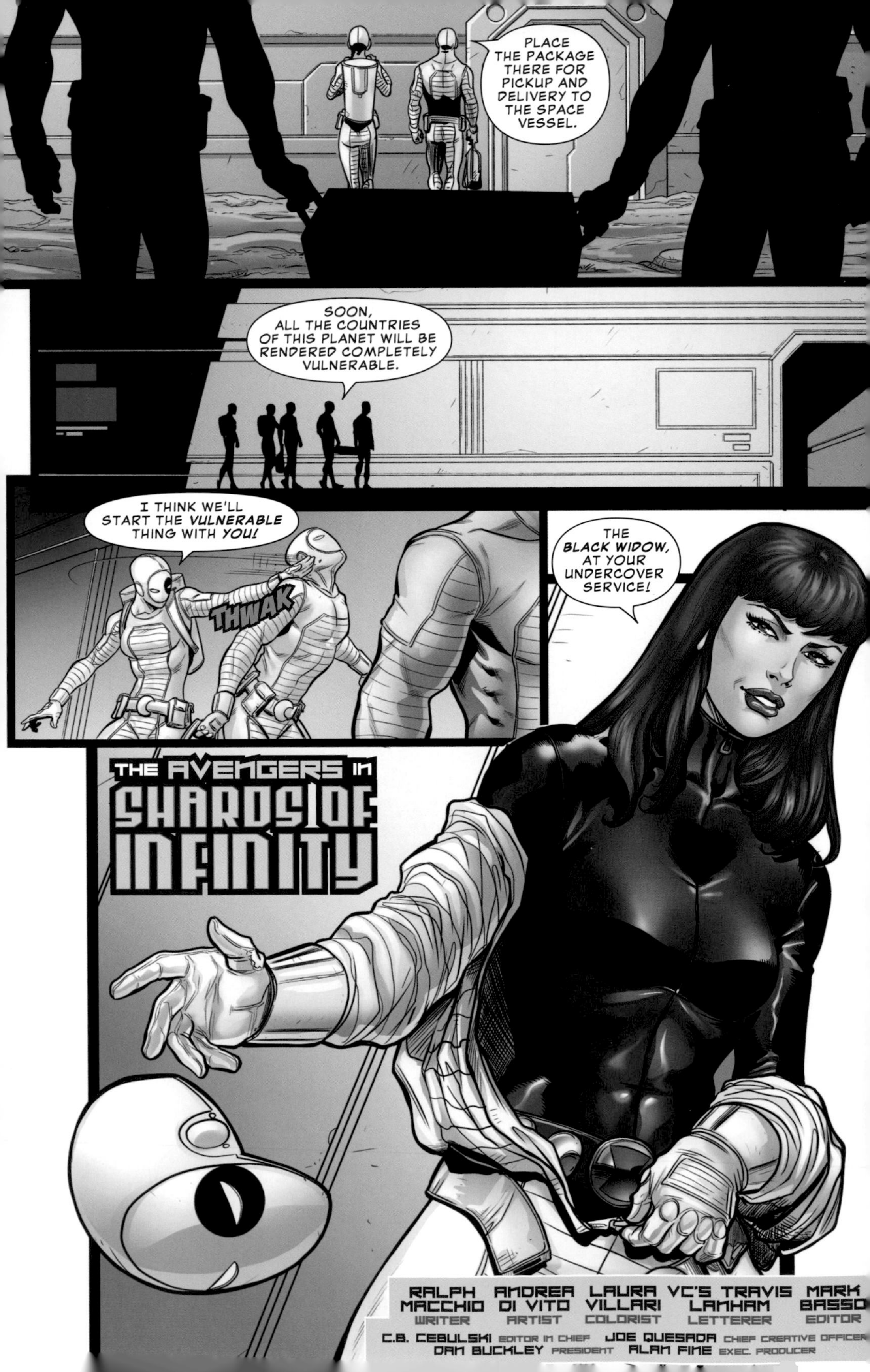

PLACE THE PACKAGE THERE FOR PICKUP AND DELIVERY TO THE SPACE VESSEL.
SOON, ALL THE COUNTRIES OF THIS PLANET WILL BE RENDERED COMPLETELY VULNERABLE.
I THINK WE'LL START THE *VULNERABLE* THING WITH *YOU!*
THWAK
THE *BLACK WIDOW,* AT YOUR UNDERCOVER SERVICE!
THE AVENGERS IN
SHARDS OF INFINITY
RALPH MACCHIO WRITER
ANDREA DI VITO ARTIST
LAURA VILLARI COLORIST
VC'S TRAVIS LANHAM LETTERER
MARK BASSO EDITOR
C.B. CEBULSKI EDITOR IN CHIEF
JOE QUESADA CHIEF CREATIVE OFFICER
DAN BUCKLEY PRESIDENT
ALAN FINE EXEC. PRODUCER

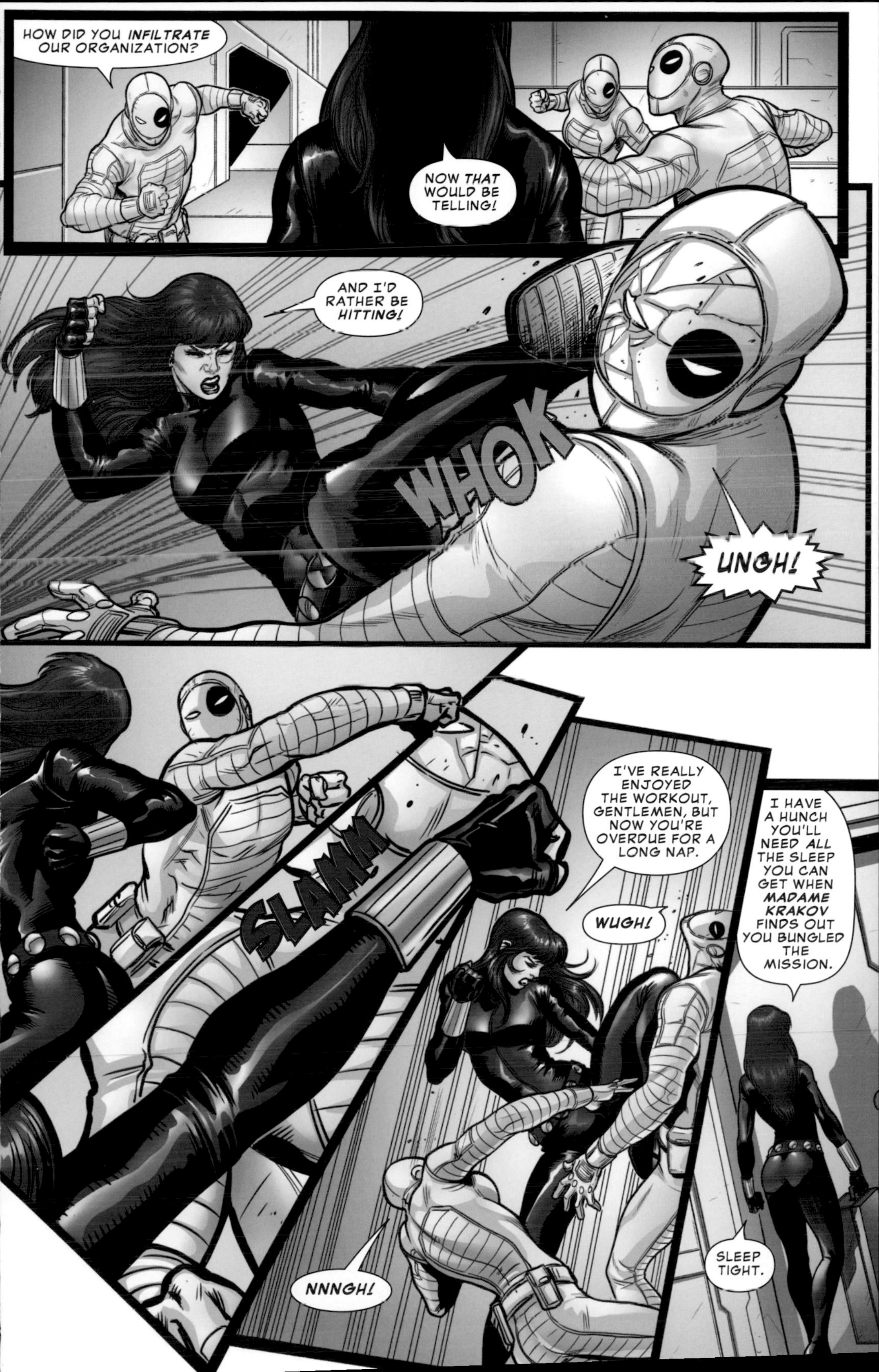
HOW DID YOU INFILTRATE OUR ORGANIZATION?
NOW THAT WOULD BE TELLING!
AND I'D RATHER BE HITTING!
WHOK
UNGH!
SLAMM
I'VE REALLY ENJOYED THE WORKOUT, GENTLEMEN, BUT NOW YOU'RE OVERDUE FOR A LONG NAP.
WUGH!
NNNGH!
I HAVE A HUNCH YOU'LL NEED ALL THE SLEEP YOU CAN GET WHEN MADAME KRAKOV FINDS OUT YOU BUNGLED THE MISSION.
SLEEP TIGHT.

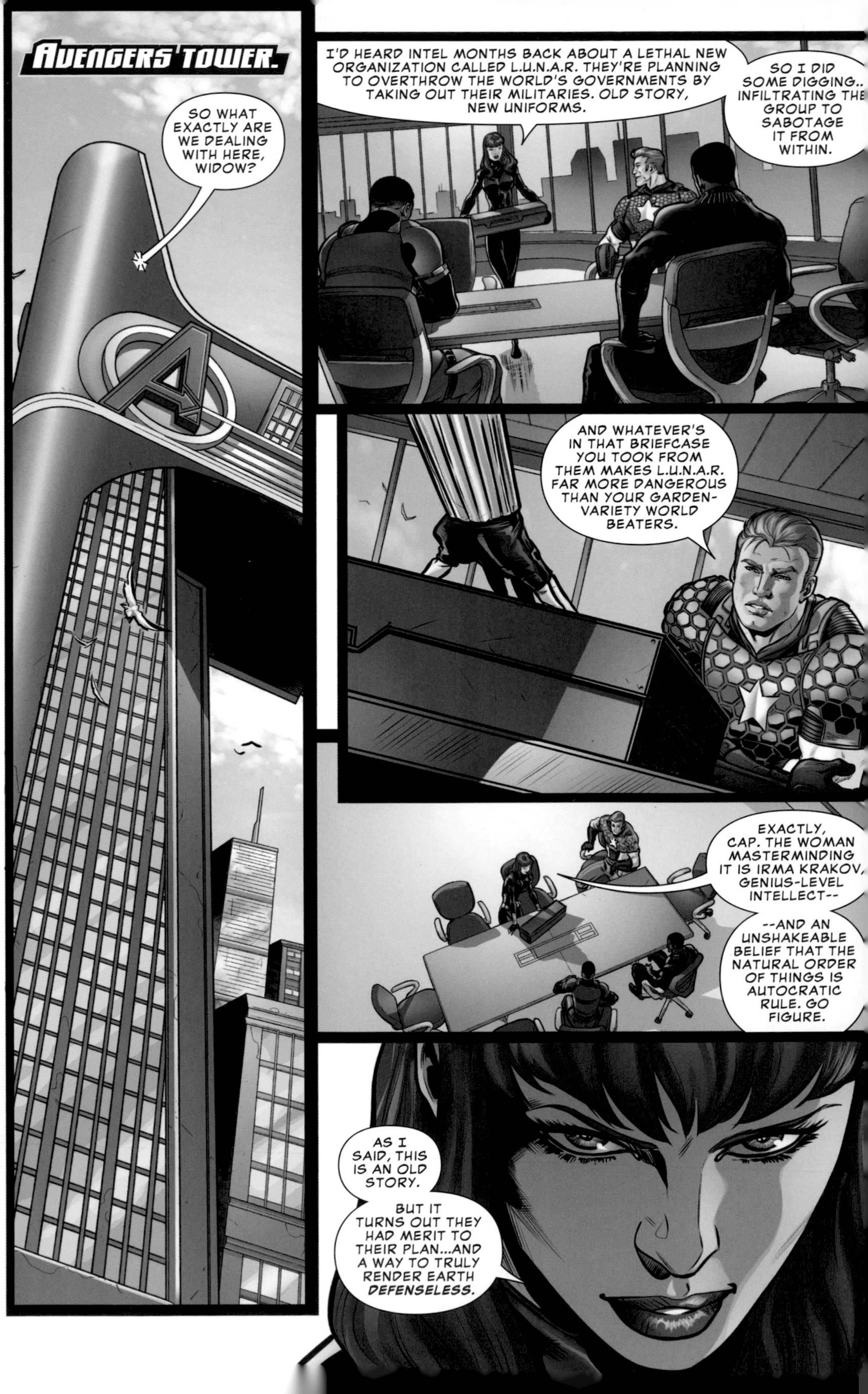
AVENGERS TOWER.
SO WHAT EXACTLY ARE WE DEALING WITH HERE, WIDOW?
I'D HEARD INTEL MONTHS BACK ABOUT A LETHAL NEW ORGANIZATION CALLED L.U.N.A.R. THEY'RE PLANNING TO OVERTHROW THE WORLD'S GOVERNMENTS BY TAKING OUT THEIR MILITARIES. OLD STORY, NEW UNIFORMS.
SO I DID SOME DIGGING.. INFILTRATING THE GROUP TO SABOTAGE IT FROM WITHIN.
AND WHATEVER'S IN THAT BRIEFCASE YOU TOOK FROM THEM MAKES L.U.N.A.R. FAR MORE DANGEROUS THAN YOUR GARDEN-VARIETY WORLD BEATERS.
EXACTLY, CAP. THE WOMAN MASTERMINDING IT IS IRMA KRAKOV, GENIUS-LEVEL INTELLECT--
--AND AN UNSHAKEABLE BELIEF THAT THE NATURAL ORDER OF THINGS IS AUTOCRATIC RULE. GO FIGURE.
AS I SAID, THIS IS AN OLD STORY.
BUT IT TURNS OUT THEY HAD MERIT TO THEIR PLAN...AND A WAY TO TRULY RENDER EARTH DEFENSELESS.

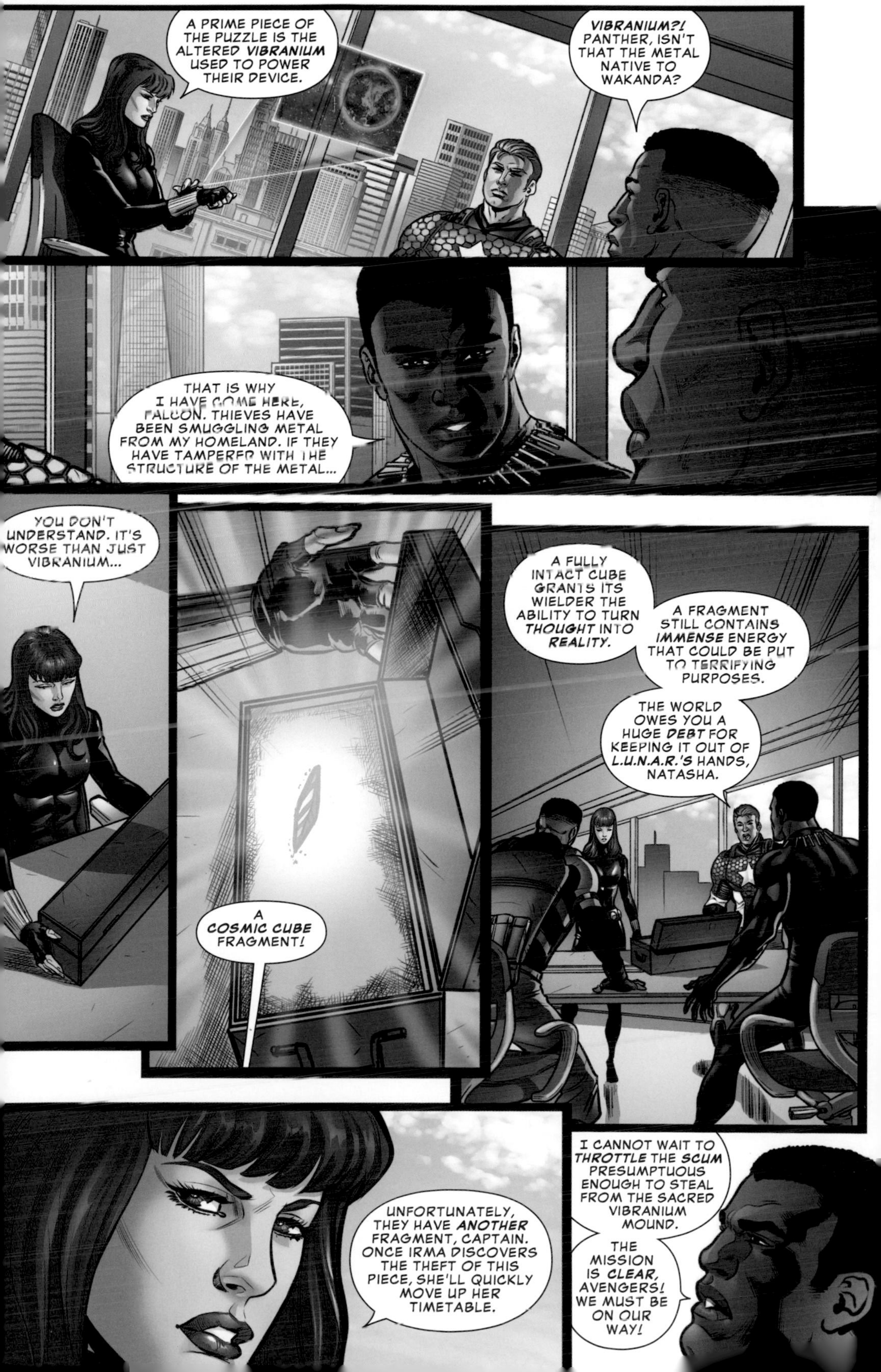
A PRIME PIECE OF THE PUZZLE IS THE ALTERED *VIBRANIUM* USED TO POWER THEIR DEVICE.
VIBRANIUM?! PANTHER, ISN'T THAT THE METAL NATIVE TO WAKANDA?
THAT IS WHY I HAVE COME HERE, FALCON. THIEVES HAVE BEEN SMUGGLING METAL FROM MY HOMELAND. IF THEY HAVE TAMPERED WITH THE STRUCTURE OF THE METAL...
YOU DON'T UNDERSTAND. IT'S WORSE THAN JUST VIBRANIUM...
A *COSMIC CUBE* FRAGMENT!
A FULLY INTACT CUBE GRANTS ITS WIELDER THE ABILITY TO TURN *THOUGHT* INTO *REALITY.*
A FRAGMENT STILL CONTAINS *IMMENSE* ENERGY THAT COULD BE PUT TO TERRIFYING PURPOSES.
THE WORLD OWES YOU A HUGE *DEBT* FOR KEEPING IT OUT OF *L.U.N.A.R.'S* HANDS, NATASHA.
UNFORTUNATELY, THEY HAVE *ANOTHER* FRAGMENT, CAPTAIN. ONCE IRMA DISCOVERS THE THEFT OF THIS PIECE, SHE'LL QUICKLY MOVE UP HER TIMETABLE.
I CANNOT WAIT TO *THROTTLE* THE *SCUM* PRESUMPTUOUS ENOUGH TO STEAL FROM THE SACRED VIBRANIUM MOUND.
THE MISSION IS *CLEAR,* AVENGERS! WE MUST BE ON OUR WAY!

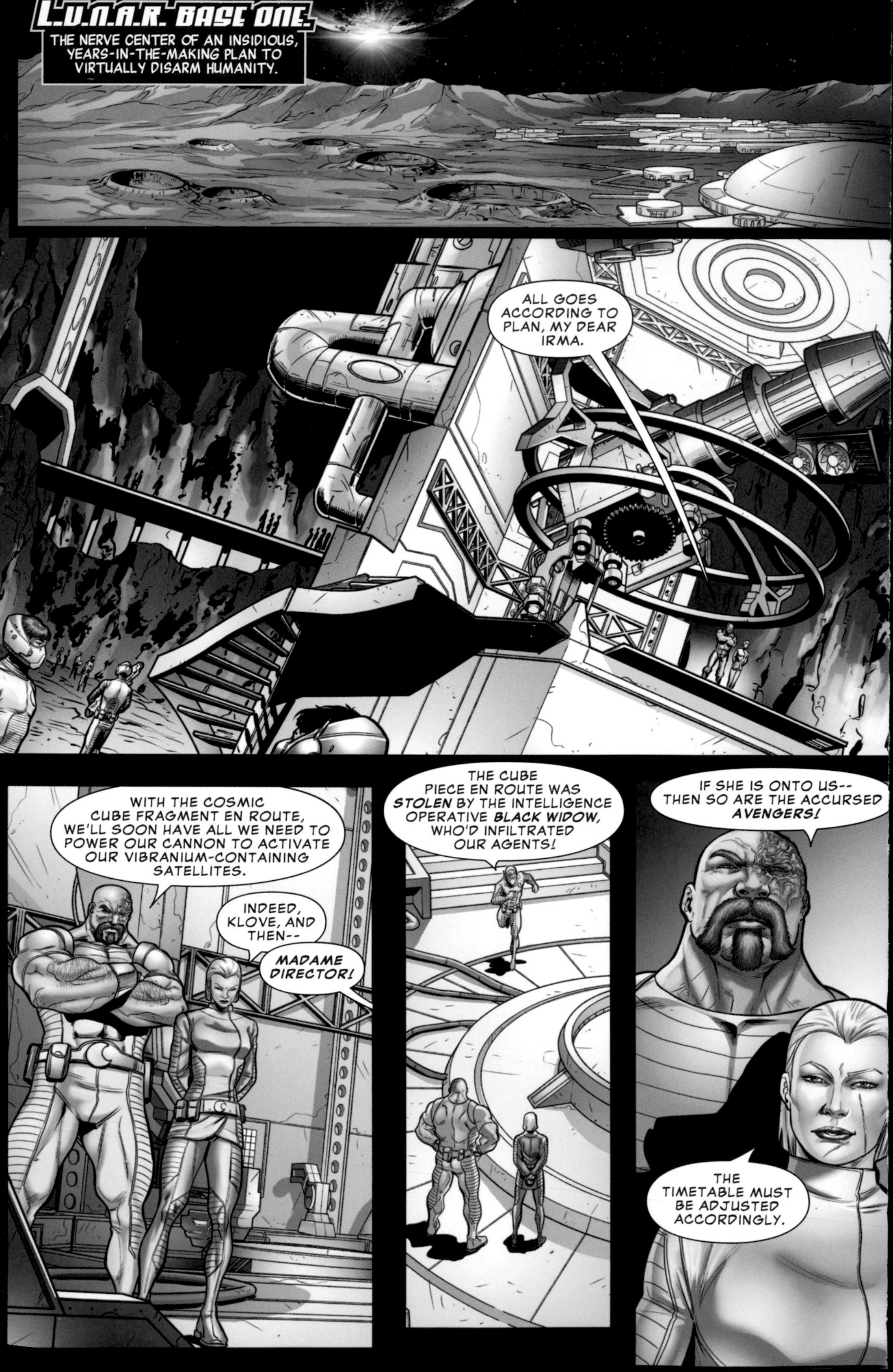
L.U.N.A.R. BASE ONE.
THE NERVE CENTER OF AN INSIDIOUS, YEARS-IN-THE-MAKING PLAN TO VIRTUALLY DISARM HUMANITY.
ALL GOES ACCORDING TO PLAN, MY DEAR IRMA.
WITH THE COSMIC CUBE FRAGMENT EN ROUTE, WE'LL SOON HAVE ALL WE NEED TO POWER OUR CANNON TO ACTIVATE OUR VIBRANIUM-CONTAINING SATELLITES.
INDEED, KLOVE, AND THEN--
MADAME DIRECTOR!
THE CUBE PIECE EN ROUTE WAS STOLEN BY THE INTELLIGENCE OPERATIVE BLACK WIDOW, WHO'D INFILTRATED OUR AGENTS!
IF SHE IS ONTO US-- THEN SO ARE THE ACCURSED AVENGERS!
THE TIMETABLE MUST BE ADJUSTED ACCORDINGLY.

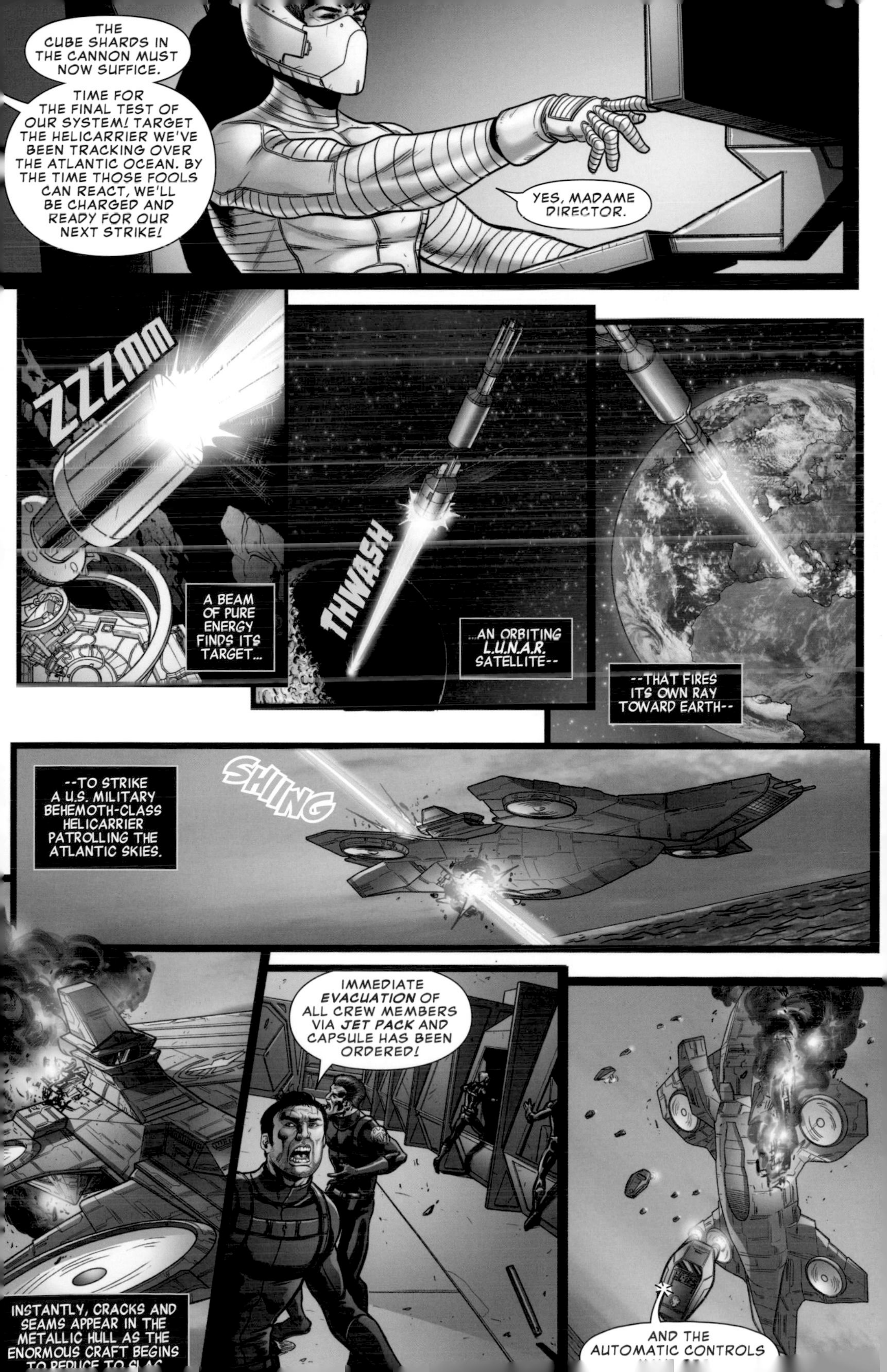
THE CUBE SHARDS IN THE CANNON MUST NOW SUFFICE.
TIME FOR THE FINAL TEST OF OUR SYSTEM! TARGET THE HELICARRIER WE'VE BEEN TRACKING OVER THE ATLANTIC OCEAN. BY THE TIME THOSE FOOLS CAN REACT, WE'LL BE CHARGED AND READY FOR OUR NEXT STRIKE!
YES, MADAME DIRECTOR.
ZZZMM
A BEAM OF PURE ENERGY FINDS ITS TARGET...
THWASH
...AN ORBITING L.U.N.A.R. SATELLITE--
--THAT FIRES ITS OWN RAY TOWARD EARTH--
--TO STRIKE A U.S. MILITARY BEHEMOTH-CLASS HELICARRIER PATROLLING THE ATLANTIC SKIES.
SHIING
INSTANTLY, CRACKS AND SEAMS APPEAR IN THE METALLIC HULL AS THE ENORMOUS CRAFT BEGINS
IMMEDIATE EVACUATION OF ALL CREW MEMBERS VIA JET PACK AND CAPSULE HAS BEEN ORDERED!
AND THE AUTOMATIC CONTROLS

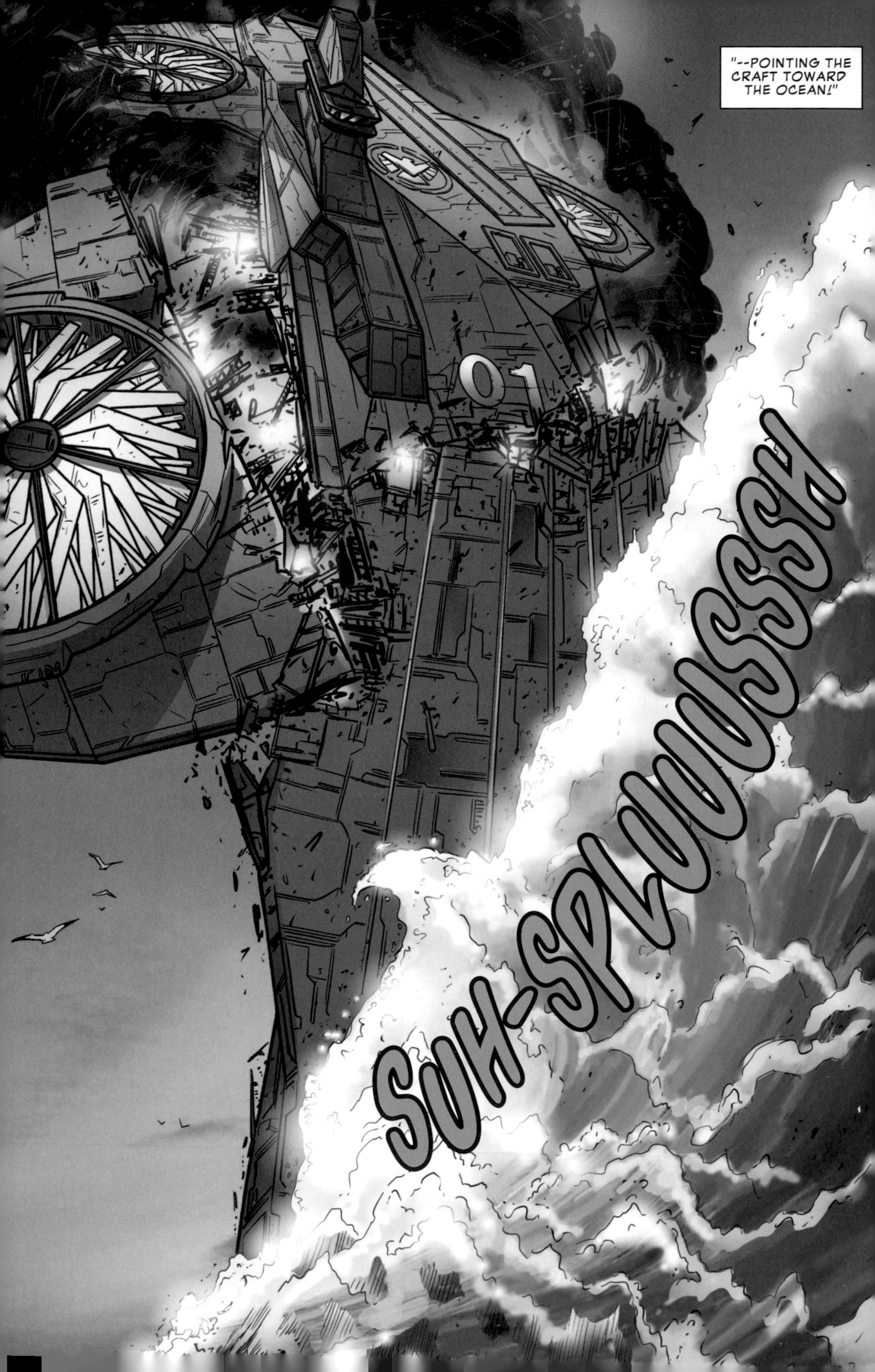
"--POINTING THE CRAFT TOWARD THE OCEAN!"
SUH-SPLUUUSSSH

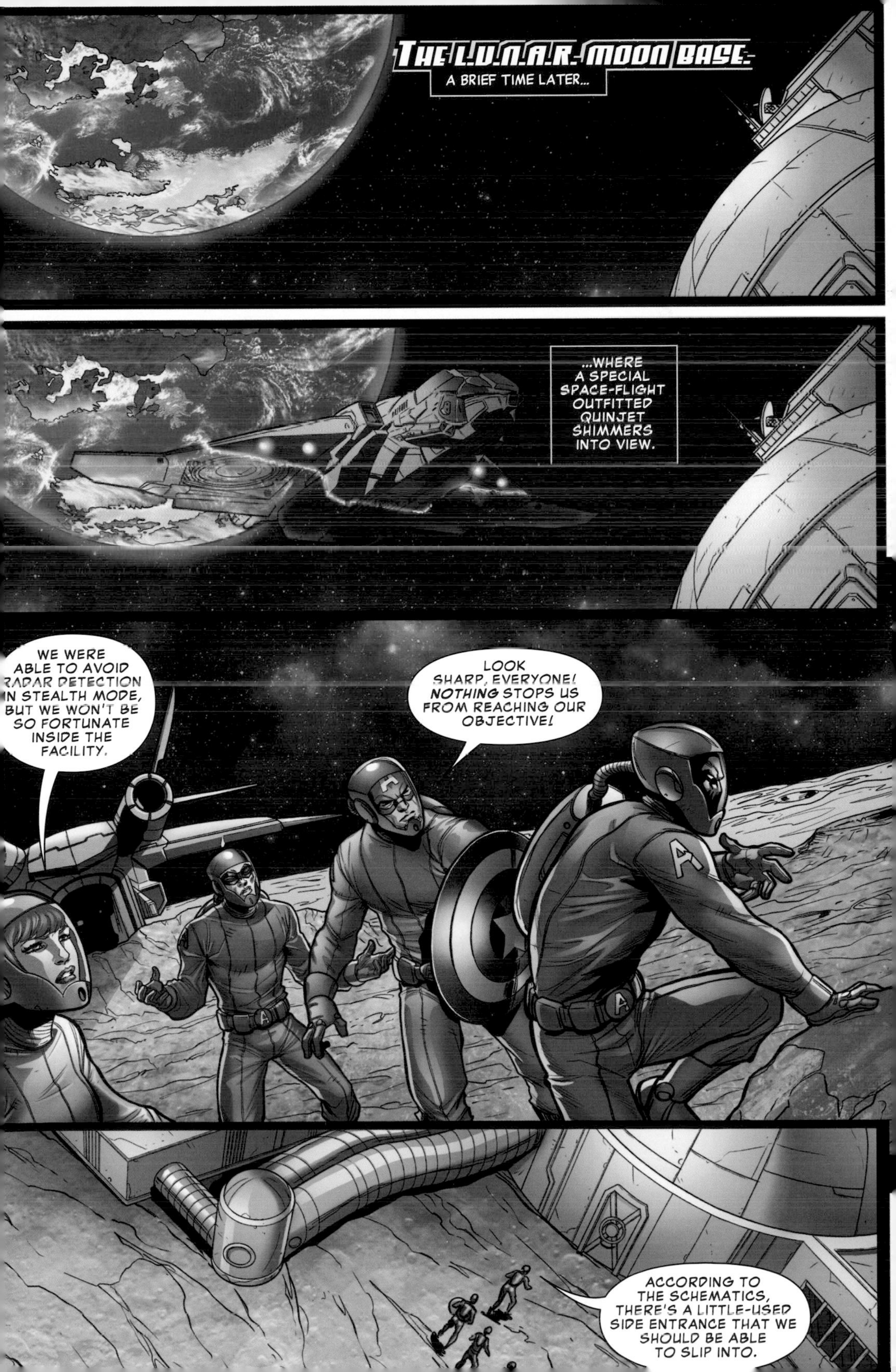
THE L.U.N.A.R. MOON BASE.
A BRIEF TIME LATER...
...WHERE A SPECIAL SPACE-FLIGHT OUTFITTED QUINJET SHIMMERS INTO VIEW.
WE WERE ABLE TO AVOID RADAR DETECTION IN STEALTH MODE, BUT WE WON'T BE SO FORTUNATE INSIDE THE FACILITY.
LOOK SHARP, EVERYONE! NOTHING STOPS US FROM REACHING OUR OBJECTIVE!
ACCORDING TO THE SCHEMATICS, THERE'S A LITTLE-USED SIDE ENTRANCE THAT WE SHOULD BE ABLE TO SLIP INTO.

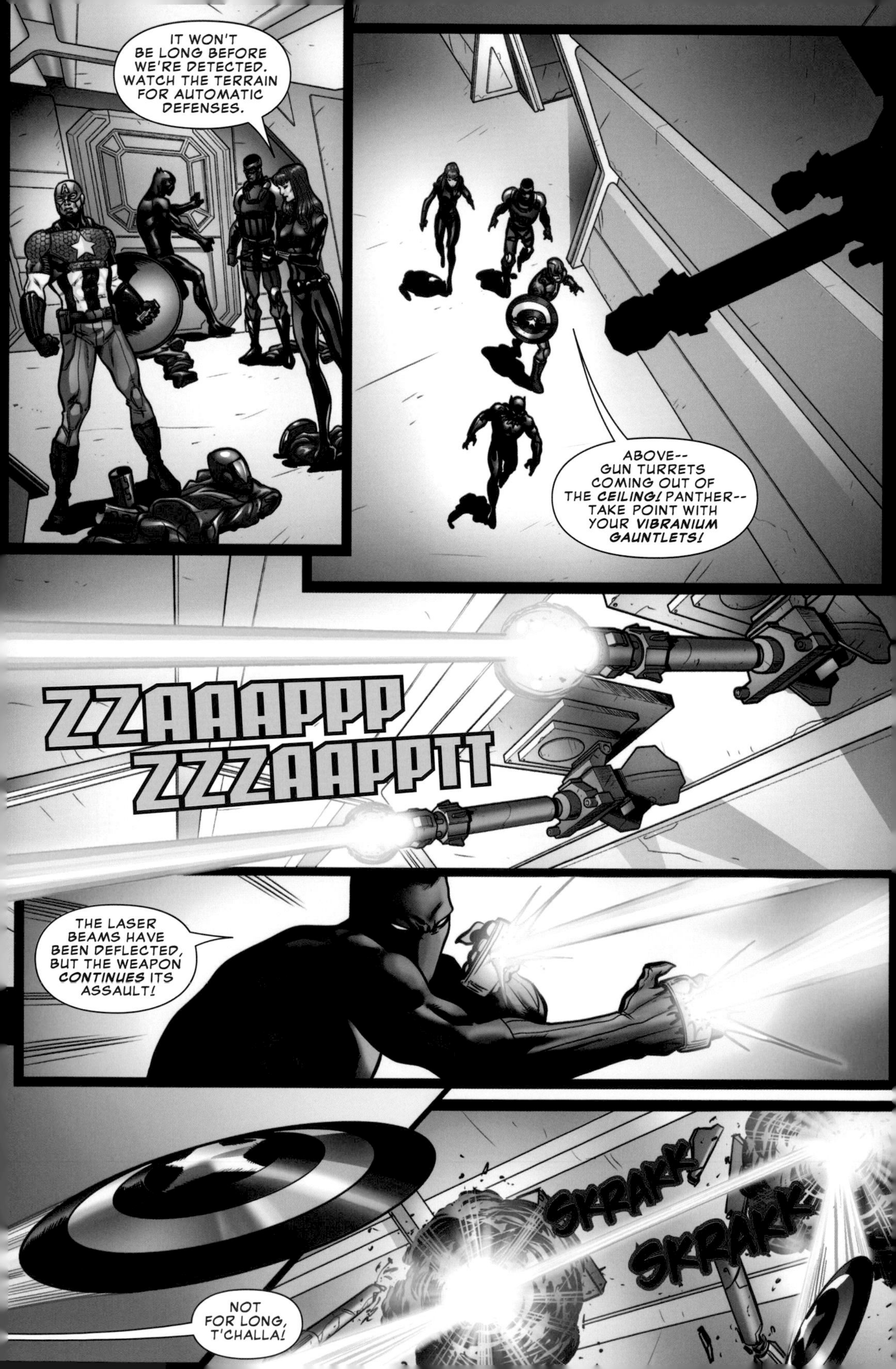
IT WON'T BE LONG BEFORE WE'RE DETECTED. WATCH THE TERRAIN FOR AUTOMATIC DEFENSES.
ABOVE-- GUN TURRETS COMING OUT OF THE CEILING! PANTHER-- TAKE POINT WITH YOUR VIBRANIUM GAUNTLETS!
ZZAAAPPP
ZZZAAPPTT
THE LASER BEAMS HAVE BEEN DEFLECTED, BUT THE WEAPON CONTINUES ITS ASSAULT!
SKRAKK!
SKRAKK
NOT FOR LONG, T'CHALLA!

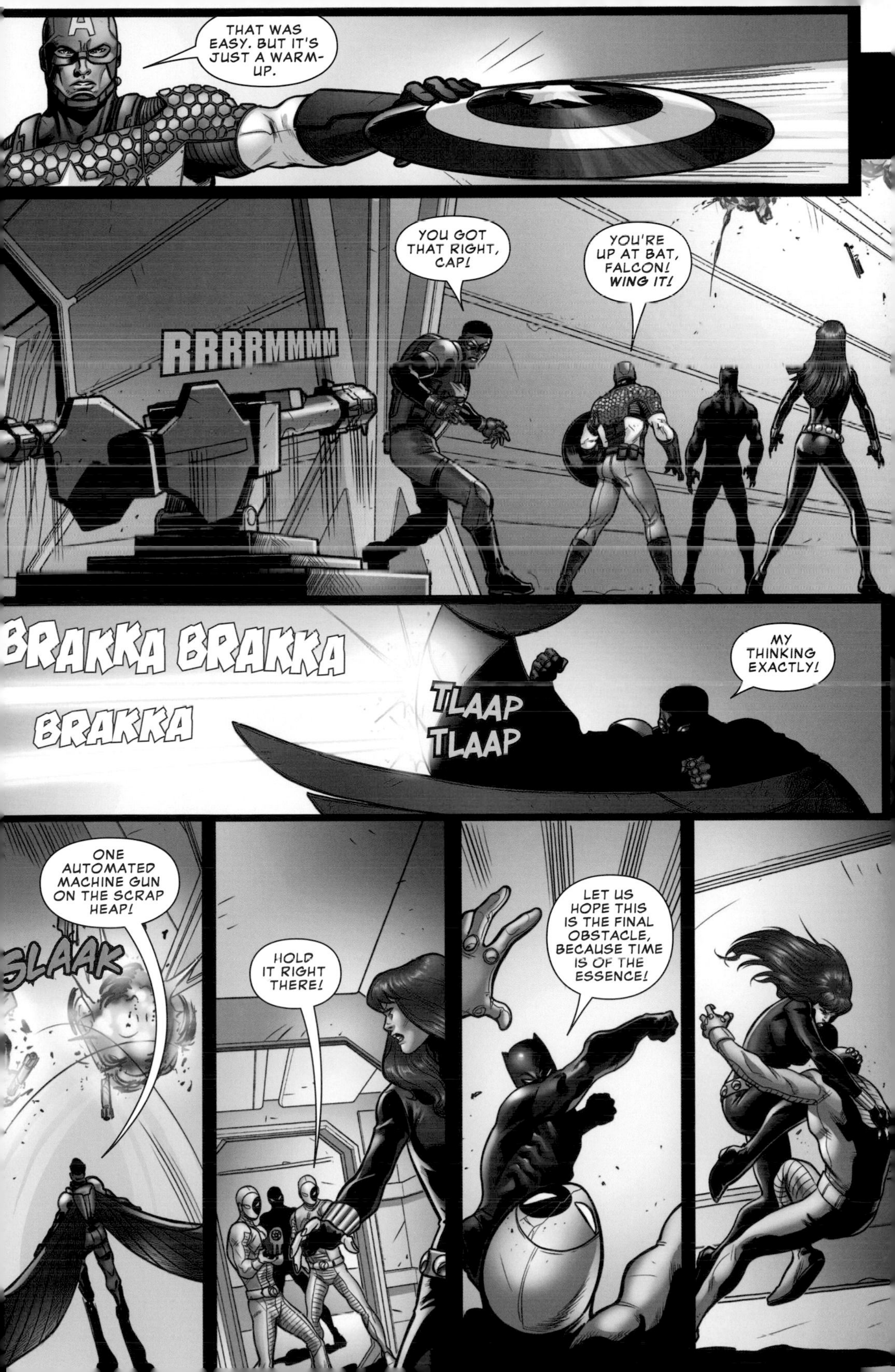
THAT WAS EASY. BUT IT'S JUST A WARM-UP.
RRRRMMMM
YOU GOT THAT RIGHT, CAP!
YOU'RE UP AT BAT, FALCON! WING IT!
BRAKKA BRAKKA
BRAKKA
TLAAP TLAAP
MY THINKING EXACTLY!
ONE AUTOMATED MACHINE GUN ON THE SCRAP HEAP!
SLAAK
HOLD IT RIGHT THERE!
LET US HOPE THIS IS THE FINAL OBSTACLE, BECAUSE TIME IS OF THE ESSENCE!

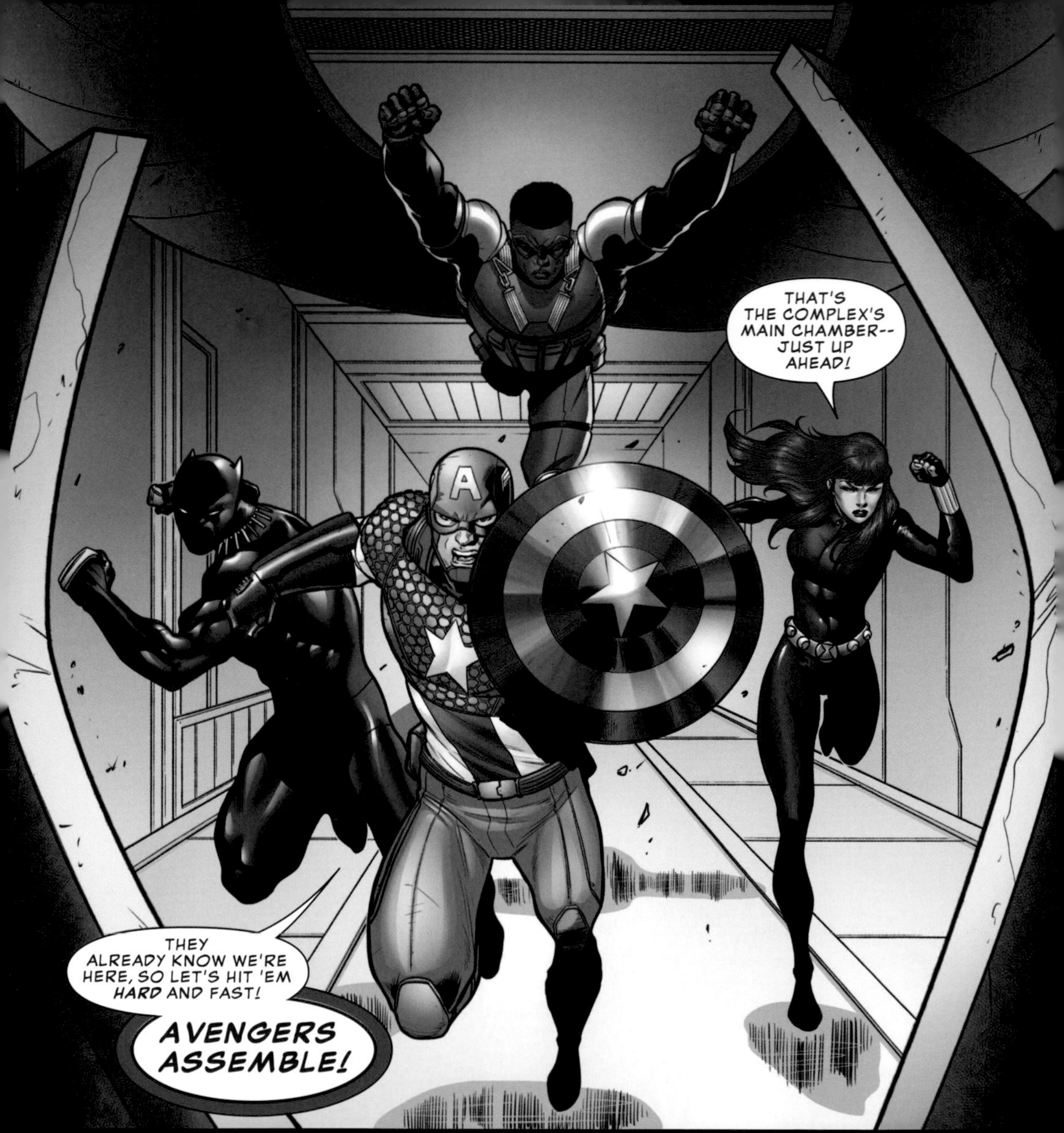
THAT'S THE COMPLEX'S MAIN CHAMBER-- JUST UP AHEAD!
THEY ALREADY KNOW WE'RE HERE, SO LET'S HIT 'EM *HARD* AND FAST!
AVENGERS ASSEMBLE!

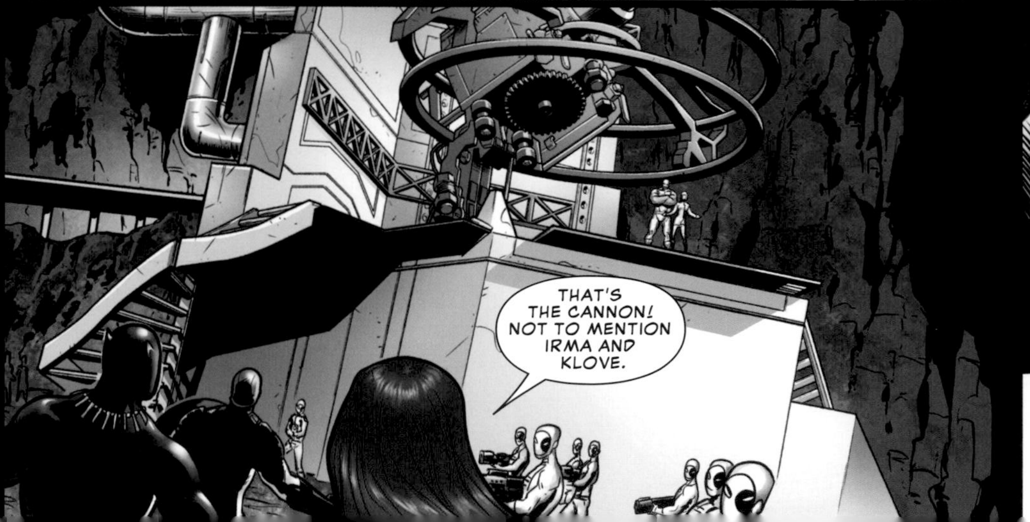
THAT'S THE CANNON! NOT TO MENTION IRMA AND KLOVE.

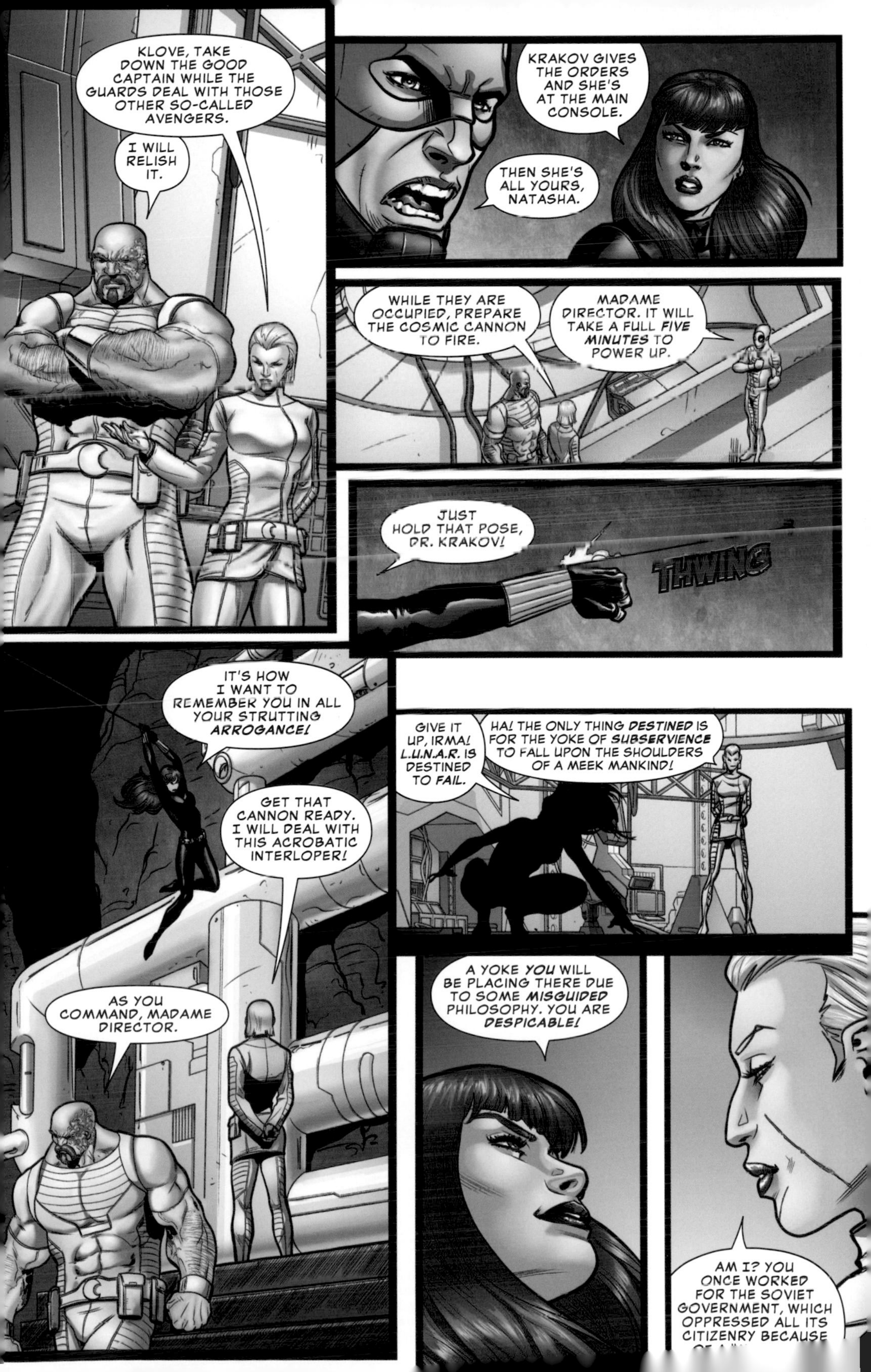
KLOVE, TAKE DOWN THE GOOD CAPTAIN WHILE THE GUARDS DEAL WITH THOSE OTHER SO-CALLED AVENGERS.
I WILL RELISH IT.
KRAKOV GIVES THE ORDERS AND SHE'S AT THE MAIN CONSOLE.
THEN SHE'S ALL YOURS, NATASHA.
WHILE THEY ARE OCCUPIED, PREPARE THE COSMIC CANNON TO FIRE.
MADAME DIRECTOR. IT WILL TAKE A FULL FIVE MINUTES TO POWER UP.
JUST HOLD THAT POSE, DR. KRAKOV!
THWING
IT'S HOW I WANT TO REMEMBER YOU IN ALL YOUR STRUTTING ARROGANCE!
GET THAT CANNON READY. I WILL DEAL WITH THIS ACROBATIC INTERLOPER!
AS YOU COMMAND, MADAME DIRECTOR.
GIVE IT UP, IRMA! L.U.N.A.R. IS DESTINED TO FAIL.
HA! THE ONLY THING DESTINED IS FOR THE YOKE OF SUBSERVIENCE TO FALL UPON THE SHOULDERS OF A MEEK MANKIND!
A YOKE YOU WILL BE PLACING THERE DUE TO SOME MISGUIDED PHILOSOPHY. YOU ARE DESPICABLE!
AM I? YOU ONCE WORKED FOR THE SOVIET GOVERNMENT, WHICH OPPRESSED ALL ITS CITIZENRY BECAUSE

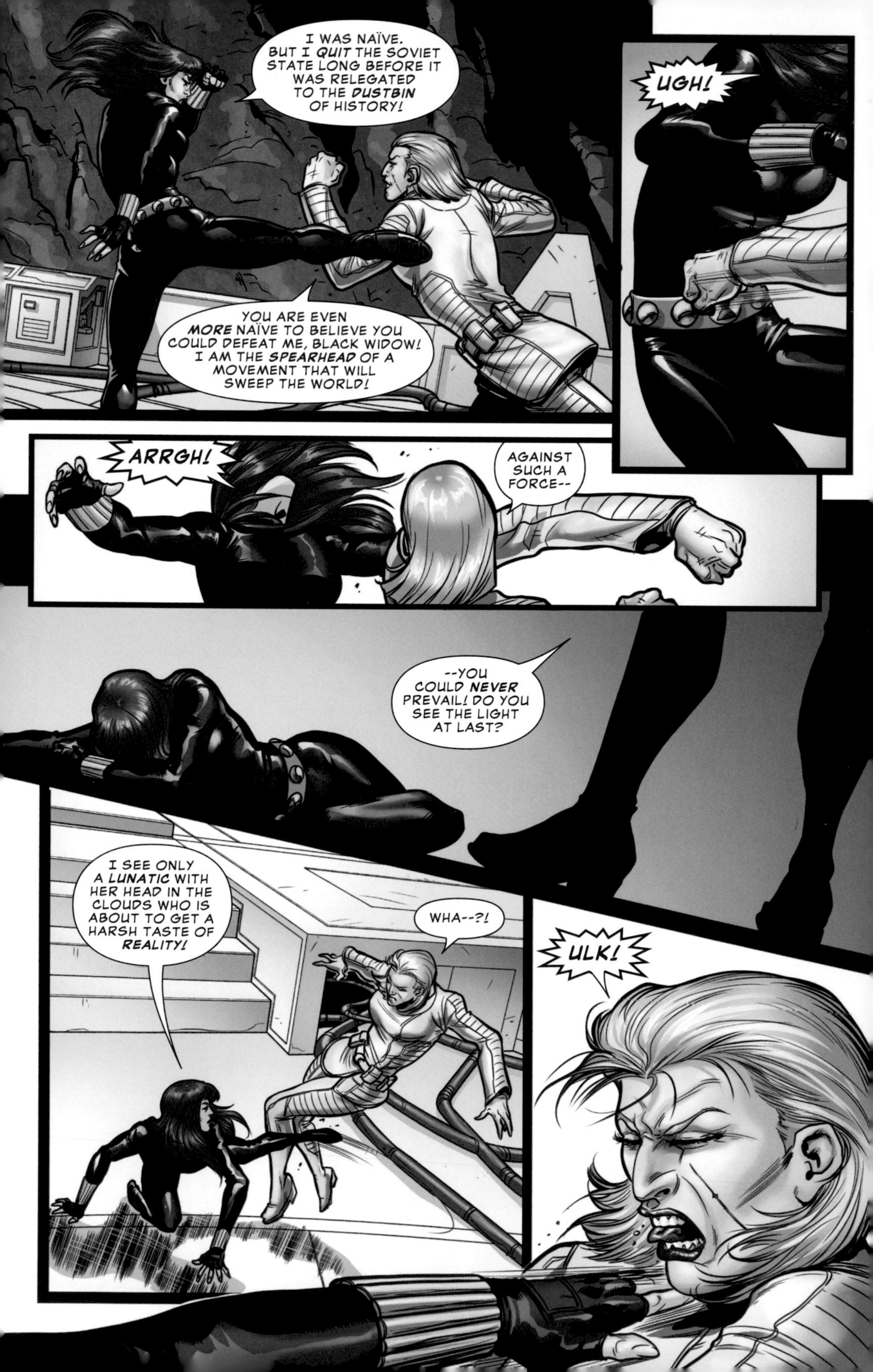
I WAS NAÏVE. BUT I QUIT THE SOVIET STATE LONG BEFORE IT WAS RELEGATED TO THE DUSTBIN OF HISTORY!
YOU ARE EVEN MORE NAÏVE TO BELIEVE YOU COULD DEFEAT ME, BLACK WIDOW! I AM THE SPEARHEAD OF A MOVEMENT THAT WILL SWEEP THE WORLD!
UGH!
ARRGH!
AGAINST SUCH A FORCE--
--YOU COULD NEVER PREVAIL! DO YOU SEE THE LIGHT AT LAST?
I SEE ONLY A LUNATIC WITH HER HEAD IN THE CLOUDS WHO IS ABOUT TO GET A HARSH TASTE OF REALITY!
WHA--?!
ULK!

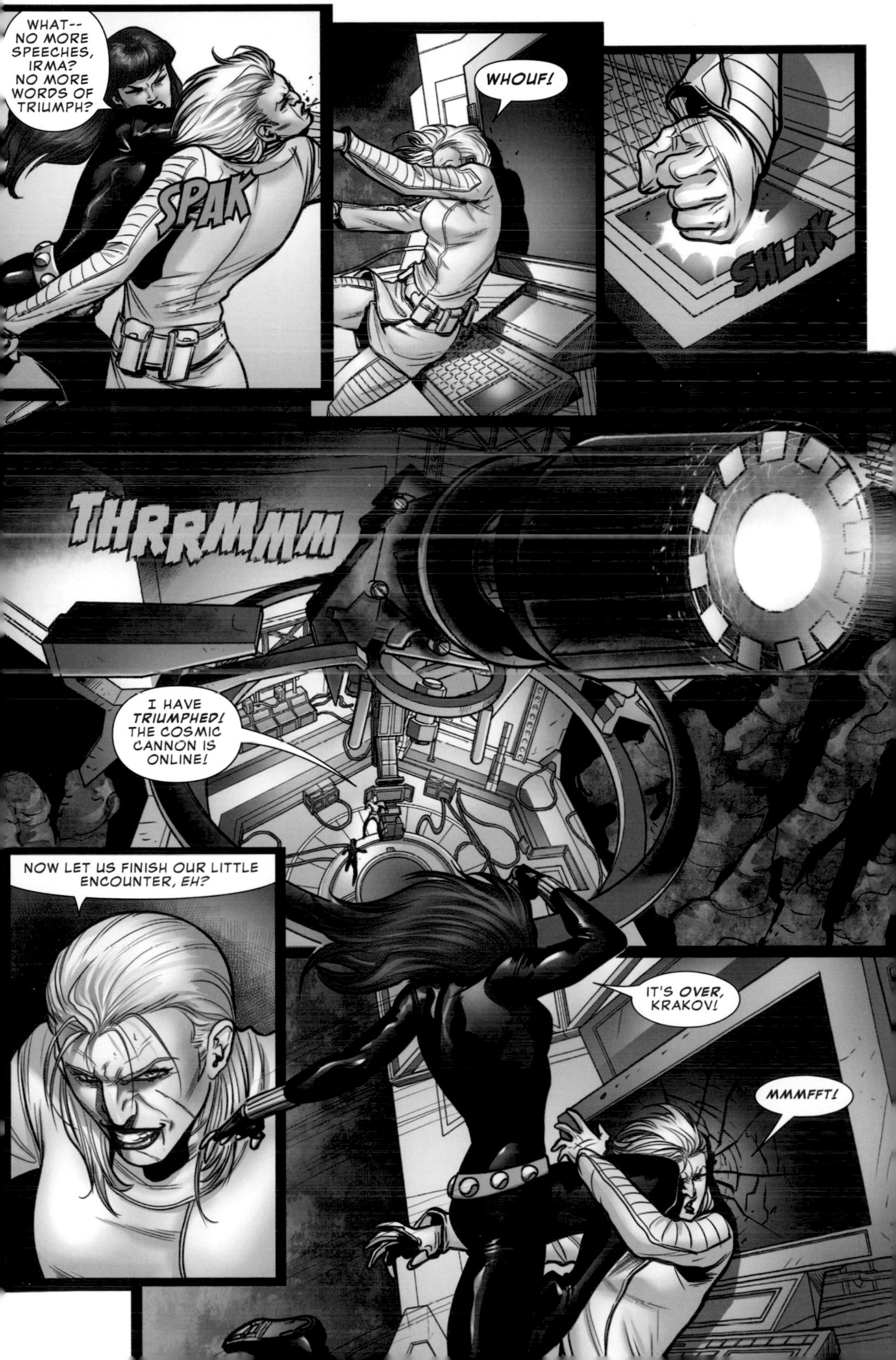
WHAT-- NO MORE SPEECHES, IRMA? NO MORE WORDS OF TRIUMPH?
SPAK
WHOUF!
SHLAK
THRRMMMM
I HAVE *TRIUMPHED!* THE COSMIC CANNON IS ONLINE!
NOW LET US FINISH OUR LITTLE ENCOUNTER, *EH?*
IT'S *OVER,* KRAKOV!
MMMFFT!

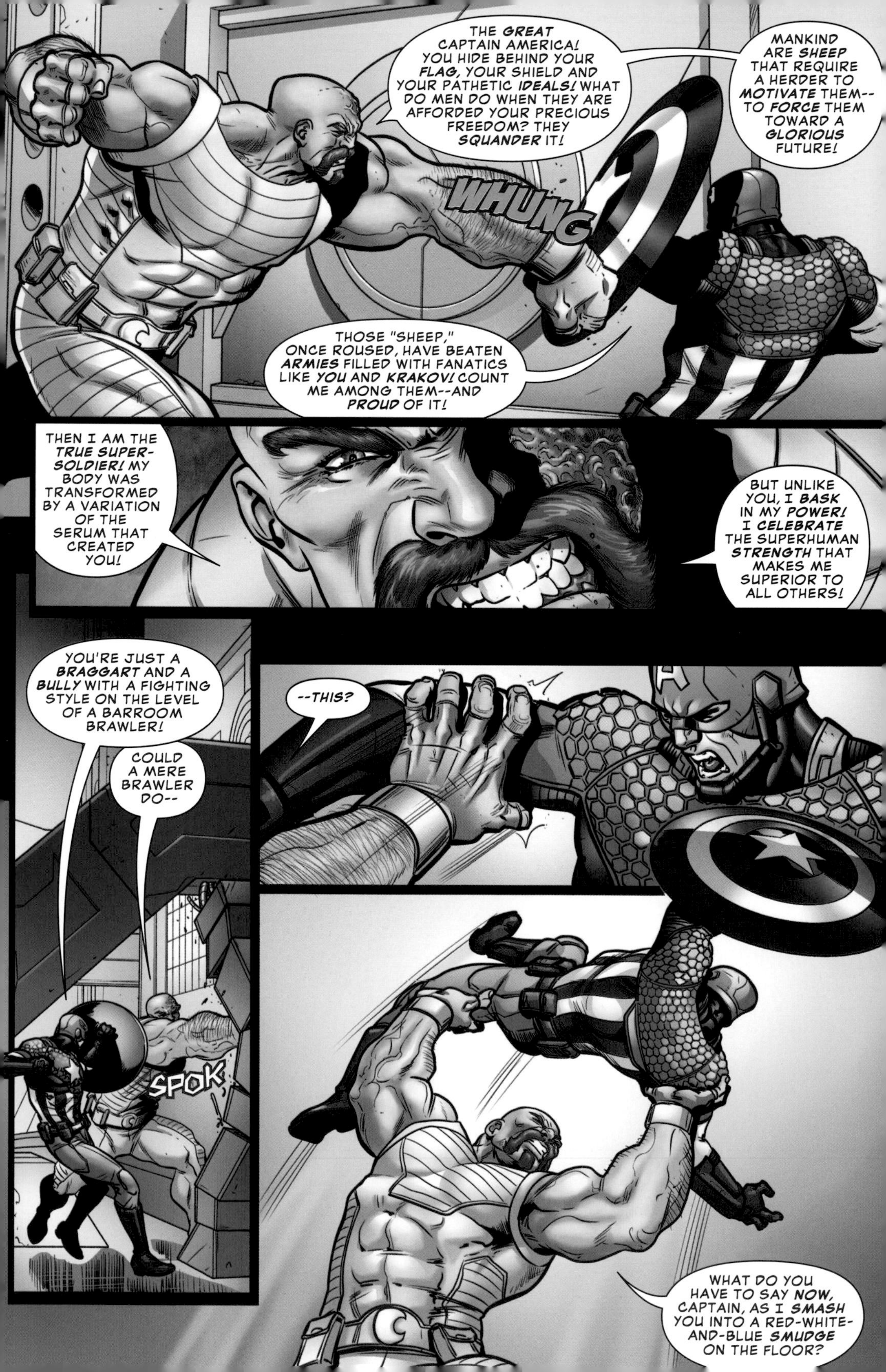
THE GREAT CAPTAIN AMERICA! YOU HIDE BEHIND YOUR FLAG, YOUR SHIELD AND YOUR PATHETIC IDEALS! WHAT DO MEN DO WHEN THEY ARE AFFORDED YOUR PRECIOUS FREEDOM? THEY SQUANDER IT!
MANKIND ARE SHEEP THAT REQUIRE A HERDER TO MOTIVATE THEM--TO FORCE THEM TOWARD A GLORIOUS FUTURE!
WHUNG
THOSE "SHEEP," ONCE ROUSED, HAVE BEATEN ARMIES FILLED WITH FANATICS LIKE YOU AND KRAKOV! COUNT ME AMONG THEM--AND PROUD OF IT!
THEN I AM THE TRUE SUPER-SOLDIER! MY BODY WAS TRANSFORMED BY A VARIATION OF THE SERUM THAT CREATED YOU!
BUT UNLIKE YOU, I BASK IN MY POWER! I CELEBRATE THE SUPERHUMAN STRENGTH THAT MAKES ME SUPERIOR TO ALL OTHERS!
YOU'RE JUST A BRAGGART AND A BULLY WITH A FIGHTING STYLE ON THE LEVEL OF A BARROOM BRAWLER!
COULD A MERE BRAWLER DO--
SPOK
--THIS?
WHAT DO YOU HAVE TO SAY NOW, CAPTAIN, AS I SMASH YOU INTO A RED-WHITE-AND-BLUE SMUDGE ON THE FLOOR?

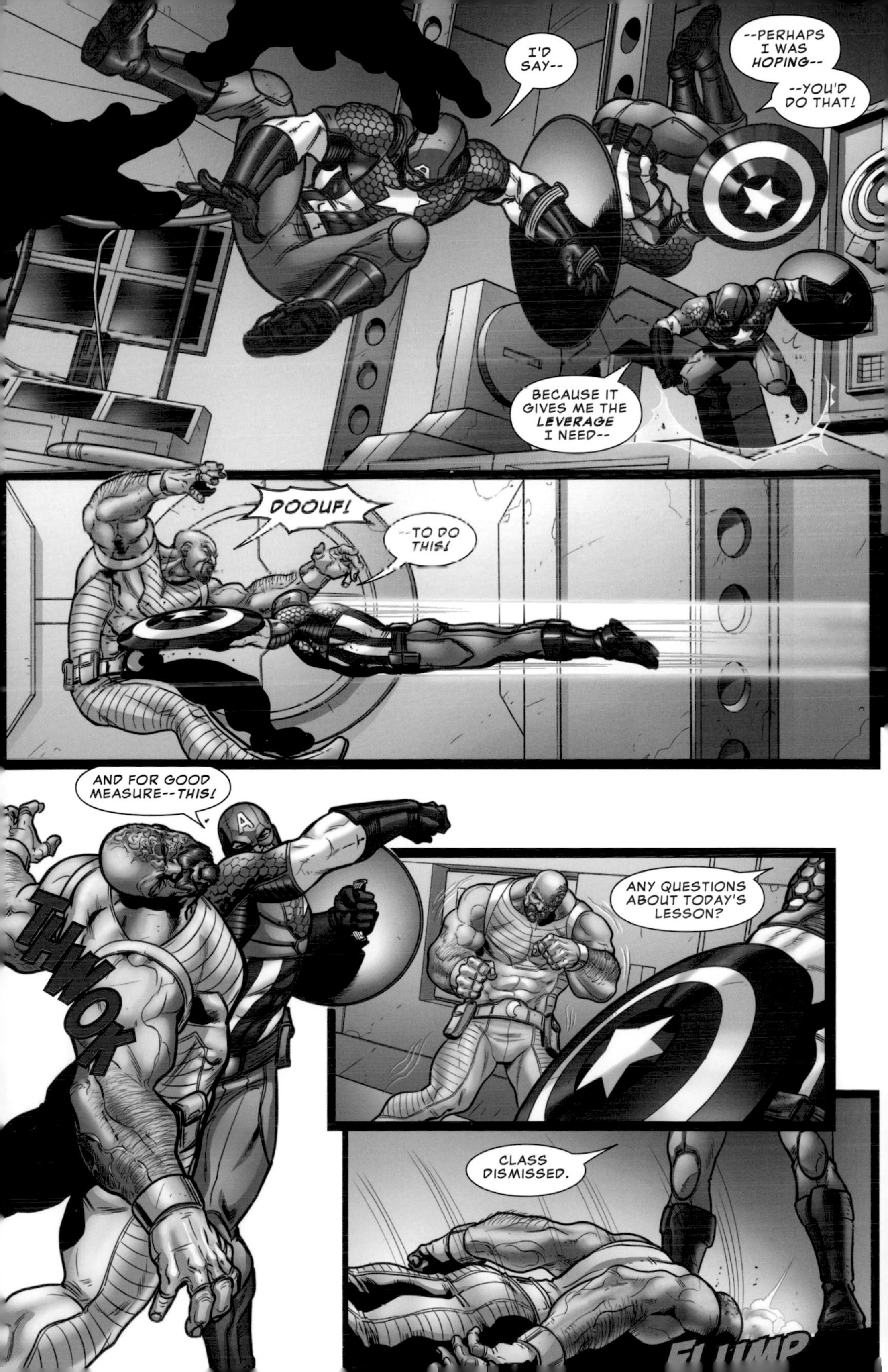
I'D SAY--
--PERHAPS I WAS *HOPING*--
--YOU'D DO THAT!
BECAUSE IT GIVES ME THE *LEVERAGE* I NEED--
DOOUF!
--TO DO *THIS!*
AND FOR GOOD MEASURE--*THIS!*
THWOK
ANY QUESTIONS ABOUT TODAY'S LESSON?
CLASS DISMISSED.

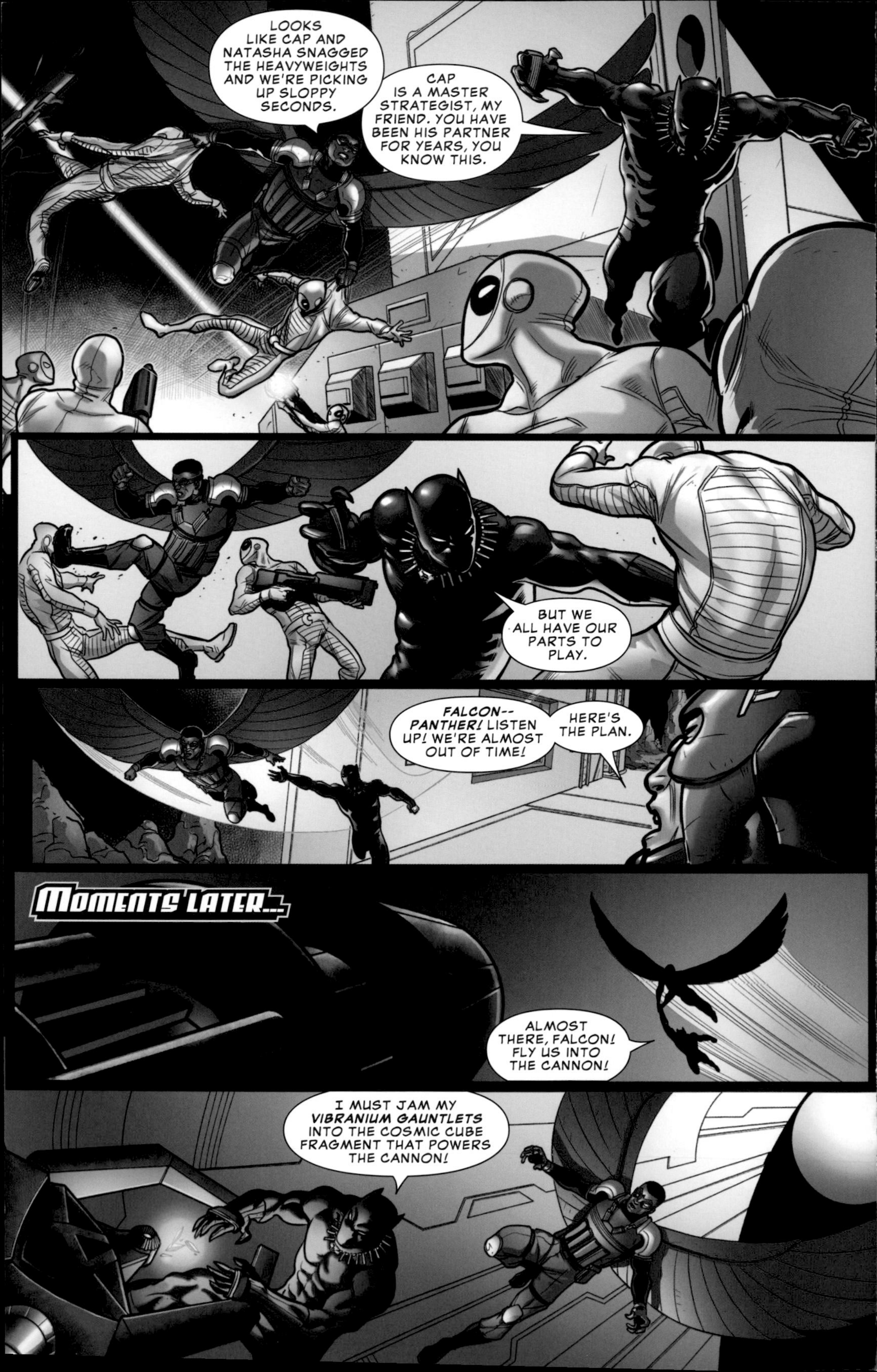
LOOKS LIKE CAP AND NATASHA SNAGGED THE HEAVYWEIGHTS AND WE'RE PICKING UP SLOPPY SECONDS.
CAP IS A MASTER STRATEGIST, MY FRIEND. YOU HAVE BEEN HIS PARTNER FOR YEARS, YOU KNOW THIS.
BUT WE ALL HAVE OUR PARTS TO PLAY.
FALCON-- PANTHER! LISTEN UP! WE'RE ALMOST OUT OF TIME!
HERE'S THE PLAN.
MOMENTS LATER...
ALMOST THERE, FALCON! FLY US INTO THE CANNON!
I MUST JAM MY VIBRANIUM GAUNTLETS INTO THE COSMIC CUBE FRAGMENT THAT POWERS THE CANNON!

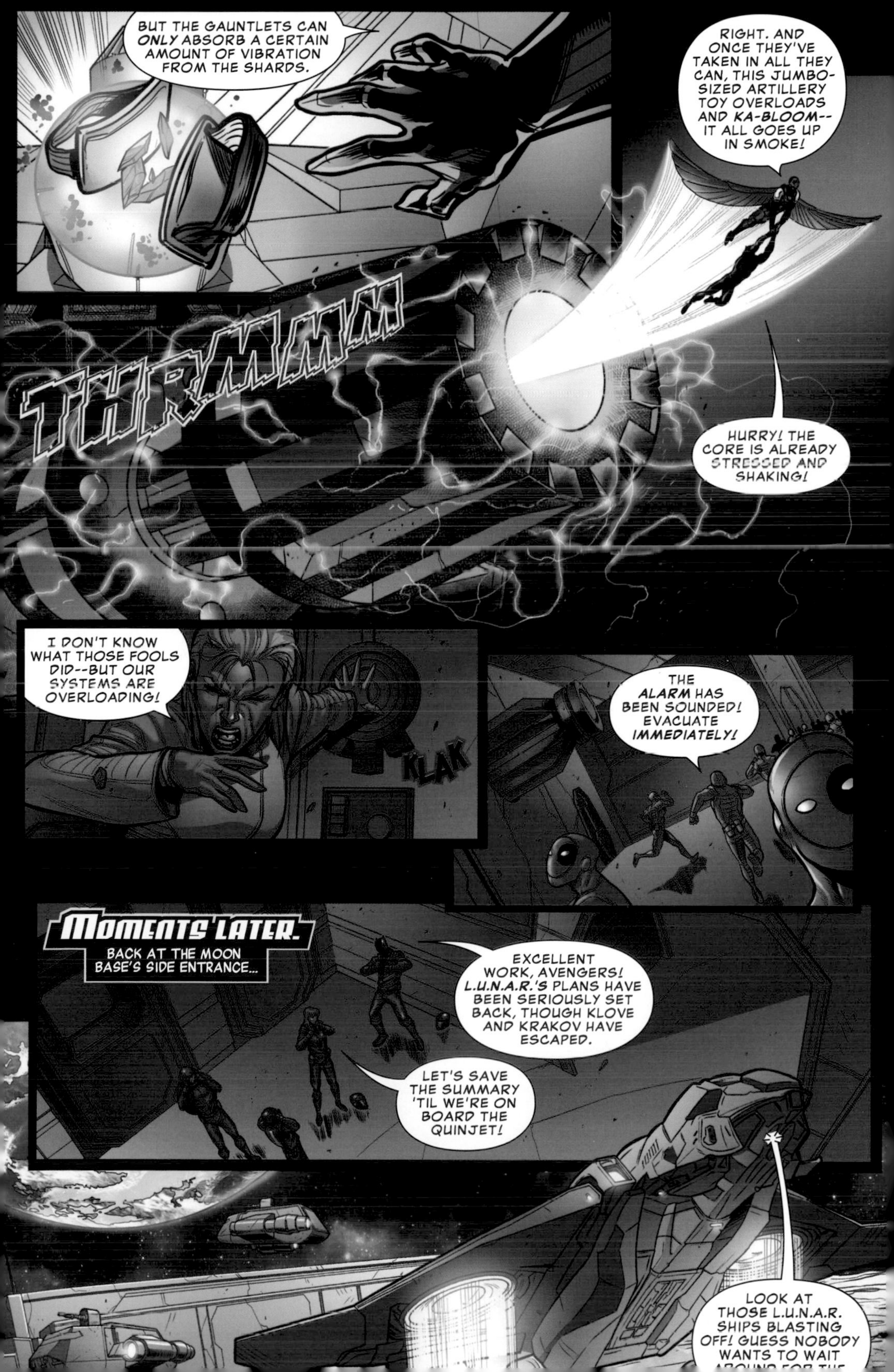
BUT THE GAUNTLETS CAN ONLY ABSORB A CERTAIN AMOUNT OF VIBRATION FROM THE SHARDS.
RIGHT. AND ONCE THEY'VE TAKEN IN ALL THEY CAN, THIS JUMBO-SIZED ARTILLERY TOY OVERLOADS AND KA-BLOOM-- IT ALL GOES UP IN SMOKE!
THRMMM
HURRY! THE CORE IS ALREADY STRESSED AND SHAKING!
I DON'T KNOW WHAT THOSE FOOLS DID--BUT OUR SYSTEMS ARE OVERLOADING!
KLAK
THE ALARM HAS BEEN SOUNDED! EVACUATE IMMEDIATELY!
MOMENTS LATER.
BACK AT THE MOON BASE'S SIDE ENTRANCE...
EXCELLENT WORK, AVENGERS! L.U.N.A.R.'S PLANS HAVE BEEN SERIOUSLY SET BACK, THOUGH KLOVE AND KRAKOV HAVE ESCAPED.
LET'S SAVE THE SUMMARY 'TIL WE'RE ON BOARD THE QUINJET!
LOOK AT THOSE L.U.N.A.R. SHIPS BLASTING OFF! GUESS NOBODY WANTS TO WAIT

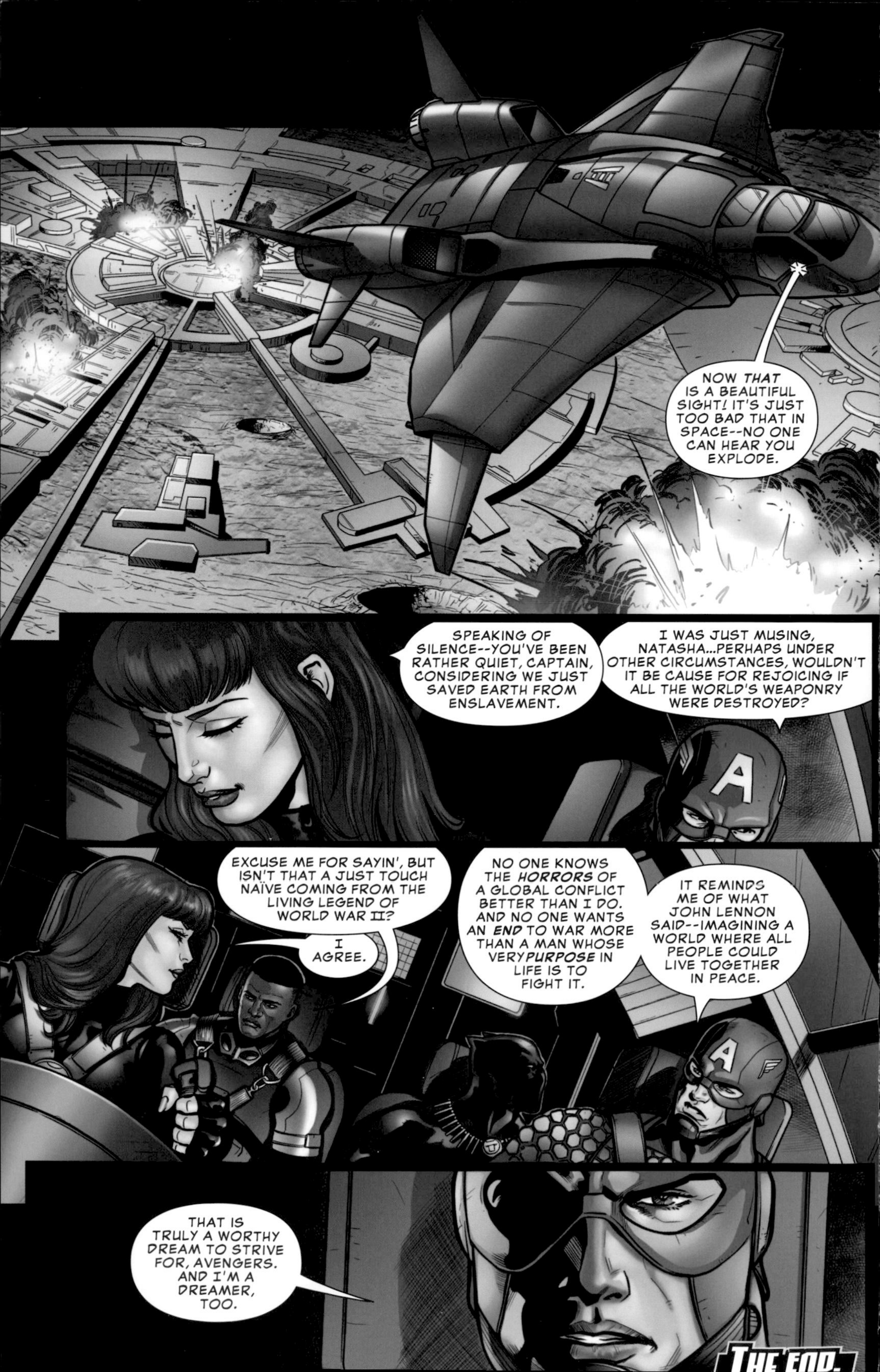
NOW *THAT* IS A BEAUTIFUL SIGHT! IT'S JUST TOO BAD THAT IN SPACE--NO ONE CAN HEAR YOU EXPLODE.
SPEAKING OF SILENCE--YOU'VE BEEN RATHER QUIET, CAPTAIN, CONSIDERING WE JUST SAVED EARTH FROM ENSLAVEMENT.
I WAS JUST MUSING, NATASHA...PERHAPS UNDER OTHER CIRCUMSTANCES, WOULDN'T IT BE CAUSE FOR REJOICING IF ALL THE WORLD'S WEAPONRY WERE DESTROYED?
EXCUSE ME FOR SAYIN', BUT ISN'T THAT A JUST TOUCH NAÏVE COMING FROM THE LIVING LEGEND OF WORLD WAR II?
I AGREE.
NO ONE KNOWS THE *HORRORS* OF A GLOBAL CONFLICT BETTER THAN I DO. AND NO ONE WANTS AN *END* TO WAR MORE THAN A MAN WHOSE VERY *PURPOSE* IN LIFE IS TO FIGHT IT.
IT REMINDS ME OF WHAT JOHN LENNON SAID--IMAGINING A WORLD WHERE ALL PEOPLE COULD LIVE TOGETHER IN PEACE.
THAT IS TRULY A WORTHY DREAM TO STRIVE FOR, AVENGERS. AND I'M A DREAMER, TOO.
THE END.

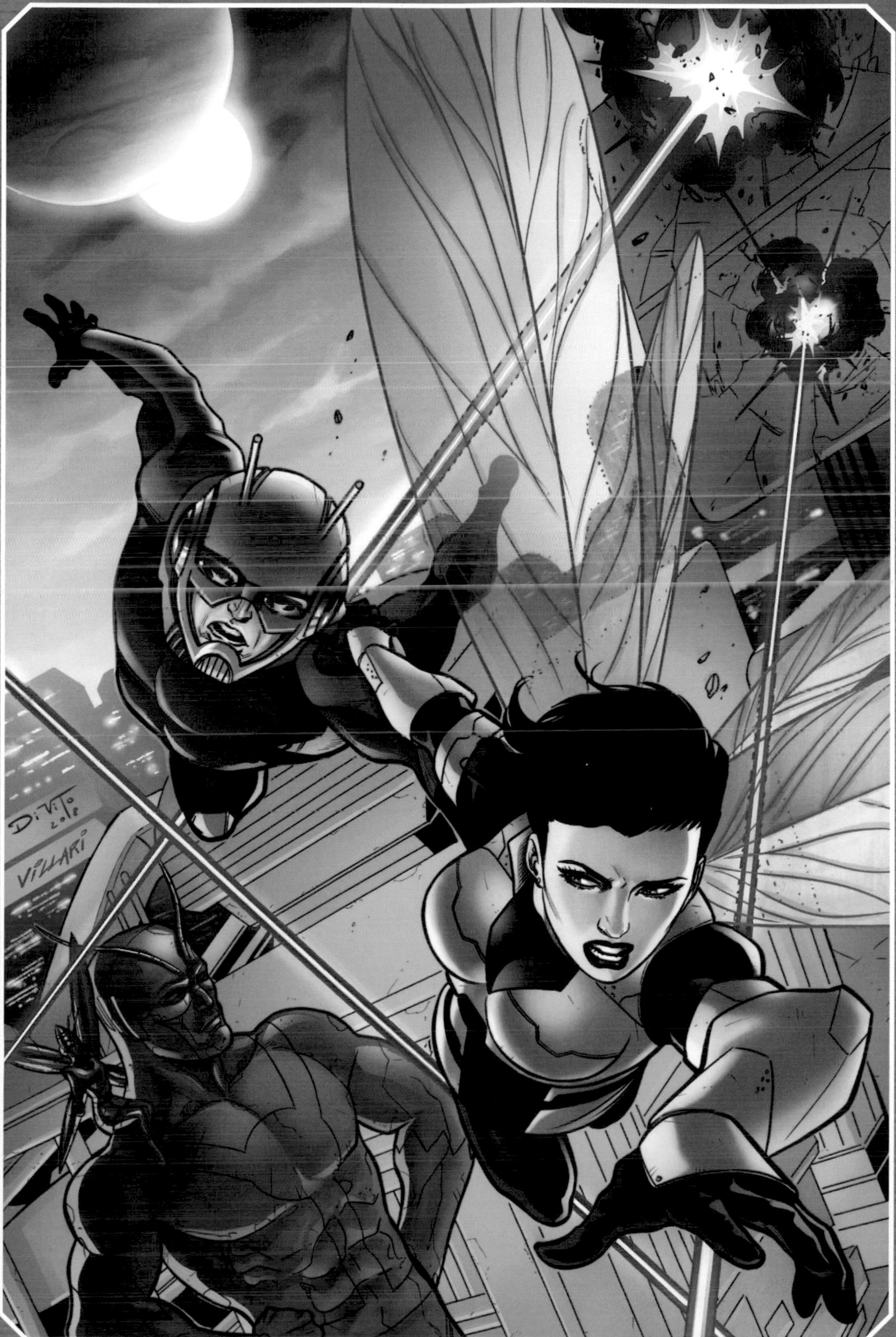
DI VITO 2018
VILLARI

ANT-MAN AND THE WASP: LIVING LEGENDS

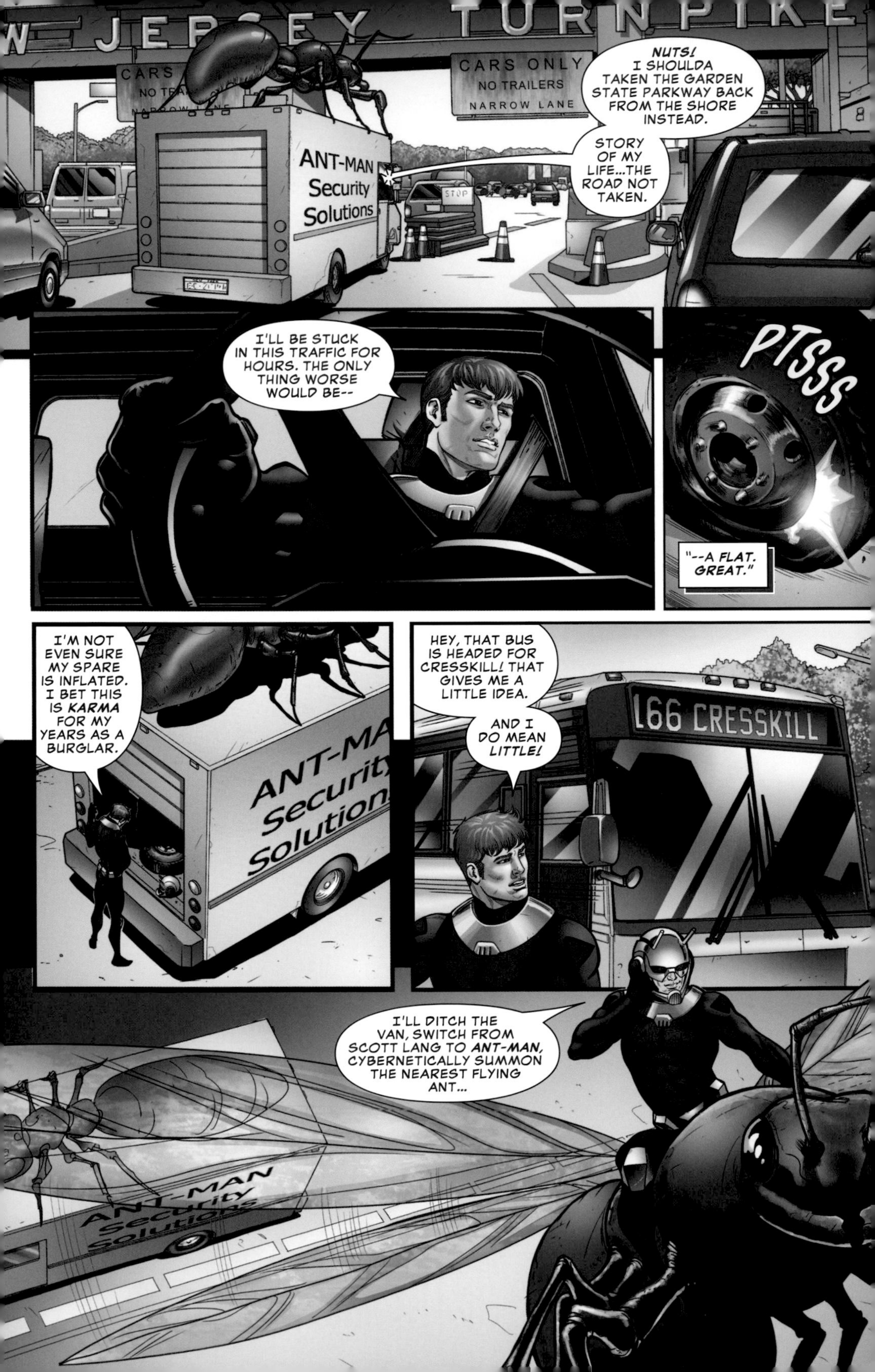
NEW JERSEY TURNPIKE
CARS ONLY
NO TRAILERS
NARROW LANE
ANT-MAN Security Solutions
STOP
NUTS! I SHOULDA TAKEN THE GARDEN STATE PARKWAY BACK FROM THE SHORE INSTEAD.
STORY OF MY LIFE...THE ROAD NOT TAKEN.
I'LL BE STUCK IN THIS TRAFFIC FOR HOURS. THE ONLY THING WORSE WOULD BE--
PTSSS
"--A FLAT. GREAT."
I'M NOT EVEN SURE MY SPARE IS INFLATED. I BET THIS IS KARMA FOR MY YEARS AS A BURGLAR.
HEY, THAT BUS IS HEADED FOR CRESSKILL! THAT GIVES ME A LITTLE IDEA.
AND I DO MEAN LITTLE!
166 CRESSKILL
I'LL DITCH THE VAN, SWITCH FROM SCOTT LANG TO ANT-MAN, CYBERNETICALLY SUMMON THE NEAREST FLYING ANT...
ANT-MAN Security Solutions

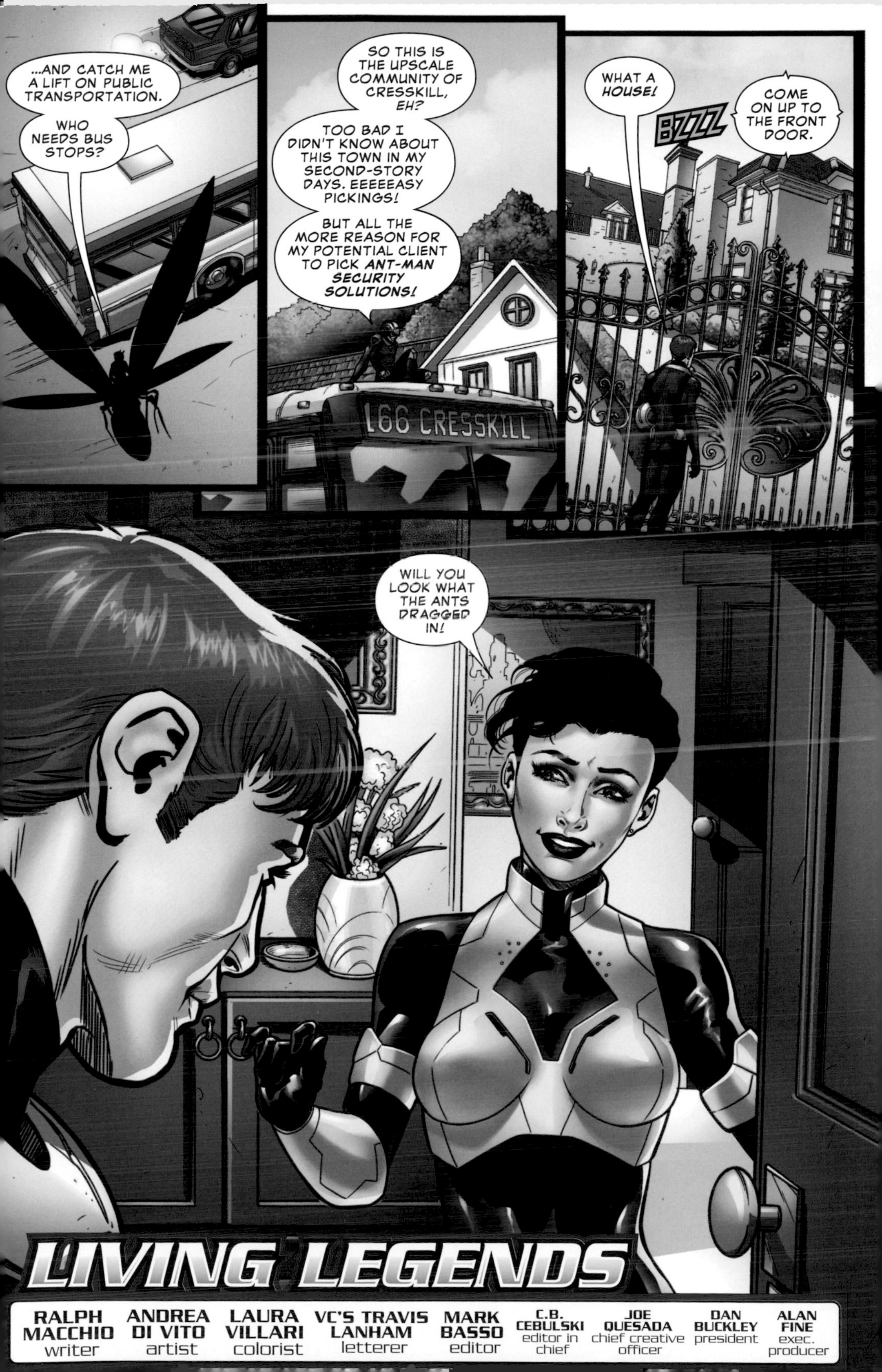
...AND CATCH ME A LIFT ON PUBLIC TRANSPORTATION.
WHO NEEDS BUS STOPS?
SO THIS IS THE UPSCALE COMMUNITY OF CRESSKILL, EH?
TOO BAD I DIDN'T KNOW ABOUT THIS TOWN IN MY SECOND-STORY DAYS. EEEEEASY PICKINGS!
BUT ALL THE MORE REASON FOR MY POTENTIAL CLIENT TO PICK ANT-MAN SECURITY SOLUTIONS!
166 CRESSKILL
WHAT A HOUSE!
BZZZ
COME ON UP TO THE FRONT DOOR.
WILL YOU LOOK WHAT THE ANTS DRAGGED IN!
LIVING LEGENDS
RALPH MACCHIO writer
ANDREA DI VITO artist
LAURA VILLARI colorist
VC'S TRAVIS LANHAM letterer
MARK BASSO editor
C.B. CEBULSKI editor in chief
JOE QUESADA chief creative officer
DAN BUCKLEY president
ALAN FINE exec. producer

GIMME A HUG, HANDSOME! I *ALWAYS* SAID THAT HELMET HID YOUR GOOD LOOKS!

WHAT TOOK YOU SO LONG? AND I THOUGHT YOU TOLD ME TO GEAR UP FOR SOME "SECURITY TEST"?

YEAH, WELL, YOU SEE, JAN--

BWEEOOP BWEEEOOP

THAT'S NOT PART OF THE TEST.

ALWAYS SOME OLD PIECE OF HANK'S TECH GOING OFF AROUND THIS PLACE--

--BUT THIS ONE SEEMS TO BE COMING FROM THE COMMUNICATIONS ROOM.

MIND IF I TAG ALONG?

NO SECRETS HERE.

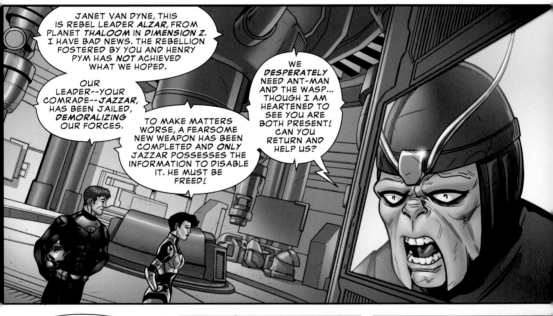

JANET VAN DYNE, THIS IS REBEL LEADER *ALZAR*, FROM PLANET *THALOOM* IN *DIMENSION Z*. I HAVE BAD NEWS. THE REBELLION FOSTERED BY YOU AND HENRY PYM HAS *NOT* ACHIEVED WHAT WE HOPED.

OUR LEADER--YOUR COMRADE--*JAZZAR*, HAS BEEN JAILED, *DEMORALIZING* OUR FORCES.

TO MAKE MATTERS WORSE, A FEARSOME NEW WEAPON HAS BEEN COMPLETED AND *ONLY* JAZZAR POSSESSES THE INFORMATION TO DISABLE IT. HE MUST BE FREED!

WE *DESPERATELY* NEED ANT-MAN AND THE WASP... THOUGH I AM HEARTENED TO SEE YOU ARE BOTH PRESENT! CAN YOU RETURN AND HELP US?

UMMM, WELL...I *AM* ANT-MAN. BUT--UH--I'M NOT *THAT* ANT-MAN. HANK PYM'S A BUDDY, Y'SEE, BUT I'M A DIFFERENT GUY ALTOGETHER.

ALZAR, HANK IS... *UNAVAILABLE*. BUT I UNDERSTAND THE *DIRE* NATURE OF YOUR PREDICAMENT.

I WON'T LET YOU DOWN. VAN DYNE OUT.

SOOOO...

HERE'S THE BRIEF VERSION. THIS DOOHICKEY IS AN INTER-DIMENSIONAL "ERASER" THAT TELEPORTS YOU BACK AND FORTH BETWEEN DIMENSIONS.

CUTZA, CALLED THE *LIVING ERASER*, USED IT TO HIJACK HANK AND ME TO DIMENSION Z.*

*WAY BACK IN *TALES TO ASTONISH* #49 --BACK-ISSUE BASSO

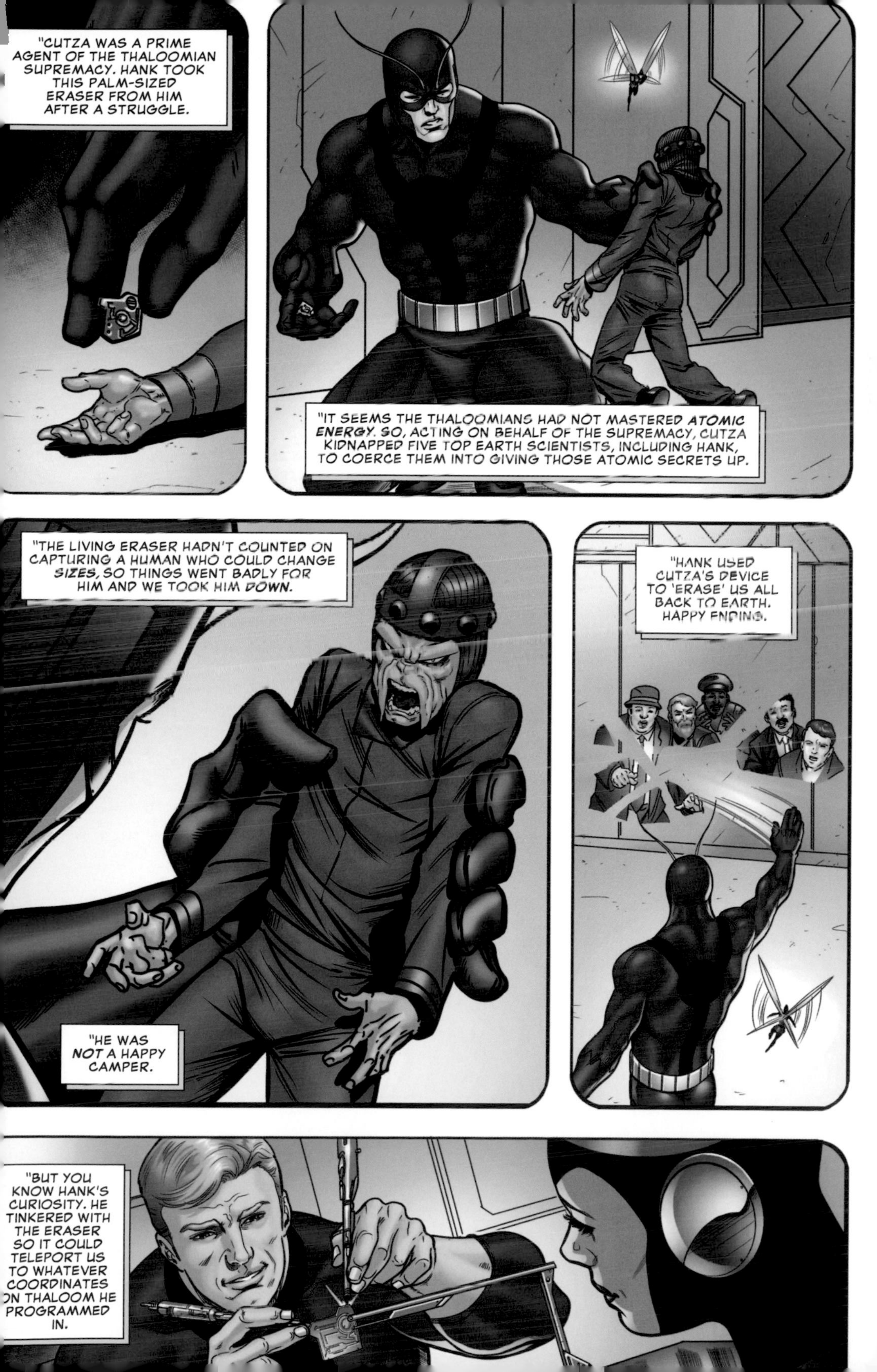
"CUTZA WAS A PRIME AGENT OF THE THALOOMIAN SUPREMACY. HANK TOOK THIS PALM-SIZED ERASER FROM HIM AFTER A STRUGGLE.
"IT SEEMS THE THALOOMIANS HAD NOT MASTERED ATOMIC ENERGY. SO, ACTING ON BEHALF OF THE SUPREMACY, CUTZA KIDNAPPED FIVE TOP EARTH SCIENTISTS, INCLUDING HANK, TO COERCE THEM INTO GIVING THOSE ATOMIC SECRETS UP.
"THE LIVING ERASER HADN'T COUNTED ON CAPTURING A HUMAN WHO COULD CHANGE SIZES, SO THINGS WENT BADLY FOR HIM AND WE TOOK HIM DOWN.
"HE WAS NOT A HAPPY CAMPER.
"HANK USED CUTZA'S DEVICE TO 'ERASE' US ALL BACK TO EARTH. HAPPY ENDING.
"BUT YOU KNOW HANK'S CURIOSITY. HE TINKERED WITH THE ERASER SO IT COULD TELEPORT US TO WHATEVER COORDINATES ON THALOOM HE PROGRAMMED IN.

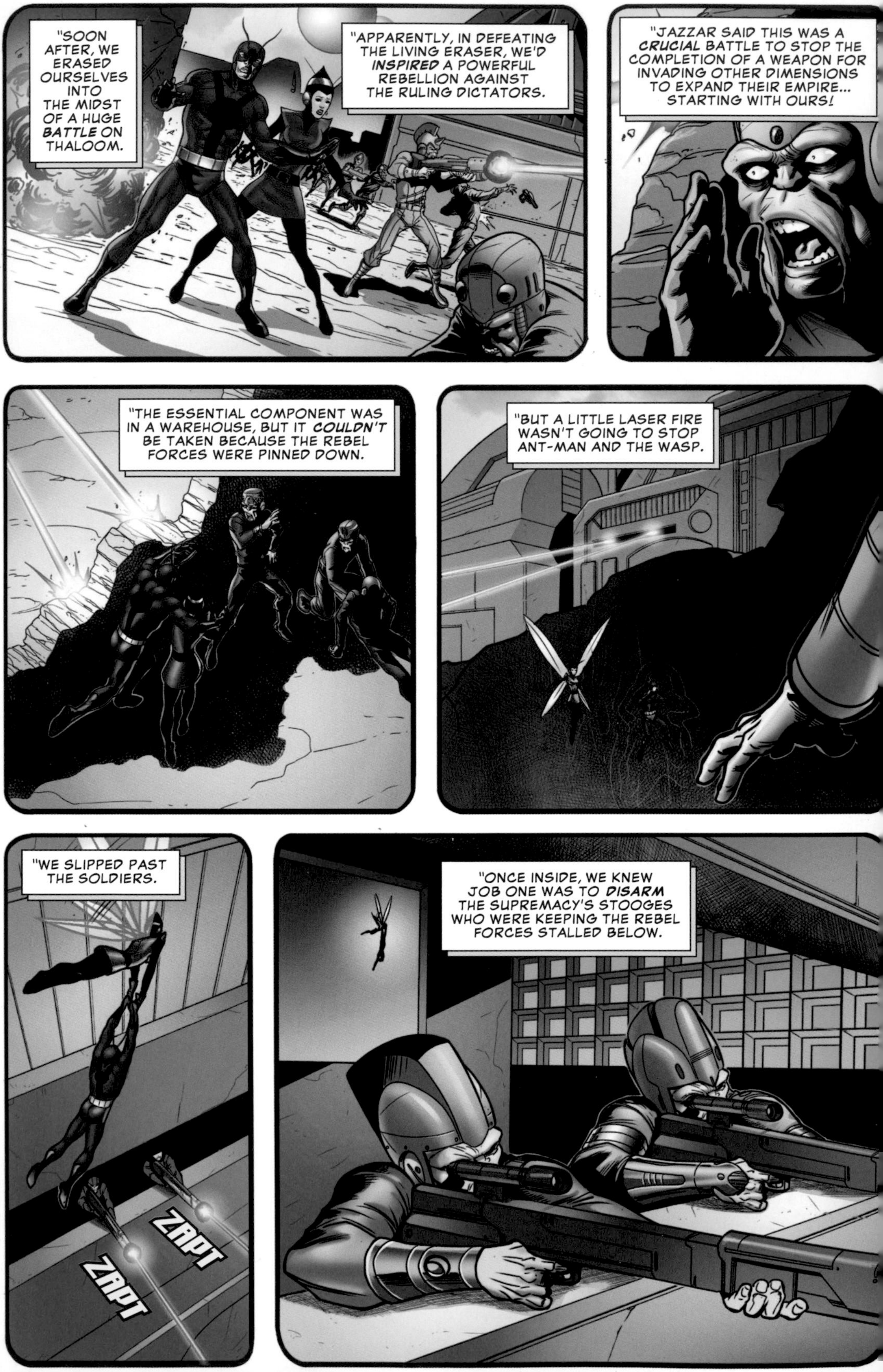
"SOON AFTER, WE ERASED OURSELVES INTO THE MIDST OF A HUGE BATTLE ON THALOOM.
"APPARENTLY, IN DEFEATING THE LIVING ERASER, WE'D INSPIRED A POWERFUL REBELLION AGAINST THE RULING DICTATORS.
"JAZZAR SAID THIS WAS A CRUCIAL BATTLE TO STOP THE COMPLETION OF A WEAPON FOR INVADING OTHER DIMENSIONS TO EXPAND THEIR EMPIRE... STARTING WITH OURS!
"THE ESSENTIAL COMPONENT WAS IN A WAREHOUSE, BUT IT COULDN'T BE TAKEN BECAUSE THE REBEL FORCES WERE PINNED DOWN.
"BUT A LITTLE LASER FIRE WASN'T GOING TO STOP ANT-MAN AND THE WASP.
"WE SLIPPED PAST THE SOLDIERS.
ZAPT
ZAPT
"ONCE INSIDE, WE KNEW JOB ONE WAS TO DISARM THE SUPREMACY'S STOOGES WHO WERE KEEPING THE REBEL FORCES STALLED BELOW.

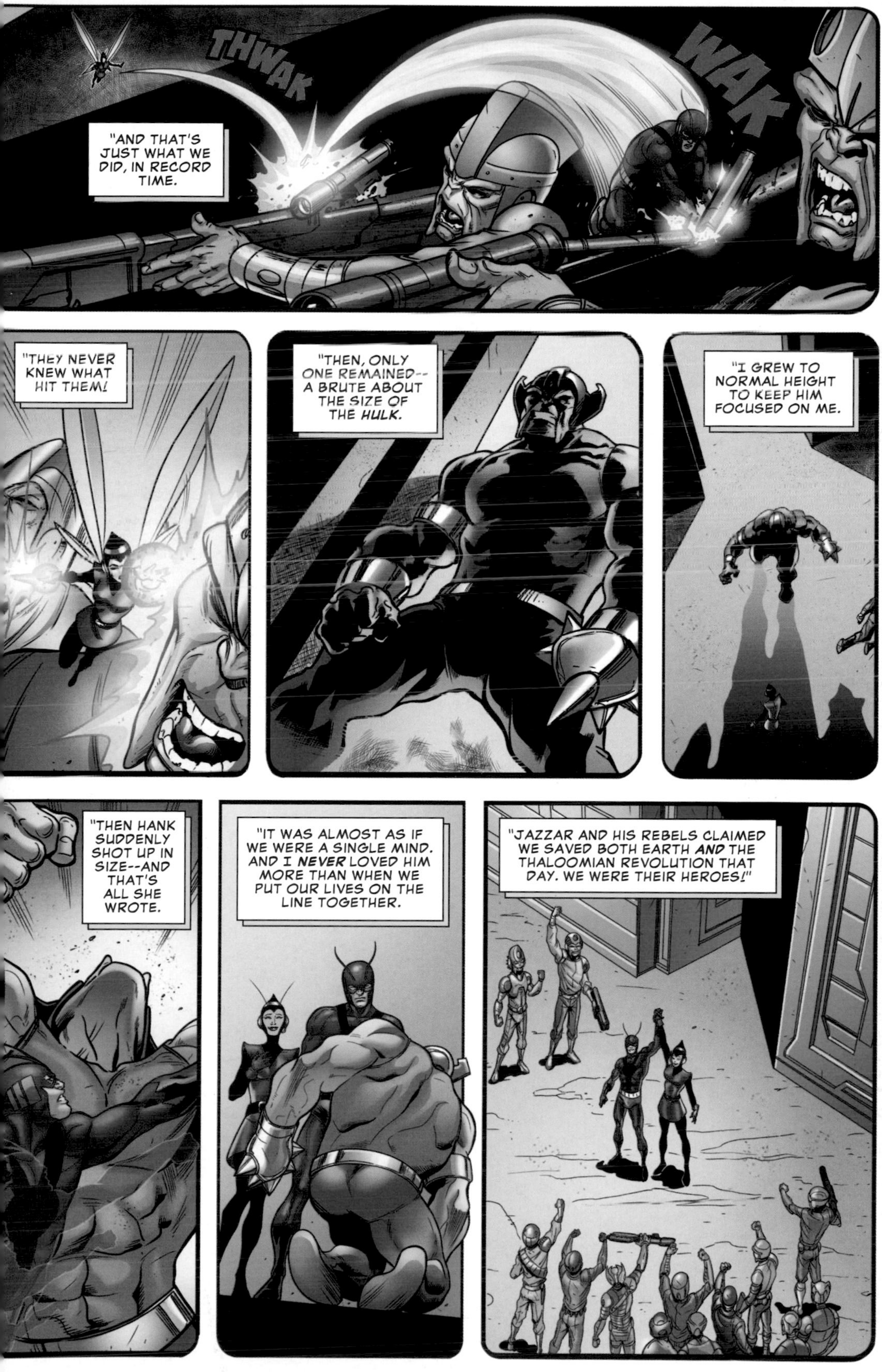
THWAK
WAK
"AND THAT'S JUST WHAT WE DID, IN RECORD TIME.
"THEY NEVER KNEW WHAT HIT THEM!
"THEN, ONLY ONE REMAINED-- A BRUTE ABOUT THE SIZE OF THE HULK.
"I GREW TO NORMAL HEIGHT TO KEEP HIM FOCUSED ON ME.
"THEN HANK SUDDENLY SHOT UP IN SIZE--AND THAT'S ALL SHE WROTE.
"IT WAS ALMOST AS IF WE WERE A SINGLE MIND. AND I NEVER LOVED HIM MORE THAN WHEN WE PUT OUR LIVES ON THE LINE TOGETHER.
"JAZZAR AND HIS REBELS CLAIMED WE SAVED BOTH EARTH AND THE THALOOMIAN REVOLUTION THAT DAY. WE WERE THEIR HEROES!"

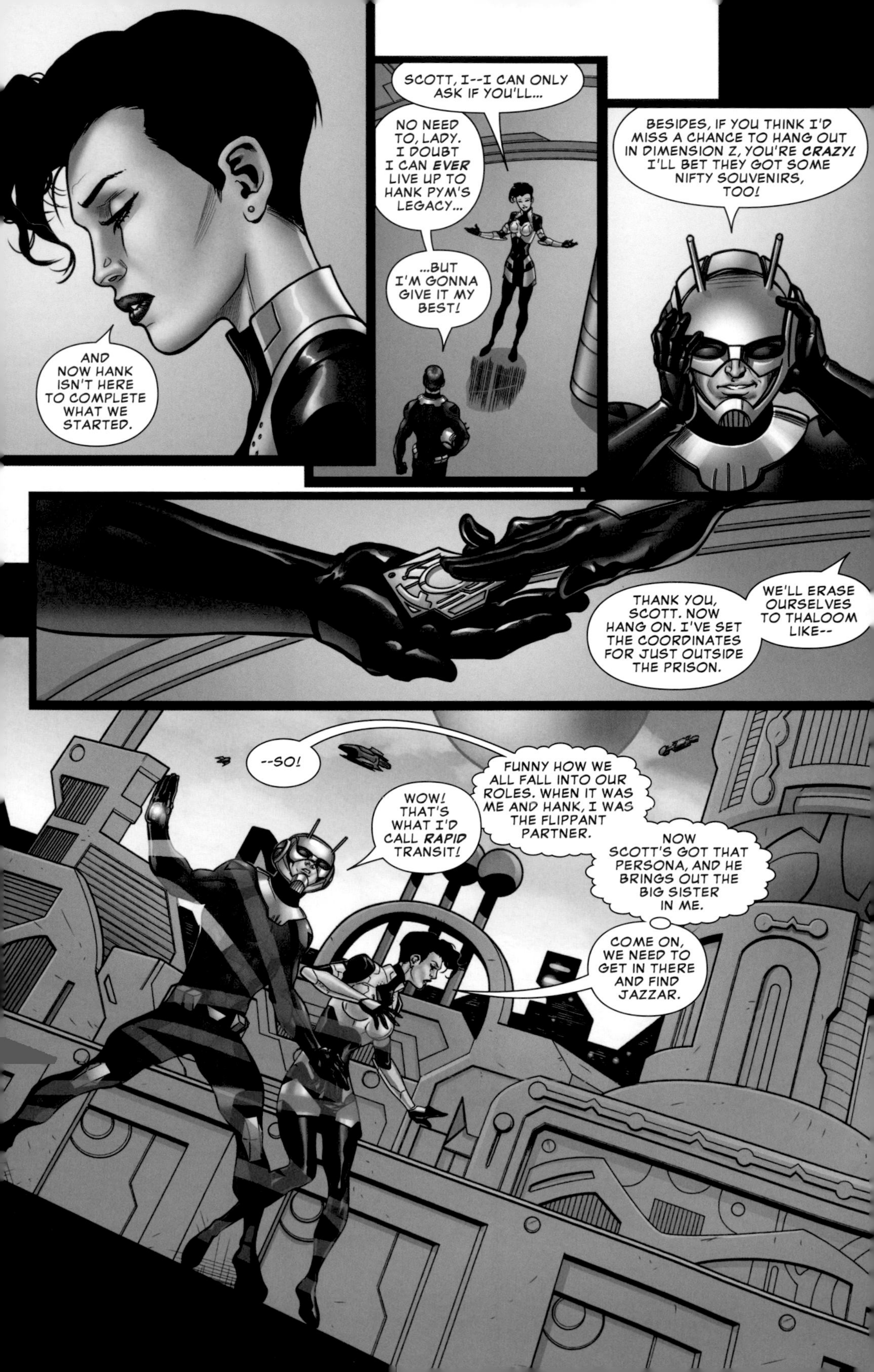
AND NOW HANK ISN'T HERE TO COMPLETE WHAT WE STARTED.
SCOTT, I--I CAN ONLY ASK IF YOU'LL...
NO NEED TO, LADY. I DOUBT I CAN EVER LIVE UP TO HANK PYM'S LEGACY...
...BUT I'M GONNA GIVE IT MY BEST!
BESIDES, IF YOU THINK I'D MISS A CHANCE TO HANG OUT IN DIMENSION Z, YOU'RE CRAZY! I'LL BET THEY GOT SOME NIFTY SOUVENIRS, TOO!
THANK YOU, SCOTT. NOW HANG ON. I'VE SET THE COORDINATES FOR JUST OUTSIDE THE PRISON.
WE'LL ERASE OURSELVES TO THALOOM LIKE--
--SO!
WOW! THAT'S WHAT I'D CALL RAPID TRANSIT!
FUNNY HOW WE ALL FALL INTO OUR ROLES. WHEN IT WAS ME AND HANK, I WAS THE FLIPPANT PARTNER.
NOW SCOTT'S GOT THAT PERSONA, AND HE BRINGS OUT THE BIG SISTER IN ME.
COME ON, WE NEED TO GET IN THERE AND FIND JAZZAR.

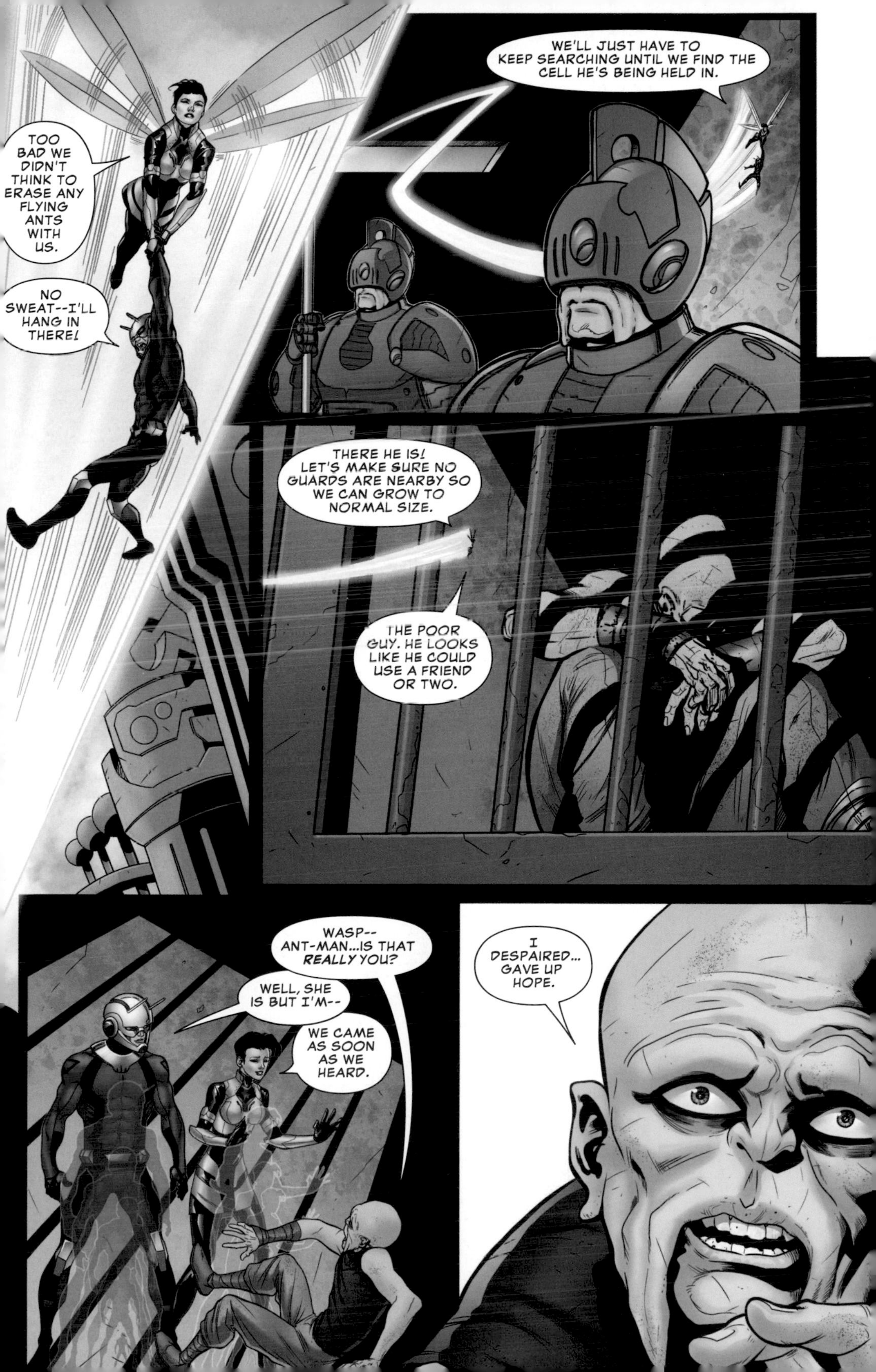
TOO BAD WE DIDN'T THINK TO ERASE ANY FLYING ANTS WITH US.
NO SWEAT--I'LL HANG IN THERE!
WE'LL JUST HAVE TO KEEP SEARCHING UNTIL WE FIND THE CELL HE'S BEING HELD IN.
THERE HE IS! LET'S MAKE SURE NO GUARDS ARE NEARBY SO WE CAN GROW TO NORMAL SIZE.
THE POOR GUY. HE LOOKS LIKE HE COULD USE A FRIEND OR TWO.
WASP-- ANT-MAN...IS THAT *REALLY* YOU?
WELL, SHE IS BUT I'M--
WE CAME AS SOON AS WE HEARD.
I DESPAIRED... GAVE UP HOPE.

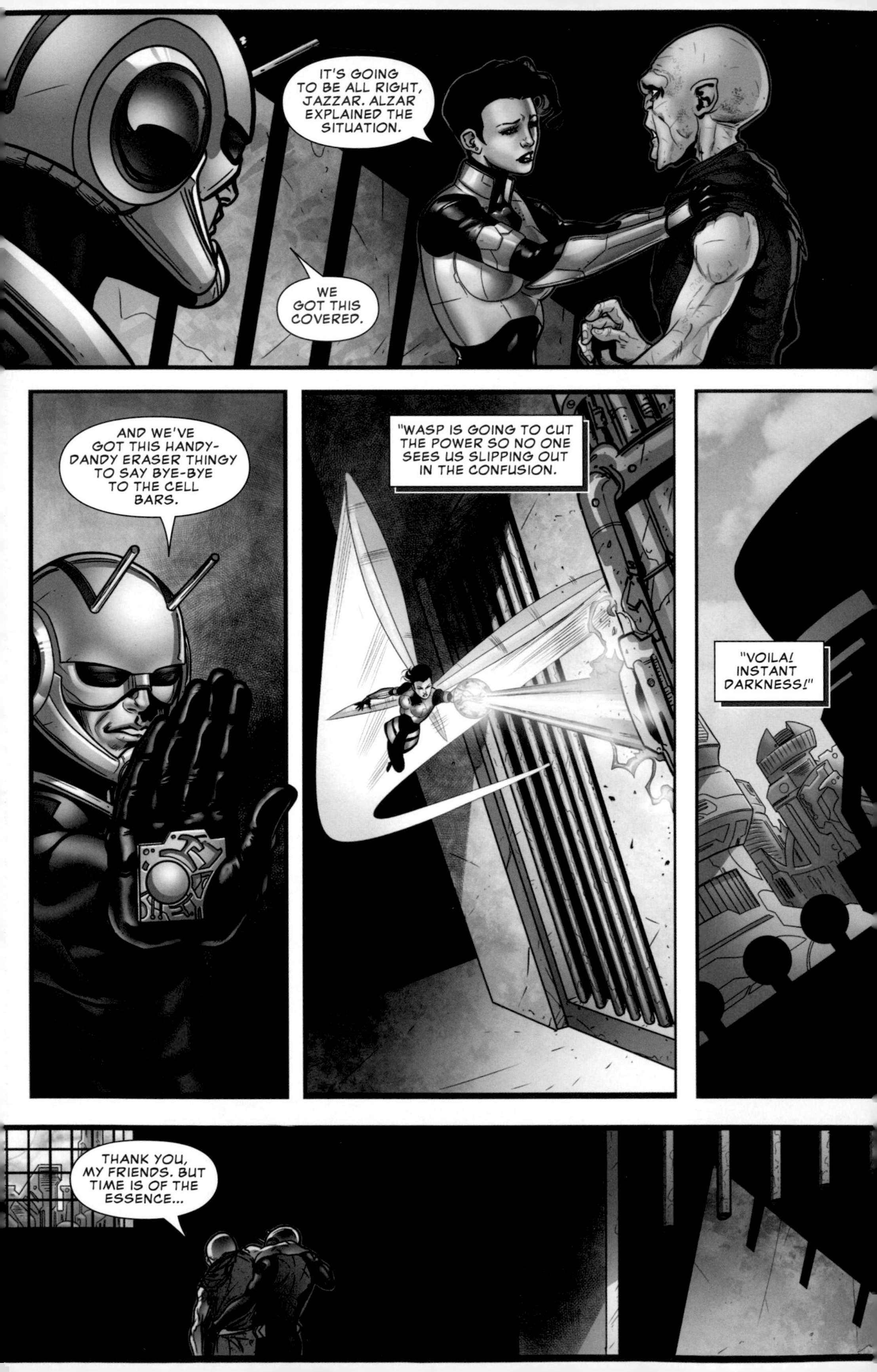
IT'S GOING TO BE ALL RIGHT, JAZZAR. ALZAR EXPLAINED THE SITUATION.
WE GOT THIS COVERED.
AND WE'VE GOT THIS HANDY-DANDY ERASER THINGY TO SAY BYE-BYE TO THE CELL BARS.
"WASP IS GOING TO CUT THE POWER SO NO ONE SEES US SLIPPING OUT IN THE CONFUSION.
"VOILA! INSTANT DARKNESS!"
THANK YOU, MY FRIENDS. BUT TIME IS OF THE ESSENCE...

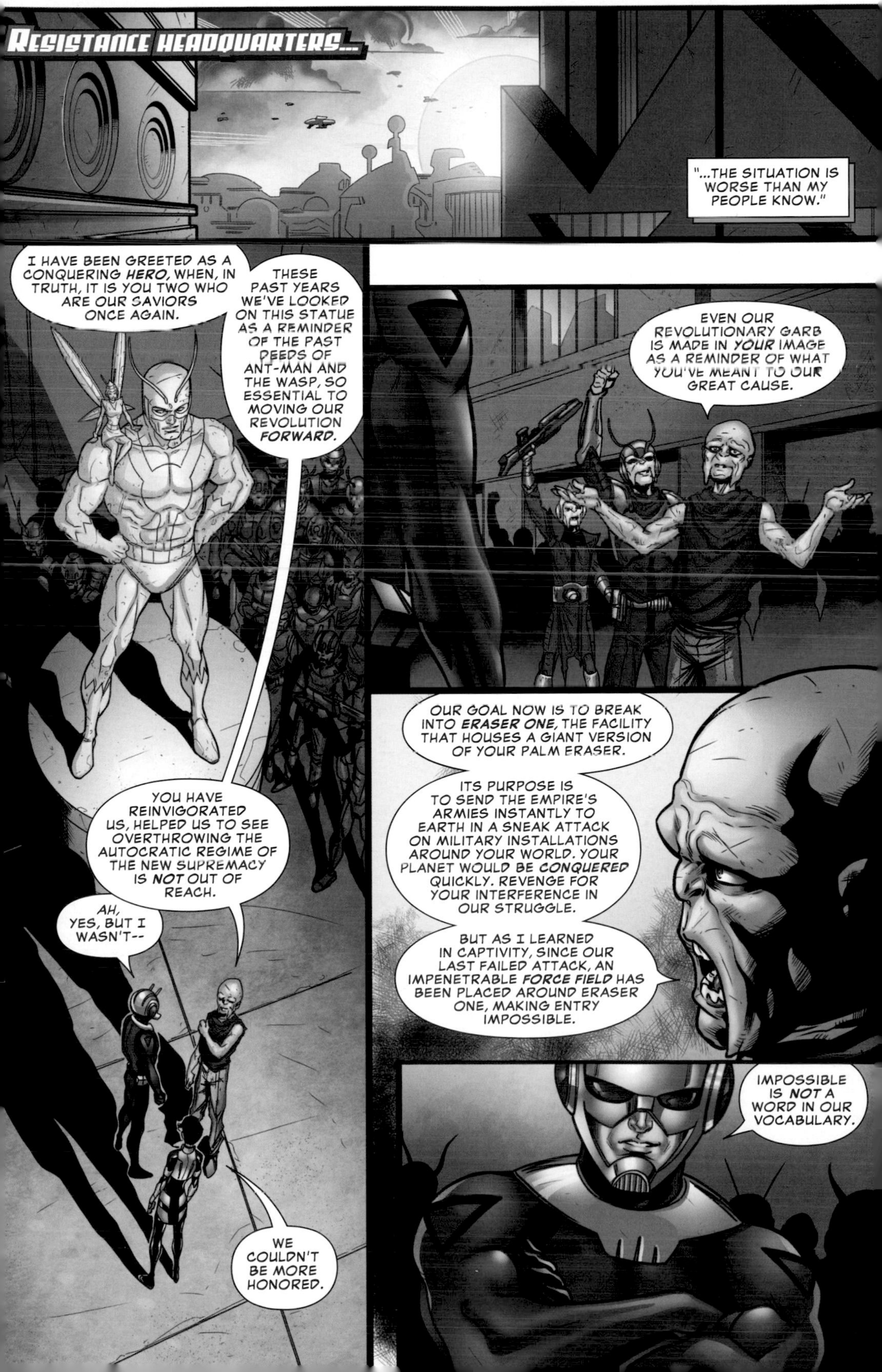

RESISTANCE HEADQUARTERS...
"...THE SITUATION IS WORSE THAN MY PEOPLE KNOW."
I HAVE BEEN GREETED AS A CONQUERING HERO, WHEN, IN TRUTH, IT IS YOU TWO WHO ARE OUR SAVIORS ONCE AGAIN.
THESE PAST YEARS WE'VE LOOKED ON THIS STATUE AS A REMINDER OF THE PAST DEEDS OF ANT-MAN AND THE WASP, SO ESSENTIAL TO MOVING OUR REVOLUTION FORWARD.
YOU HAVE REINVIGORATED US, HELPED US TO SEE OVERTHROWING THE AUTOCRATIC REGIME OF THE NEW SUPREMACY IS NOT OUT OF REACH.
AH, YES, BUT I WASN'T--
WE COULDN'T BE MORE HONORED.
EVEN OUR REVOLUTIONARY GARB IS MADE IN YOUR IMAGE AS A REMINDER OF WHAT YOU'VE MEANT TO OUR GREAT CAUSE.
OUR GOAL NOW IS TO BREAK INTO ERASER ONE, THE FACILITY THAT HOUSES A GIANT VERSION OF YOUR PALM ERASER.
ITS PURPOSE IS TO SEND THE EMPIRE'S ARMIES INSTANTLY TO EARTH IN A SNEAK ATTACK ON MILITARY INSTALLATIONS AROUND YOUR WORLD. YOUR PLANET WOULD BE CONQUERED QUICKLY. REVENGE FOR YOUR INTERFERENCE IN OUR STRUGGLE.
BUT AS I LEARNED IN CAPTIVITY, SINCE OUR LAST FAILED ATTACK, AN IMPENETRABLE FORCE FIELD HAS BEEN PLACED AROUND ERASER ONE, MAKING ENTRY IMPOSSIBLE.
IMPOSSIBLE IS NOT A WORD IN OUR VOCABULARY.

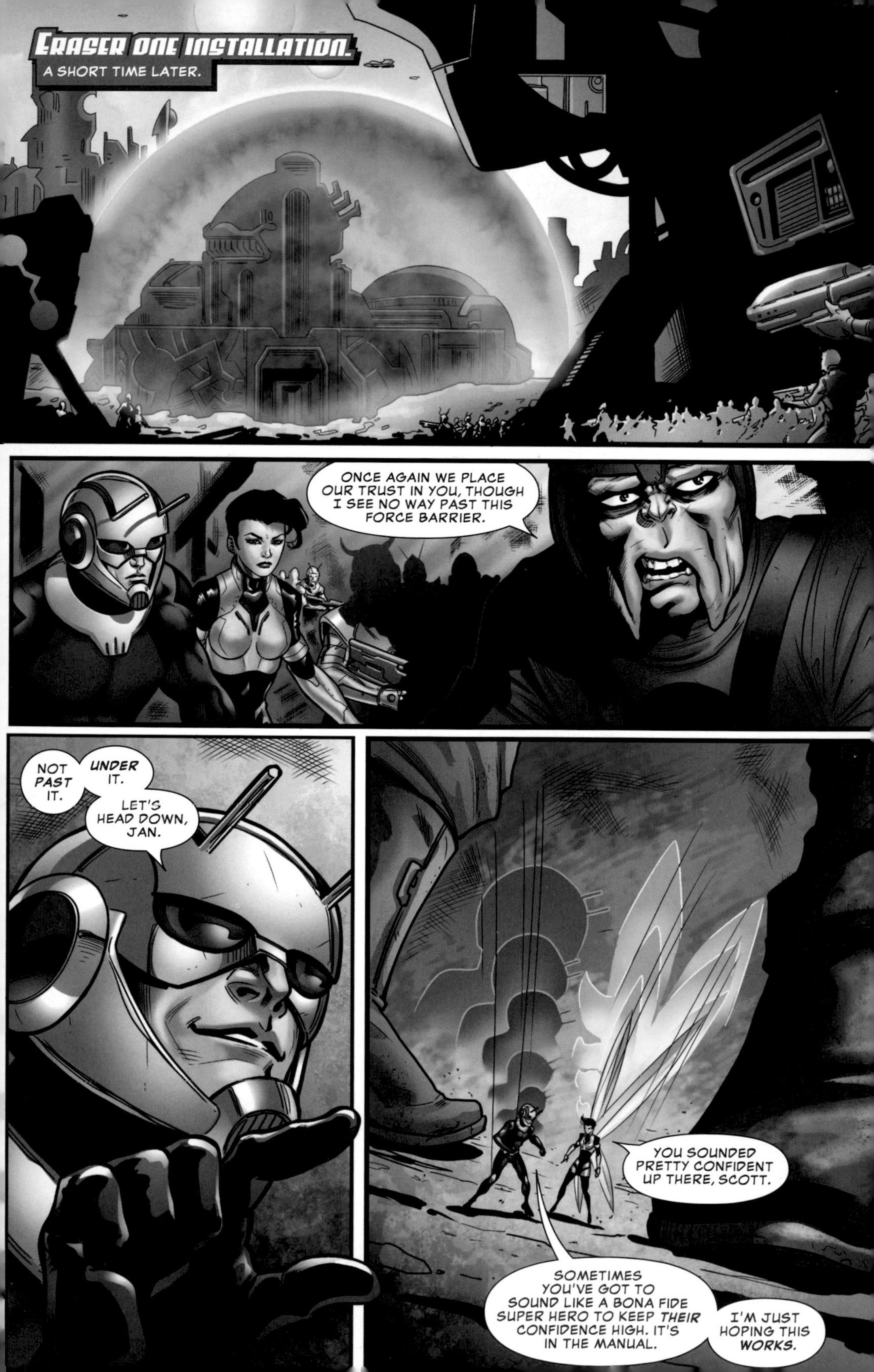
ERASER ONE INSTALLATION.
A SHORT TIME LATER.
ONCE AGAIN WE PLACE OUR TRUST IN YOU, THOUGH I SEE NO WAY PAST THIS FORCE BARRIER.
NOT PAST IT.
UNDER IT.
LET'S HEAD DOWN, JAN.
YOU SOUNDED PRETTY CONFIDENT UP THERE, SCOTT.
SOMETIMES YOU'VE GOT TO SOUND LIKE A BONA FIDE SUPER HERO TO KEEP THEIR CONFIDENCE HIGH. IT'S IN THE MANUAL.
I'M JUST HOPING THIS WORKS.

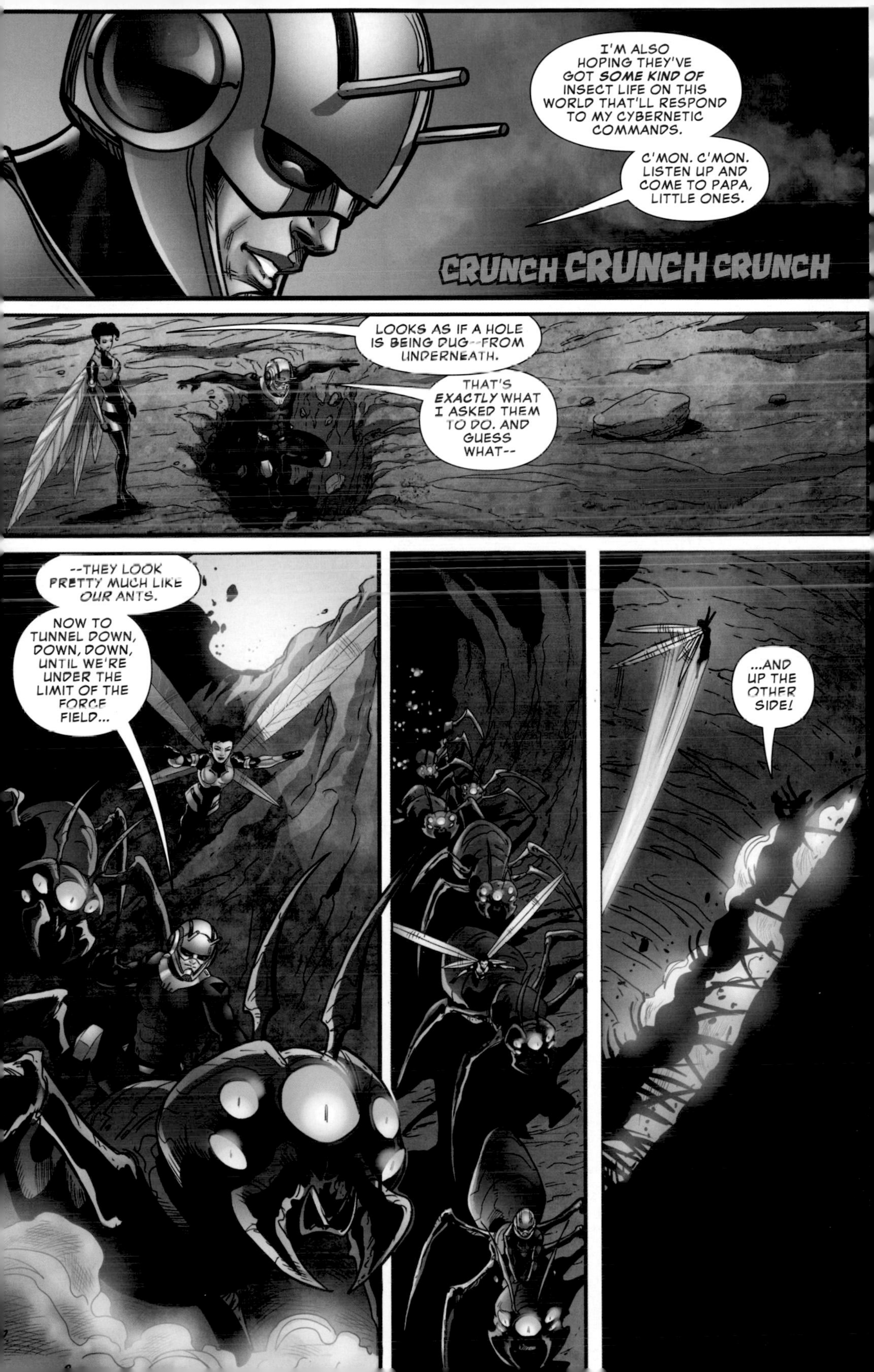

I'M ALSO HOPING THEY'VE GOT SOME KIND OF INSECT LIFE ON THIS WORLD THAT'LL RESPOND TO MY CYBERNETIC COMMANDS.
C'MON. C'MON. LISTEN UP AND COME TO PAPA, LITTLE ONES.
CRUNCH CRUNCH CRUNCH
LOOKS AS IF A HOLE IS BEING DUG--FROM UNDERNEATH.
THAT'S EXACTLY WHAT I ASKED THEM TO DO. AND GUESS WHAT--
--THEY LOOK PRETTY MUCH LIKE OUR ANTS.
NOW TO TUNNEL DOWN, DOWN, DOWN, UNTIL WE'RE UNDER THE LIMIT OF THE FORCE FIELD...
...AND UP THE OTHER SIDE!

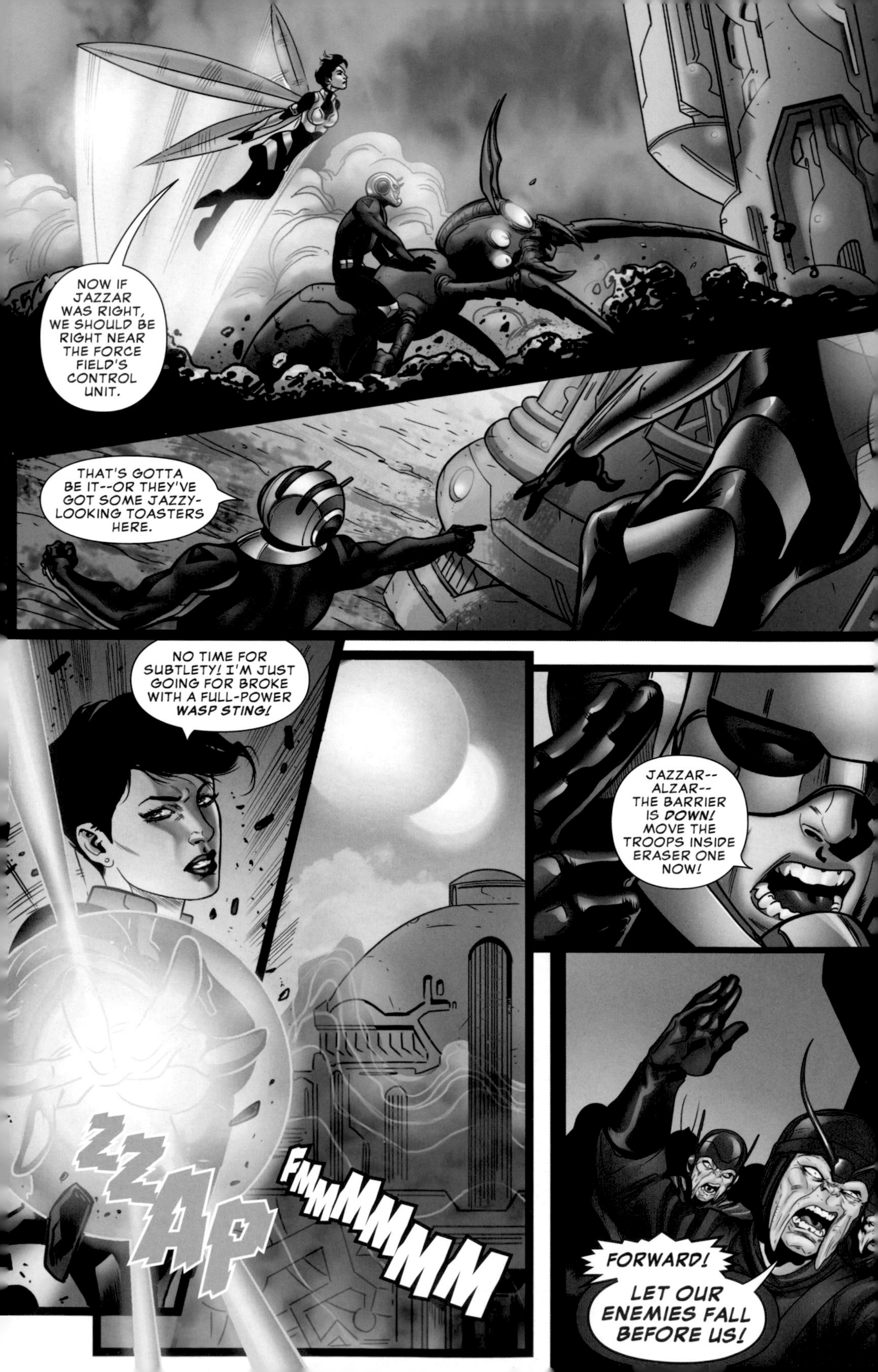
NOW IF JAZZAR WAS RIGHT, WE SHOULD BE RIGHT NEAR THE FORCE FIELD'S CONTROL UNIT.
THAT'S GOTTA BE IT--OR THEY'VE GOT SOME JAZZY-LOOKING TOASTERS HERE.
NO TIME FOR SUBTLETY! I'M JUST GOING FOR BROKE WITH A FULL-POWER WASP STING!
ZZZAP
FMMMMMMMM
JAZZAR-- ALZAR-- THE BARRIER IS DOWN! MOVE THE TROOPS INSIDE ERASER ONE NOW!
FORWARD!
LET OUR ENEMIES FALL BEFORE US!

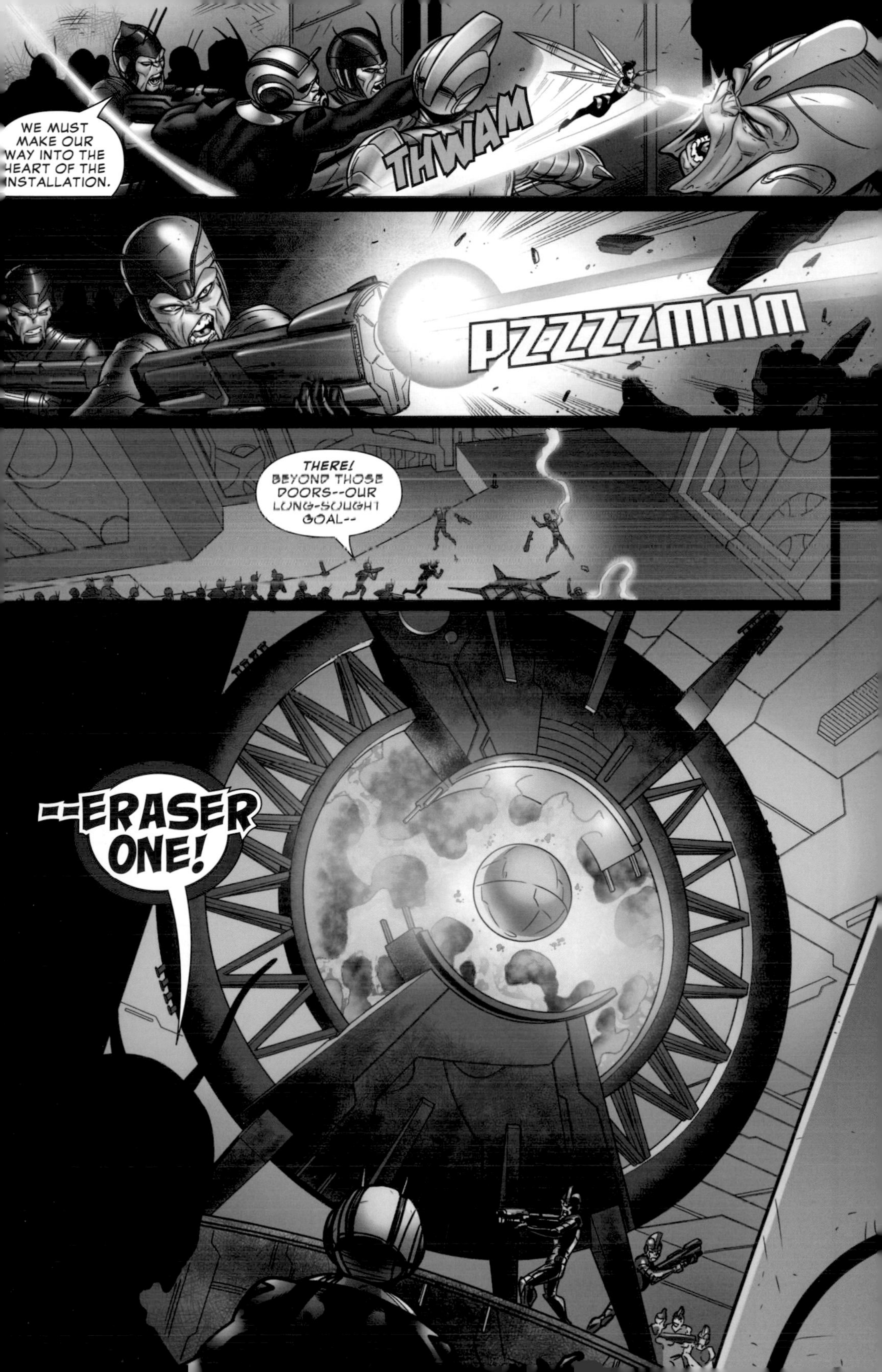

WE MUST MAKE OUR WAY INTO THE HEART OF THE INSTALLATION.
THWAM
PZZZZMMMM
THERE! BEYOND THOSE DOORS--OUR LONG-SOUGHT GOAL--
--ERASER ONE!

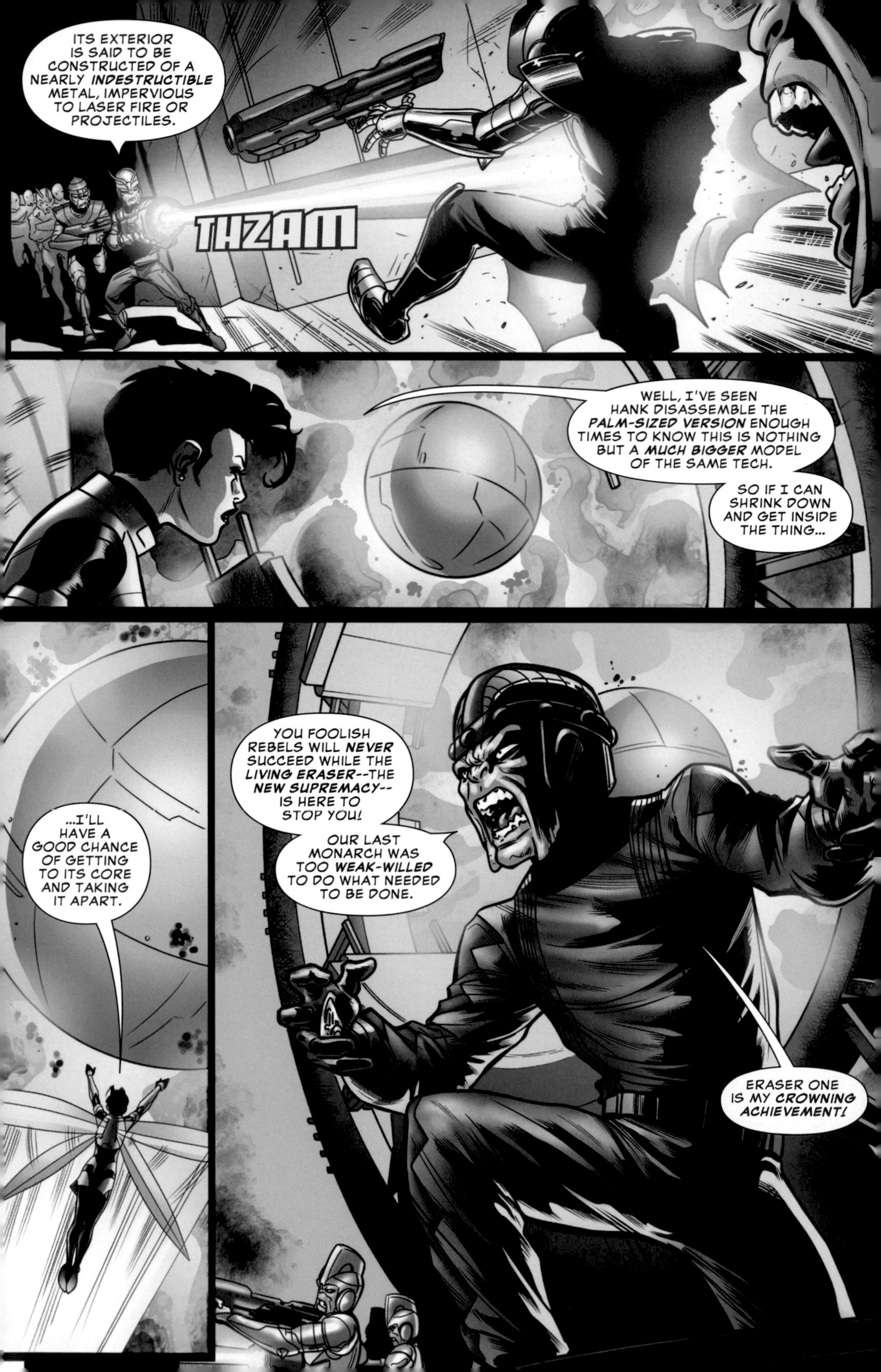

ITS EXTERIOR IS SAID TO BE CONSTRUCTED OF A NEARLY INDESTRUCTIBLE METAL, IMPERVIOUS TO LASER FIRE OR PROJECTILES.
THZAM
WELL, I'VE SEEN HANK DISASSEMBLE THE PALM-SIZED VERSION ENOUGH TIMES TO KNOW THIS IS NOTHING BUT A MUCH BIGGER MODEL OF THE SAME TECH.
SO IF I CAN SHRINK DOWN AND GET INSIDE THE THING...
...I'LL HAVE A GOOD CHANCE OF GETTING TO ITS CORE AND TAKING IT APART.
YOU FOOLISH REBELS WILL NEVER SUCCEED WHILE THE LIVING ERASER--THE NEW SUPREMACY--IS HERE TO STOP YOU!
OUR LAST MONARCH WAS TOO WEAK-WILLED TO DO WHAT NEEDED TO BE DONE.
ERASER ONE IS MY CROWNING ACHIEVEMENT!

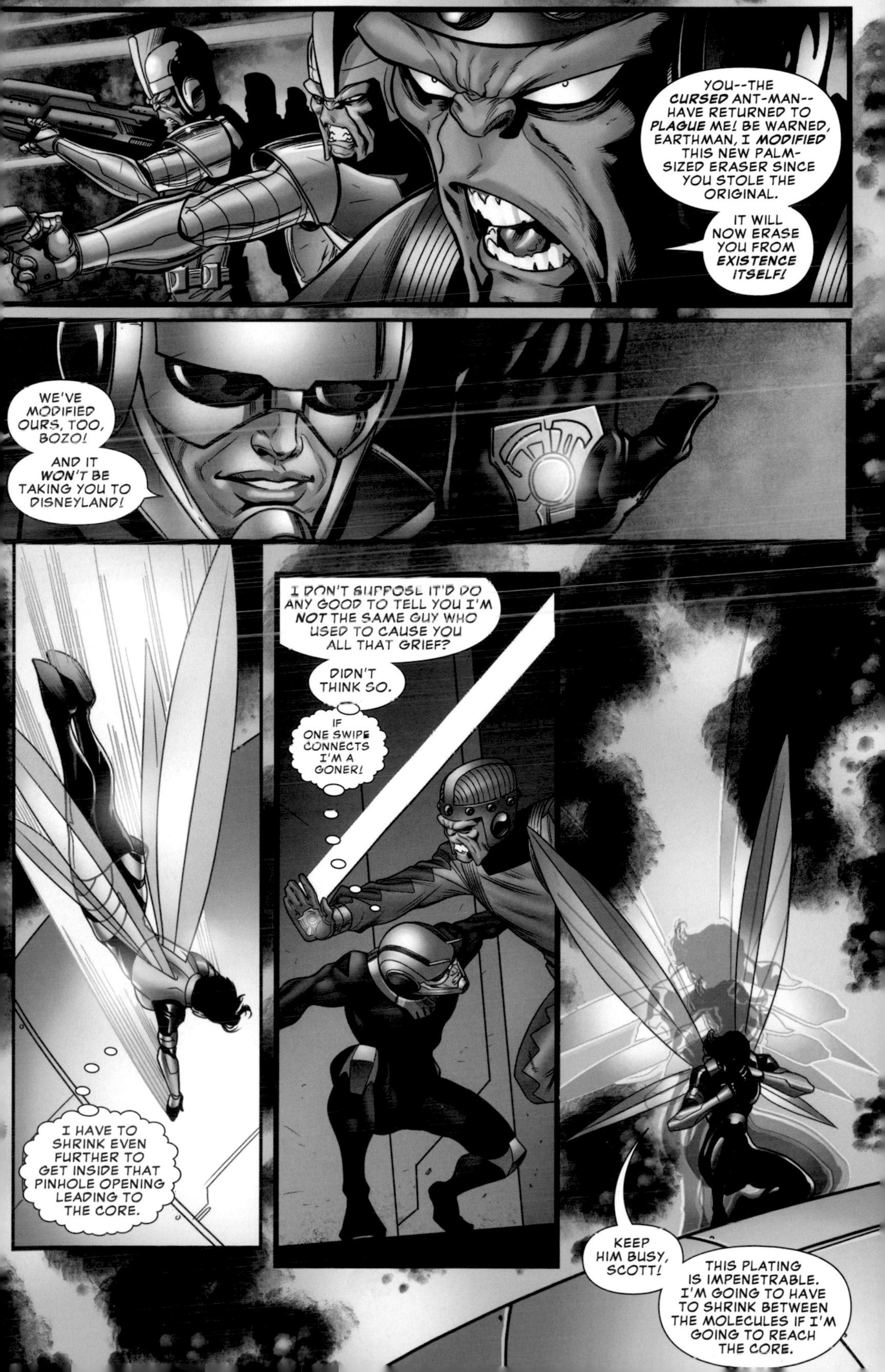
YOU--THE CURSED ANT-MAN--HAVE RETURNED TO PLAGUE ME! BE WARNED, EARTHMAN, I MODIFIED THIS NEW PALM-SIZED ERASER SINCE YOU STOLE THE ORIGINAL.
IT WILL NOW ERASE YOU FROM EXISTENCE ITSELF!
WE'VE MODIFIED OURS, TOO, BOZO!
AND IT WON'T BE TAKING YOU TO DISNEYLAND!
I HAVE TO SHRINK EVEN FURTHER TO GET INSIDE THAT PINHOLE OPENING LEADING TO THE CORE.
I DON'T SUPPOSE IT'D DO ANY GOOD TO TELL YOU I'M NOT THE SAME GUY WHO USED TO CAUSE YOU ALL THAT GRIEF?
DIDN'T THINK SO.
IF ONE SWIPE CONNECTS I'M A GONER!
KEEP HIM BUSY, SCOTT!
THIS PLATING IS IMPENETRABLE. I'M GOING TO HAVE TO SHRINK BETWEEN THE MOLECULES IF I'M GOING TO REACH THE CORE.

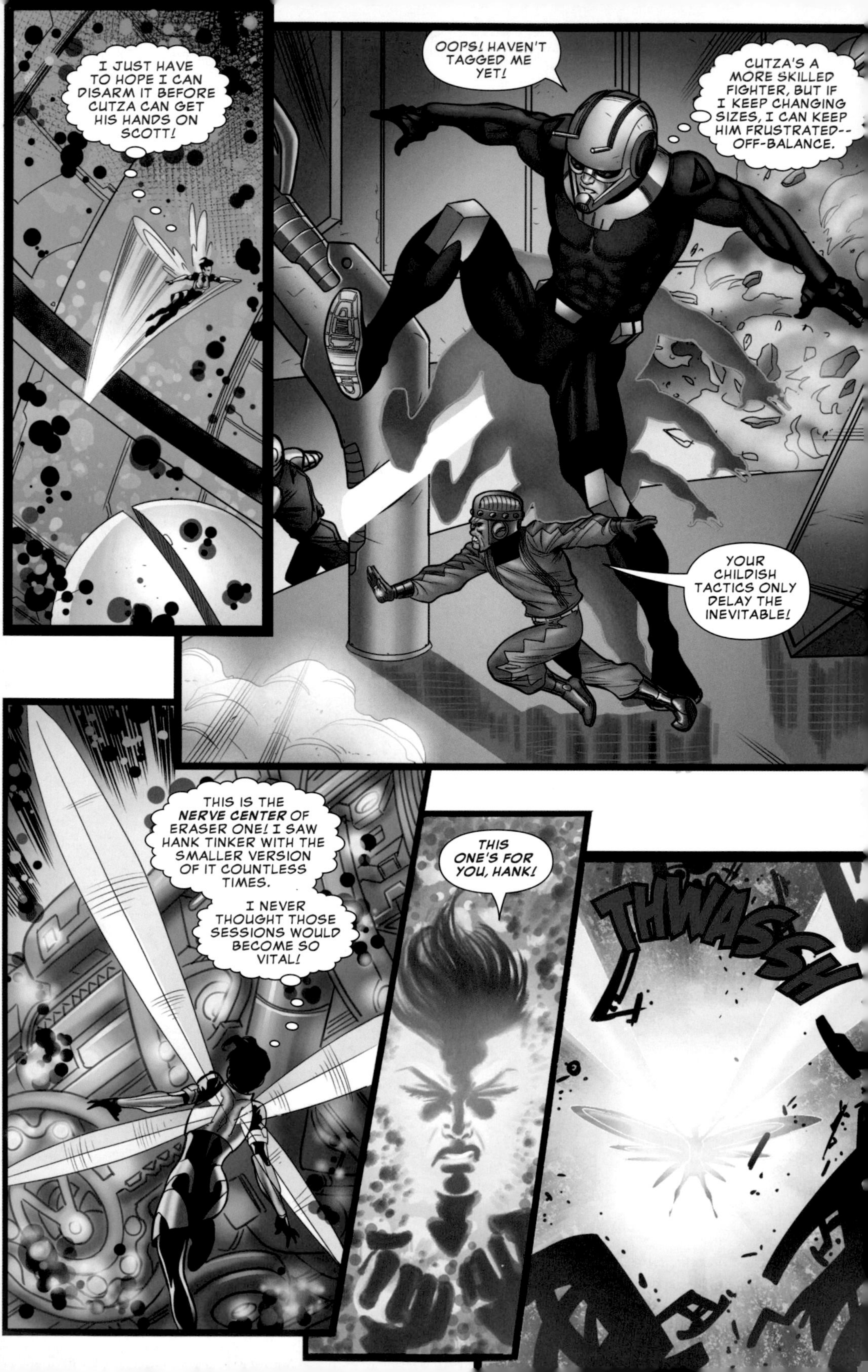

I JUST HAVE TO HOPE I CAN DISARM IT BEFORE CUTZA CAN GET HIS HANDS ON SCOTT!
OOPS! HAVEN'T TAGGED ME YET!
CUTZA'S A MORE SKILLED FIGHTER, BUT IF I KEEP CHANGING SIZES, I CAN KEEP HIM FRUSTRATED--OFF-BALANCE.
YOUR CHILDISH TACTICS ONLY DELAY THE INEVITABLE!
THIS IS THE NERVE CENTER OF ERASER ONE! I SAW HANK TINKER WITH THE SMALLER VERSION OF IT COUNTLESS TIMES.
I NEVER THOUGHT THOSE SESSIONS WOULD BECOME SO VITAL!
THIS ONE'S FOR YOU, HANK!
THWASSH

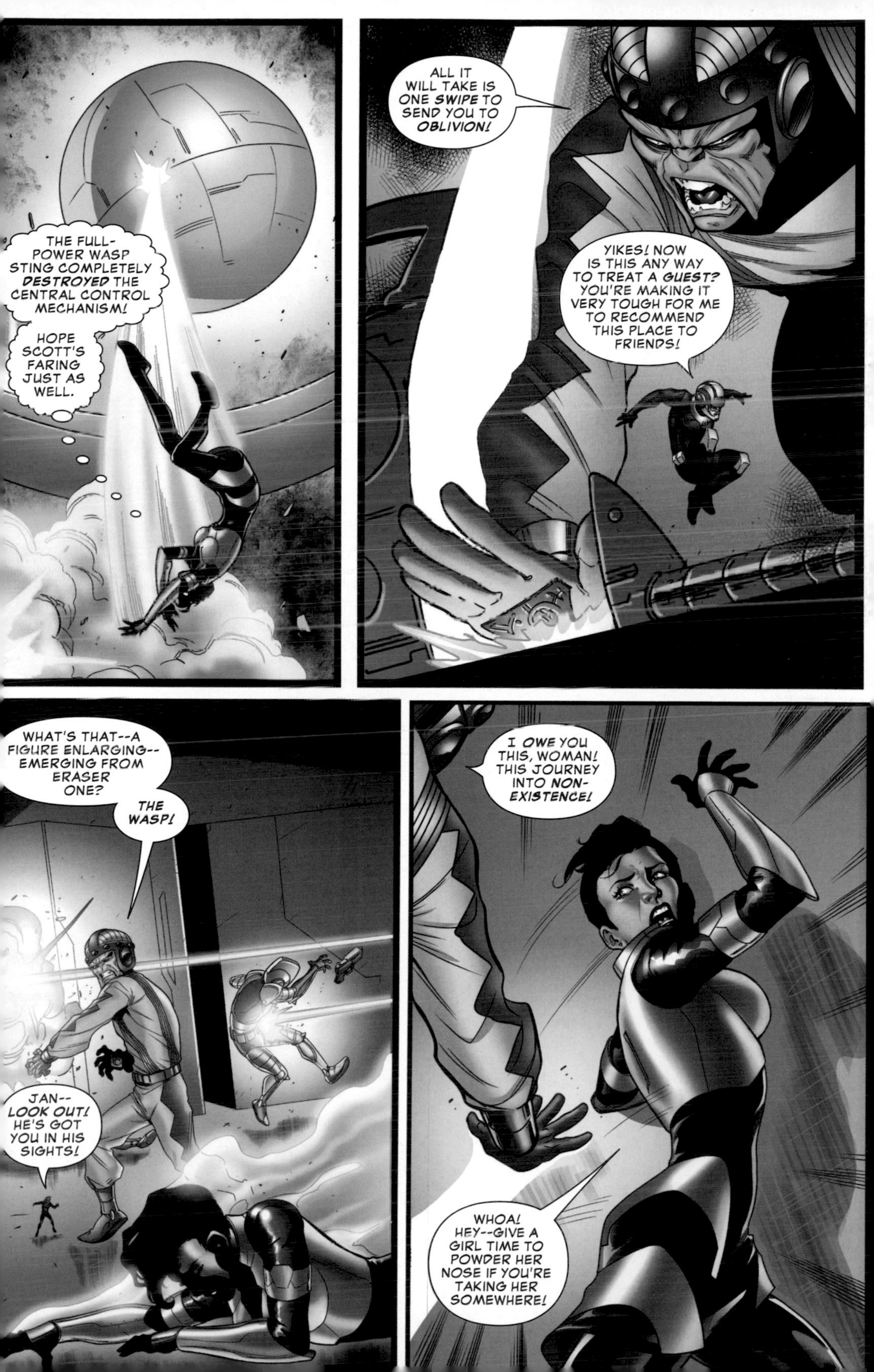
THE FULL-POWER WASP STING COMPLETELY DESTROYED THE CENTRAL CONTROL MECHANISM!
HOPE SCOTT'S FARING JUST AS WELL.
ALL IT WILL TAKE IS ONE SWIPE TO SEND YOU TO OBLIVION!
YIKES! NOW IS THIS ANY WAY TO TREAT A GUEST? YOU'RE MAKING IT VERY TOUGH FOR ME TO RECOMMEND THIS PLACE TO FRIENDS!
WHAT'S THAT--A FIGURE ENLARGING-- EMERGING FROM ERASER ONE?
THE WASP!
JAN-- LOOK OUT! HE'S GOT YOU IN HIS SIGHTS!
I OWE YOU THIS, WOMAN! THIS JOURNEY INTO NON-EXISTENCE!
WHOA! HEY--GIVE A GIRL TIME TO POWDER HER NOSE IF YOU'RE TAKING HER SOMEWHERE!

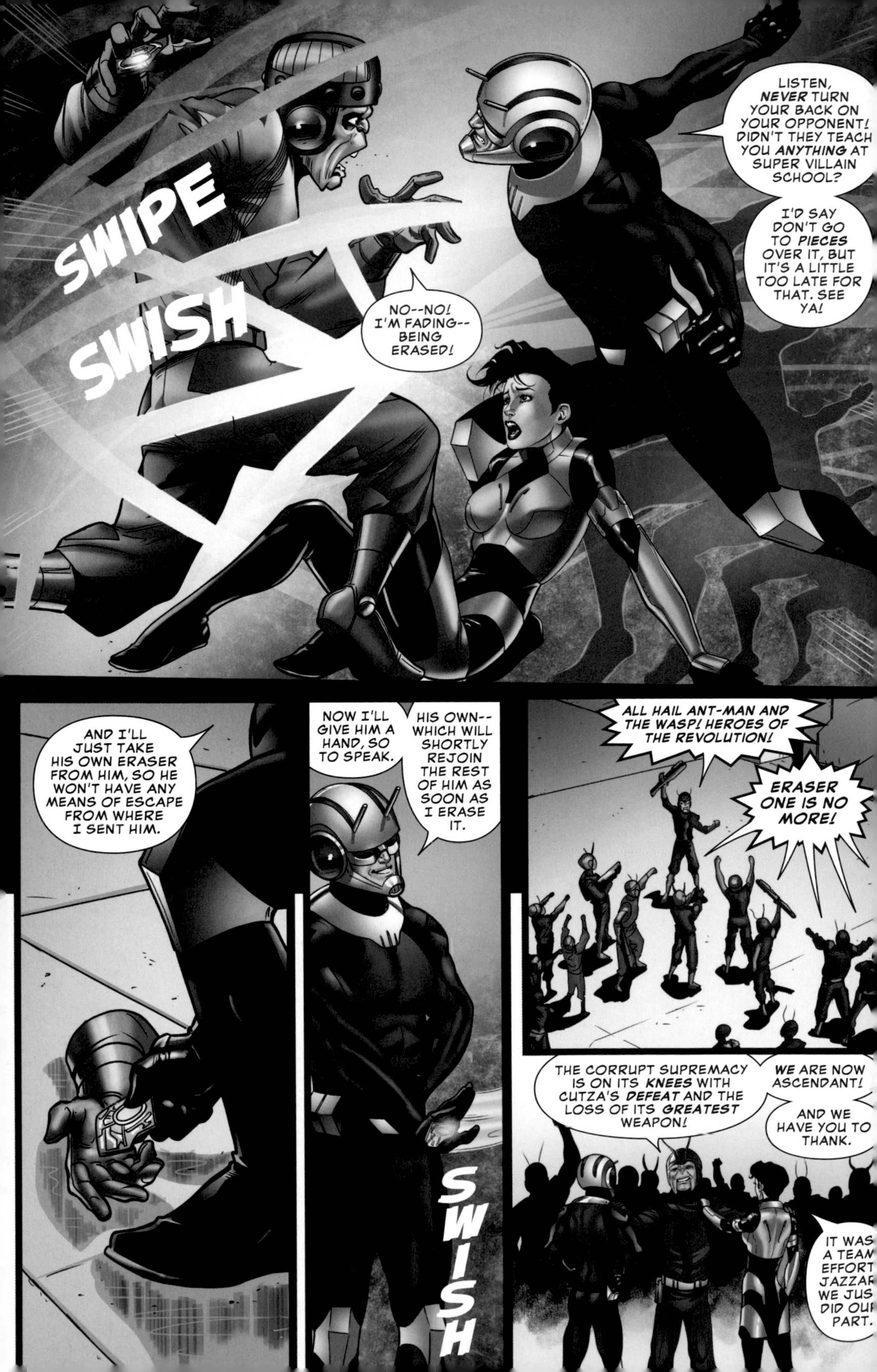

LISTEN, NEVER TURN YOUR BACK ON YOUR OPPONENT! DIDN'T THEY TEACH YOU ANYTHING AT SUPER VILLAIN SCHOOL?
I'D SAY DON'T GO TO PIECES OVER IT, BUT IT'S A LITTLE TOO LATE FOR THAT. SEE YA!
SWIPE
SWISH
NO--NO! I'M FADING-- BEING ERASED!
AND I'LL JUST TAKE HIS OWN ERASER FROM HIM, SO HE WON'T HAVE ANY MEANS OF ESCAPE FROM WHERE I SENT HIM.
NOW I'LL GIVE HIM A HAND, SO TO SPEAK.
HIS OWN-- WHICH WILL SHORTLY REJOIN THE REST OF HIM AS SOON AS I ERASE IT.
SWISH
ALL HAIL ANT-MAN AND THE WASP! HEROES OF THE REVOLUTION!
ERASER ONE IS NO MORE!
THE CORRUPT SUPREMACY IS ON ITS KNEES WITH CUTZA'S DEFEAT AND THE LOSS OF ITS GREATEST WEAPON!
WE ARE NOW ASCENDANT!
AND WE HAVE YOU TO THANK.

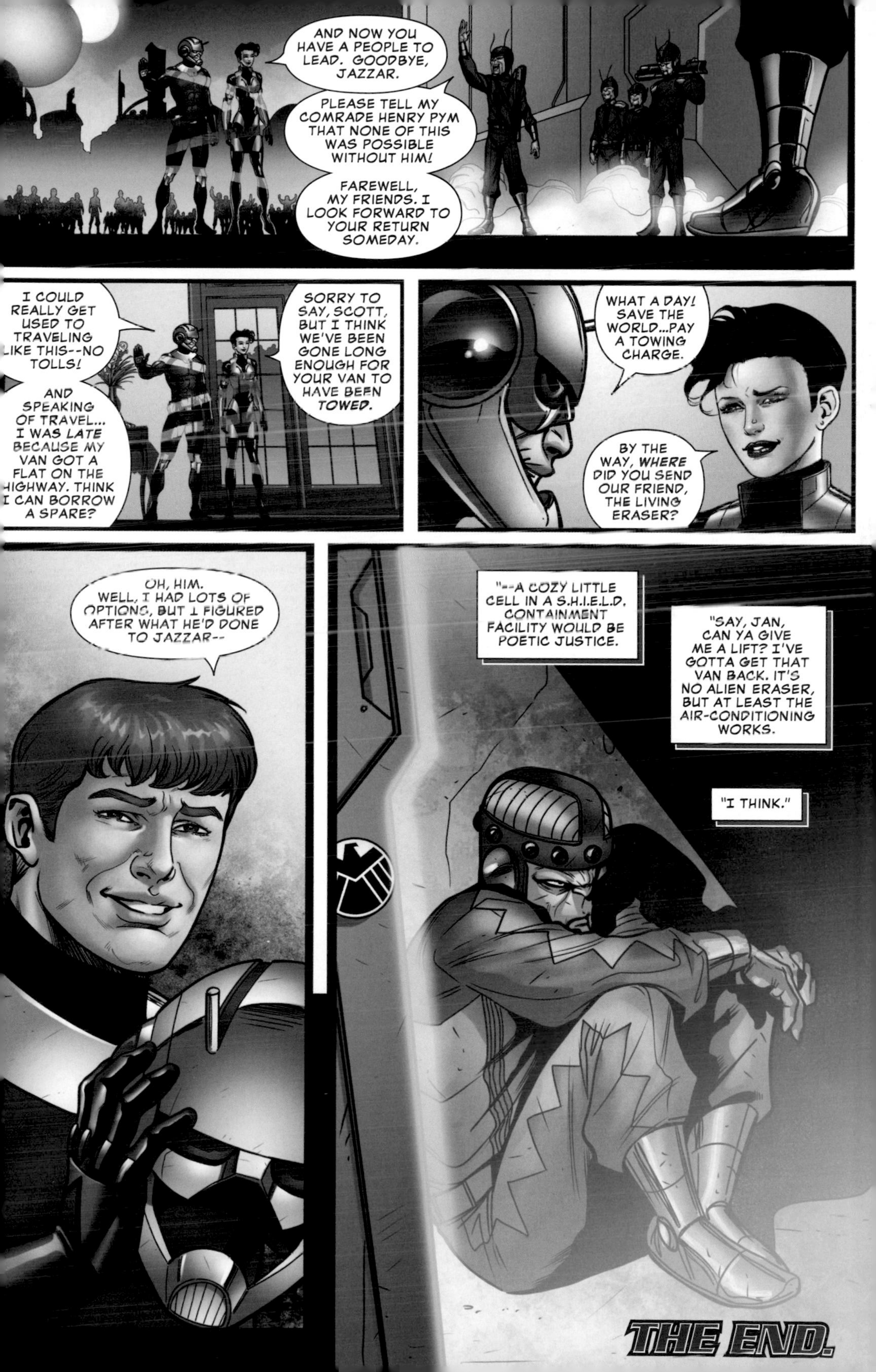
AND NOW YOU HAVE A PEOPLE TO LEAD. GOODBYE, JAZZAR.
PLEASE TELL MY COMRADE HENRY PYM THAT NONE OF THIS WAS POSSIBLE WITHOUT HIM!
FAREWELL, MY FRIENDS. I LOOK FORWARD TO YOUR RETURN SOMEDAY.
I COULD REALLY GET USED TO TRAVELING LIKE THIS--NO TOLLS!
AND SPEAKING OF TRAVEL... I WAS LATE BECAUSE MY VAN GOT A FLAT ON THE HIGHWAY. THINK I CAN BORROW A SPARE?
SORRY TO SAY, SCOTT, BUT I THINK WE'VE BEEN GONE LONG ENOUGH FOR YOUR VAN TO HAVE BEEN TOWED.
WHAT A DAY! SAVE THE WORLD...PAY A TOWING CHARGE.
BY THE WAY, WHERE DID YOU SEND OUR FRIEND, THE LIVING ERASER?
OH, HIM. WELL, I HAD LOTS OF OPTIONS, BUT I FIGURED AFTER WHAT HE'D DONE TO JAZZAR--
"--A COZY LITTLE CELL IN A S.H.I.E.L.D. CONTAINMENT FACILITY WOULD BE POETIC JUSTICE.
"SAY, JAN, CAN YA GIVE ME A LIFT? I'VE GOTTA GET THAT VAN BACK. IT'S NO ALIEN ERASER, BUT AT LEAST THE AIR-CONDITIONING WORKS.
"I THINK."
THE END.

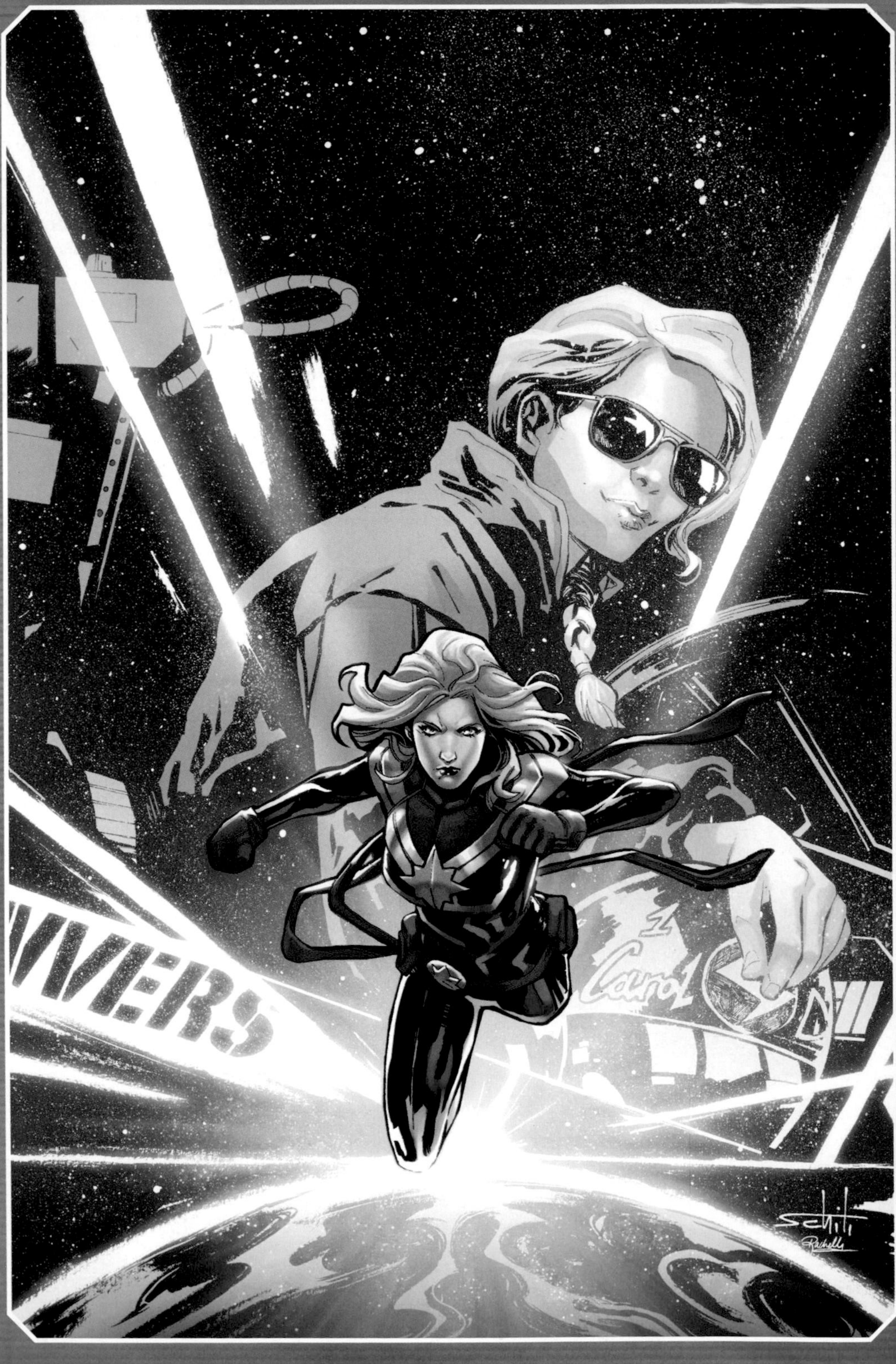
VVERS
Carol

CAPTAIN MARVEL: BRAVER & MIGHTIER

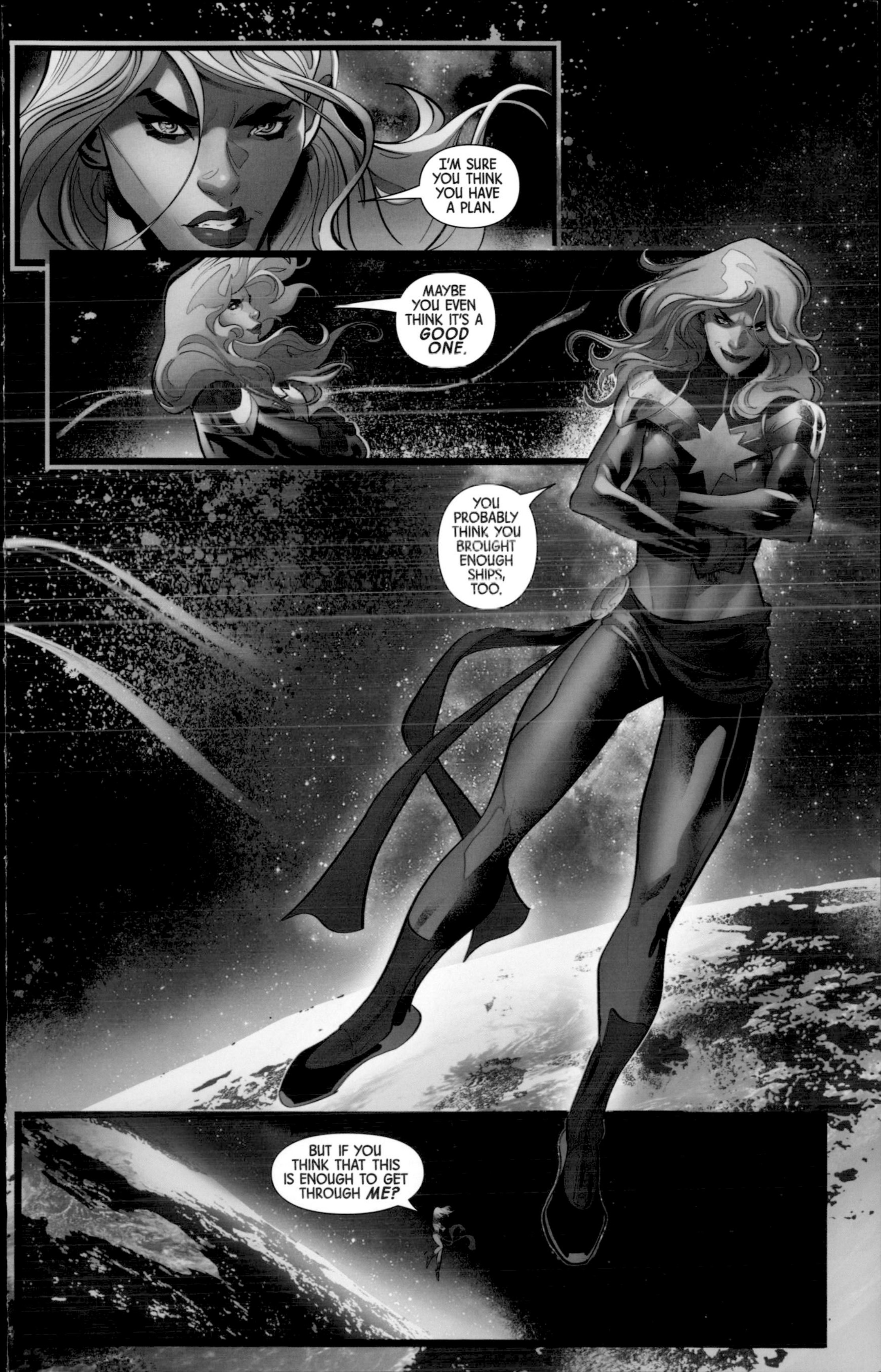
I'M SURE YOU THINK YOU HAVE A PLAN.
MAYBE YOU EVEN THINK IT'S A *GOOD ONE.*
YOU PROBABLY THINK YOU BROUGHT ENOUGH SHIPS, TOO.
BUT IF YOU THINK THAT THIS IS ENOUGH TO GET THROUGH *ME?*

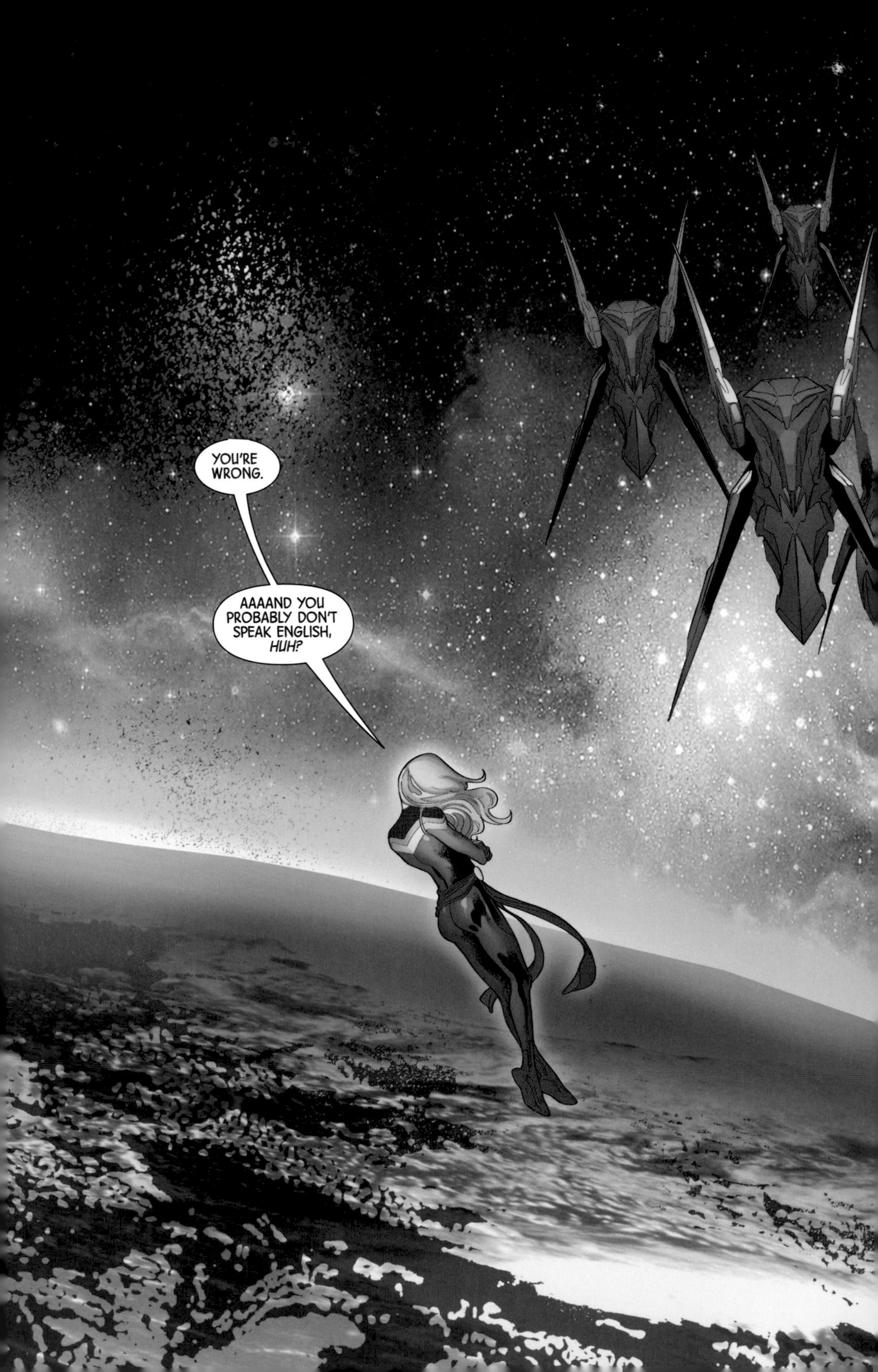
YOU'RE WRONG.
AAAAND YOU PROBABLY DON'T SPEAK ENGLISH, *HUH?*

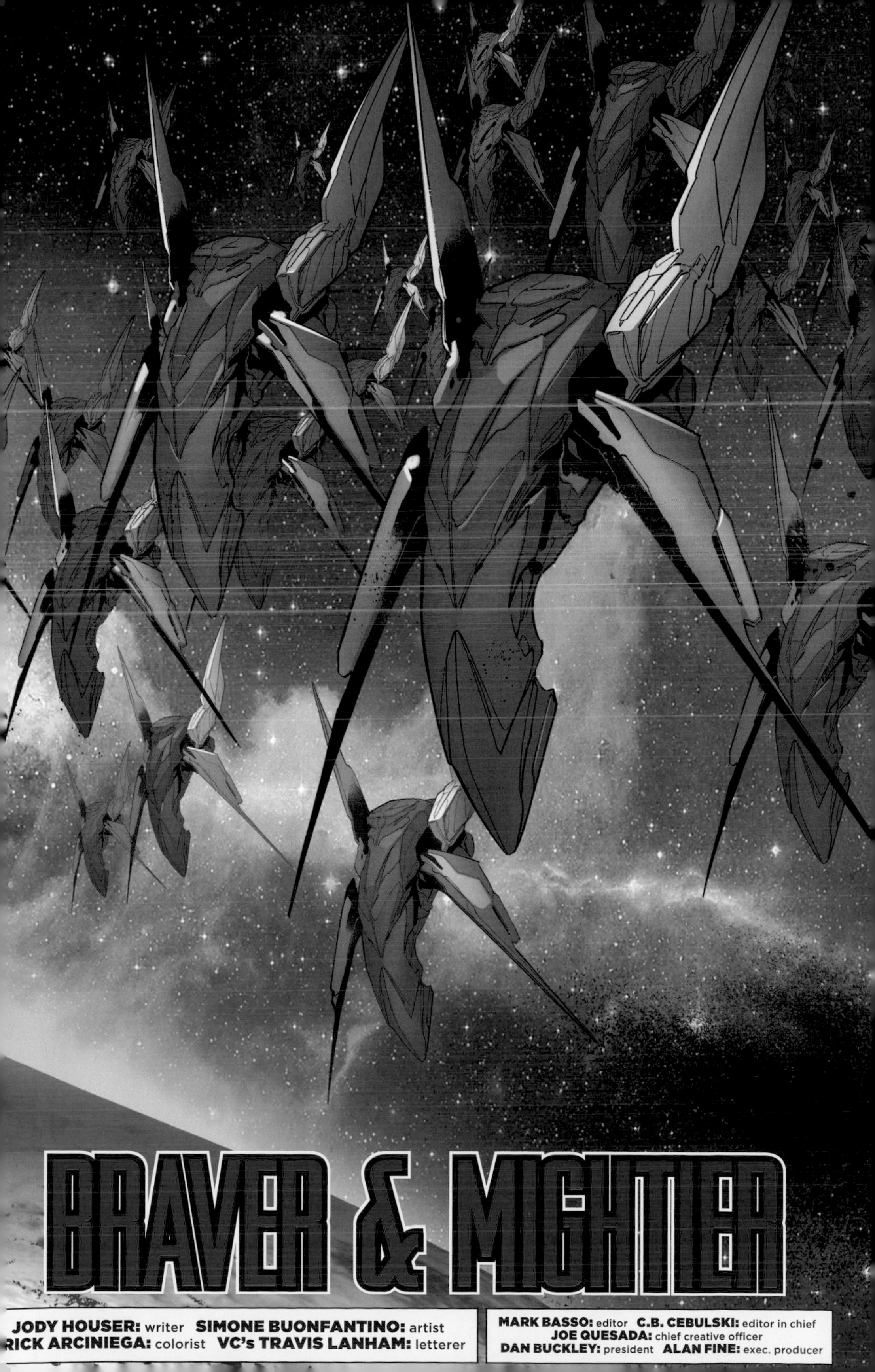
BRAVER & MIGHTIER
JODY HOUSER: writer SIMONE BUONFANTINO: artist
RICK ARCINIEGA: colorist VC's TRAVIS LANHAM: letterer
MARK BASSO: editor C.B. CEBULSKI: editor in chief
JOE QUESADA: chief creative officer
DAN BUCKLEY: president ALAN FINE: exec. producer

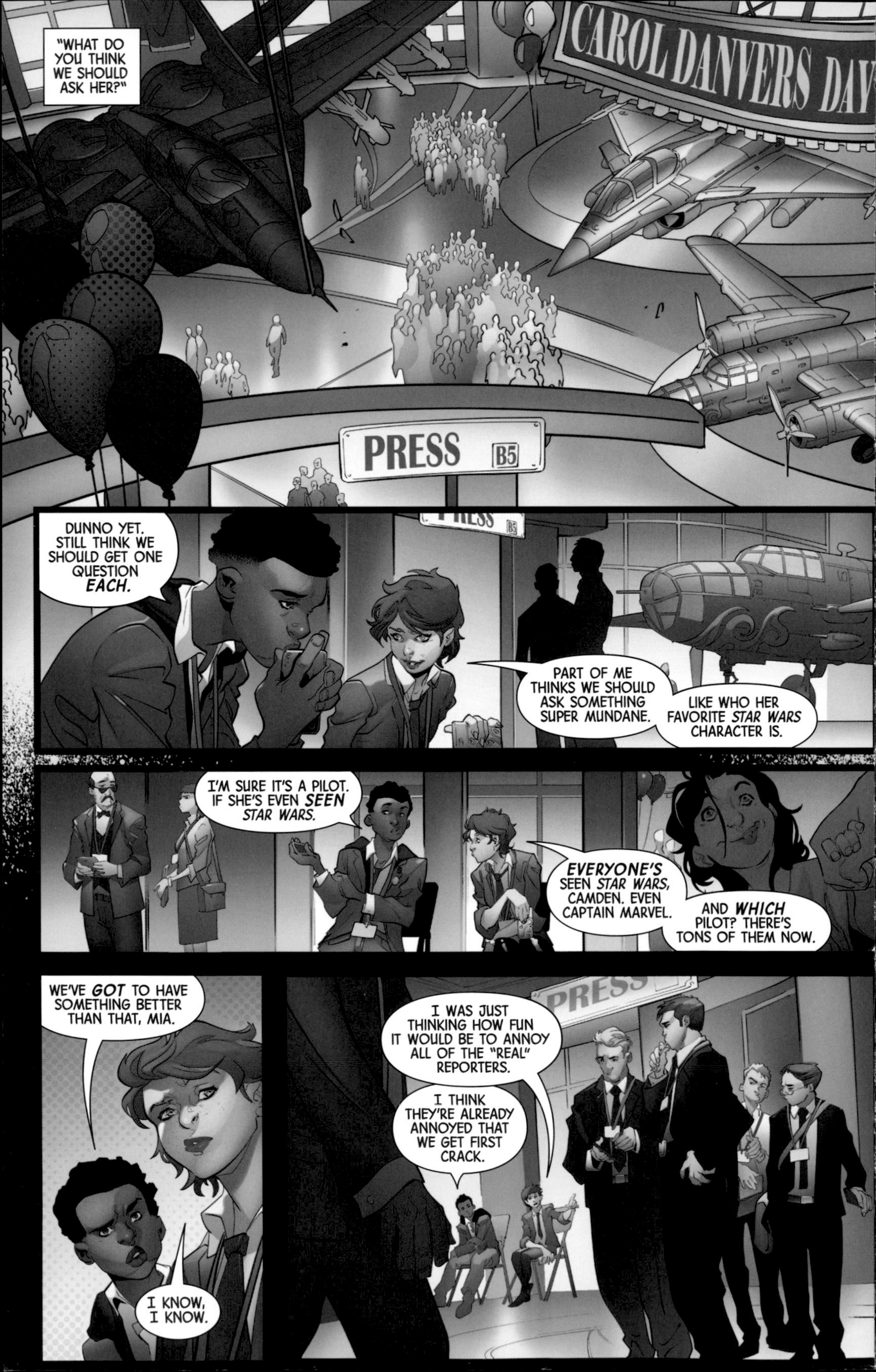
"WHAT DO YOU THINK WE SHOULD ASK HER?"
CAROL DANVERS DAY
PRESS B5
DUNNO YET. STILL THINK WE SHOULD GET ONE QUESTION *EACH.*
PART OF ME THINKS WE SHOULD ASK SOMETHING SUPER MUNDANE.
LIKE WHO HER FAVORITE *STAR WARS* CHARACTER IS.
I'M SURE IT'S A PILOT. IF SHE'S EVEN *SEEN* *STAR WARS.*
EVERYONE'S SEEN *STAR WARS,* CAMDEN. EVEN CAPTAIN MARVEL.
AND *WHICH* PILOT? THERE'S TONS OF THEM NOW.
WE'VE *GOT* TO HAVE SOMETHING BETTER THAN THAT, MIA.
I KNOW, I KNOW.
PRESS
I WAS JUST THINKING HOW FUN IT WOULD BE TO ANNOY ALL OF THE "REAL" REPORTERS.
I THINK THEY'RE ALREADY ANNOYED THAT WE GET FIRST CRACK.

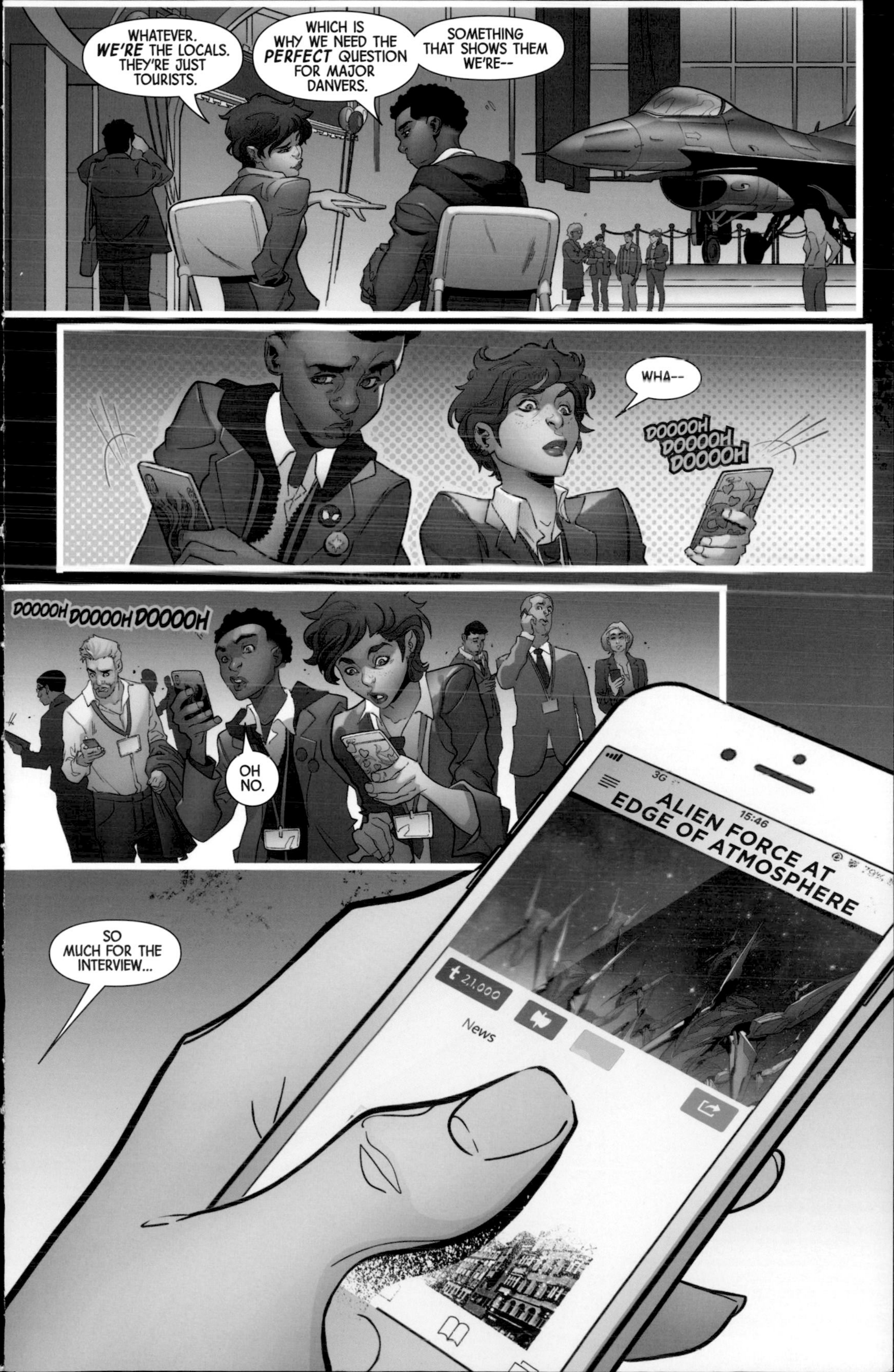
WHATEVER. WE'RE THE LOCALS. THEY'RE JUST TOURISTS.
WHICH IS WHY WE NEED THE PERFECT QUESTION FOR MAJOR DANVERS.
SOMETHING THAT SHOWS THEM WE'RE--
WHA--
DOOOOH DOOOOH DOOOOH
DOOOOH DOOOOH DOOOOH
OH NO.
ALIEN FORCE AT EDGE OF ATMOSPHERE
15:46
3G
21,000
News
SO MUCH FOR THE INTERVIEW...

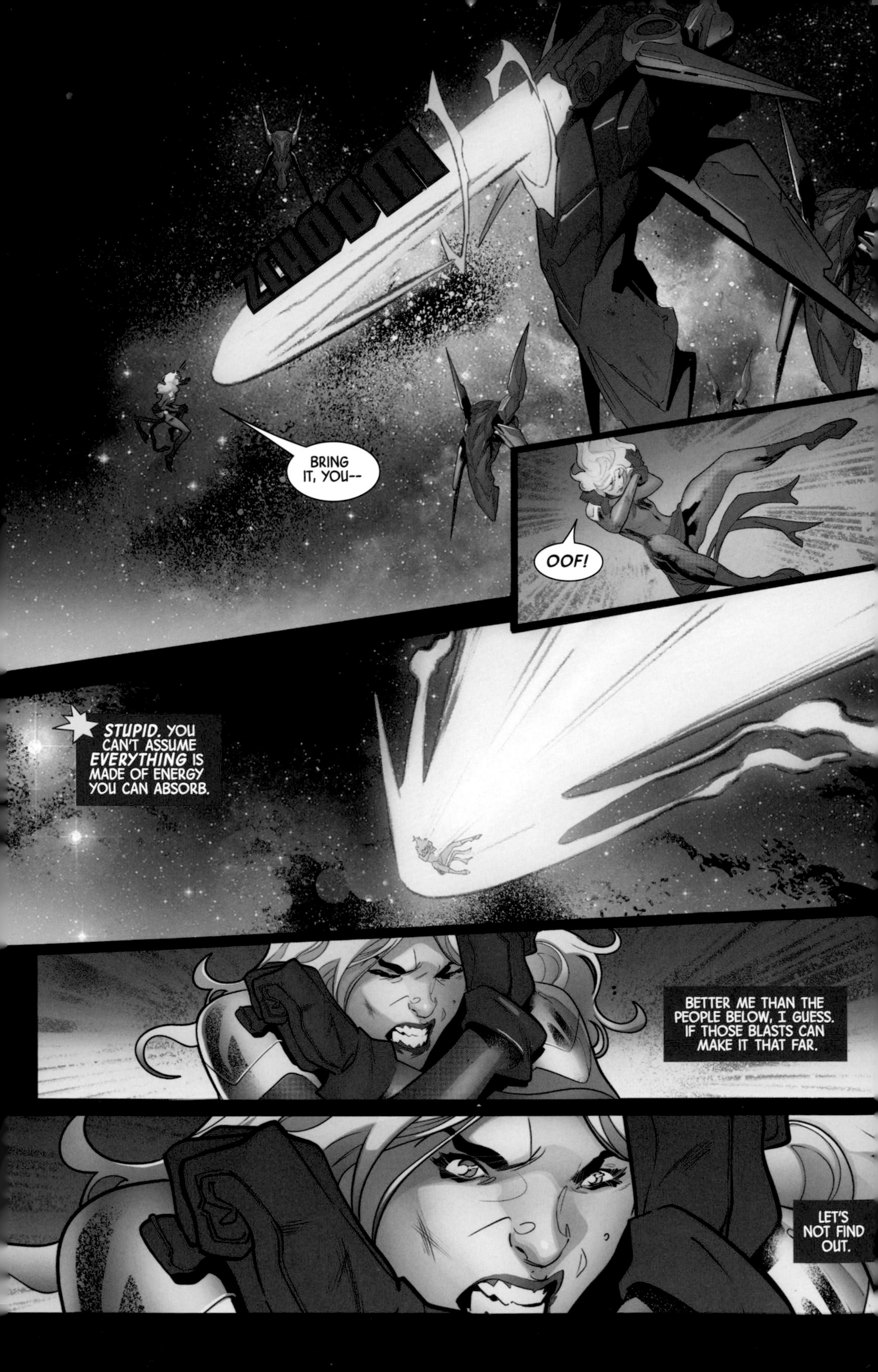
ZZHOOOM
BRING IT, YOU--
OOF!
STUPID. YOU CAN'T ASSUME EVERYTHING IS MADE OF ENERGY YOU CAN ABSORB.
BETTER ME THAN THE PEOPLE BELOW, I GUESS. IF THOSE BLASTS CAN MAKE IT THAT FAR.
LET'S NOT FIND OUT.

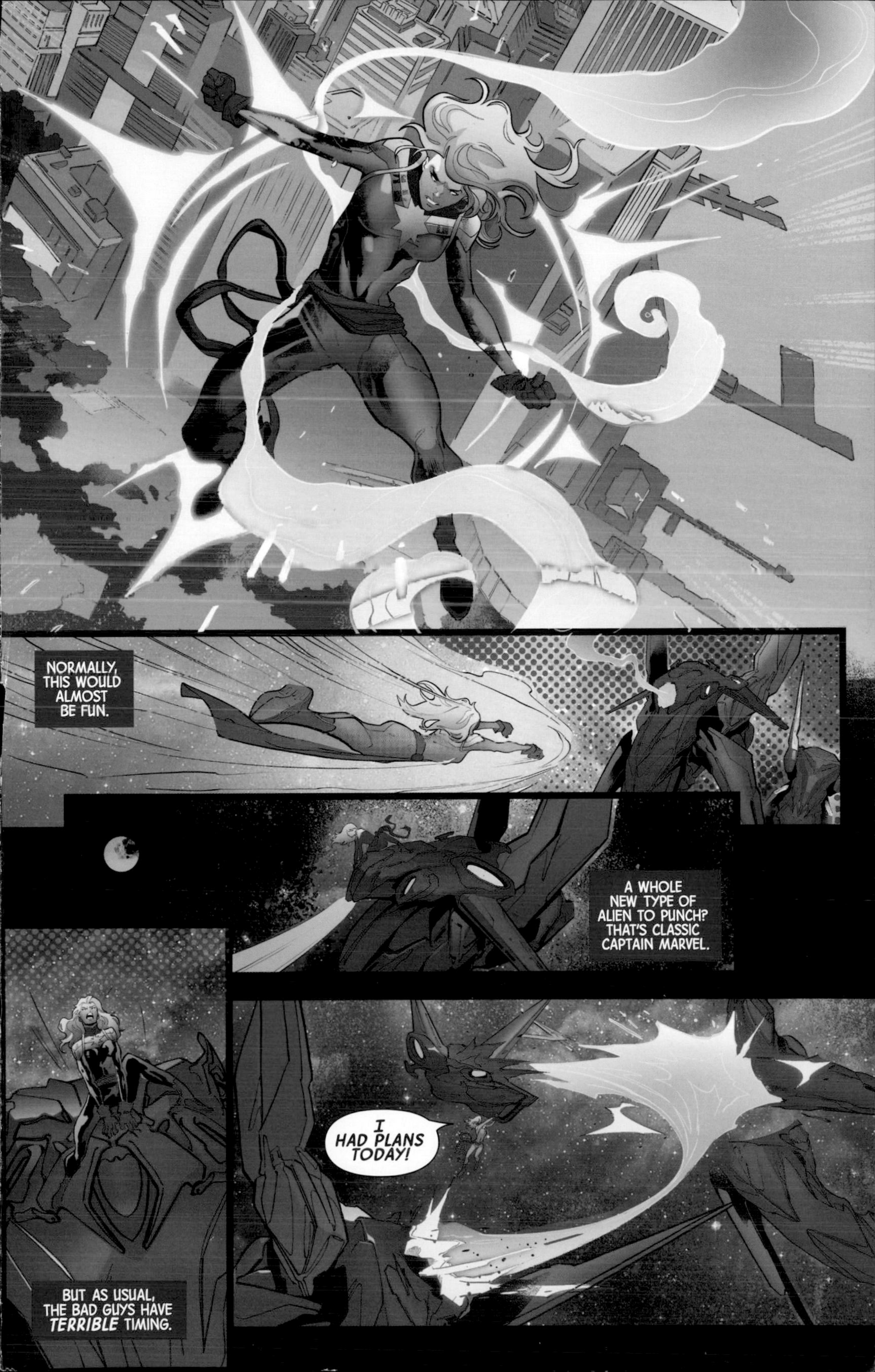
NORMALLY, THIS WOULD ALMOST BE FUN.
A WHOLE NEW TYPE OF ALIEN TO PUNCH? THAT'S CLASSIC CAPTAIN MARVEL.
BUT AS USUAL, THE BAD GUYS HAVE TERRIBLE TIMING.
I HAD PLANS TODAY!

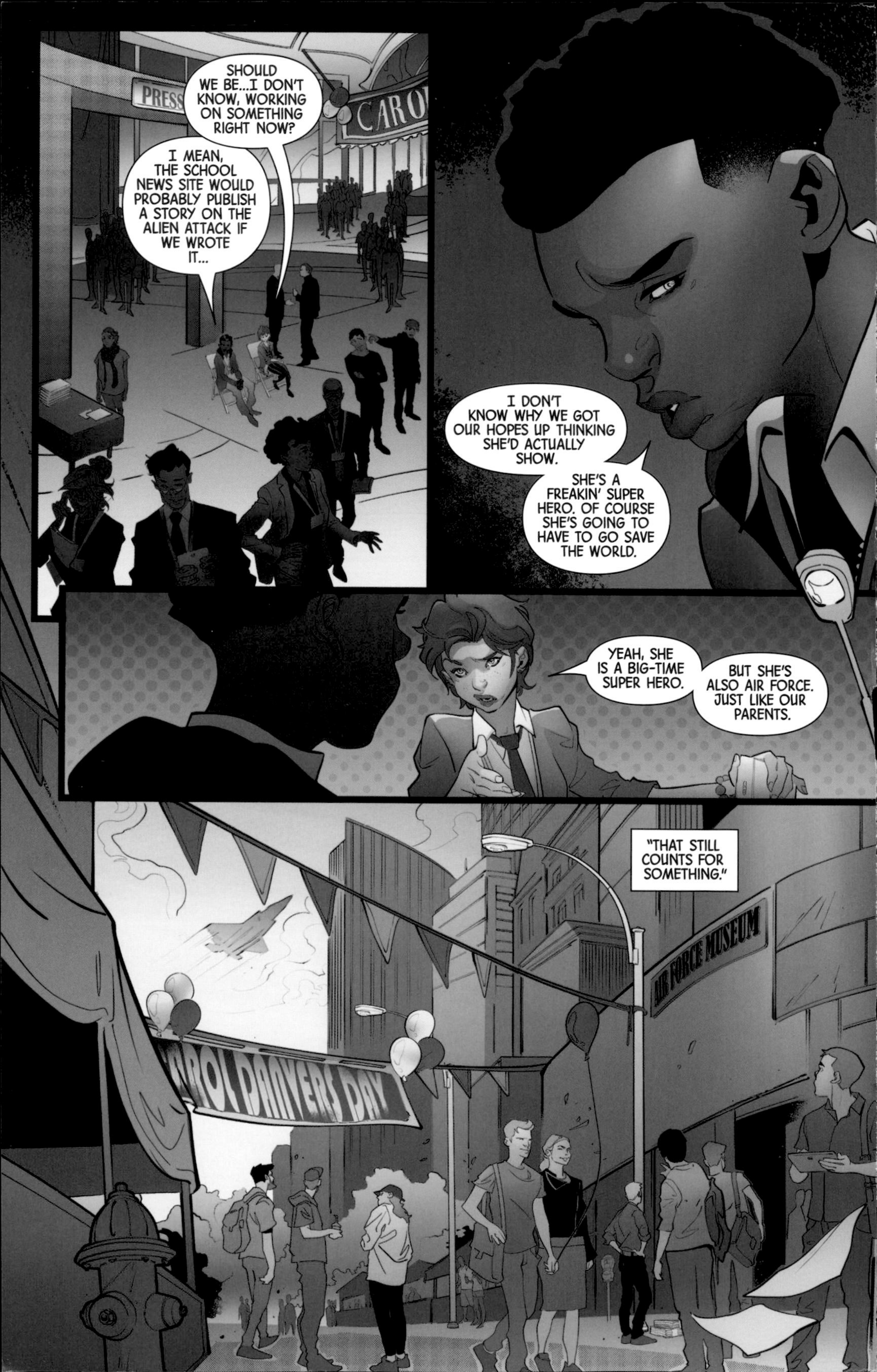
PRESS
CARO
SHOULD WE BE...I DON'T KNOW, WORKING ON SOMETHING RIGHT NOW?
I MEAN, THE SCHOOL NEWS SITE WOULD PROBABLY PUBLISH A STORY ON THE ALIEN ATTACK IF WE WROTE IT...
I DON'T KNOW WHY WE GOT OUR HOPES UP THINKING SHE'D ACTUALLY SHOW.
SHE'S A FREAKIN' SUPER HERO. OF COURSE SHE'S GOING TO HAVE TO GO SAVE THE WORLD.
YEAH, SHE IS A BIG-TIME SUPER HERO.
BUT SHE'S ALSO AIR FORCE. JUST LIKE OUR PARENTS.
"THAT STILL COUNTS FOR SOMETHING."
AIR FORCE MUSEUM
CAROL DANVERS DAY

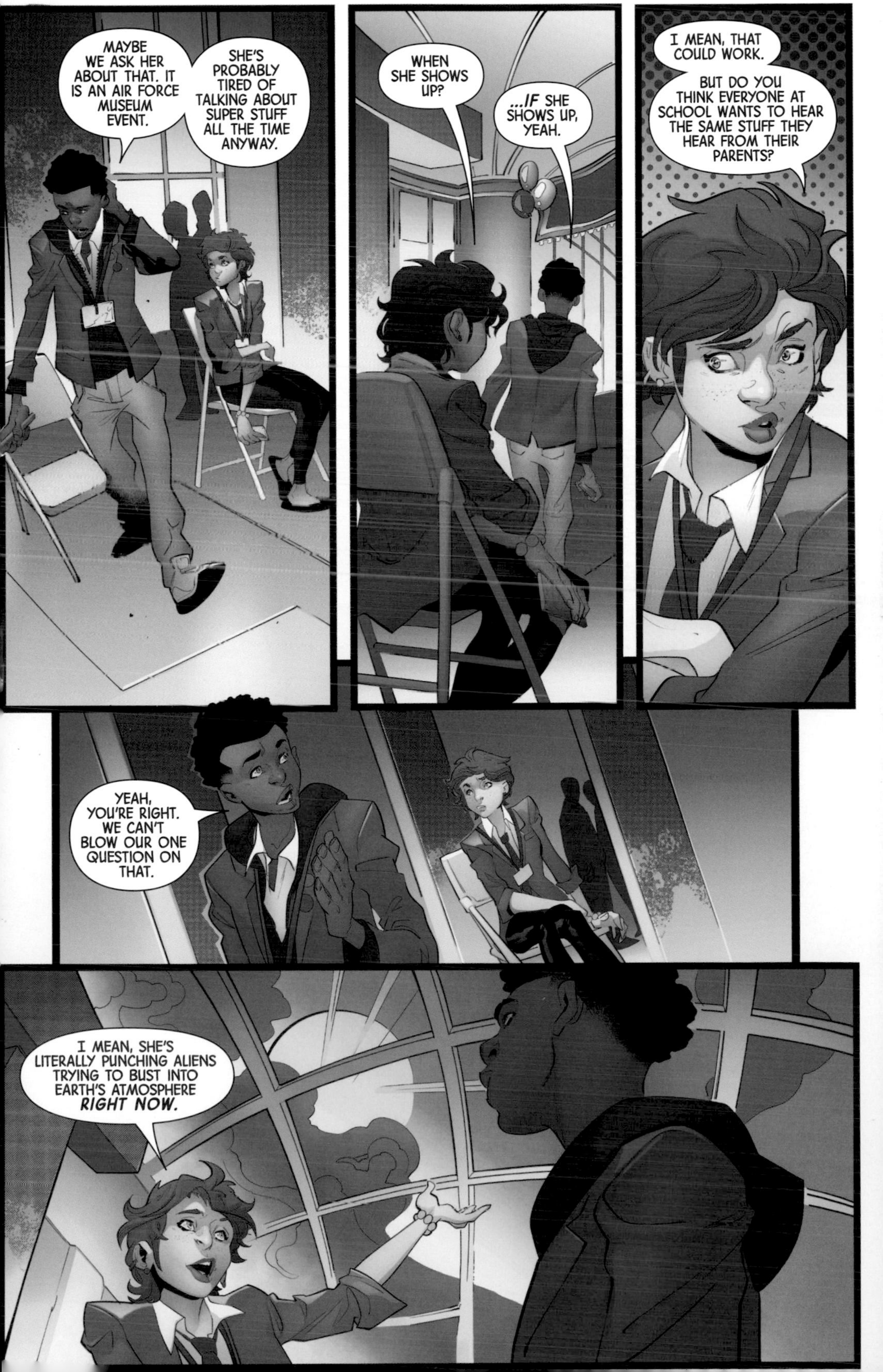
MAYBE WE ASK HER ABOUT THAT. IT IS AN AIR FORCE MUSEUM EVENT.
SHE'S PROBABLY TIRED OF TALKING ABOUT SUPER STUFF ALL THE TIME ANYWAY.
WHEN SHE SHOWS UP?
...*IF* SHE SHOWS UP, YEAH.
I MEAN, THAT COULD WORK.
BUT DO YOU THINK EVERYONE AT SCHOOL WANTS TO HEAR THE SAME STUFF THEY HEAR FROM THEIR PARENTS?
YEAH, YOU'RE RIGHT. WE CAN'T BLOW OUR ONE QUESTION ON THAT.
I MEAN, SHE'S LITERALLY PUNCHING ALIENS TRYING TO BUST INTO EARTH'S ATMOSPHERE *RIGHT NOW.*

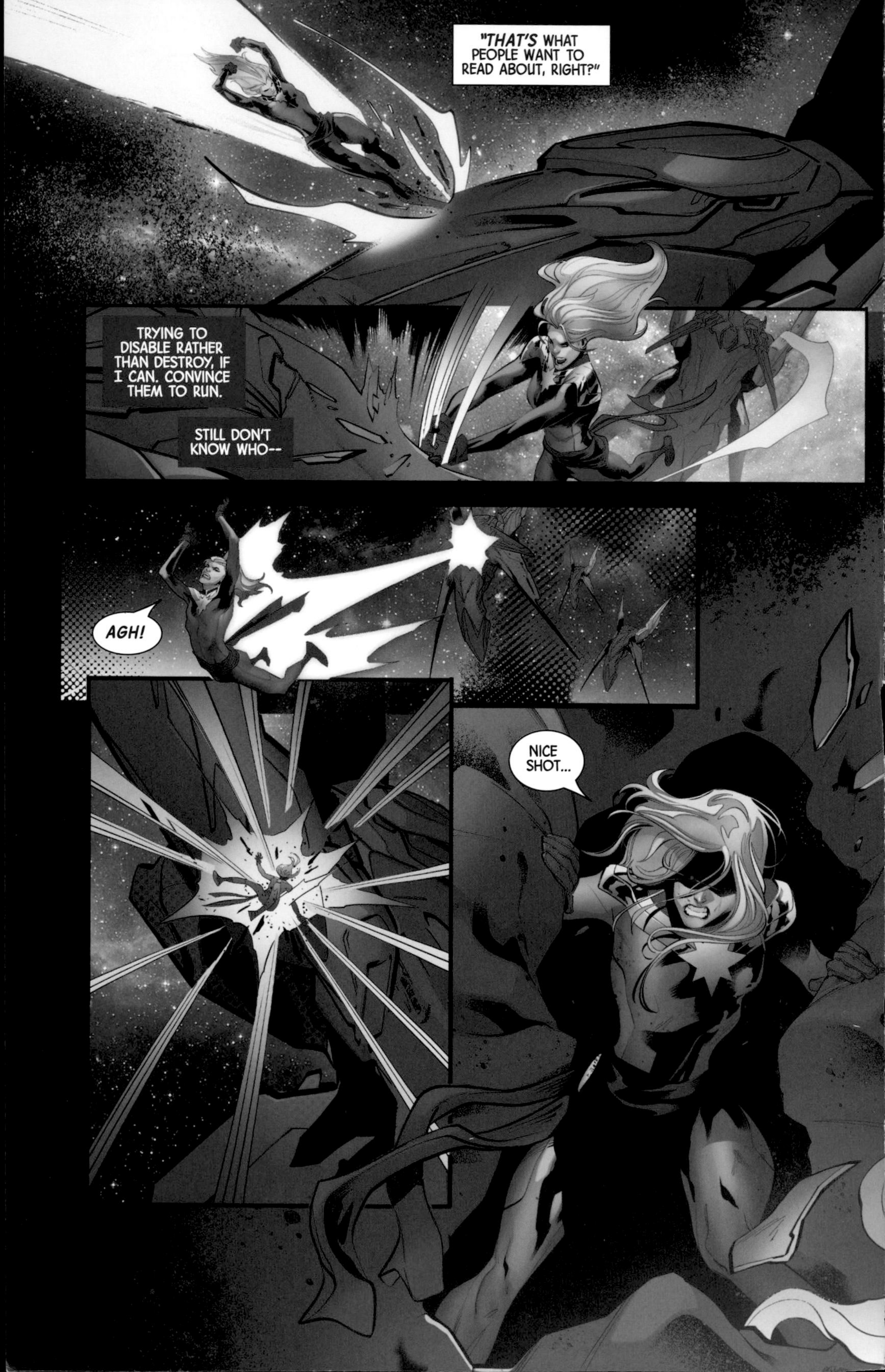
"THAT'S WHAT PEOPLE WANT TO READ ABOUT, RIGHT?"
TRYING TO DISABLE RATHER THAN DESTROY, IF I CAN. CONVINCE THEM TO RUN.
STILL DON'T KNOW WHO--
AGH!
NICE SHOT...

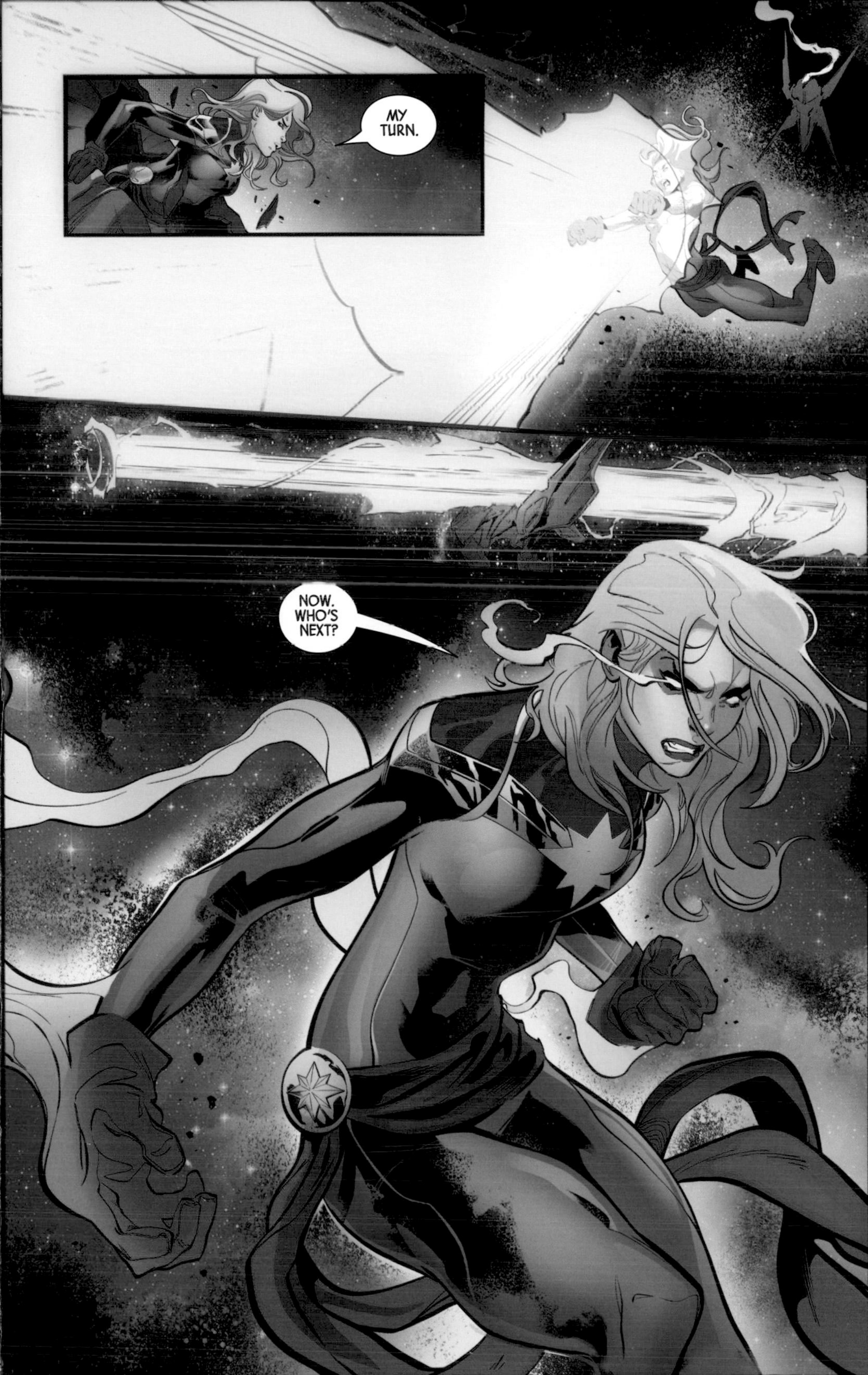
MY TURN.
NOW. WHO'S NEXT?

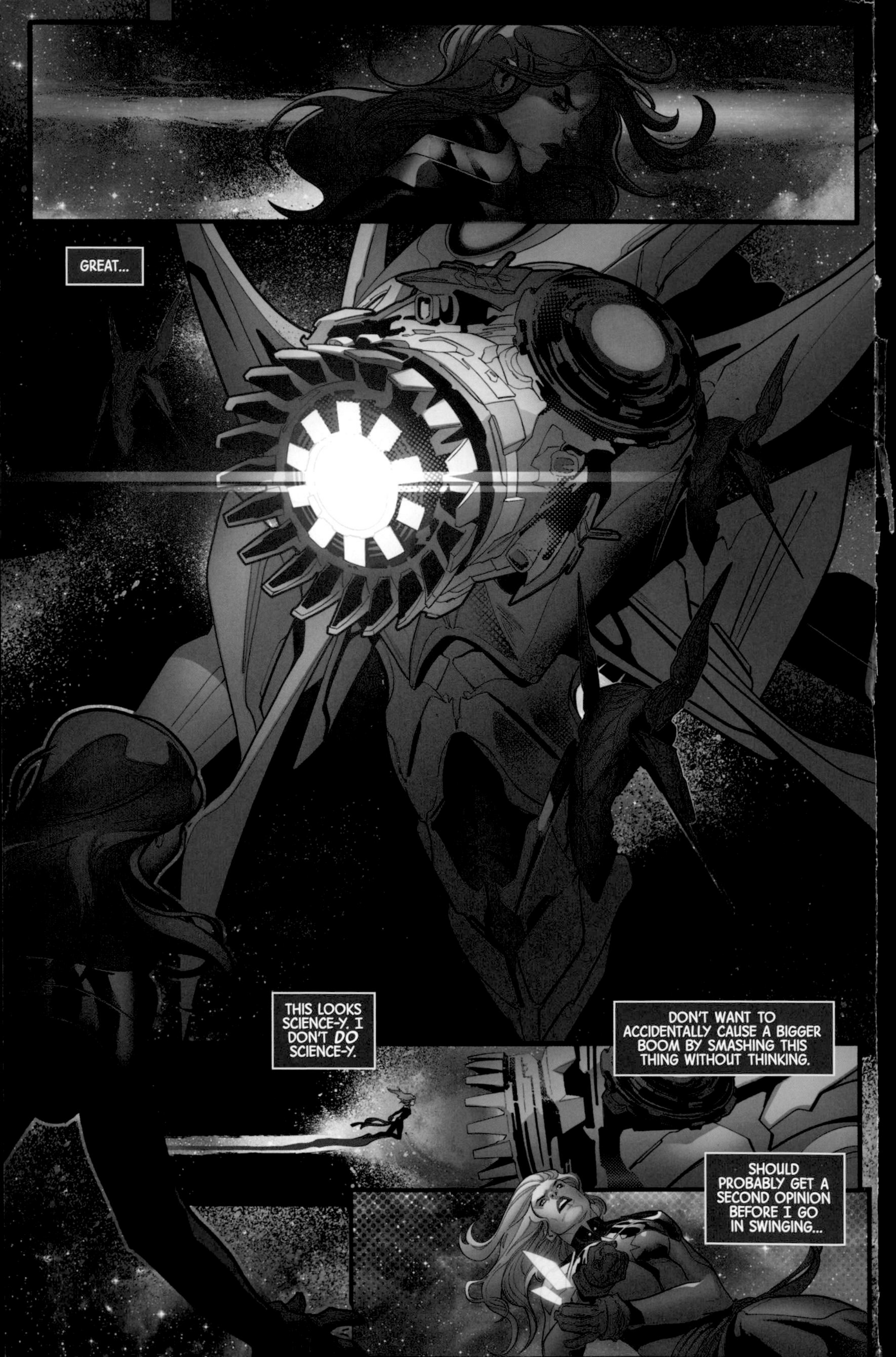
GREAT...
THIS LOOKS SCIENCE-Y. I DON'T *DO* SCIENCE-Y.
DON'T WANT TO ACCIDENTALLY CAUSE A BIGGER BOOM BY SMASHING THIS THING WITHOUT THINKING.
SHOULD PROBABLY GET A SECOND OPINION BEFORE I GO IN SWINGING...

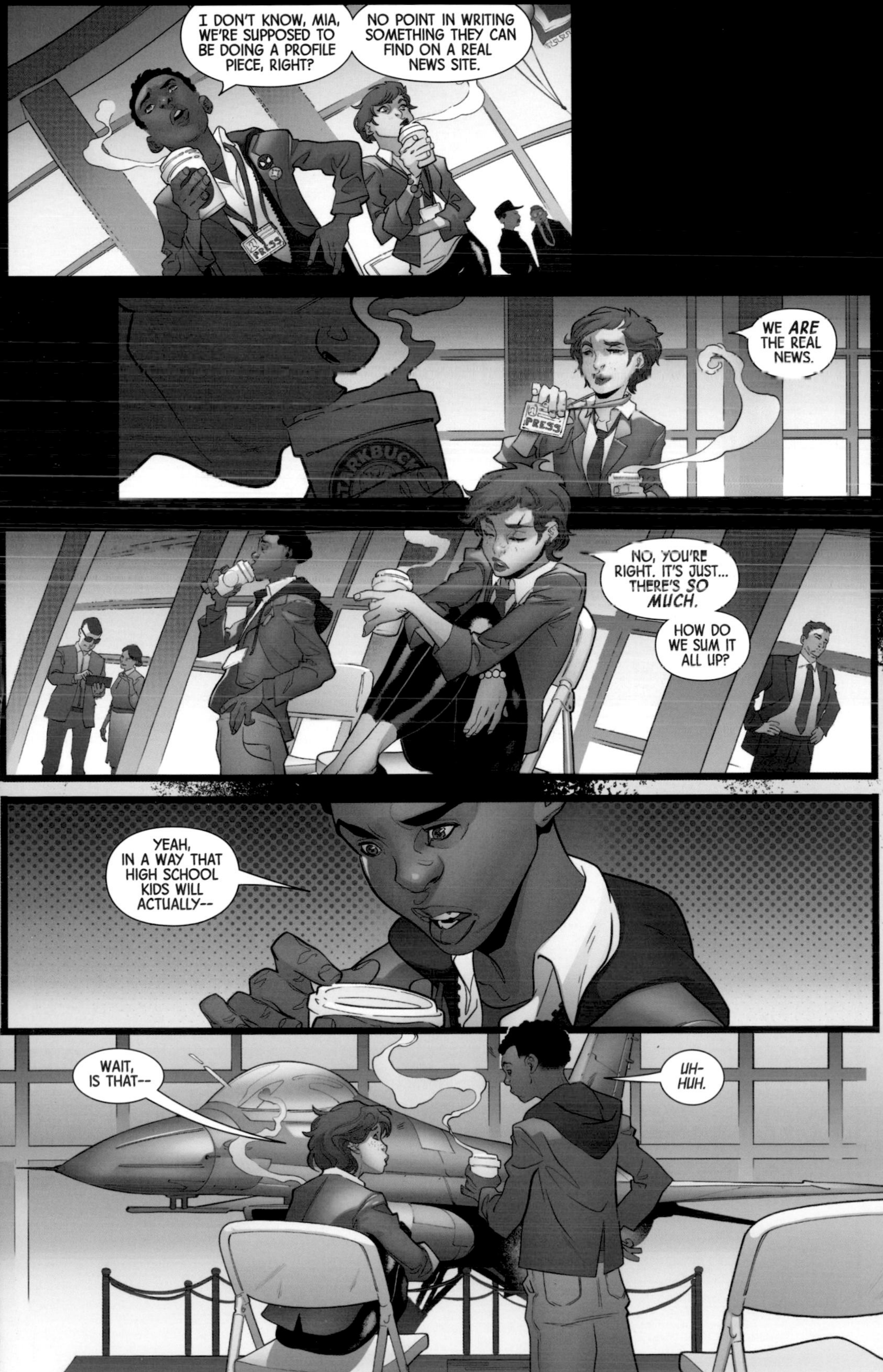
I DON'T KNOW, MIA, WE'RE SUPPOSED TO BE DOING A PROFILE PIECE, RIGHT?
NO POINT IN WRITING SOMETHING THEY CAN FIND ON A REAL NEWS SITE.
PRESS
WE *ARE* THE REAL NEWS.
PRESS
NO, YOU'RE RIGHT. IT'S JUST... THERE'S *SO MUCH.*
HOW DO WE SUM IT ALL UP?
YEAH, IN A WAY THAT HIGH SCHOOL KIDS WILL ACTUALLY--
WAIT, IS THAT--
UH-HUH.

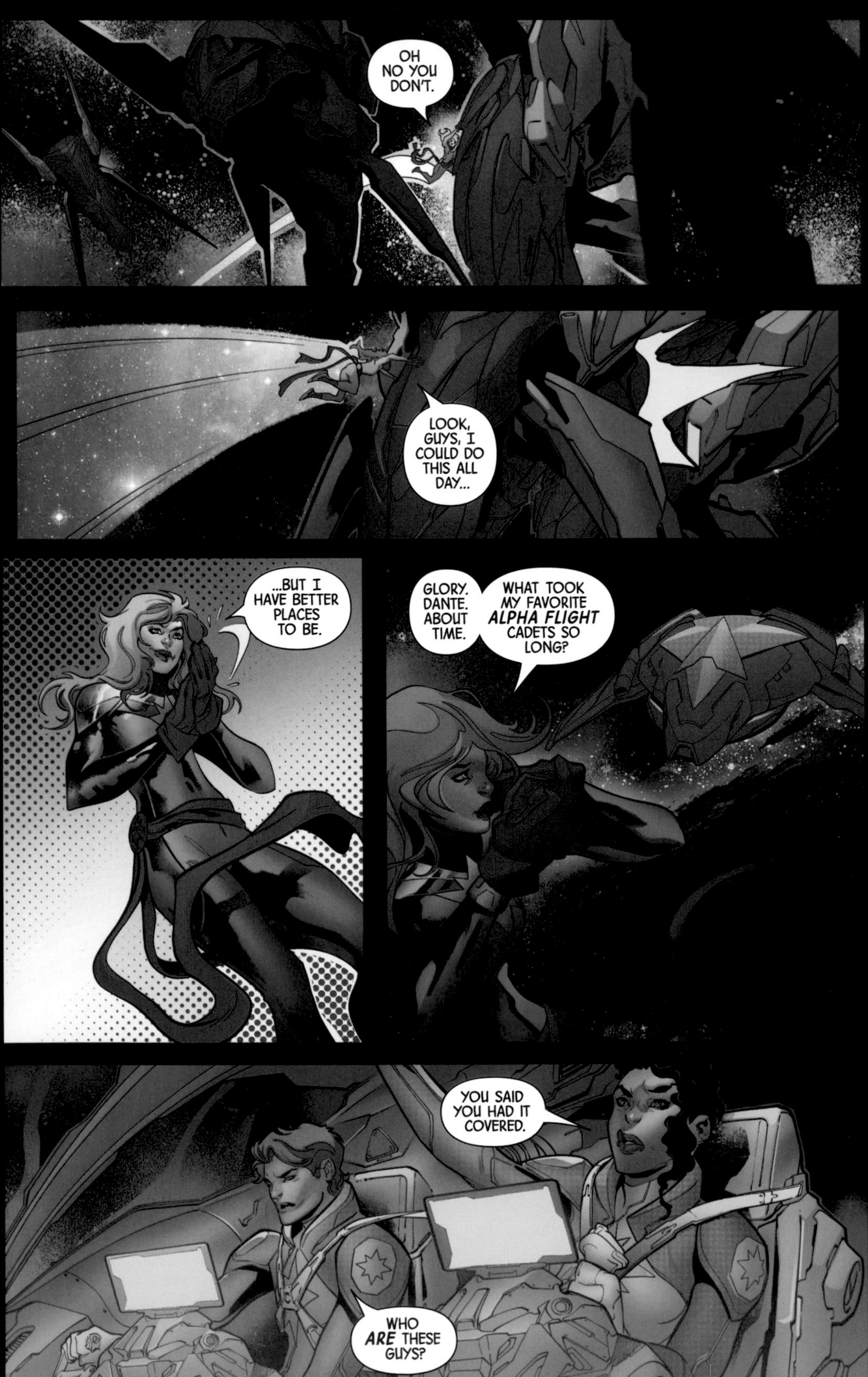
OH NO YOU DON'T.
LOOK, GUYS, I COULD DO THIS ALL DAY...
...BUT I HAVE BETTER PLACES TO BE.
GLORY. DANTE. ABOUT TIME.
WHAT TOOK MY FAVORITE ALPHA FLIGHT CADETS SO LONG?
YOU SAID YOU HAD IT COVERED.
WHO ARE THESE GUYS?

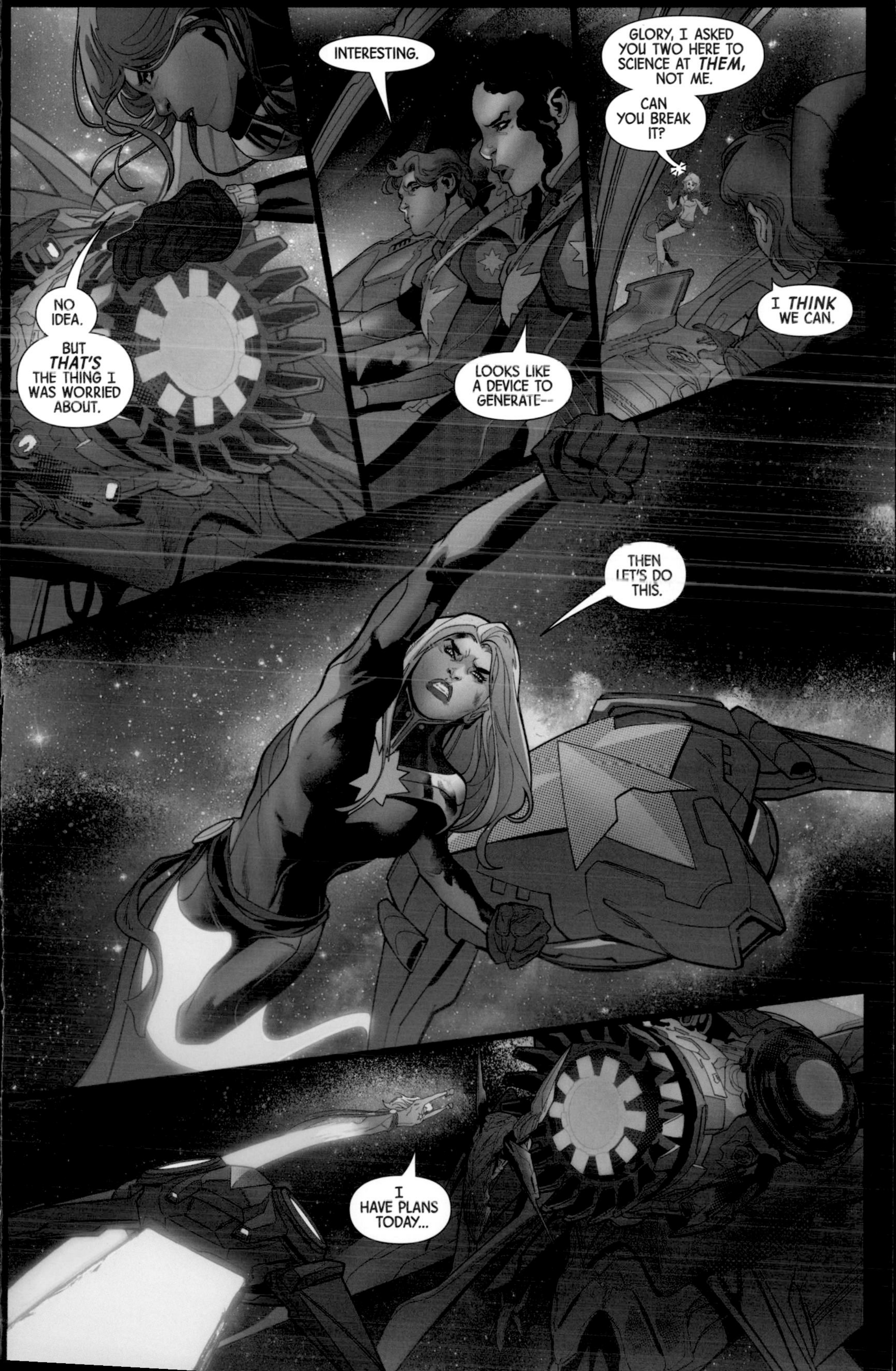
NO IDEA.
BUT THAT'S THE THING I WAS WORRIED ABOUT.
INTERESTING.
LOOKS LIKE A DEVICE TO GENERATE--
GLORY, I ASKED YOU TWO HERE TO SCIENCE AT THEM, NOT ME.
CAN YOU BREAK IT?
I THINK WE CAN.
THEN LET'S DO THIS.
I HAVE PLANS TODAY...

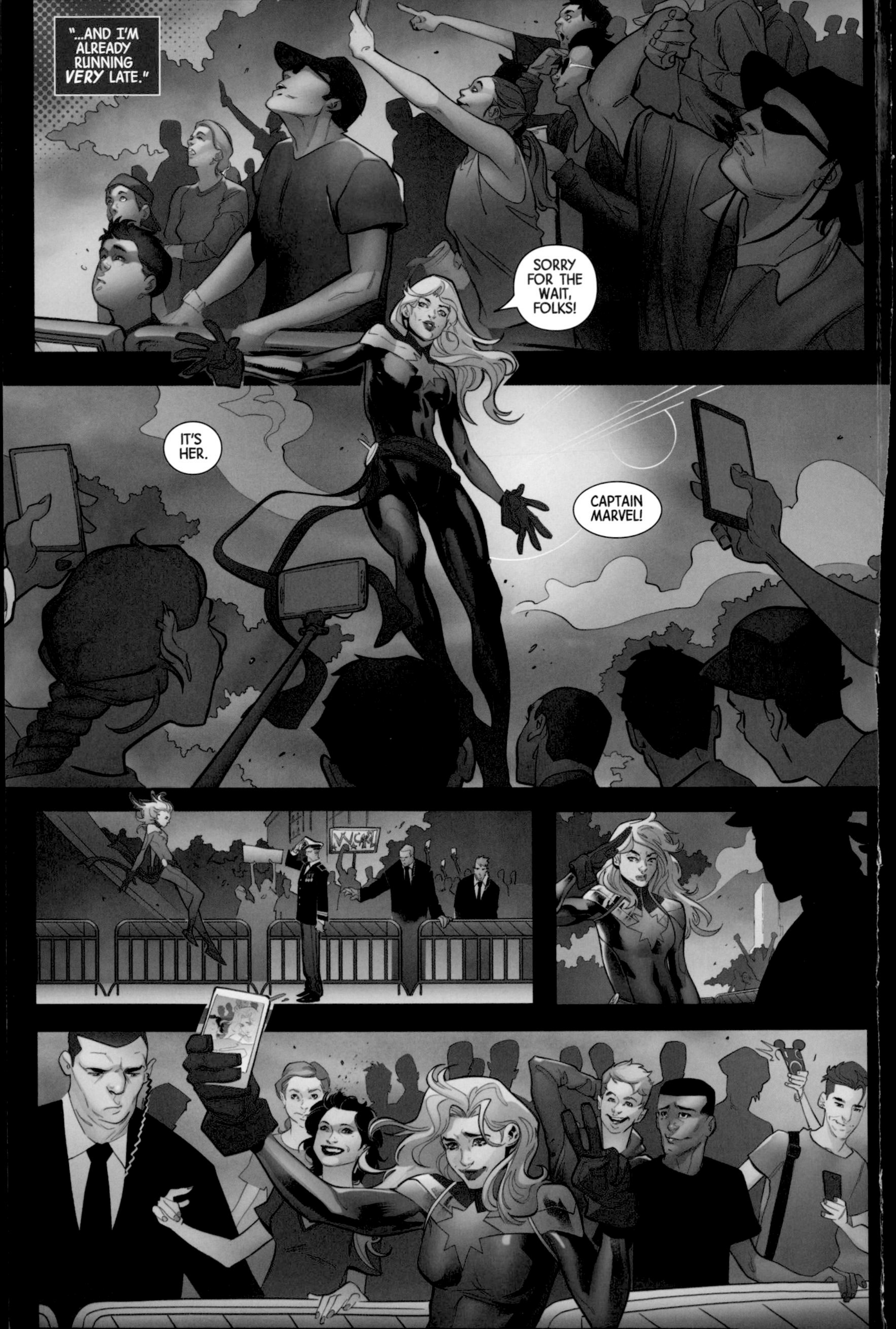
"...AND I'M ALREADY RUNNING VERY LATE."
SORRY FOR THE WAIT, FOLKS!
IT'S HER.
CAPTAIN MARVEL!

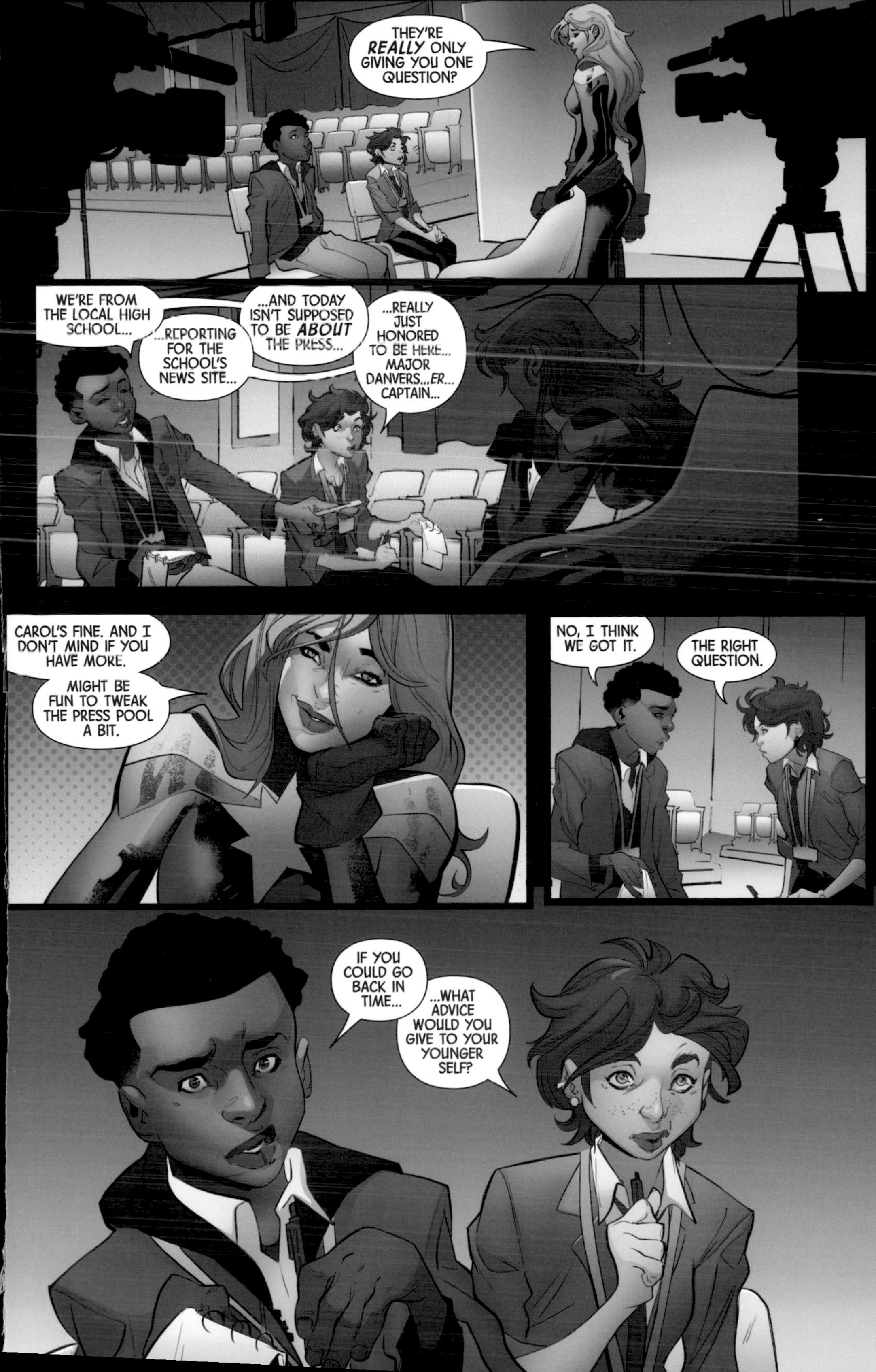

THEY'RE *REALLY* ONLY GIVING YOU ONE QUESTION?
WE'RE FROM THE LOCAL HIGH SCHOOL...
...REPORTING FOR THE SCHOOL'S NEWS SITE...
...AND TODAY ISN'T SUPPOSED TO BE *ABOUT* THE PRESS...
...REALLY JUST HONORED TO BE HERE... MAJOR DANVERS...*ER*... CAPTAIN...
CAROL'S FINE. AND I DON'T MIND IF YOU HAVE MORE.
MIGHT BE FUN TO TWEAK THE PRESS POOL A BIT.
NO, I THINK WE GOT IT.
THE RIGHT QUESTION.
IF YOU COULD GO BACK IN TIME...
...WHAT ADVICE WOULD YOU GIVE TO YOUR YOUNGER SELF?

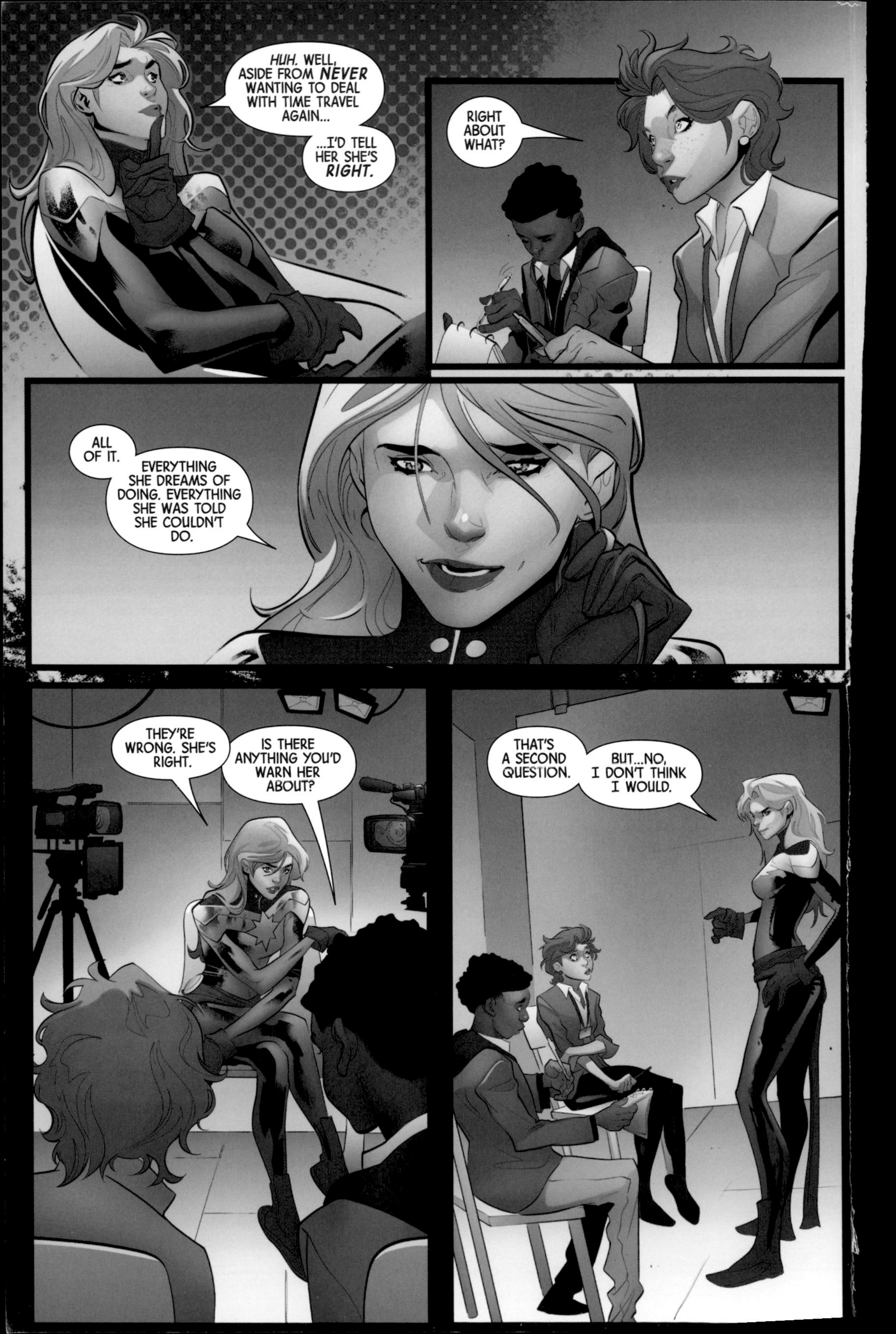
HUH. WELL, ASIDE FROM NEVER WANTING TO DEAL WITH TIME TRAVEL AGAIN...
...I'D TELL HER SHE'S RIGHT.
RIGHT ABOUT WHAT?
ALL OF IT.
EVERYTHING SHE DREAMS OF DOING. EVERYTHING SHE WAS TOLD SHE COULDN'T DO.
THEY'RE WRONG. SHE'S RIGHT.
IS THERE ANYTHING YOU'D WARN HER ABOUT?
THAT'S A SECOND QUESTION.
BUT...NO, I DON'T THINK I WOULD.

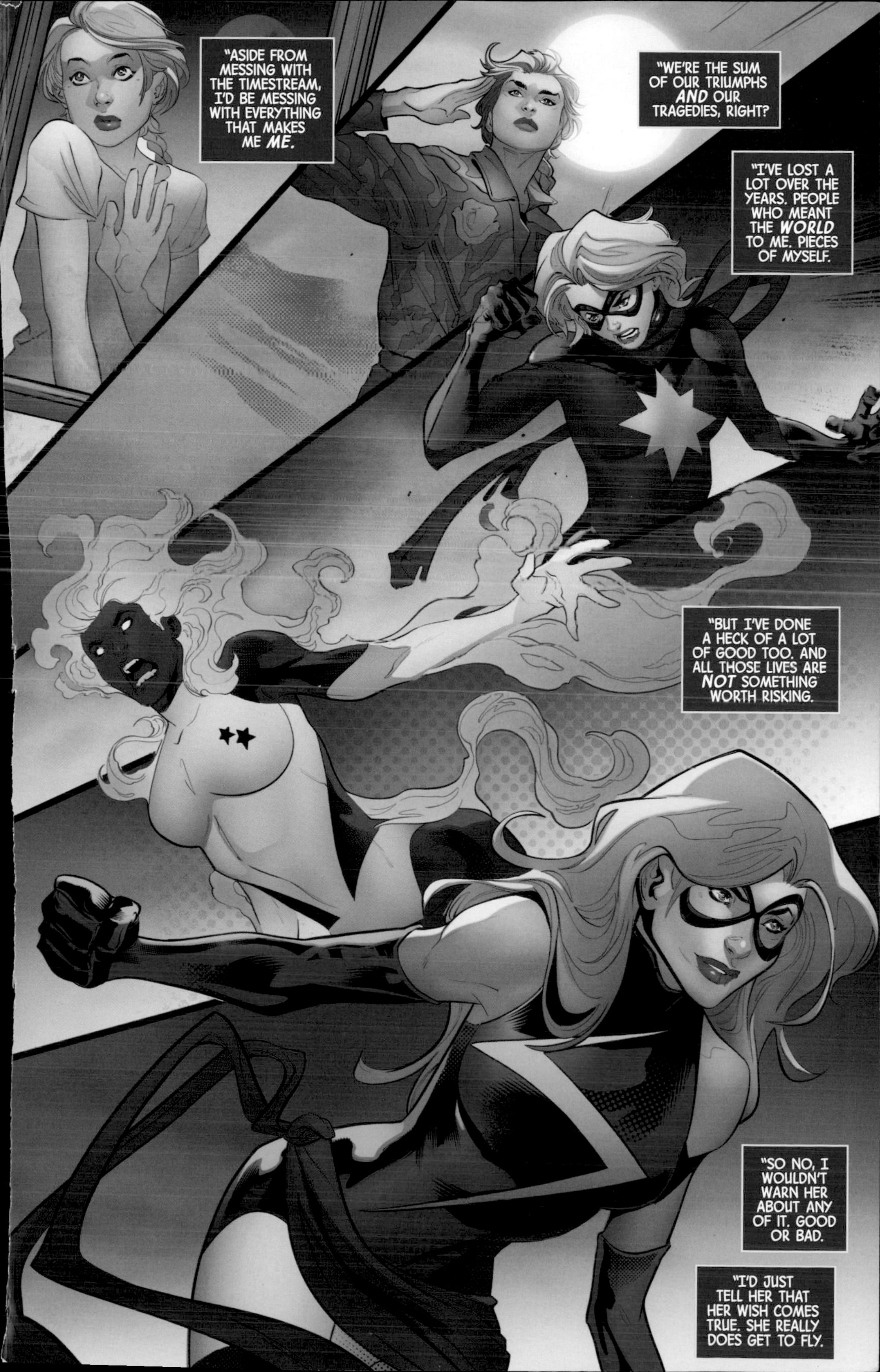
"ASIDE FROM MESSING WITH THE TIMESTREAM, I'D BE MESSING WITH EVERYTHING THAT MAKES ME *ME*.
"WE'RE THE SUM OF OUR TRIUMPHS *AND* OUR TRAGEDIES, RIGHT?
"I'VE LOST A LOT OVER THE YEARS. PEOPLE WHO MEANT THE *WORLD* TO ME. PIECES OF MYSELF.
"BUT I'VE DONE A HECK OF A LOT OF GOOD TOO. AND ALL THOSE LIVES ARE *NOT* SOMETHING WORTH RISKING.
"SO NO, I WOULDN'T WARN HER ABOUT ANY OF IT. GOOD OR BAD.
"I'D JUST TELL HER THAT HER WISH COMES TRUE. SHE REALLY DOES GET TO FLY.

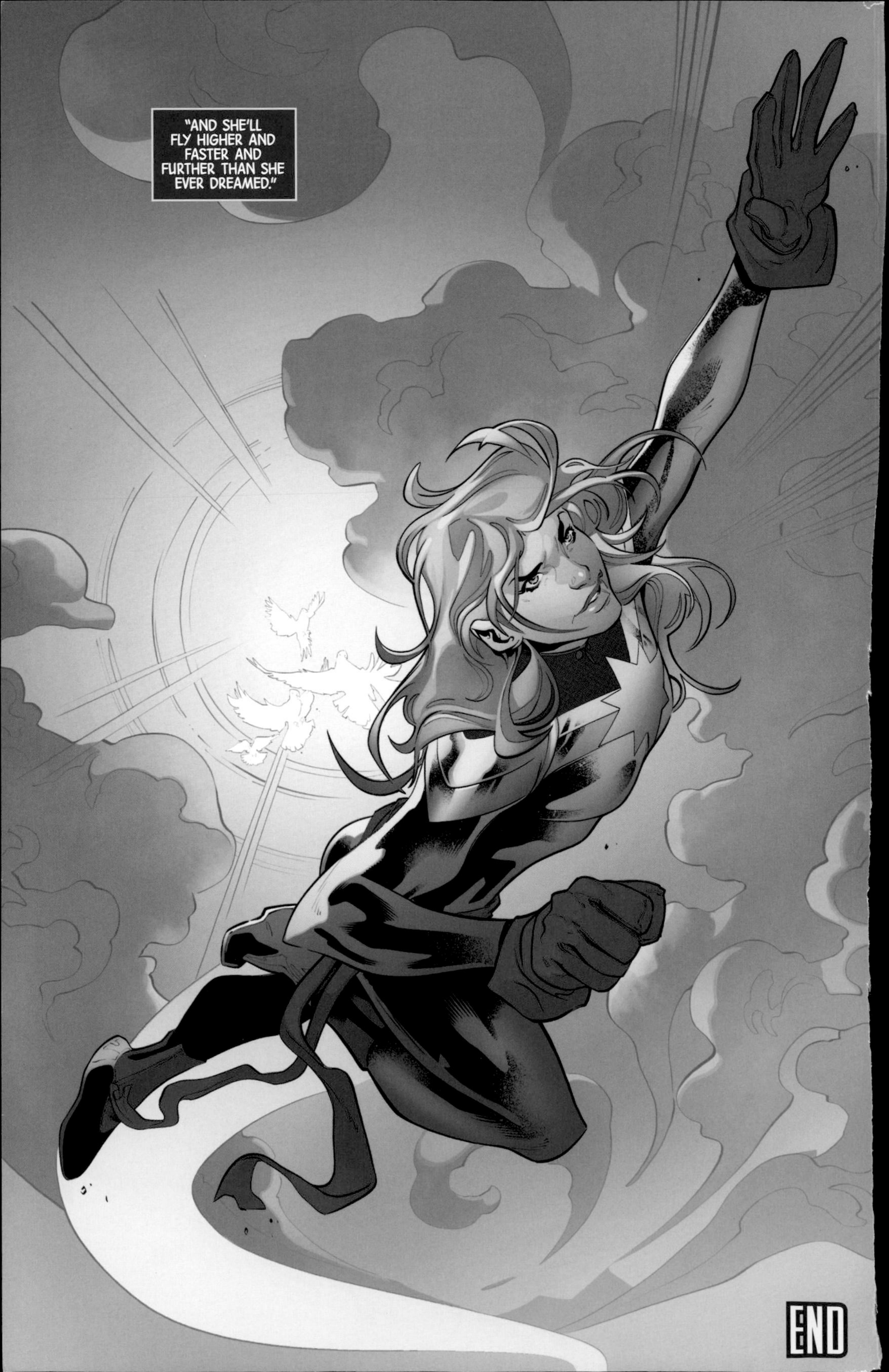
"AND SHE'LL FLY HIGHER AND FASTER AND FURTHER THAN SHE EVER DREAMED."
END

Zach Howard & Federico Blee
THOR: WHERE WALK THE FROST GIANTS variant

Ron Lim & Rachelle Rosenberg
BLACK PANTHER: THE SOUND AND THE FURY variant

Kalman Andrasofszky
AVENGERS: INFINITY SHARDS variant

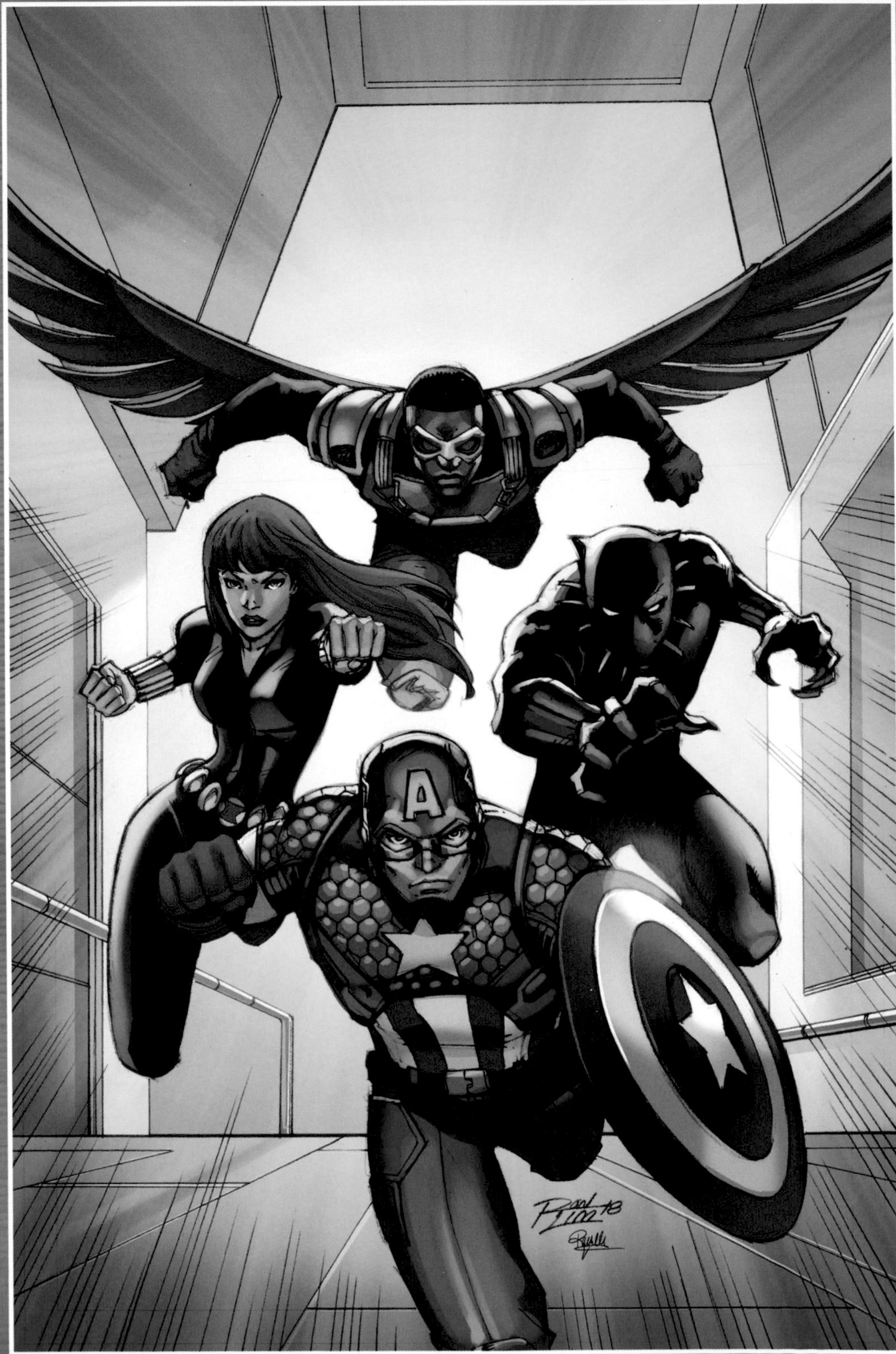

Ron Lim & Rachelle Rosenberg
AVENGERS: INFINITY SHARDS variant

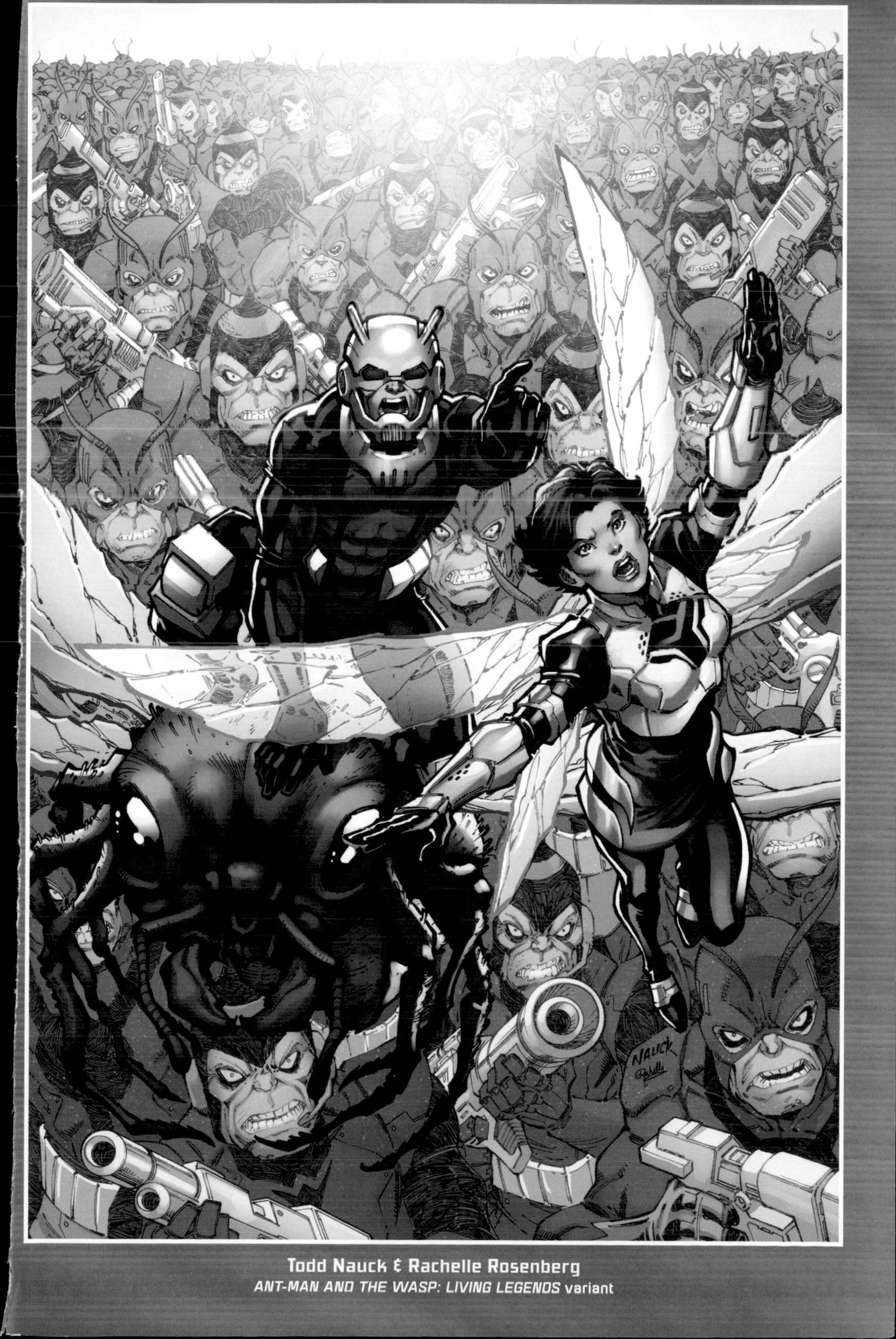
NAUCK

Todd Nauck & Rachelle Rosenberg
ANT-MAN AND THE WASP: LIVING LEGENDS variant

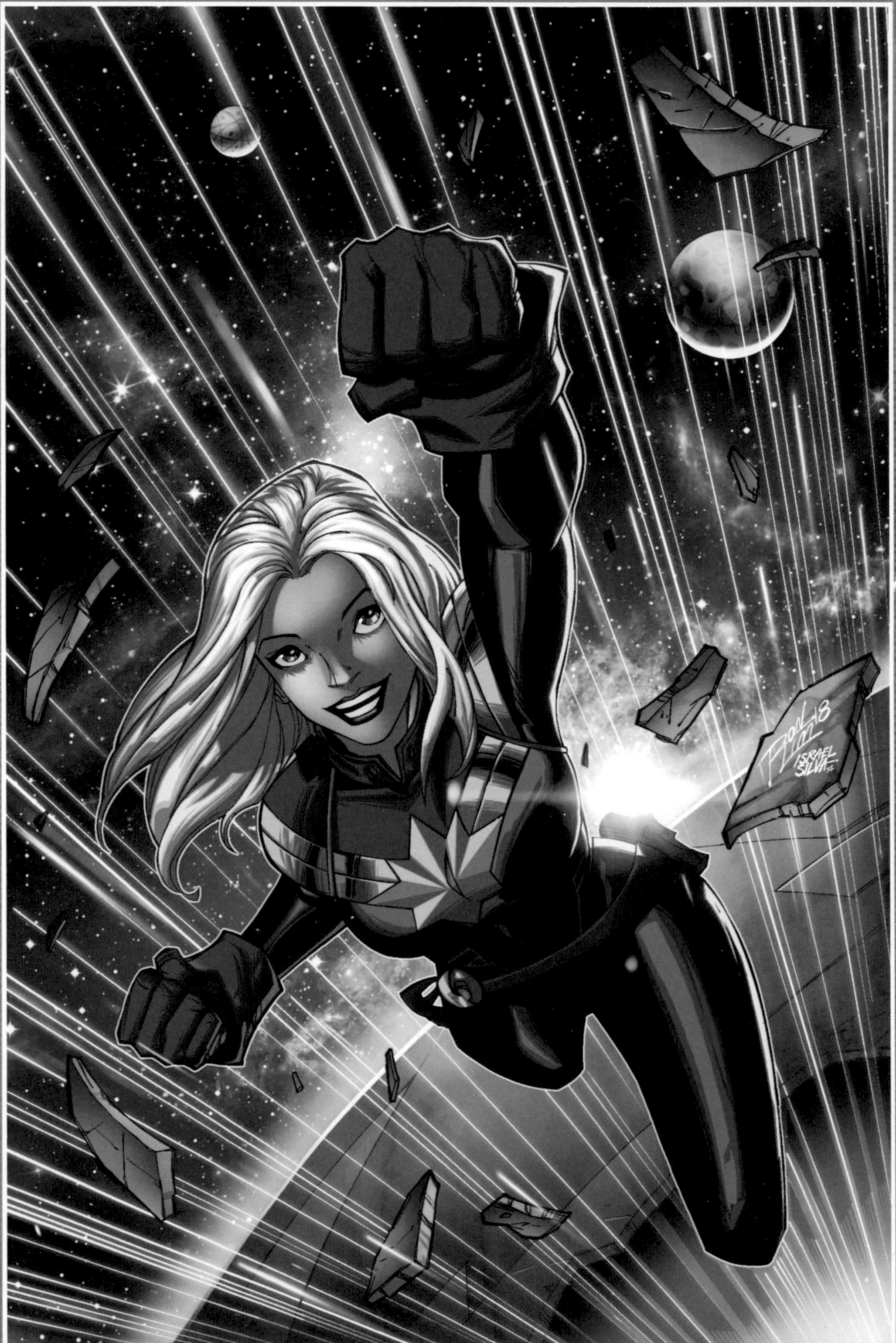

Ron Lim & Rachelle Rosenberg
CAPTAIN MARVEL: BRAVER & MIGHTIER variant